Broken Glass

By the same author

Angel's War
Mirror on the Wall
Mirror Images
To Reason Why
Ties of Blood
All Manner of Things
The Foolish Virgin
A Lesser Peace
A Chained Satan
Season of Sins
The Decent Thing
Silk Stocking Spy
Looking Glass

Broken Glass

C. W. REED

ROBERT HALE · LONDON

First published in Great Britain 2007

ISBN 978-0-7090-8311-5

Robert Hale Limited
Clerkenwell House
Clerkenwell Green
London EC1R 0HT

2 4 6 8 10 9 7 5 3 1

Typeset in 10/13pt Baskerville
by Derek Doyle & Associates, Shaw Heath
Printed and bound in Great Britain
by Biddles Limited, King's Lynn

PART I

LET THE REST OF THE WORLD GO BY

CHAPTER ONE

'There's another letter from your admirer. PC Brown. Doesn't he know there's a war on? That's the second this month.' Beth Hobbs nodded towards the brown envelope that was lying on the plain wooden table, at the opposite end to where she sat before a pile of blue exercise books. Her soft, corn-gold hair hung down at the sides of her face, and stood up untidily from the brow, pushed up by the hand in which she had been resting her head while she got on with the tedious task of marking.

'Jealous?' Alice Glass grinned. Her own hair, also fair but of a much darker tint than her friend's, was also much shorter: a snug cap of tight curls made even snugger by the close fitting woollen cap she had been wearing out of doors during the chilly autumn day, and which she flung onto the old dresser as she came in. Her face was a healthy, scrubbed-looking red, and she brought a fresh whiff of the cold dusk in with her to the stuffy warmth of the room.

'Of who?' Beth asked, with a luxurious disregard of grammar which would have shocked her young pupils. 'Him or you?'

'What you on about, you daft 'aporth?' She strode over to the seated figure, put both hands heavily on the thin shoulders, bent and kissed her below her left ear, on the side of her neck. She felt the shoulders heave violently, as Beth shrugged and squirmed.

'Brr! Your nose is freezing!'

Alice rubbed it deliberately against the fragrance, and savoured the sweet soft brush of the wisps of hair on her face before she withdrew. 'Well, some of us have to work for a living, tha knaas, not sit yammering in a cushy classroom all day like some I could mention!'

Alice's assumption of the broad Dales' accent of the village was a comic exaggeration which both girls delighted in using, though in truth Alice's normal speech was hardly less distinctive. She came from the north-east coastal town of Margrove, no more than forty miles away. So did Beth, though her way of speaking was much more 'refined' – 'like talking with a gobful of alleys' was Alice's teasing expression for it. It emphasized the strong social distinction which marked the girls, in spite of the few miles which separated their families' homes, and which, if it hadn't been for the disruption of the war, would have ruled out the likelihood of their paths ever crossing. Or, rather, recrossing, for they had met first more than ten years before, at Lister Road Infant and Junior School. But they hadn't shared the closeness which characterised their present relationship, for, in spite of her violent reaction to the embrace, Beth immediately and penitently reached up behind her and caught hold of Alice's rough and icy hand, and clung onto it, holding it to her cheek.

'Gosh! You're freezing, poor thing! Sit down by the fire. I'll make a fresh pot of tea.' She jumped up and tugged the short, stocky figure, made bulkier by the pale dungarees and the slacks beneath them, towards the brightly burning coal fire in the small grate. She picked up the envelope and handed it to Alice when she had squatted on the low stool close to the narrow little hearth. 'Aren't you going to open it? You know you're dying to hear from your passionate policeman, your bedazzled bobby!'

'Shut up! I'll wait till I've had me cuppa first, if you don't mind! He's just about given up on his declarations of undying love now, any road. Besides, there's only one bobby dazzler for me round here. *You* should know that, kidder!' She made a pretend grab, and Beth skipped away out of reach, with a little squeal. Alice noted the faint, characteristic hint of embarrassment and pleasure lightly pinking the lovely face. She sighed with contentment as Beth moved out to the tiny kitchenette, no bigger than a pantry, to make the tea. Alice held her roughened hands out to the warmth, her forearms resting on her knees. She had kicked off her wellingtons in the tiny porch at the foot of the steep stairs which led up to the flat. The feet of her over-generous grey woollen socks trailed out in front of her like tentacles. Her muscles were aching. They had had a long and arduous day out in the estate grounds, the vast majority of which had been turned over to vegetable growing. The last of the potatoes were in now. Even the snooty little madams of St Anne's, the posh boarding school, billeted on the Denby Estate as evacuees, had helped, in their scarves and hats and wellies, their well-bred cherry noses running and their delicate little hands black with unaccustomed graft. All jolly good fun, doncher know!

Beth's voice floated in over the sound of the kettle, the pouring of water, the chink of the crockery. The heat from the fire struck through the thick layers of clothing and Alice felt a responsive stirring, a deep thrill of both physical and spiritual bliss. I've never felt this happy before! The thought, or at least the acknowledgement of it, was almost scary. She shouldn't be feeling like this. She didn't deserve it.

In spite of her indifferent words, she didn't wait any longer, but tore open the envelope. She wanted to see what Davy had to say. She might be able to joke about it with Beth, but his growing feeling for her during his time in Howbeck, and their friendship, meant a lot to her. She couldn't help feeling guiltily proud that he had wanted it to develop into something more, had even asked if she would consider moving away with him to York. She had made it plain that there could never be that kind of relationship between them, though she was anxious that they should remain good friends. And they *had* been close. In fact, she had been his only friend when he had first come to the village, not many months after the Margrove contingent of children and adults had established themselves in their new surroundings. He had been virtually shunned, as a conscientious objector who had served a term in gaol. With typical cussedness, she had been determined to demonstrate that she did not agree with the entrenched attitude of most of the villagers, and had gone out of her way to show her friendliness.

When she learnt of his history, she was even more determined that others should acknowledge his right to his viewpoint, however unpopular it might be. He had fought in the Spanish civil war, witnessed the violence and atrocities, committed on both sides, and had been lucky to escape physically unscathed. Eventually, he had told her of his love for a French girl – 'Lou', he had called her – whom he had become really close to during the months he had spent in Paris, before the outbreak of war. Unfortunately, Lou had not reciprocated his feelings, at least not in the intense way he wished. Poor Davy! Disappointed in love in France, and then rejected a second time in the Yorkshire village to which he had been sent after his imprisonment. But he had taken it well, and she was grateful, for she had not wanted to lose his friendship. She welcomed his letters, and even the resigned, wry humour with which he was able to refer to his dashed and ever fainter hopes of winning her.

'Well? What's he got to say for himself?' Beth brought the wooden tray laden with the enamel mugs, the chipped milk jug and sugar bowl, and the already cosied teapot to the fire and laid it on the worn hearthrug. She knelt and put her hand on Alice's knee. 'Apart from all the broken hearted bits? I couldn't bear it.'

'Cheeky monkey!' Alice gave her a vigorous shove. 'Listen to this.' She read aloud. ' "*I've been on night shift this week, stumbling around York again in the blackout. I still hardly know my way around. Talk about asking your friendly local bobby for directions! It's the other way round for me. I had to stop one old girl and ask her the way back to the station!"* ' Skipping ahead a paragraph, she swiftly absorbed its content and lapsed into silence. She searched for a light riposte, but Beth, of course, had spotted her hesitation.

'Do you miss him? You can tell me, you know. There's nothing wrong in admitting it, Al.'

'I know that!' Alice's tone was defensively sharp. She put her hands out to the stooping shoulders, drew Beth in close against her warm limbs. 'He was a good mate, that's all. I miss him as a mate. But you know, don't you? There isn't anywhere I'd rather be than here right now.'

It was true, and they both knew it. In the big, creaky, comfortable old bed a couple of hours later, snug against the chill under the sheet and two blankets and lumpy eiderdown, Alice fitted herself around the curving back and buttocks of her friend, hugging her lovingly, savouring the feel of the thick winter nightie, its fragrant smell as it rubbed against her cheek, and the caress of Beth's woollen socked heels against her own bare feet. She pressed her nose against the soft golden curls, her lips nuzzled. 'Snug as bugs, eh? Happy?'

Beth's hands closed over the hands clasped about her midriff. 'Ecstatic!' The arms hugged her even tighter, the body fitted even closer to hers.

'You and your posh fancy words!'

'You don't have to keep coming round to check up on me, you know. I'm getting on fine.'

Doreen Glass, Alice's eleven-year-old sister, gave her neatly brushed dark brown curls a haughty flick, and Alice felt the involuntary tugging of a smile begin, in spite of her annoyance. She was getting more like her benefactor and guardian, Miss Ramsay, every day. She certainly looked the part in her smart new winter outfit: the pretty knitted tam, the checked coat, the brown woollen stockings and ankle boots. A right little toff! Even her accent had lost all its rough edge; the Margrove twang was virtually absent from her rounded speech. Almost as elegant as her own dear Beth, Alice acknowledged wryly. The youngster was transformed, and all in a single year. 'Aunty Elizabeth' had certainly done a good job on her all right. Whoops! No. Not 'aunty'. 'Aunt Elizabeth', she had to be called. 'Aunty' was common. Shows your 'browtins-up', as they said back home in Margrove. Young Doreen had come a long way from there – and wouldn't be going back if she had anything to do with it.

Alice could not help but cynically admire the way Doreen had begun her campaign, right from their first day in Howbeck, newly off the train, when she had stood in the village hall with her label and her gas mask, alongside all the other evacuees from Lister Road School. As soon as she had clapped eyes on the smartly dressed spinster – 'money folk' was the immediate classification Miss Ramsay came under – and recognized the approval of her winsome waif looks, Doreen had capitalized on it. 'I don't mind going on me own!' Doreen offered hastily, when Miss Ramsay had turned away on realizing that the girl was part of a job lot, which included the grubby, smeary nosed Algy, aged five, to say nothing of their big sister and adult helper, Alice. And that was it. Now Doreen was the official ward of Elizabeth Ramsay, all signed, sealed and delivered, with the approval of Fred and Maggie Glass, for an unknown and not-to-be-discussed financial reward. Purchased like any slave from the shores of Africa, or one of those eastern markets. Except, Alice acknowledged, never was a slave more willing to offer herself up for captivity, and so far Doreen seemed to be getting everything that was best from the bargain: new lifestyle, new clothes, new education. She had even begun attending the girls' grammar school, travelling in on the train every day with all the other little clever-clogs or rich little bitches from up the dale.

But be fair, kidder! Alice uncomfortably chided herself. You're no better. You jumped at the chance to escape from 19 Maudsley Street, Margrove, when chance came along in the form of kitchen assistant and general dogsbody in the Lister Road evacuation to Howbeck. Now that that was all over, a year later the school had moved back home, but she, just like Doreen, had clung to the chance to remain here with her beloved Beth.

Alice suspected that Miss Ramsay was as unenthusiastic as Doreen about Alice's brief but regular appearances at Northend Cottage. Some cottage! A double fronted Georgian house, ivy on its grey walls, and other impressively deterring drystone walls around its substantial gardens, front and back. You could have fitted practically the whole of 19 Maudsley Street into just one of its imposing rooms. Not that Miss Ramsay would have liked the comparison. She was doing her best to wipe the memory of such things from Doreen's mind. So the all too solid reminder of her humble roots in the shape of her elder sister was not to Miss Ramsay's liking at all. In the year during which the three junior members of the Glass family had been present in Howbeck, not once had Alice been invited to a meal, not even at Christmas time, the second of the war, with its new let's-all-pull-together spirit.

But Alice was obstinately determined to make her presence visible, as a reminder to her sister of her family ties and her origins. In answer to Doreen's surly remark about 'checking up on her', Alice said, 'If I didn't keep coming round I'd never see you. You never come up to t'Big 'Ouse to see me.'

She could sense Doreen's inner wince at her rough usage of the common village phrase for Howe Manor, where Alice and Beth shared the tiny flat, former servants' quarters, over the stables, most of which had been converted to garages.

'Ooh, I wouldn't want to intrude on you and Miss Hobbs. I know how cosy you are over there, just the two of you!'

Alice felt the familiar itch to bring her palm into sharp contact with that sneering, pretty little face, and was even angrier at the heat she could feel mounting in her own features. 'What the hell you mean by that?'

'Nowt! Nothing at all!' the young girl answered lightly, smiling.

Alice fumed, choked back her flare of rage. Even the use of the dialect word was mocking.

'It's nice to see you and Miss Hobbs such good friends. Who'd have thought it? She's lovely, isn't she?' Doreen smiled so sweetly, Alice's fingers curled inside her gloves.

'Yes, she is. Elsbeth's a good mate.' Elsbeth! Why had she used her full name like that? She was Beth now. That's what she wanted. Mind you, Alice wanted to be Al, but she was only Al when they were alone together. She was quite sure Doreen was needling her, being deliberately nasty under that simpering smile. But she couldn't challenge her. Not about that. 'You writing home regular?' she asked abruptly.

The young girl nodded. 'Look, I'd better go. I've got some work to do. They give us bags of prep now.'

'Aye, right-oh. Listen – you getting on all right at school? Making friends and that?' she added awkwardly.

Doreen gave that cool look again, the brown eyes wide, unfathomable. She nodded. 'Yes, thank you. I haven't stolen anybody's pocket money or made anyone pee their pants with fright. Well, I must go. Ta-ra, our kid!' The broad accent of the farewell was the last vindictive flick as she turned and went through the gate.

Alice remained staring after her for a few seconds. She felt the sting of tears behind her eyes, and a sigh as she stood in the louring afternoon sky. God, I'm turning soft in me old age! It's all your fault, Beth Hobbs! I'm not the hard little bitch I used to be. Not since you came on the scene. Doreen's reference to the stealing and the knicker-wetting brought back all the powerful memories of the reasons leading to Beth's re-entry into her life. Just before the evacuation to Howbeck, Doreen and some others had been involved in a bullying incident. The newly appointed infant teacher, Elsbeth Hobbs, had alerted Alice and helped to defuse what might have been a much more serious situation. She had done it because, of course, she had known Alice during their own time as juniors in that very school. Ironic, too, that one of their chief shared memories was of a similar incident, when Alice had been the perpetrator and Beth the recipient, of a jug of water poured over her head and down the neck of her blouse. They laughed often about it now.

'I was scared stiff of you!' Beth readily confessed. 'And I envied you so much. You weren't scared of anybody – or anything! I so much wanted to be like you. And for you to like me.'

Well, the last part of her wish had certainly come true. How much almost frightened Alice sometimes, it seemed so close to being too good to be true. Except that it *was* truer than anything she'd ever known or felt before. And there was nothing she could do about it. Except to enjoy it, to wallow in it, and be bursting with gratitude for the unbelievable joy of it.

CHAPTER TWO

When Beth saw Luke Denby he was surrounded by the usual cluster of leggy senior pupils, at the foot of the wide staircase which led down to the imposing entrance hall of Howe Manor. It had become the gathering place for the girls between lessons and, as now, at the end of morning school. As she descended the last of the shallow stairs, she knew it was too late to avoid him, and knew, by the callous way he cut through the knot of admiring adolescents, that he had no intention of letting her do so.

'Ah! The divine Miss Hobbs herself! May I carry your books, Miss?' He stepped forward with that wide, infuriatingly cocky grin, one hand already raised to take her arm, and she felt the hot colour rushing up to her face. The girls snorted and sniggered. She felt their knowing, worldly eyes on her, and her own beet-coloured, helpless inadequacy. She flustered and stumbled verbally. His grip imprisoned her, and led her away through the noisy, staring throng. He was wearing his uniform. The wings over the breast had that tarnished appearance, the much sought after veteran look. He was bare-headed. She remembered how he had self-mockingly confessed to her back in the spring how they all used to crumple up their caps and rub at the badges to get rid of the 'new boy' label they proclaimed.

He *was* a veteran now, she supposed, after several months on active service in Bomber Command. She wondered how many missions he and his crew had flown already.

'It's good to see you.' Her face burned anew. She must be glowing like a beacon. Surely he must know how untrue her statement was? She blundered on. 'I mean . . . I'm glad . . . you're all right, I mean. Safe and sound.' He laughed. She wanted to pull her arm free of his hold, but she didn't dare.

'So far so good! Just got a couple of days' leave. Thought I'd pop up and see how the old folk at home are doing. And of course in the hope of catching a glimpse of my number one girl. You're even more beautiful than in my dreams!'

'Don't! Please!' She turned her face towards him appealingly. Her blue eyes were filmed with tears. The vivid recall of the scene in the tiny room above she had occupied earlier in the year, part of the quarters allocated to St Anne's, caused her to feel trapped and helpless again. And scoured with shame. He was tormenting her, she was sure, knowing full well her horror of what had taken place there; what she had, in her monumental ignorance and foolishness, allowed to happen.

'Oh, come on, Beth!' His tone was harsh, upbraiding. He held her arm tightly, like an arresting policeman. 'You can't expect me just to forget everything. Do you really think that little of me?'

'No! It's not . . . it was all a mistake. It's over and done with. I just want to . . .' She was about to use the very word he had just used, and realized how absurd it was. She could *never* forget it, no matter how much she longed to. 'Put it all behind me,' she ended pitifully. At last she summoned up the resolve to pull her arm clear of his restraining grip.

'I hear you're settled in over the stables. With that tough little chum of yours, Alice. Taken over the Land Girls' billet. Nice and cosy, are you? Just the two of you!'

Oh God! she thought miserably. If she turned any redder she'd spontaneously combust.

'I thought she had something going with the conchie chappie? Davy Brown. Patrick Barr tells me he's gone off to York. Joined the police. Hope he can square his conscience with what he's doing. Probably rounding up the call-up dodgers and deserters. Making sure they get roped in to go off and fight for the cause. Rum do, eh?'

'He did plenty of fighting in Spain,' Beth answered. 'He saw lots of action.'

'I'm sure he did. Good luck to him, wherever he is. I always thought he was a decent sort. Mind you, he put a few people's backs up in the village, eh? Along with your little roommate! Over that business with Gus Rielke. You should hear Vera Rhodes going on about them. I trust the pair of you don't frequent the Oddfellows these days? You're liable to get your drinks tipped over you if you go in there with Alice!'

'Mrs Rhodes is lucky she didn't lose the pub altogether. She could have been thrown out. She should be ashamed of herself!'

Gus Rielke had been an exotic square peg in Howbeck's round hole. Norwegian by nationality, he had suddenly appeared in the village soon after the fall of his country to the Nazi occupation. His account of his dramatic escape by boat from his homeland, during which he had picked up the hip injury which rendered him unfit for military service, had made him something of a hero to the country folk, for whom the war had so far meant little more than minor irritations caused by the rationing of certain foodstuffs and fuel. Even the air raids, which had begun in the north-east towards the end of 1940, were no more than distant rumbles of thunder and the occasional red flicker over the horizon – nothing to get out of bed for – during nights undisturbed by the rising and falling wail of sirens heard in the towns and cities. Big of stature, and with a personality to match, the bluff Scandinavian had swiftly made himself popular with the villagers. He was always ready to lend a hand, to take on casual work. His popularity was only slightly dented even when he made himself apparently indispensable to the landlady of the village inn, whose soldier husband was a POW after the fall of France. Gus took his place not only behind the bar but also in the marital bed. Gradually, he acquired a reputation as a 'Mr Fix-it'. If there was something which, through the exigencies of the war, had become difficult or impossible to obtain, from silk knickers to cans of petrol, Gus was your man.

It was Alice who, by her persistence, and with the vital help of Davy Brown, had exposed the flourishing black market and sheep-stealing network of which Gus Rielke had been a prominent member. The Norwegian had somehow escaped the trap the authorities had set, disappearing the very night of the police raid, never to be seen again. Though officially the villagers tut-tutted in righteous outrage, there were several, including the embittered Vera Rhodes, who privately regretted the passing of the extrovert Scandinavian. Luke Denby, the squire's son, was one of them. He gave the knife of Beth's acute personal discomfort a delicate little twist. 'Have you still got my present, or have you assigned them to the virtuous flames of penitence for our sins?'

With cruelly precise skill, he had brought together the various strands of her discomposure, for the 'present' he referred to had been purchased through the good offices of Gus Rielke, had been in a very real sense an essential part of her own downfall, and, finally, highlighted the hypocrisy of her tone of moral indignation at Mrs Rhodes' misbehaviour. Beth had been wrong also in her belief that the full extent of her embarrassed ruddiness had been achieved; her blushes deepened. Even his wickedly accurate use of the plural pronoun 'them' was an added barb, for the present Luke had bought her those eventful months ago had been an exquisite pair of cami-knickers, almost literally a silken web to ensnare her in the loss of her virtue.

Not that she had done anything so gross as to surrender her virginity for some pretty underwear. Of course not. But, enmeshed in the wild uncertainties that war had brought, with compassionate feelings for the handsome young warrior who, after months of training was about to embark on the perilous task of carrying the fight to the enemy in the skies, and filled with patriotic notions of selflessness and duty, but mainly with guilt at the notion of denying him, she had all too literally laid aside her instinctive inhibitions and reluctance and let him make love to her.

She had known before the act was consummated that she had made a terrible, perhaps unforgivable, mistake. In her memory of it, it would always be a kind of rape, despite her utterly passive non-resistance, her stunned acceptance. Something told her in his look afterwards that he was somehow aware of how she felt. He was as glad to escape as she was to see him go. Of course he could not accept the truth. From his new posting in Lincolnshire, he had even tried to woo her on paper, and on his dashes back to his home whenever opportunity presented itself during the early part of the summer, he had striven increasingly desperately to achieve his aim, to express his 'need and love' for her, between the sheets. He had been bitter – vituperatively so – when it finally dawned on him that she would not relent. Since then, silence, and avoidance.

This was the first time in more than three months that she had even seen him. She was disturbed by the fact that he had apparently come to seek her out again, and anxious at his reappearance. She felt his threat to her happiness. And she *was* happy now, happier than she had ever dreamt it was possible to be. It was a happiness so precious, and so absorbing, so utterly apart from the rest of this violent, dangerous world, that she feared for it almost constantly.

'I see his nibs is back again.' Alice's flat statement made the air between them quiver almost visibly. The tide of red which swept up Beth's features was more eloquent than any words. 'You've seen him then? Spoken to him?' Alice's lips were thin as a line on paper, and Beth felt them as an accusation.

She nodded, swallowed hard, tried not to sound guilty. 'He was in the entrance hall. With all the girls there. I couldn't avoid him.'

'Oh aye? And what did he have to say then?'

Beth flashed her a look of appeal. She almost said, 'Don't be angry with me.' Then thought how foolish it would be. Why should she feel so guilty, so ashamed, when she was simply telling the truth? He had waylaid her, knowing very well that she would never cut him dead, make a scene, with the girls all looking on. She suffered badly now from a sense of inadequacy, as though she had somehow let Al down. 'Nothing, really. Just chit-chat. We didn't talk for more than a minute or so.' Of course, Al knew all about Beth's one-night affair. She was the only one Beth had confided in. Alice had come round the following morning, found Beth still in a state of weeping shock. Beth almost smiled at the memory, in spite of her unease, when she recalled Al's somewhat unorthodox method of alleviating her distress – a good, solid slap to the face that had left a mark on her cheek for several days, immediately followed by an engulfing hug and tears that mingled with Beth's as she rocked her tightly in her arms. It had been the first really open acknowledgement of the depth of feeling between them.

'I just hope he doesn't dare to show his face round here, that's all!' Alice declared grimly, and Beth hoped so, too, fervently, for she could not bear the thought of a confrontation between them. She was afraid that he might just do that, turn up at the door of their little refuge, out of a wicked desire to stir up more trouble, or maybe from a vindictive wish to punish her some more for her rejection of him. For she *had* rejected him, she could take some comfort from that, even though she had made that terrible mistake of yielding up her virtue to him on that one fatal occasion. And still that was how she thought of her moral lapse, in those old-fashioned terms, though it hurt to acknowledge even to herself that she had been the chief instigator of her own downfall. She had not seen him for weeks, and his importuning letters had stopped ages ago. His parents had had nothing more to do with her, even though she had been living in the same building – no more teatime chats or invitations to cosy informal suppers in the drawing room. From the first, Letitia Denby had made plain her anxiety at the thought of any lasting attachment between her son and the daughter of a lowly tradesman, even if Beth's father did own his own printing works, and was doing better than ever despite wartime restrictions. So at least Beth could take some comfort from the thought that the squire and his lady would be relieved. Mind you, that fact alone might be enough to make Luke start trying to renew his suit to her – not that he had even the remotest intention of offering a proper relationship. Alice's indelicate remarks about getting into drawers and between the sheets were much nearer the mark.

'Please don't say anything to him if you do run into him,' Beth pleaded that night, when they sat before the glowing coals with their mugs of cocoa before retiring. 'I just don't want any more rows. He'll be gone again soon. And he knows – he won't bother me again, I know it.'

'He'd better not. He'll be glad to get back to dropping bombs on the Germans if he tries 'owt round here!' She took the mug from Beth and carried them through to the sink.

He didn't. In fact, he left two days later without seeking out Beth again, who learnt of his departure from one of the sniggering fifth-formers. As an unqualified assistant mistress, Beth taught only the lower forms, but she came into daily contact with the senior pupils because of the various extra-curricular tasks she was required to perform. As an assistant housemistress, she supervised prep, and was on the rota for early morning and lights-out duties. She was also roped in to help with games. The enlightened Miss Bell, the headmistress of St Anne's, had instituted a system whereby those girls who were determinedly non-sporty could opt for an afternoon walk of at least three miles – the 'route march', as both scholars and staff had dubbed it. Beth had misguidedly welcomed this assignment, especially as winter was approaching, as an alternative to the mud and violence of the hockey or lacrosse pitch. But 'Dinger' Bell was adamant: come fair weather or foul the walks would take place. For a start, there was the arduous feat of assembling all the names on the list, which involved an energetic combing of classrooms, dormitories and lavatories to ensure success. Then there was the danger of miscreants falling by the wayside as soon as they had left the grounds of Howe Manor, and branching off on their own expeditions to various favoured hideouts for illicit ciggies and scandalous gossip, or for a precipitate return to the cosy warmth of the dens back at the house from which they had only recently been extricated.

Beth quickly began to have more sympathy for the scurrying sheep dogs so frequently seen about the dale side or on the moors. It was while striving, with no great success, to inject a little enthusiasm for the walk, that she found herself alongside a group of the fifth year, always favourites for sudden, mysterious disappearances. 'I expect you're feeling a bit down in the dumps, aren't you, Miss?' The speaker was Felicity Gould, a lanky girl already several inches taller than Beth. Her eyes were wide with innocent sympathy. 'With Flying Officer Denby having to go back so soon. Is it true he writes every day to you, miss?'

'Be quiet!' Helplessly, Beth felt the heat mounting to her cheeks. 'Don't be impertinent!'

'I'm not, Miss!' Felicity cried out in hurt protest, amidst the smirks and audible sniggers around her. 'I just know he thinks a lot about you. It's common knowledge. He told one of the girls—'

'I said be quiet! Or you'll find yourself on report for insolence! I don't – my private life is no concern of yours. You need to learn some manners.'

'I was only trying to be friendly, Miss!' Still the tone of outraged innocence was there, as were the snorts and the giggles, and, not for the first time, Beth felt almost sick with rage, and with a helpless sense of her inability to cope with these supercilious creatures.

'I wish he'd write to *me* every day!' another voice said, hoarse with passion, and others joined in.

'I heard that some girls write to him!'

'They say he gave Edie Crowther a picture of him standing by his Spitfire.'

'He's a bomber pilot!' Beth couldn't stop herself from interjecting, and there was a chorus of laughing exclamations, as though she had admitted some deep intimacy.

Beth gave a small cry of frustration and anger. 'Oh! You girls! You think you're so clever. You're so rude and arrogant. Just shut up if you can't think of anything pleasant to talk about.'

She was well aware that as a riposte her answer lacked the authority of a teacher, and, in spite of all that had happened to her recently, she felt more like the bullied victim of these mocking, privileged fifteen or sixteen-year-olds.

CHAPTER THREE

There was a steely glint in Miss Ramsay's gaze and an extra firm set to her strong jaw as she surveyed Alice. 'We've been invited to spend the Christmas holiday with my brother and his family. In Hertfordshire. I haven't seen them since the war started over two years ago, and they're very much looking forward to meeting Doreen. I've told them so much about her. I'm planning to travel down on the twenty-second. We'll stay until after New Year.'

Alice cleared her throat. She glanced down at her feet, the toes in the thick grey socks curling against the patterned rug. She resented the embarrassment and sense of inferiority she experienced in these unfamiliar, affluent surroundings. As usual, she had shed her boots in the porch, and, as usual, she had not even been invited to take a seat in the comfortable drawing room, where the fire burnt cheerfully, the brasses and the fire irons twinkled, and there was a fragrant smell of polish and an air of luxurious ease. What was it Beth was always saying about their own disorganized untidiness? 'A place for everything and nothing in its place.'

Alice cleared her throat again. Her husky voice sounded even coarser in her discomfort and her resentment. 'I think me mam was counting on her being home for Christmas. They haven't seen her since the summer.'

'Oh, Alice!' Doreen was sitting at a small, baize-covered folding card table, whose surface was covered with books and papers. A long wooden pencil case was aligned neatly at one end. Her cry was a mixture of protest and plea. 'You know there's hardly room for all of us to fit in if we're all going to be at home. Are you going to be home for all the holiday?' There was a clear challenge in the petulant voice, which added to Alice's irritation as it twinged the nerve of her own guilt. It was true enough. She had already been hoping and scheming for her and Beth to spend as much of the holiday as they could together in their haven above the stables. They could surely plead work as an excuse for cutting down on the time they had to spend with their families in Margrove.

'I'll be there for the Christmas, at least!' she said reprovingly. 'It's a time when families ought to be together. Especially these days. Nobody knows what's going to happen, do they? We might never have another chance, the way things are now. Don't you *want* to be with mam and dad – and our Algy and Ethel – and George?'

The snort of disgust and disagreement was eloquent, if somewhat uncouth. 'Come off it! They couldn't care less if they never see me again! I mean our Ethel and George,' she added, with the merest shade of apology in her tone. 'They never write to me, any of them.'

'And do you? Have you written to *them*?'

'Doreen writes a letter home practically every week.' Miss Ramsay's eye glittered coldly, despite the fire's warmth. She rose from the armchair, putting aside the newspaper and brushing invisible crumbs from her Tweed skirt. 'School doesn't finish until the nineteenth. And we're travelling on the Monday. We'll need the weekend for packing and so forth. But we'll be returning on 5 January. There's still a week before the start of term. I'll arrange for Doreen to come through to Margrove one day during that week. I'm sure she'll have lots to tell you all. Travel broadens the mind, even if it's only as far as Hertfordshire.' She gave a low, modulated chuckle, and Doreen gave a responsive little snicker.

Toadying little bitch! Alice glowered, but submitted to the inevitable defeat.

'Now, I really think you'd better get on, sweetheart, don't you?' She beamed a smile at her ward, then turned again towards Alice. The smile was there, but transformed to one of implacable triumph. 'Your sister has the end of term tests coming up and we're expecting great things. She'll make us all proud of her one day, I'm sure.'

'Aye. She always was a crafty little so-and-so!' Alice's sense of inadequacy was only slightly eased by this mark of churlish defiance, and she moved towards the door, and the outer cold, glad to be escaping in spite of her anger.

Miss Ramsay came with her into the hallway, with its ticking clock, and high, mirrored coat stand. 'We must hope for better things in 1942. Surely the Americans will be joining us at long last. And the Russian winter will do for Herr Hitler what it did for Napoleon. Things are looking up.'

News had come through of the previous day's sudden attack on the United States' fleet at Pearl Harbour. There were also reports of the halt to Hitler's drive on Moscow because of the severe weather, and talk of a possible Russian counter-offensive. Alice thought of the early morning air attack, which had caught the Americans on the hop. There had been considerable loss of life, as well as damage to the assembled warships. She had to admit that most folks in

Howbeck seemed, like Miss Ramsay, to view the attack as a good thing for Britain. Funny way of going on, when you welcomed the news of people who were supposed to be our friends being blown to bits! She thought suddenly of Davy Brown and his unpopular stance against the violence the whole world was now caught up in. She had a strong wish to see him again, to see that warmth in his brown eyes, to feel that gentleness, and his liking for her. Why did she shy away from putting a name, the proper name, to it? It went much deeper than liking on his part, as she well knew.

He would be pleased if he knew how her opinion had swung from her vigorous and unthinking support of the war with which she had bludgeoned him in the earliest days of their acquaintance, even when, to everyone else who condemned him for his pacifism, she had stoutly defended his right to be wrong. She knew he had witnessed at first hand some terrible things during the fighting in Spain, which had left their lasting mark on him. It was only gradually, as they had grown much closer, that she realized how deep their effect had been. It was ironic that his youthful repudiation of his Quaker family's pacifist beliefs had been the cause of his enlisting in the International Brigade, only to have his own conviction of fighting for 'freedom' shattered by such brutal first-hand experience.

But there had been an equally intense if not deeper experience, which had occurred after he had returned home from France, soon after the outbreak of the war. It was even more painful for him to recall; *too* painful, so that Alice had to judge more by what he did not tell her just how terrible the months in the English gaol had been. He had eventually been discharged, after suffering both a mental and physical breakdown, and after the strenuous, unflagging efforts of his father and others to secure his release.

'They won in the end, Alice,' he had confessed, one golden, late summer afternoon, as they sat on one of their favourite rocky outcrops on the moor beyond High Top Farm. 'They broke me in there. That's why I'm here, working on the land. They let me off easy.'

She had put her hands on his arm, gripped him tightly, almost surrendering to the sudden urge to fling her own arms around him, to hold him tight against her. 'No!' she said fiercely. 'You're not carrying a gun, are you? You're not part of the killing. Growing food for people. That's not helping the war!'

He laughed quietly, sadly, and now it was he who slipped an arm round her shoulders. But it was an easy, comradely move, and he pressed his forehead briefly against her burnished curls, in tender friendship. 'If they'd forced me – if push had come to shove – I think I'd have ended up carrying one of their blasted rifles, rather than go through all that again.'

She wanted desperately to comfort him, to give him strength. Maybe to offer him more than just friendship. And it was what *he* had wanted, too, despite the love he had felt for the French girl he had told her about – another of his 'confessions', their 'secrets', which he had shared with no one but her. Lou had not wanted that kind of love. And now she was out of his life, in a country occupied by the enemy he didn't want to fight, and there was no way he could learn even of her whereabouts.

Alice could see how lonely he felt, how much life had scarred him already, even though he was only a little more than four years older than she was. She could also see the dangers of the closeness which was developing between them. Perhaps he misinterpreted her readiness to be friends, the spontaneous ease with which she opened up to him, just as he had misinterpreted her later caution, and her insistence on remaining 'just good mates'. It was probably one of the things that endeared her to him, this open, unsophisticated intimacy, which carried little of the male-female undercurrent with it. So that when, towards the end of his time in Howbeck, he had become involved in the exposure of Gus Rielke and his illegal dealings, and through that had become enthused with the idea of joining the police force, he was hurt and dismayed at her rejection of him as would-be lover and lifetime partner.

She was ashamed of her secret pride in his desire for her, as well as startled by it. She had never entertained feelings of that kind throughout her teenage years. Her disinclination, and even inability, to behave as her contemporaries did as she passed through adolescence had occasionally disturbed her, but she had grown used to feeling 'different'. Then fate had reunited her with Elsbeth Hobbs, thrown them together in these new and totally foreign surroundings, and all the cloudy uncertainties, all the secret fears, had become clear. She knew what she was, knew what it was that had always made her feel different, and she was fiercely glad of it, despite the shame that came with it.

She hadn't the right vocabulary to express it. In any case, Beth would never discuss it, even in their most intimate moments, except in the conventional terms which applied to normal relationships, and even then, only with the greatest reluctance. She hardly ever volunteered 'I love you'. Alice had to put the question, press her for an answer, which itself came out almost grudgingly. 'You know I do! You don't have to keep asking!' But sometimes Alice did. She needed the reassurance of it, because it all seemed so unbelievable. It sometimes frightened her how intense her own passion was for the lovely golden girl, how dreamlike the magic of their precious time together. At those special moments, Beth seemed to bring a kind of innocence to their love, as if it were the most natural thing in the world; as if there *was* no world outside of their room, their bed. Nothing, no one waiting to condemn or deny them.

How could Alice tell the truth, even to Davy? There was a part of her that wanted to, to end the hope that she sensed he still clung to, even after she had gently refused his offer of love; his letters after he had left for York told her as much, in spite of their tone of wry, humorous acceptance of non-requital. Just as there had been an even briefer, more treacherous part of her which had seen a possibility of a way out, an escape from her own 'abnormality', when he had first proposed to her. But she was even more ashamed at the very notion that she could consider such a betrayal of the essential truth of her.

It was still dark when Davy came off shift. The December early morn was black and there was a biting penetration in the air which hung about the river. He felt it through the thickness of his greatcoat, and the uniform beneath it, and the thickness of the underwear beneath that. The cold struck up through the still squeaky boots as he groped for the bicycle propped in the yard at the rear of the station, numbed his gloveless fingers as he fumbled to get the slitted lamp adjusted, to direct its feeble, pencil-thin beam down to his front wheel and its battered mudguard. It wasn't adequate to stop him bumping into things, but it might just be enough to prevent things bumping into him.

Even at this early hour the city streets could be hazardous, with the crowds of railway workers and the Rowntree's factory hands, the majority mounted on cycles like himself. Then there were the buses and trams, the vans and the odd taxi or private car, not to mention the horse drawn carts and hand pushed barrows. Accidents caused through the blackout had become the bane of every special constable's life, to say nothing of the nurses and auxiliaries at hospital or first aid posts, especially now that the winter darkness had well and truly set in. 'Roll on the light nights!' became the beat bobby's heartfelt cry, even if it made the Luftwaffe's task that much easier.

He sensed rather than saw the bulk of Clifford's Tower looming up into the sky, perched on its mound to his left, and the heavy boards around the foot of the grassy knoll, which narrowed the pavement and made pedestrians an added hazard on the busy road. Peering ahead through the dimness, he swung over to the right, negotiated the junction with Skeldergate Bridge, and crossed the river. A quick, involuntary glance over the parapet gave a suggestion of a slightly paler, oily sheen to indicate the water's surface, but he was concentrating too much on the traffic, most of it now coming towards him, to pay it any attention. Once over the bridge, he followed the curve of Bishopthorpe Road round to his left, noting the pale glimmers of paint on the lamp posts becoming spectrally visible in the reluctantly dawning day, counting them, his heart lifting at the prospect, of the fire-lit warmth of Mrs Lumley's kitchen, only a minute away, and the satisfaction of the mug of hot tea and the substantial breakfast spread on the chequered oilcloth of the large table; the stretching of stockinged feet towards the glow of the high fire in the range, then the welcome if initially icy embrace of the sheets in the room he shared with Bob Noone, whom he had probably passed heading in the opposite direction, towards Tower Street Police Station and his early start on the morning shift.

He turned into the closely intersected network of streets of terraced houses that made up the district of Clementhorpe, found Dubry Street and gave a growling cough at the richly pungent effluvium of soot and smoke, cast like a blanket over the narrow streets from a thousand discharging chimneys. The curtained blanks of the windows were just visible now, and the dark oblongs of the front doors, the faint paleness of the holystoned front steps. The door of No. 25 was unlocked. He pushed it open, and swiftly wheeled his bike into the long, narrow hall, closing the door hastily behind him. The wardens were wickedly keen around here, and were certainly not above lurking to catch any unfortunate transgressor of the blackout regulations.

'Morning, Mrs L. Only me. By lad, it's freezing out there this morning! We'll have snow before Christmas, I'll bet on it.'

He was aware of how lucky he was to have found digs as good as 25 Dubry Street, and a landlady as amiable as Irene Lumley. 'Reeny' was the pronunciation of the diminutive by which all her friends and intimates, including her husband, Dick, knew her, and doubtless that was the way they would spell it, too. It caused Davy some private amusement to contemplate how she and they would react to his own French version of the name. 'Renée' would be foreign in every sense to them. He settled for 'Mrs L', and she seemed pleased enough to be addressed thus. It was familiar but respectful, and recognized her position and authority. However her name was spelt or sounded, Davy knew how lucky he was that chance and timing had landed him here.

She was there, now, with that welcoming smile, as he propped his bike against the wall in the passage – he would wheel it out into the yard at the back later – and entered the brightly-lit heat of the kitchen. He resolutely pushed aside his roommate's enthusiastic, ribald comments from his consciousness. 'By heck! She's a cracker is our Reeny, eh? Imagine cuddling up to that in bed, eh, Davy?' He concentrated on fixing his gaze on her wide, clear-eyed smile, and away from the full splendour of her figure, the curves of her flesh which the thick woollen dressing gown could not disguise. The hairnet and the two metal crimps holding her dark honey-coloured hair at the front ought to have served to distract his thoughts from their wayward appreciation of her physical attraction, but they failed to do so. Maybe it was because she was still in her night attire – not that there could be anything more decent than that ankle length, checked gown. Or because of the exclusive intimacy of these early morning rendezvous in the kitchen. Her four-year-old boy, Micky, was still fast asleep, and her husband would most likely be asleep upstairs, too, if he were home, which, a lot of the time, as now for instance, he was not. He worked for LNER as a driver and was away from home most of the time, it seemed, in these hectic days. Perhaps that was why Davy entertained these wayward thoughts and beating impulses. They seemed to be stronger than ever at the end of his shift, when he was dog-tired and aching for his bed. Ready for bed! There you go again, he chided helplessly. Surely his libido should be flagging at these weary times? He tried not to catch a glimpse of her trim, bare ankles as he eased himself into his place at the table and she moved over to the blackleaded stove to pick up the teapot.

'Mr Lumley not home yet?' he asked, as she served him his breakfast of porridge oats, followed by a rasher of bacon, a portion of kidney and some fried bread, washed down with a mug of strong tea.

'Nay, he's not back till late tonight or maybe tomorrow morning. I never know.' She chuckled and tapped the side of her nose. 'Too hush-hush to tell me what's going on. He could be anywhere, from Land's End to t'other place, for all I know! He could have a fancy woman in every town!'

Davy searched desperately for some reply that would not be considered over-familiar or risqué. Bob Noone would have come up with something quick enough, and cheeky enough, too. 'He wouldn't do that, Mrs L. He's not that stupid,' he offered awkwardly, and she reached out and patted his sleeve. What dainty hands! As pretty as her ankles! With a silent groan, he admonished himself for his licentiousness. 'You shouldn't be getting up at this ungodly hour. We can fend for ourselves, you know. We know how to make tea – and there's a canteen of sorts at work.' She must have been up before five to get Bob Noone his breakfast.

'Nay, lad! I'll not have my lodgers going out without summat warm inside them, not in this weather. Oh! I slipped a hot water bottle in your bed. I hope you don't mind.'

'I couldn't be better cared for at home. You spoil us, Mrs L.'

'Get away with you! You get up them stairs. I'll try to keep our Micky quiet, if I can. His nana'll be coming round later on. She'll take him out of the way for a bit.'

She stood, leant over to take his plate away, and he saw the ruffled neck and the sprigged pattern of her nightdress between the lapels of the dressing gown.

'You haven't had a letter from that young lady of yours for a while now.' She smiled encouragingly. 'There'll be one in the post I expect. It'll be there when you wake up. You'll see.'

'Now now, Mrs L. She's just a good friend, that's all. I just got to know her when I was working in the Dales.'

'You don't fool me. Good-looking young feller like you! Bet you've broken a few hearts along the way already.'

'No such luck.' There was a slight pause, before he yawned exaggeratedly and stood. 'Well, I'll head on up.'

'Aye, off you go. I'll bring you a cuppa about two, when Bob gets in. I'm doing mince and dumplings for tea.'

'Great! 'Night. Whoops! I mean Morning!' Just like his mum, he thought as he mounted the dark stairs. Then again, he thought, perhaps not.

CHAPTER FOUR

'Davy! You awake, luv? It's half past two gone! Your mate's not in yet. I bet he's called in at t'Mucky Duck, the rascal! Here's a nice cup of tea. And there's a letter from that lass of yours. I told you there'd be one today, didn't I? Here you are then.'

She made enough cheerful noise and bustle, half opening the door and fussing before she came in, to make sure he would be decent when she entered. All that was showing was a tousled dark head, and a face emerging from the mound of blankets, as he groaned and blinked his way to consciousness. The room was in deep darkness, for he had not drawn back the heavy blackout drapes, and the light which filtered through the doorway from the little landing was a gloomy grey.

'She's not my lass, Mrs L.' She chuckled derisively. A little more of him emerged as he struggled up onto his elbows, and he displayed the top of his striped pyjama jacket, fastened to the uppermost button, and one sleeve as he snaked out his hand to take the mug from her, with a murmur of thanks.

'She must think summat of you to write as often as she does. I'm sure I've never had anywhere near as many letters in all my married life, and that's five years and more now.'

Davy grinned. 'Have you ever been apart?'

'You what? You know yourself our Dick spends more time away than he does at home. Not that it's his fault, I know. There *is* a war on!' She trotted out the trite phrase in a humorous tone. 'There's plenty of hot water. I'd get your wash and shave before your mate Bob gets at it. I don't know what that lad does in that bathroom. Worse than a lass, he is! He'd have a bath every night if he had his way!'

But after she had departed, he swung out of bed only to draw back both sets of curtains to allow the murky daylight in, then scrambled back under the bedclothes with a sense of decadent luxury and tore open the envelope. At least Alice had stopped apologizing for her poor spelling and lack of linguistic skill, which he had never failed to assure her, truthfully, were more than adequate. In fact, there were a good number from far more privileged backgrounds that were nowhere near as good. 'You'll have to take me as you find me.' One of her most favoured sayings, and delivered with that pugnacious defensiveness he had come to know so well during the months of their acquaintance. Which he was more than happy to do, as he found her more and more delightful the more he got to know her. He admired her straightforward, full-speed-ahead approach, her undaunted cheerfulness, and her determination not to be knocked down, or to stay down if she *did* take a fall. There was absolutely no side to her, which made her so different from almost all the girls he had known – except for one, he acknowledged, as he strove to push the pain of Lou's memory away from him. Alice just didn't give a damn about clothes or looks or using her feminine wiles or anything like that. It was what he loved her for. And he *did* love her. Perhaps not with the depth and blend of spirituality and passion he had felt for the unattainable Lou, but with a feeling strong enough to ensure that he could find happiness and comfort in spending a lifetime with her.

He felt the sadness of her absence as he stared at the familiar, square script, smiled tenderly at the remembrance of her awkwardness, her ineptness when he had first kissed her properly, passionately, taken her in his arms. 'I can't be doing with all that!' she had declared, close to tears he could see, when he had asked her to accept his proposal. And though he couldn't quite understand it, he had to accept it, for he knew she was being truthful with him, as she always was. He still clung to a half-hope that she might change her mind some day, though he had to admit there was little chance while they remained apart. As he read this latest letter and the bubbling, full account of the minutiae of her existence, and the characters of Howbeck and their doings, her enthusiasm made the hope of winning her even fainter. She was happy enough. He had to face it. She sounded enthusiastic about her life with Elsbeth Hobbs. It struck him that she sounded perfectly fulfilled with her relationship with the pretty blonde girl. It used almost to exasperate him the way she would so good humouredly put herself down when comparing herself with her friend. 'She's so lovely!' she would say, with clearly heartfelt appreciation, and with no sense of envy. The young teacher was pretty, it was true, but he had always thought her rather insipid, too much the shrinking violet, in great contrast to Alice. Not that he would ever say so – Alice would have gone for him like a terrier after a rat! Well, he supposed he should be glad she was so content, but he couldn't help feeling more than a little envious himself of the teacher's good fortune in living under the same roof as her staunch champion.

We're going home for the Christmas break next week. Beth's dad is coming through to pick us up on the 23rd. There's posh, eh? I'll have to get him to drop me off at the end of our road, otherwise the whole street'll turn out to gawp. You don't get motors in Maudsley Street every day. I'm hoping we can come back here together on 27th – I'll have to be back for work anyway – your old boss, Mr Barr, can be a bit of a slave driver. Mind you, I shouldn't call him! As you know, now that I've turned twenty (last Sunday and I've already thanked you for my card and my present. I'm still reading it when I get time. I try reading in bed but Beth gets mad – I'm usually snoring after five minutes with the book on my chest and the lamp still on! I don't mean it's boring or anything, it's just I'm so dead beat at night. All this working outside – you know what it's like!)

I've lost myself now! Oh yes! I have to register now I'm twenty. I was a bit worried that they wouldn't recognize the job here, but Mr Barr's doing his best and has written a letter about the work, how it's war work and I'm working with the land girls and all that – Evelyn and Beryl are still here, still as bitchy as ever and causing ructions down in the Oddfellows! So I'm hoping I'll be all right and won't have to go off anywhere for training or anything. Beth isn't twenty till March, but I'm sure she'll be fine with her teaching job. So hopefully we'll be able to stay on here for as long as the war lasts – I do hope so, as I'm really happy here the way things are – except for missing you, of course! XX

He smiled again, a little sadly. So much for keeping his hopes burning. He had bought her a book for her birthday. He had wondered what she would think of such a gift. He had considered a scarf, or a brooch; something distinctly feminine. But he knew how little concern she had for such fripperies. He smiled when he remembered her fury when Gus Rielke had, with calculated maliciousness, presented her with the item of silk underwear, in the humiliating public environs of the bar of the Oddfellows. At that moment the crooked Norwegian had sealed his fate, if only he'd known it. She'd been spitting blood for days!

So Davy had decided to take the risk and send her a copy of Graham Greene's latest novel: *The Confidential Agent*. He was a writer Davy admired. There was far more to his books than the hard, fast paced thrillers they appeared to be. At least it was far from the romantic women's fiction which he was certain Alice would have nothing but contempt for, if she ever read such stuff. Mind you, she wasn't exactly wild with enthusiasm over Greene, either. No doubt she'd tell him what she really thought of it when she'd finished reading it.

He heard the faint sound of music from the wireless drifting up, and then the sound of the front door. Bob Noone called out a greeting, and Mrs L replied. Swiftly Davy kicked back the bedclothes, swung his feet out to the cold. He remembered the landlady's warning. He'd better get to the bathroom quick, before his hygiene-conscious roommate struck.

When he entered the kitchen again half an hour later, he was freshly shaven, hair neatly parted and combed. He was wearing his uniform shirt, and the serge uniform trousers, but he was without collar and tie. A dark blue sleeveless pullover hid the white canvas braces. Bob, similarly casual, but minus the pullover and with his front stud unfastened, was lounging in one of the two easy chairs, his stockinged feet resting on the upper rim of the solid mesh fireguard. He was glancing through the newspaper but more concerned with chatting to Irene Lumley, who, with a daunting pile of clothes in the basket beside her was ironing away, face flushed. At the same time, she was keeping an eye on her son, Micky, playing with his wooden animals and Noah's ark at her feet. The electric light was on, and the window looking out onto the back yard already showed a faint reflection of the room because of the murky remains of the daylight.

'Bunch up, you, and let the dog see the rabbit,' Irene said to Bob, as an indication that he should let Davy have access to the fireside. She beamed her wide smile at Davy, and as always he noted appreciatively the prominent, high cheekbones, the exceptional quality of her even teeth, the dimples and the open warmth of the grey-blue eyes. The hairnet of the early morning had been replaced by the scarf tied turban fashion about her hair and knotted high at the front, the ends sticking up like two little rabbit ears, just over the metal clamps of the curlers still in place. The flowered pinafore over the old skirt and blouse, and even the wrinkled lisle stockings and the soft felt slippers could not disguise her attractive form, nor prevent the involuntary flash of lustful thought before he banished it sternly.

'Still hasn't snowed. The sky's looked full of it all day.'

'Too cold for snow,' Bob observed, moving his feet and drawing back his long legs a little as Davy sat down in the remaining cushioned chair in front of the fire. 'Hey! Did you see that report? Our friend was out again. You let him slip through your fingers again, eh?'

'See it? I had to type up the blessed thing!' Davy answered. 'Wasn't on my beat, thank goodness! Up Micklegate. Not far from the Bar. Just after chucking out time.'

Bob laughed. 'That's what you get for being educated, see? You get all the rotten jobs. Me, I'm still on me ABCs. Leastways, that's what I tell the duty sarge. He wouldn't even send me for the fish and chips, in case I get the change wrong.'

The criminal activity they referred to was becoming an increasingly recurrent one – of robbery, perpetrated by their very own 'Sandshoe Charlie'. It was a name used in several towns and cities to indicate the fleet footed robbers, so called because of the rubber soled, light canvas pumps they favoured. The blackout provided excellent cover for their crimes. They preyed on women who were out after dark, speeding out of the shadows and snatching handbags or shopping bags and sprinting away again, usually with no more violence than that required to wrench the bag from the startled victim's grasp. The swift and sudden assault often caused far more lasting distress than the physical violence or the material losses involved, to say nothing of the inconvenience of losing essential documents like a national identity card, or ration books. And in one case at least in York, an elderly lady had bravely or instinctively clung on to her bag, and been flung violently to the ground before her attacker could tear it from her hold. She had received a fractured arm, and severe bruising all down one side of her body, as well as the shock, which might well have done further damage to her heart.

Although descriptions were of necessity very vague, there was a similarity about them – the dress of the victim: black or dark Balaclava, a long, flapping, much stained mackintosh, dirty white pumps, as well as the height, and the growling cry he gave as he struck, like that of an angry dog – that suggested this was the work of one person. The attacks had been reported in the *Evening Press*, and women were being warned about being out alone or carrying substantial sums of money with them. Sandshoe Charlie's reputation was such that many women were now avoiding going out after dark if possible. But with so many women working these days, and with darkness descending by four o' clock, it made life difficult.

'You want to hurry up and catch this devil.' Irene Lumley's iron thumped with extra firmness down on the narrow board. 'He's making us prisoners inside our own homes! Get him behind bars and keep him there till the war's over.'

Easier said than done, though, Davy thought. They were stretched enough as it was to man all the beats in the city. More than half the force was made up of specials now, and most of them were part time, not full timers like himself and Bob.

Irene spoke forcefully again. 'In fact, prison's too good for him. Too safe!

They should stick him in the front line somewhere, in the desert. Or send him up in one of those bombers flying over Germany. The rotten little coward! Staying safe at home to attack women!'

While Bob made some typical light-hearted remark to take the edge off Irene's sudden flare of righteous indignation, Davy, not for the first time, was disturbed by the direction of his inner thoughts. Too safe in prison. The phrase reverberated in his brain, as he recalled the grimness of the northern gaol, which had quickly become a nightmare, then a hell for him, in which he had seriously contemplated seeking death as a way out. It was an option he probably would have chosen if he had not been rescued. His hold on reality had faltered so much, especially when that reality was such a drowning sense of hopelessness.

Another phrase of hers throbbed like an old wound on his conscience. 'Rotten little coward. Staying safe at home . . .' As far as he knew, no one in York was aware of his past, incredible though it seemed. Norman Holden, the detective inspector from the North Yorkshire Constabulary he had worked with to break up the racket Gus Rielke had been involved in, had assured him it could be kept secret. It was D. I. Holden who had first suggested Davy should apply to join the police force. 'There's not just baduns abroad, Davy, lad, as you well know.' He did, too, for the ring which he had, in his undercover role as police informant, allowed himself to be dragged into by Gus, was a large scale and highly organized group operating throughout the north-east.

The scholarly looking, authoritative figure of Holden quickly saw beyond Davy's diffident reserve. He recognized the deep-seated sense of morality which underlay Davy's character, empathized with it, so that the forty-year-old husband and parent, and the young, spiritually bruised Davy developed a closeness which both valued. Davy finally agreed to make an application to join the force, supported by Holden, who pulled more strings than Davy was aware of to ensure his success.

'You fought in Spain, spent a year in France, and returned home. You've got a C-3 medical category. Your time in Spain explains that. What happened afterwards isn't part of your recorded history. Not as far as our lot are concerned, all right? They'll take you on as a special. Three months' training. Posting to the City of York Force. Good place to start. I'll have my eye on you. See how you take to it. Get in a bit of beat bashing, then, if you're still keen we'll find something for you in our branch. Plain clothes.'

The inspector was as good as his word. He did keep a friendly eye out, and made no secret of his interest in the new recruit, dropping in at Tower Street now and then for an informal chat about his progress.

Irene's laugh rang out, and dispersed his sombre reflections. It hurt to think of how she might feel if she learnt the truth about him. He was not ashamed of any of it, except for that final weakness which had broken him down in prison. But he was glad enough to let it remain secret, and to be guilty of a number of lies of omission. Maybe he would make a reasonable detective after all.

CHAPTER FIVE

Beth looked suitably wretched and penitent, and her big blue eyes pleaded for understanding. 'I *have* to stay at home over New Year, Al! I can't get out of it. Mummy – mum and dad,' she quickly corrected herself, 'would have a fit if I said I was coming back to Howbeck before then. The term isn't starting until the fifteenth. As it is, I'll have to fib and tell them I have to come back early for some work. It'll have to be the fourth or fifth at the earliest!' She gave a penitent little moan and reached for Alice's hand.

Alice allowed it to be captured, but let it lie limply unresponsive in her friend's hold. 'Bloody hell, Beth! I've got to be back here on the twenty-eighth. To start work next day, on the Monday. And I'll probably have to travel on the twenty-seventh, to make sure of a train. You know what Sundays are like. I'll be here on my own for more than a week.'

'You won't be on your own, will you? You'll have Beryl and Evelyn.'

Alice's hand suddenly came alive. It broke free of Beth's hold, to seize her thin wrist, its grip tight as she held Beth close to her and watched the redness mount in Beth's face, the soft eyes flicker away from her direct gaze. 'Not exactly the same, is it, sweetheart? Eh?' The bitterness of her disappointment forced the element of fierce accusation into her tone. She could not help herself, even as she realized she was being unfair, could appreciate and had anticipated the difficulty Beth was faced with.

'I'm sorry, Al,' Beth murmured miserably. 'You know I'd rather be with you. But I can't get out of it.' She made a small movement and Alice released her. There was a faint circle of redness on the skin where Alice had held her.

'Not half as sorry as I am, kidder!' The bitterness was still there, so that the attempted lightness came as a barb. Nor could she prevent herself from continuing it, with the same sarcastic flippancy. 'But then you never are, are you? Seems I'm the one who has to make all the running, all ways up. You're never that bothered, are you?'

'Don't, Al! Please!' Those lovely eyes were begging now, and filled with tears. The hands moved, reached for her, and Alice stood woodenly, allowed the arms to hold her, felt the thin body press close to hers, the face nuzzle into her with another soft moan. Almost reluctantly, Alice's hands came up to take in the bent, yielding frame, hug it to her, stroking the blonde head, the proffered curve of the back.

Alice wondered yet again why she let these strange moods spoil things, felt this sudden intense dissatisfaction that crept in to spoil the bliss. She had found more happiness than she had ever imagined possible with this lovely girl. Why wasn't it enough? Most of the time, their private time together, it was. So what more could she possibly yearn for? What else was there?

But there *was* something, and every now and then she could not ignore it. Beth would rarely speak about it, about their love. The trouble was, Alice could understand that, how her lovely, beloved girl found it nigh on impossible to express their love. Except in the glorious and tender actions of their bodies in their exclusive union. And that was the heart of the trouble. There were no words for it; at least no decent words, none that could truly acknowledge what they felt for each other. Beth blushed, deeply ashamed, at Al's clumsy efforts to do so, looked haunted, frightened by those attempts, trapped by them. And Al ended up as always, defeated, secretly hurt and feeling hopeless. Outside of these rooms, this little haven and shabby heaven, they were just friends. 'Best mates', in the crude terminology of Al's background. And Beth was content, went on sunnily in that other world, the one outside, as though she could keep the two worlds entirely separate. And which one was the real one, did she think?

Alice let her go, moved towards the kitchenette, spoke gruffly over her shoulder. 'Forget me. I'm just a grumpy old bitch! Listen. The lasses were saying there's a special do tomorrow. The hop. Last Saturday before Christmas. Supper laid on and everything. In the village hall. They're going. I said I'd see if you fancied it. How about it? Get us in the mood for the holidays. What do you reckon?'

There was only the slightest hesitation before Beth answered, 'I don't mind. I'm game if you are.'

'Right! You're on! They're starting off with a drink in the pub first. All right?'

'Oh!' The hesitation and reluctance were even plainer now. 'Is that a good idea, do you think?'

'Yes, I do. And I know what *you're* thinking an' all! Listen, the place'll be packed out. Old Ma Rhodes probably won't even know we're there. And anyway she won't dare say 'owt. She's not that daft. Good will to all men, eh? Even us!'

They made sure of getting over to the main house early on the Saturday afternoon, soon after their lunch, and bagging the cold, old bathroom shared by the staff, well before the two Land Girls and any of the others could ensconce themselves in the bare, brick-walled room. 'You hop in first,' Alice commanded, and Beth was happy to obey. She squealed, and paused before lowering herself gingerly into the steaming heat. 'Shut up, you little fairy! At least you haven't got all *my* muck in there with you. And I want it to be a bit warm still when it's my turn. So come on. Bend forward and I'll do your back for you. And hurry up. I'm freezing here!'

Beth turned and glanced up mischievously. 'Jump in with me if you want! There's room if we squinsh up a bit.' She squealed as Alice thrust down the baggy bottom of her siren suit and kicked it free, then hauled the top up over her head. 'You sure the door's bolted?' She squealed again as Alice descended with a foamy splash in a tangle of limbs.

Alice was right about the Oddfellows being busy. The four girls had to squeeze their way into the public bar and stand patiently in line waiting to be served. She was wrong, however, about Vera Rhodes not noticing them. Though she and the two barmaids were going at full stretch, she had time to direct a glitteringly hostile look at Alice. Her voice was loud above the babel of conversations. 'My word! What do we owe this honour to? Long time since you've shown your face round here, i'n't it?'

'Season of good will, eh?' Alice stared straight back at her, her face wreathed in a challenging smile.

Annie Hogan was the one who was serving them. She was one of the villagers who had worked with Alice preparing the meals during the time when Lister Road pupils had been evacuees in Howbeck. Annie was in her early thirties and did a variety of domestic jobs to supplement the wages of her farmhand husband. Alice had crossed verbal swords with her on more than one occasion, especially over Davy Brown. Annie had been one of his most wickedly outspoken enemies during his stay. The relationship between Alice and Annie had never been an easy one. The residue showed now, as she gave a malicious smirk and said, 'Buying your own drinks, lasses? That's a shame. Haven't any of you got fellers to get 'em in for you? Don't know what the world's coming to, women buying drinks over the bar! And two such bonny lasses as Evelyn and Miss Hobbs there an' all!'

'Ta very much, Annie! You say the nicest things!' Alice was unperturbed.

'Just as well you're wearing the trousers then!' Annie sniped, as she handed over the change to Alice.

Evelyn Hughes, whose auburn hair was piled in an elaborate combination of waves and curls, and whose full bosomed figure was displayed to advantage in her flowered dance frock, grinned and winked a mascara-clad eye, then glanced around, saying eloquently, 'We don't want to waste ourselves on this lot. We're saving ourselves for them Americans. They reckon there'll be hordes of them flocking over here soon!'

Alice noticed the inevitable blush which had covered Beth's features, and felt a sudden, disloyal stab of irritation. Why does she always have to look like that, at the least little thing? So bloody mortified about it all. Unable to prevent herself, she slipped her free arm about Beth's slim waist and gave her a squeeze. 'We don't need no clodhoppers flinging us about like a sack of tatties, do we, luv?'

'Chance would be a fine thing for some!' Annie retorted, then, with added malevolence as she turned to the next clamouring customer, 'Shame young Mister Luke's not here, eh, miss?'

Beth looked as though she would turn and run at any second, and Alice eased them away from the dripping counter. They could feel the gritty sawdust beneath the thin soles of their best shoes. 'Wonder how Ma Rhodes is managing these days without Gus?' Beryl Ennis snickered through her long nose, and Alice's grin widened. 'I mean for getting her booze, you mucky tyke! I'm sure there's plenty of dirty sods round here who'll keep her well supplied with the other!'

'It's not funny!' Beth protested over the sniggering of her three companions. 'Think of her poor husband. A prisoner in France.'

'Germany,' Beryl corrected her. 'They've moved them to camps in Germany.' Beryl was not in the least abashed by Beth's earnestness. 'And don't you worry, chuck. There's plenty more not so far away as Germany whose wives are having a bit on the side. And blokes, too. Eh, our Evelyn?'

The attractive girl gave a squeal of delighted outrage. 'How dare you! That's slander, that is!'

'Oh! Is that what they call it?' Beryl answered wryly, her thick eyebrows raised in high arches, and even Beth giggled a little, in spite of her sense of moral discomfiture.

It was after midnight when Alice and Beth got into their cold bed and hugged each other's shivering frames until they had created once more their blissfully warm cocoon against the chill outside. 'Enjoy yourself?' Alice probed, savouring the feel of Beth's head against her breast and the softness of her hair across her mouth and cheek. 'Tell you what. I don't know about Evelyn and her goings-on, but I reckon poor old Malcolm's well and truly smitten.'

Malcolm Aygarth was married to Eileen. They had three children and farmed at Howbeck Side, on the northern slope of the dale above the village. Alice and her little brother, Algy, had been billeted there, and had quickly been made to feel part of the family. Eileen had been deeply sorry to see both of them go. Alice made a point of making the long climb up the hill out of the village to call in at their cottage once a week or so. Beth was well aware that Al was merely teasing her because Malcolm had gallantly asked Beth for a dance, as he had Alice, and had clearly enjoyed steering the pretty blonde around the crowded floor.

'Our last day together tomorrow,' Alice said, against the fragrant hair. 'Alone, I mean. I'm not counting Monday. We'll be with your dad. We'll be back in Margrove by dinner time.' She felt Beth's arms tighten against her.

'It's only for a couple of weeks. We'll soon be back here again.'

Alice grunted. 'It'll be next year.' Beth had said nothing about the time they would be in Margrove. Their houses were scarcely two miles apart, but the social gulf between them was enormous. Did Alice really expect Beth to invite her up to that posh house, with a front *and* back garden, up by the park, where all the nobs lived? Or for Beth to come tripping down to Maudsley Street, looking as gorgeous as a dainty butterfly, and sit in their kitchen? With dad probably coming in black as the ace of spades from the steelworks and stinking of ale from the Black Horse, and George with his mucky, spotty, leering grin and his eyes undressing her as she sat there? And how would she feel seeing her lovely girl picking her way out into the yard and the netty with its draughty wooden door rattling, and the squares of Titbits hung on a nail?

But still she wished for it to be different. I'd be on my best behaviour, she vowed to herself, and I'd dress up real smart. I'd even wear a frock if you wanted me to, and dab make-up on my face and lipstick on my gob! 'Oh, I'm really going to miss you, lass!' she whispered forlornly, and felt all the weight of her heavy heart when silence followed her confession.

The following morning, Alice gave the little flat a thorough clean, which took no longer than the duration of the morning service at St John's, which Beth attended. She would normally have been required to do so as part of her official duties, escorting the crocodile of schoolgirls down into the village, but the St Anne's pupils had departed the previous week for the holiday. 'Why don't you come? Sing some carols? And the church looks lovely.'

Alice laughed. 'What? Me? Go in with your lot? You must be joking!

Blooming roof might fall in, or get struck with lightning or summat! I've told you, I'm a right heathen. Eileen's always trying to get me to go to chapel, but it's not for me, none of it! No. I'll give this place a bit of a clean-up while you're out, otherwise your dad's gonna think we live in a right tip! Say one for me, kidder, while you're in there.'

Alice even had time to prepare the dinner – she still couldn't bring herself to call it 'lunch', in spite of Beth's influence – and have it ready to serve when Beth returned. 'Sit yourself down. Your cheeks look rosy. Still nippy out there, eh?'

'There's snow on the tops. I hope we don't have a fall tonight. Daddy might not be able to get through if the road's bad.'

'Can't wait to get away from me, eh? Only joking!' Alice added quickly, over Beth's protest. 'Here, get stuck in. It's the mutton stew warmed up, but there's some of Eileen Aygarth's bread, still nice and fresh. We need to use it up today.'

Beth sat at the table and Alice served both plates from the saucepan she brought from the stove. 'You'll have to get used to doing things right and proper from tomorrow,' she said as she joined her. There was a pang of regret behind her light tone. 'I hope you can remember the right knives and forks to use. My rough and ready browtins-up might've rubbed off on you.'

Beth shrugged and shook her head in disagreement. 'Don't be daft! We're just ordinary – we're not toffs, you know. Not like up at t'Big 'Ouse!' She mimicked the local accent accurately.

'See? You're even starting to sound like me now! Your folks'll kill me!' No they won't, she thought. They won't see me. Except for your dad, and I'll be as good as gold. Sit like a mouse and keep me gob shut and say yes please and no thank you.

'I wish you wouldn't.' Beth stopped eating and gazed at Alice reproachfully.

'What?' Alice affected innocence, arching her brows and staring questioningly at her.

'You know darned well what! Making out like we're from two different worlds or something. It's just not true.'

'Isn't it?' Suddenly, at the simple question, all pretence at playfulness had gone. That pleading look came over Beth's features, as though she were begging her not to go on. 'It couldn't be truer. And you can't say different.'

Beth laid down her knife and fork, stared at Alice with that hurt expression and a helpless vulnerability. 'Don't, Al! Don't spoil things. Everything's fine.' She gestured eloquently about them at the shabby cosiness. 'When we're here, like this. It's just us. It's lovely.'

'Aye. With the door shut and bolted and the curtains drawn and us all snug. You're right, lass. It's great.' Her curly head jerked as she nodded behind her. 'But the world's still out there. It hasn't gone away because we've shut the door. It's still waiting.'

'But it's not like that in *here*!' The colour showed on Beth's face and her blue eyes shone with her tears. 'As long as we've got this, to ourselves, just—'

'Just the two of us?' Alice completed fiercely. 'Aye. But we can't stay hiding ourselves away in here for ever! Like I said. The world out there doesn't just disappear.'

The golden head drooped. Beth whispered, 'It does when I'm here with you.' She looked up again. 'Don't let's spoil it while we've still got it.'

Alice felt an overwhelming rush of despair, and tenderness and love – and a great frustration that she could not put into words, or even clarify in her thoughts. 'I love you!' she said.

Beth said nothing, simply nodded, and they both sat, eyes wide and shining with tears, holding each other's gaze as the food slowly cooled and congealed on their plates.

CHAPTER SIX

It dismayed Alice to discover how far her alienation from her family and life in Maudsley Street had progressed, and in little more than fifteen months. Even the 'Christmas spirit' and the dangerous times could do nothing to lift her – if anything, they emphasized it all the more. In her own defence, she acknowledged that she had rarely, after puberty, felt blissfully happy here. There had been a keen sense of isolation, in spite of scarcely ever being alone, apart from the chilly sanctuary of the backyard netty and its bolted door. She must have become good at fooling people, she guessed, for her school report on leaving Lister Road had spoken of her 'cheerfulness', and Miss Laverton, only a few months ago, when the Lister Road evacuees had left the village of Howbeck to return home, had written a recommendation applauding her 'indomitable spirit of cheerfulness and determination'. In fact, she must have become pretty damned good at fooling people, that's all she could say of herself.

She felt guilty, especially when she saw how pleased mam was to have her back. There was precious little sign of it from the others, except for little Algy, of course. She felt a nostalgic pang that first morning when she woke to feel his scrawny frame burrowing into hers in the warmth of the lumpy old bed in the front bedroom, and his sleepy grin of contentment at the feel of her arms going around him; in great contrast to the scowl from her sister, Ethel, sleeping on his other side, and her crabby complaints at having to sleep three instead of two to the bed. It was amazing how that scowl could transform what was rapidly blossoming to genuine beauty into the mean stamp of dissatisfaction that reflected life in these terraced streets. At fourteen, Ethel was already showing the delicate, graceful lines which Alice could admire without envy. It was a beauty her younger sister, Doreen, would acquire, too, as she matured. So why not me? Alice wondered wryly, but without any real rancour. First born but not first served, certainly not in the looks department, anyhow. I got the brains instead! And a lot of good they've done me, she thought. Doreen was the one going to the grammar school in Whitby. Let's just hope she had enough sense to make the most of her ticket to freedom.

Guilt weighed even more heavily on her at seeing Doreen's opportunity in those terms. Alice knew how much mam had been hurt by Doreen's failure to return home for Christmas, though she was so quick to excuse it. 'Miss Ramsay wanted her with her. All the way down to wherever-it-is, eh? Just think! Travelling all that way. And we'll see her after New Year. Summat to look forward to, after the Christmas and all that. Perk us up a bit, eh?'

Dad just made the bile rise in Alice's throat with his show of righteous anger and parental indignation. 'Too high and mighty for us now, is Miss lah-di-dah Doreen! Forgetting where she's come from, if you ask me!'

Miss Ramsay *did* ask you, didn't she, dad? she felt like saying. All nice and legal. You signed a paper, solicitors and the lot. And don't make out you didn't know what you were doing, handing her over. And for a tidy sum, too, though none of us will ever know how much. All mam had said was, 'Miss Ramsay's been very good. Helped us out a bit. She insisted.' And Maggie Glass had looked so wretched and ashamed that Alice hadn't the heart to press her any more. And it was for her mam's sake that Alice was struggling so hard to keep the lid on the simmering saucepan of her rage at her dad's supremely hypocritical exhibition of patriarchal sensibility.

At least mam had a new dining suite – the first of their twenty years of married life – and a new outfit: a costume in the 'utility' style, in navy blue. 'Skirt's far too short,' Maggie complained. 'I can't be showing that much of me legs!' She'd used a great number of the coupons which had become obligatory with the advent of clothing rationing in June.

'A right waste!' Ethel told Alice, in scornful confidence. 'When's she ever gonna go anywhere to wear it?' Probably with some justification, Alice acknowledged. But Maggie wore it for Christmas Day and Boxing Day. She had her hair done by Daisy Liddle a few doors down, and with her face made up, and cheeks flushed with unaccustomed drinks of brandy and sherry, she looked startlingly different from the mother drudge they had all known and ignored for so long. There was even a ghostly glimmer of the looks so evident in Ethel and Doreen – and conspicuously absent in her own case, Alice self-mockingly noted.

But even Alice washed her hair, softened it with the water from the rain barrel in the backyard, fluffed and brushed up her bronzy curls. She wore a white short-sleeved blouse, with the chocolate-brown slacks, one of the pairs Beth had given her a few months back, and which Jess Corbett had altered for her. 'Beth's an inch or two longer in the leg than me but my backside's twice as fat as hers, so you've got your work cut out!' But Jess had made a good job of the alterations, and Alice thought she looked quite smart.

It stung her all the more when, as they gathered for the festive meal on Christmas Day, her dad said, 'God! Haven't you got a skirt you could put on? I've never seen you in 'owt but trousers since you were a bairn!'

'Tek no notice of him, luv! You look right smart.'

Before she could take comfort from her mother's words, her brother George leapt joyously to the attack. 'By heck! Look at the arms on her, eh? Muscles like Samson the Strong Man!'

'Only thing big about you is your gob!' she fired back. She was angrier with herself at being so hurt than at the gibes themselves. Once again she found herself wondering if Beth's gentle influence on her was turning her soft.

'That's all *you* know!' George's leer raised her anger to murder level. 'But then, you wouldn't know about that kind of thing, would you? Not interested, are you?'

Now it was a snickering Ethel who seized her chance to join in. 'Oh, I dunno. How's that conchie feller you're pally with? The one that helped catch that gang of crooks last summer? Still good mates, are you?'

Alice was startled at how vulnerable she felt. 'Yes, we are!' she answered roundly. 'Shows how interested you are in what goes on. I told you ages ago – he went to York. Joined the police. He writes now and then.'

And back came her father, the leader of the pack, the foam from the stout unattractively coating his sneering lips. He gazed round the table in triumphant appeal. 'Wouldn't you know it, eh? The only feller she can get to show any interest is some yeller-bellied bloody conchie who's too scared to do his bit!'

'Like you, you mean? And *you*?' she rounded back on her brother, her eyes blazing. 'Making money hand over fist, taking all the overtime you can get and boozing it away in t'Black 'Oss?' Her voice had risen, and shook with emotion, and, to her horror, she could feel tears welling behind her eyes.

'Now that's enough! You can shurrup, the lot of you!' Maggie had risen, and she flourished a knife round the table at all of them. The strength of her outburst startled and silenced them, and they gawped open-mouthed. 'It's Christmas Day. We weren't together last Christmas, and God knows where we'll be next Christmas. We're all together now, except for our Doreen, God bless her, and we're gonna enjoy it! All right?'

There was no answer. She probably didn't expect one, but, as Sir Thomas More once observed in a court of law, *Qui tacet consentire videtur.*

*

The Christmas meal in the Hobbs household began in a much less volatile and more harmonious fashion. The blackout and the velvet winter curtains were already drawn against the afternoon murk, for what looked like becoming a heavy fall of snow over on the moors, which had begun the day before Christmas Eve, had at the coast deposited no more than a sprinkling of white, like the icing on a cake, before changing to a freezing sleet, which had all the biting wintry chill and none of the picture postcard attractiveness. There was even a precious log crackling in the red tiled, low hearth, necessitating the placing of the fireguard before they moved to the dining-room and its less traditional but more efficient gas-fire glow. The black spidery stumps of the rose bushes and the neatly trimmed privet hedge were shivering under the slanting grey onslaught, which rattled the windows impotently, as though furious at the solid, warm haven of the house. Its name, 'Holmlea', engraved and painted in white letters on its varnished oak sign, swung on the ends of the two short chains which secured it to the hooks in the curved arch of brickwork over the entrance to the outer porch.

'Come on, Arthur. Take a seat. In between our Bill and Elsbeth. Beauty and the beast, eh?' The chuckle which accompanied these words took away from the ascetic look of Elsbeth's father, Cedric. His face was thin, and he was almost completely bald on top, with dark hair neatly trimmed about his ears. A pair of black framed spectacles with circular lenses added to the studious look, and his dark moustache, though fully covering the space between nose and upper lip, was chopped off sharply at the corners of the rather small, prim mouth. A bit like Mr Attlee, Elsbeth thought – or, rather, a shamefully disloyal comparison – like Adolf Hitler's. All in all, together with his conservative taste of cut and colouring in his three-piece suits, he could appear somewhat stern, and formal, like an academic, or a cabinet minister.

Their guest was still a little unsure of him. Beth could tell by the quick but uncertain smile Arthur Clark threw at him. The young man had been quite a shock to Beth, who had had no idea that he was coming. She hadn't expected her eldest brother, Bill, to be there at all, but here he was, unexpectedly given leave until the twenty-ninth, and bringing this stranger with him, a fellow second lieutenant from the same detachment of the Royal Signals Corps. They were both in the late stages of a training which had lasted six months or more, and were expecting a posting in another two months. 'Far East is the favourite buzz,' her brother told them breezily. 'Now that the Japs have joined in, they'll be shipping boatloads out to India to hold back the yellow hordes.' His words had been delivered lightly, his manner feigned or otherwise, as they all sat round the fire on Christmas Eve. An hour later they listened to the nightly wireless bulletin, and the reader's solemn tones as he announced the grave threat to Hong Kong.

When they were all gathered round the table for the meal on Christmas Day, Mildred Hobbs tried to insist on banishment of all talk of the war, but it was not easy. Rob, at fifteen,the youngest of the three children, bombarded the two fledgling military men with questions and speculations as to which theatre of operations they might be posted. He was at school near Harrogate, and full of the exploits of his OTC unit. In spite of his eagerness, he did manage not to express his most fervent wish, that hostilities might continue until he could rush to the colours. Beth's older brother succeeded in maintaining an atmosphere of lightness by highly humorous accounts of incidents during their training, diffidently supported by his companion, who appeared rather shy. Beth warmed to him at once, for she recognized his reserve, and the tendency for the youthful freshness of his complexion to colour up when the spotlight was diverted onto him. 'Call him Arty!' Bill instructed them heartily. 'We all do.'

'Sounds like a bandleader,' Mr Hobbs said, and Beth noted the pink tide flooding the sensitive features.

His hair was fair and very fine, and though cropped above the ears and at the back of the neck in true regulation manner, a little tuft of wayward, corkscrew curls sprouted at his brow, adding to his already boyish looks. He was only a few months younger than her brother, who would be twenty-three next month, but he looked far younger. He was slim and delicate looking, not at all the young warrior. His battledress had hung upon him, its ill fit highlighting his slight build and generally non-belligerent air. He looked much more at home now, in clean white shirt and starched collar and, probably, old school tie, with a Fair-Isle sleeveless pullover showing beneath his open, informal sports jacket.

Beth was attracted to his unthreatening physical appearance and graceful gentleness. Almost pretty, she thought, and was surprised at the adjective that came to mind. Did she mean unmanly? She felt uncomfortable at the idea that she might. It disturbed her to acknowledge how much her attitude towards young men had been coloured by her experience with Luke Denby; that dangerous masculine power he exerted, and the fatal weakness of her own response to it. Then Al had come along, taken her over, saved her, and taught her about love, and . . .

No! She did not want to explore that, did not want to allow their world to infiltrate into this completely different, familiar background. She strove hard, pushed it away from her mind, turned towards the young stranger, encouraged by his shyness to overcome her own. In the familiar setting, and with the people around her she had known her whole life, she was confident, animated, and concentrated on making Arty Clark feel at home here, to draw him out a little. Bill had quickly filled in the details of why Arty was to be their guest, during a hasty phone call from down south to warn them of their arrival. 'I feel sorry for him, poor chap. His mother's dead. Father's away at sea. Merchant Navy. There's only an aunt and uncle. He can't stand them, and they feel the same about him, apparently. He was going to spend the holiday up in London, I think. He's a good chap. You don't mind?'

What could there possibly be about him not to like? Beth wondered. She went out of her way to charm him, and by Boxing Day it was obvious that she had succeeded. He was sleeping on a camp bed in Bill's room, but left his comrade-in-arms snoring in the decadent luxury of a long lie-in, and rose reasonably early, in order to take a walk with Elsbeth. It had been a little hard for Beth to get used to being Elsbeth again, but by Christmas Eve she was at home with it once more. She decided she was quite happy to be Elsbeth for Arty, but shied away from self-examination as to her reasons for it.

They went no further than the neighbouring park. They almost had the place to themselves, apart from dog walkers and a gang of children, and one or two pram pushers. Arty offered her his arm, and she linked him in a perfectly proper manner, while they strolled round the frosty paths and black, empty flowerbeds. The weird, silver barrage balloon, moored on the ground at its site in one corner of the park, was an unavoidable reminder of the times they were living through. The rounded fins, like giant ears, gave it a comic elephantine appearance as it rolled slightly in the wind, though Beth could recall people fleeing homeward in fear when it had suddenly been sent soaring aloft one Saturday afternoon soon after the outbreak of the war. More than two years ago now. She had not long finished her schooling, and had been looking forward to university.

There was a long, raised embankment marking the presence of a communal shelter in the vicinity. It was covered with grass now, blending in with the surrounding greenery, apart from the concrete structures at either end. She remembered how, those two long years ago, the rawness of the newly dug earth had made it a much more livid scar on the landscape. She gave Arty's arm a little squeeze and bumped her hip companionably against his as they moved towards the pond, where a thin, shifting film of ice clung to the dark water at the rim. 'I hope you're enjoying yourself, Arty! Two more whole days before you have to go. We want you to feel at home with us. I hope we'll see you again.'

She pinked a little at her own fervour, but she wanted him very much to be happy. His grey eyes showed the warmth of his response to *her* warmth, and his colour, too, as he reassured her. 'It's been wonderful. You've made me so welcome. All of you!'

But his feeling for her was evidently rather stronger than for the other members of the family, maybe including her brother Bill. At any rate, the night before the two warriors returned to the battle, he seized a snatched moment alone with her to beg her to write to him, and for permission to reply. 'I'd like—' He never completed his sentence, but she guessed at its meaning when he suddenly clasped her and held her crushingly against him. The edge of the kitchen table cut into her behind, and his leg pressed against her thighs in a most un-Arty-like fashion, while his lips covered hers, and he kissed her, with little finesse, but with undoubted fervour. When she had recovered enough to breathe and think, by which time they were embracing again, slightly more decorously, she reflected that, however much of a bosom chum her brother might be to this sweet, shy lad, she was willing to bet they had never kissed like that.

'Arty! We mustn't. I hardly know you!' She clamped her open mouth against his again and tightened her arms about his neck to make sure he was helpless to obey her injunction.

CHAPTER SEVEN

On the other side of the world, the Japanese seized Hong Kong on Christmas Day, and by the second day of 1942 they had occupied Manila. They were unreal names in an atlas, though real people were dying there. A little nearer home, physically at least, the 8th Army was making ground in North Africa, retaking those foreign names which many at home had already read of: places like Benghazi in the Libyan desert. Bleak enough, no doubt, but certainly livelier and warmer than Howbeck. Alice had arrived late, by train from Middlesborough, so that it was dark as she trudged through several inches of melting snow along the rutted lane from the station to reach the road that led down the rest of the hill to the village at its bottom. The snow, piled in high banks at its margins, glimmered palely, in spite of the crust of soot and the dirt flung up by passing vehicles. It was Saturday evening, and though it was probably too early for the Oddfellows to be packed, its squat shape and smoking chimneys, the odd chinks of light through its door and closed curtains, and, as she passed close by, the noise of laughter and voices, made her feel even lonelier. It almost tempted her to turn aside into the warm bar, but then the thought of the chilly reception from the hostess and maybe more than one or two of the regulars deterred her.

Not that she couldn't do with cheering up. Mam had cried this morning at parting from her, making Alice feel even more wretched for that part of her which was so glad and relieved to be getting away. However, full penance was exacted when she groped in the darkness of the cobbled yard to open the front door of the flat, then again on the wall to search out the tit of the light switch. Habit forced her to scramble to drag the heavy curtain into place at the foot of the narrow stairs, even though she had seen no sign of anyone since passing between the pillars of Howe Manor's entrance; there was no admonitory voice to tell her to 'put out that light!'

The unshaded bulb at the head of the stairs cast a pale, unfriendly illumination. The painted brick wall to her right, to which a wooden handrail was fixed, seemed to shine with an icy patina. She could almost feel its cold as an ache as she ascended. The room at the top was just as cold, and dead, with none of the special welcome she had known. No Beth, no warmth, no life.

She put her case on the floor, gazed about at the emptiness, tried to drive away her sense of despond. You soppy ha'p'orth! You're like some daft swooning lass shut up in a tower, she admonished herself. Get that grate cleared out, get a fire going, and get a kettle on. A cuppa tea, a wash and some of that good grub mam loaded you down with, a hot water bottle in the bed. No Algy squirming and turning in the middle, and no Ethel whimpering and dragging the blankets over to her side – and no Beth to warm yourself against, for another endless week or more! No wonder you're bloody miserable! What do you expect when the lass you care about more than anyone in the world is miles away and not coming back for nine more days?

Alice was dismayed by the flow of resentment which crept up on her, as she thought of her darling tucked up in her own bed, cherished in the bosom of her family – all the nice things she'd no doubt missed. The luxuries and the comforts, the posh, educated talk. The world Al would never know, would never be admitted to. Why couldn't they have met up? Why couldn't she have asked Al up just once, to call for a cuppa? Or at least to meet up in town? At the swanky Regent café, where she'd met her once before, just after Al had walked out of her job at the co-op, and Beth had come up with the news about the move to Howbeck, and thus opened the way to transform entirely her life? Both their lives, she swiftly reassured herself. For Beth had never known anything like this either, this *love* that they felt for each other.

Alice decided against lighting a fire. She had thought how cosy it would be, to get a real blaze going, and to settle down in one of the two chairs pulled up to the little hearth. She had even promised to herself that she would make a really determined effort to finish her birthday present from Davy. She felt bad about that, and the way she evaded his questions in his letters about her thoughts on it. She had put it aside after struggling through the opening chapters, and Beth had read it in no time at all. 'It's good,' Beth told her, and so it must be. To be honest, though, Al couldn't see what they saw in this Greene bloke. Right weird, she'd thought it, but hadn't said so. And why not? What was happening to her in her advancing years? Was this yet another example of what being in love was doing to her? Before Beth, she would have had no hesitation in telling Davy, by post or to his face, what a load of old rubbish she thought it. But then that was typical of the old her, straight in, feet first, and usually right into her gob!

The old her was gone, for ever. All at once, like a nasty warning twinge of a bad bellyache, she felt an uneasiness – about her and Beth and the happiness they had discovered in each other here. It's just cos you're alone here for the first time, you silly bitch! Because it's Christmas, and because you're missing her already, so much, after only a week apart – and another one to go. And because you're afraid that she won't be feeling the same, that she might even be relieved being back with her family in that world you know nothing of. Might not even lie awake thinking of you, missing you so much.

The weather was so miserable back at work the next morning that Dick Pearson, the grumpy head gardener, still under the influence of the season, set the three girls working in the long greenhouse, cleaning out implements and sorting out plant pots and seed boxes, and other 'bits and pieces' to keep them occupied. Alice listened to Evelyn and Beryl's accounts of their brief but lively leaves at their respective homes. 'How about you and Elsbeth then? How did you get on?' Beryl asked finally.

'Beth? How would I know? I haven't seen her.'

A gruff defensiveness in her tone was picked up at once, and Beryl's long face assumed an expression of comic surprise. 'Ooh! What's wrong? You two haven't had a falling out, have you?'

'Don't be daft! Just cos we live in the same town, it doesn't mean we have to spend every minute together! We see enough of each other here, don't we?'

'Yes, of course,' Beryl agreed smoothly. 'It's just with you two being so close, best pals and everything, I thought you'd have seen *something* of her over the Christmas. She didn't come back with you then?'

'She's not back till after New Year. She's got another two weeks' holiday.'

'Lucky little cow!' the pretty Evelyn observed. The big eyes were turned on Alice with unconvincing innocence. 'Bet you miss her, though. Must be lonely, all by yourself in that big bed, eh, Beryl?'

Beryl gave a neighing laugh. 'Oh, sure! I don't half miss getting my shins kicked black and blue by madam here every night. But I'm sure you and Elsbeth don't have any of that, eh?' She winked at Alice, who felt herself growing red. 'Cosy as little birds in the nest, you and your girlfriend, isn't that right?'

The prospect of spending New Year's Eve alone was too daunting for Alice to turn down Eileen Aygarth's enthusiastic invitation to spend it with them up at Howbeck Side, and glad she was that she hadn't, for they welcomed her as they always had to their fireside. Work finished early, and she climbed the long hill in the louring daylight. The main meal would be eaten in the afternoon.

Eileen had already insisted that Alice should stay the night, in the bed she and Algy used to share in the old, rambling cottage, which had grown piecemeal with the generations of Aygarths until it was a roomy four bedroom house of uneven passageways, stone walls and low beams, with brick and plaster and high ceilinged additions. 'Bit of everything, like us,' Malcolm had acknowledged contentedly.

'You look right nice,' he told her comfortably, and Alice blushed. She had hesitated long and hard before she finally decided to forego slacks and sweater for the thick, muted check of a dark woollen dress, with nipped in waist and wide belt, and over it a knitted cardigan in dark blue. She had even worn her best brassiere, and the pink step-ins, with stockings clipped to the suspenders. The unaccustomed constriction of these garments almost made her change her mind, and her clothes, at the last minute, but with a hint of defiance, and even of self-mortification, she resisted the temptation.

'He's getting a right Casanova in his old age,' Eileen laughed. 'But he's right enough. You look real bonny, you know. You ought to dress up more often. You'd soon have the lads' heads turning, just like your pal Elsbeth.' But Alice was glad she'd packed her siren suit in the carrier bag along with her night things and wash bag, and vowed that as soon as she could after the family dinner she would change out of all the female frippery that felt like torture to her.

They saw the New Year in, with one of the young Aygarth cousins, suitably dark if not handsome, acting as first foot. Alice, along with ten-year-old Becky Aygarth and other Aygarth relatives, stood outside the cottage with him, waiting for the moment when blackout regulations would be flouted and the door cast wide open to welcome him in, with the salt and coal and bread to bring good luck along with the new year. Alice was reminded of a similar dark night a year ago, the day after her December birthday, when they had heard a frantic cry, and found poor, wounded, bedraggled Beth, covered in mud and sobbing with fright, in the ditch by the garden wall. That was the first night they had shared a bed. Alice remembered how strange she had felt, awkward and stiff, afraid to let any part of her make contact, until Beth had turned and reached out to her.

'Not like proper New Year,' Mr Aygarth senior, Malcolm's dad, grumbled, when they were safely inside and drinks were being passed out. 'No church bells ringing, horns sounding. You could hear ships' hooters going if wind was in right direction.'

About four hours previously, Alice had gratefully slipped away up to the room she was sleeping in, and which was so familiar to her, to heave and twist and wriggle out of her finery, grunting with distaste at the clamminess of her skin and the red marks. Despite the loose comfort of the siren suit and thick grey socks, she found herself waylaid about one in the morning by the first foot Aygarth cousin, a young man about her own age whom she had known for over a year now. He trapped her in one of the narrow passages between the kitchen and the 'back-kitchen' as it was called, where she had been helping to wash and stack dishes. 'You look reet grand, Alice!' he assured her, with the earnestness of one for whom alcohol had opened the way to truth. 'You're smashin'! Ah've always thowt so, though ah've nivver said nowt.'

His arms were round her shoulders, he wrestled her against the cold, varnished wallpaper, and his face searched for hers. She let him kiss her, then turned her face away as she felt his tongue wet on her lips, and she thrust him back. 'Booze talking, Derek. Be a good lad.'

'Come on,' he whined plaintively. 'Ah've always fancied yer. Yer must know it.'

'I know you've had a skinful. Now gerroff me and leave me alone!'

He moaned and thrust his slobbering face at her again, heaved his body blatantly against hers. She decided diplomacy would not suffice. She reached down against their conjoined bodies, scrabbled, felt the bulge of crotch and the rough texture of his trousers. She dug in her fingers, gathered a handful of flesh and cloth and twisted it upward, squeezing as hard as she could. His importuning changed to a shrill bleat and his hips jerked as far from her as he could remove them, while his arms dropped from her shoulders, to clutch frantically at his own genital area. He sank to a crouch, knees pressed together, turned away from her. A stream of hissed profanities came from him in his agony.

'And happy New Year to you an' all!' She made a fist of the hand which had already done such damage, extended the knuckle of the forefinger, and jabbed it hard behind his ear. He squeaked rather than cried, and tumbled sideways. 'Careful, Derek!' she called as she headed to the lighted end of the passage and the people gathered there. 'Poor lad's slipped and hurt himself. I think he's had a bit too much!'

When she got back to Howe Manor after lunch on New Year's Day, she found a wan looking Evelyn and Beryl standing straddle legged in the staff bathroom attempting to wash the streaks from their stained legs. They had tried the increasingly common alternative to silk stockings: gravy browning and an eyebrow pencil wielded by a steady hand for the seams. 'It works.' Evelyn smiled tiredly in reminiscence. 'Mind you, it's tricky if it's raining. And it looks a bit odd when you get to grips, if you know what I mean! Still, by that time they wouldn't care if you were covered in sky-blue-and-pink spots, would they, Beryl?'

Beryl shrieked. 'Don't ask me! *I* wouldn't know, you mucky cow!'

Alice was already heading for the door and she spoke over her shoulder. 'Sorry? Was that mucky you said, or lucky?'

Alice was bitterly disappointed when she went into work on the first Saturday of 1942 to find a message waiting from Beth. She had telephoned the Estate Office the previous evening, to say that she would not be able to return to Howbeck on 5 January after all, and that she would be writing to Alice to explain. The letter came on Monday, the day she should have been back, and it was full of contrite apology, but light on detailed explanation.

> *Some family things have cropped up. My brother got some unexpected leave, and one or two other things need to be sorted. But I'll definitely be back on Thursday some time, so it's only another two and a bit days really! Not long! Have the place nice and warm for me. See you soon,*
>
> *Love,*
> *Beth xx*

Alice tried to reason herself out of the sense of injury again, but once more she was unsuccessful. There was just something about the note – that's all it was, not a proper letter, not even wishing her a happy new year, and the only reference to her own doings was almost like a snub. *Some family things*. That only made Alice feel even more excluded. In other words, keep your neb out, it's got nothing to do with you. Yet again, it came down to that feeling that Beth wanted everything about the two of them to remain separate, to be cut off from everything else going on around them. She had never liked to acknowledge in words the real thing they had between them. *Love*, she'd written. And two little crosses. What sort of kisses were they, Al wondered? Pecks on the cheek? No *I love you*, or *All my love.* No. That would be too near the nitty-gritty.

She thought of the passion they had both discovered and shared with such rapture inside these walls. She, too, knew how exclusive it was, how wonderfully apart from everything they had known, or dreamed possible. But the painful difference was that Alice took that feeling everywhere with her, even though she was at pains to hide it from the rest of the world. Of course they had to, she knew that well enough. It was hard sometimes but she understood the necessity for it. But for Beth – it seemed to Alice that her golden girl could drop it, all of that rapture, that feeling, as soon as they were outside, as though she could leave it behind the closed door of the flat. Even inside, Beth didn't want to talk, didn't want the words Alice groped to find to express her love. She knew they made the lovely girl uncomfortable, that Beth would stop her with kisses. 'Don't talk!' she would whisper, even as she offered herself. Why not? It always hurt Alice, that even in the feverish activity of it all, Beth didn't want words, didn't want to hear the truth.

Alice felt deeply uneasy about this break, there was no getting away from it. They had not been separated this long since the summer, when you could say they had really found each other, even though they had been friends for a year. She told herself she was just being foolish, there was no cause for her alarm. Another day or two and everything would be wonderfully back to the way it was. But she wanted her, needed her with her.

She seized on an excuse just to hear her voice. On the fifth, Miss Ramsay and Doreen returned from their trip to Hertfordshire, and Alice was round at Northend Cottage the following afternoon, as soon as she had finished work. She stood as usual in her stockinged feet until Miss Ramsay invited her to 'please take a seat', and she perched on the edge of one of the hard backed chairs against the wall and listened to Doreen's enthusiastic account of the holiday. 'Why don't you take your sister up and show her your presents?' Miss Ramsay smiled. It was only the second time Alice had penetrated beyond the drawing room and up the elegantly carpeted staircase to Doreen's small but comfortably appointed room.

'It would have been nice if you'd bothered to seek *me* out for a change!' Alice said, as soon as they were alone.

'We were tired. It was quite late when we got back here, and we had our unpacking to do. I would have come round . . .'

'Aye! When? Next Christmas?'

'I'm going through to Margrove tomorrow,' Doreen said importantly. 'On the train. On my own. The guard will get a porter to see me on to the train at Middlesborough. I'll stay the night with mam and dad. Come back Thursday. I've got some gifts for them.'

'Hey! Thursday? Wait a minute. I might be able to fix up a lift for you.'

Mr Barr himself made the trunk call from his office, and waited for the operator's, 'You're through to Margrove, caller,' before he handed over the receiver to Alice. Her heart was racing.

'Could I speak to Elsbeth please, Mrs Hobbs? It's Alice Glass.'

And seconds later, she heard Beth's voice, breathless and taut with anxiety.

'Alice? Is that you? What's wrong?'

Alice heard the tension. 'Nothing. Just a favour to ask, that's all. There's nothing wrong, love.' But was that true? she wondered.

CHAPTER EIGHT

Alice's secret fear was confirmed, from the first seconds, when she had rushed up the narrow stairs to find the room transformed by the sight of Beth standing there, the shabby room lit by her presence, as well as the fire which Alice had laid in readiness for her return. 'I put a match to it,' Beth said. 'I thought I'd have the place warmed up for you. You're early.' She was still in her smart travelling outfit and looked wonderful.

'Oh God! It's good to see you. I've been on edge all day. Old Pearson let me off early. Come here! You look gorgeous. I won't mucky your clothes, sweetheart, but let me wish you Happy New Year!'

They embraced and Alice kissed her eagerly. But she knew, felt the instinctive awkward stiffness under her touch, and saw it in the start of colour to the face, the mix of reluctance and appeal in the blue eyes. She swallowed her dismay and broke the embrace quickly. 'By heck! I've missed you, lass! That bed – it's been like lying in the middle of a football field.' She shouldn't have mentioned the bed. She realized it as soon as she saw Beth's deepening blush. She turned away from the tension, went through to the sink in the tiny kitchen. 'Hey! Great news about my registration, eh? It's official! I am an Agricultural Worker. Classified. I don't have to worry no more. We're here to stay, kidder!' She pushed away her disappointment at the lukewarmth of Beth's murmured congratulations. 'Good journey, was it? Everything all right? Listen! I'm sorry about our Doreen! Your dad wasn't mad, was he? I bet he thought what a flipping cheek, eh? But it just seemed—'

Beth grabbed swiftly at the safe topic, over-compensating with her enthusiasm. 'No! It was fine! Really! She's a lovely girl. So polite – a real little lady. Daddy was very impressed. We dropped her off at Northend. We even had a cup of tea with Miss Ramsay. She insisted!' Beth laughed. 'Can't quite match her grandeur, I'm afraid, but the tea's ready. I'll just pop the kettle on again. Two minutes.'

The awkwardness was there and Alice's alarm was growing, because it had never been there before in the little flat. She felt worse because she had somehow been expecting it, while at the same time trying to dismiss her fears as all nonsense, as she waited for Beth's return from her home. And now that she was here, Alice was all at once and very uncharacteristically afraid to tackle it. Instead she took Beth's way out, of not acknowledging it. It's just because we've been away from each other, Alice falsely reassured herself. It'll be right, once we settle down together again.

When they sat in their dressing gowns in front of the fire, with their mugs of cocoa watching the little heap of red coals dim, they talked easily enough once more, though it was on the surface, over that underlying other feeling. Alice made her laugh with her mocking portrait of the festivities at 19 Maudsley Street. She was aware of Beth's reluctance to talk of her own family, of her time with them. Casually, she asked Beth how things had gone.

'Yes, it was nice having Bill home. A real surprise. He didn't think he'd get leave. Didn't know until the last minute.' There was another hesitation, and Alice, sensitive about everything to do with Beth, picked up on the hint of unwillingness in her next offering. 'He brought someone with him. A chap from his unit. Nice boy. Very quiet, though.'

'Oh aye?' Alice was prepared to tease, but held back on her inclination. 'Didn't he have a home of his own to go to?'

'Not really. His mother's dead and his father's a sea captain. He was away abroad or at sea somewhere.'

'Oh dear! Poor chap! Still, I expect you made up for it. Gave him a good time, I mean.' She waited for more, but didn't press when nothing more was offered.

In bed, with the lamp out, Beth moved quickly, her hands on Alice's reaching arms in a companionable touch. 'Just cuddle me, Al. I – my tummy feels a bit upset. Maybe it's the travelling, or the change of water. All right?'

Alice was glad of the dark as she felt the heat rise to her face, and a burning in her throat. A great ache of dismay and disappointment engulfed her, tightened every muscle. 'Aye, all right, love. A good night's sleep'll put you right, I expect. I'll try not to disturb you when I get out in the morning. You have a good lie-in. Make the most of it.'

They managed to carry on in this strange manner, together in every way as they had been formerly, except in that most important, most wonderful way of all, with Beth coming up with other excuses when they climbed into bed: 'I'm worn out. I've been swotting up and preparing lesson notes all day. They want me to take Scripture this term. Can you imagine?' Or: 'I've been helping Molly

Richards, the PE mistress, to sort out the games kit. That changing room's a nightmare!' Alice felt sick and lost, and thoroughly unsure of herself.

But on the third day she rose and decided she could take this strange state of affairs no longer. It was Saturday and she finished work at lunchtime. 'We have to talk!' she said before leaving in the gloomy morning, and from the fixed expression of the face that peeped out blearily over the blankets at her, she knew that Beth understood very clearly what she meant.

Alice told herself she must remain calm whatever happened. She did not want to hurt Beth, or to bully her. It was too important, and she loved her too much for that. And Beth, for her part, afraid as she was, was also determined to be reasoned and unemotional, but firm. She would not allow Alice to browbeat, or overwhelm her, strong as she was.

It didn't work out like that, for either of them. 'Come on then! Out with it! What's wrong?' Alice's desperate effort to get the cards on the table had all the subtlety of a hammer blow.

And in spite of a whole morning psychologically gearing herself up for a tender but impermeable argument, Beth's response was a hunted look, like a child caught rifling her mother's purse, and a hoarse squawk of 'Wrong? What do you mean?'

But at least the confrontation had got under way. The crisis had surfaced, and 'wrong' was a word that figured largely in the opening rounds. Beth used it, came out with it as a tortured rasp, as if a crumb had lodged in her gullet, and Alice echoed it in a disbelieving, interrogative squeak.

'You can't deny it, I don't care what you say!' Beth sounded desperate from the first, and the tears came quickly and unintentionally, against all her predetermination to keep them at bay. And the awful, unpalatable truth was that, in the last analysis, Beth was right. Alice couldn't deny it. Or she didn't think she could. She had known it all along, resisting the knowledge within herself, striving to oppose it. But finally, here it was, that insurmountable barrier that had been there all the time, that both of them had been struggling so hard to ignore.

'We're *different*!' Alice cried desperately. She wondered if Beth had felt it as long as she had, from her childhood.

'We're – we're *abnormal*!' Beth wept.

Alice was at last dumb with despair. *Wrong*! They were back to that word, clanging, tolling like the sound of a funeral bell, as solid and inescapable as all the 'Thou shalt nots' of the Commandments blackly imprinted on the sombre walls of Lister Road school.

There were no other words, none that they could come up with to counteract all those negatives, no way of supporting Alice's weary, whispered, genuinely puzzled query. 'How can it be wrong, feeling like this, the way we do?' But Beth didn't any more, not from that moment of tormented recognition.

It wasn't a clear-cut, clean break, go forth and sin no more. Affairs of the heart rarely are. That night they both cried and wondered what they should do, and lay miserably in the suddenly cheerless bed side by side and a mile apart. Alice dozed, woke in the blackness of the early hours, felt Beth's weeping, the sniffles of her grief, and she groaned with love, reached out, and they clung desperately together, comforting, loving, and in the tired music hall parlance of nudge-nudge, wink-wink, one thing led to another, and another, and so on . . . they were lovers again. But still, it was never the same again.

'We can still be just the same, except for . . . you know.' Again, the flame in Beth's face drove Alice to despair, and she felt a wicked desire to shake and slap her. But the dying 'you know' brought them up against that brick wall once more, the wordless impasse, the leering, shameful, muckiness that was so far from all that Alice felt, and Beth, too, Alice was sure, if only they could break through. If ever words were needed, they were needed now. All Alice could find were the phrases of convention, the boy-girl stuff, nightingales in Berkeley Square, wherever the hell that was, and Beth wouldn't listen to those. Only once, in the early days, her darling had gone burbling on about some old dame and a bunch of lasses playing harps and making up poems on some old Greek island in the year dot, which is where the word 'lesbian' came from, but so what? That was just another of the mucky words people used, like 'fairy' and 'queer'.

Alice felt helpless and afraid for the first time in her life, in spite of all that had taken place in the past two years of general madness. There was no one she could talk to. Once that great storm of emotion had whipped up and blown itself out, the peace that followed was never the same, never sure.

'We're all right, aren't we?' Beth would say, seeking her hand, even kissing her, but it sounded more like a genuine question, rather than a reassurance, and neither could truly answer it. Alice only had one real friend of the kind with whom you could share secret, deep confidences, and that was Davy Brown. He was sixty miles away. If he were here, he would be well aware that things were far from right with her. Maybe it was just as well he wasn't around, for how could she share her secret, even with him? He wouldn't understand. How could he? She couldn't understand herself, only how she felt in her heart. Her mind was nothing but confusion, all muddied up. What was that word Beth had used, her face streaked with tears? *Perverted.* That was it. Alice knew what it meant. It was like that old feller who used to wander round town when she was a kid. He wore an old army coat, trailing the floor, in all weathers, and he used to open it up in front of women, exposing his willy. All the old girls round Maudsley Street used to laugh and shake their heads even when they were saying how 'disgusting' it was. Or like the feller that hung round the park and tried to take little lads off behind the bushes for a 'sweety'.

It was all to do with shame and wickedness and sin. Ungodly. Meanwhile, they both suffered and tried to carry on, and lay stiff and apart from each other in their bed, except occasionally, when she couldn't stand it any longer, and neither could Beth, and they would come together, frantic with need and love. But the sense of sin, and the dumb suffering, would be there, mercilessly waiting the next day.

An HM Forces envelope came addressed to Beth in early February. Alice was on her way out to work. Dick Pearson was a bugger for punctuality, so Alice was out before Beth had even stirred, usually. She picked up the flimsy envelope from the worn and dirty piece of coco matting at the foot of the stairs and looked at the sender's name on the back. *2nd Lt. A. Clark.* The address was some army camp. All abbreviations and numbers, apart from the first line, which read *c/o Officers' Mess*. There's posh. Alice guessed this must be the chap Beth had mentioned, the guest for Christmas, the mate of her brother. She hadn't said very much about him at all, not that Alice had pumped her for information. 'Nice boy'. 'Quiet'. That's all Alice recalled. She thought suddenly of Luke Denby, and felt that little stirring in her gut of hate for what he had done to Beth. She laid the letter on one of the lower steps and left.

'Got a secret admirer?' she asked lightly, when she had got in from work that evening, and was settled in front of the fire in her stockinged feet, thawing out.

Beth hadn't volunteered any information, but then, Alice conceded, she hadn't given her much chance, having only been in a few minutes. 'Eh?' She matched Alice's jocund tone as she carried out the little ritual of making the pot of tea and carrying the tray in. She put the tray down between them, waiting to let the tea mash. She sat in her own chair, on the other side of the small hearth. It was only a few feet away, but the space was significant. Before Christmas, Beth would always park herself on the floor, at Alice's feet, leaning in against her, arms folded on Alice's knees. She didn't do that any more. 'Oh! The letter?' She played out the fiction of failing to interpret Alice's query. 'It's from Bill's friend. That boy who stayed with us. I said he could write if he wanted.'

'He's left it a bit late, hasn't he? Slow starter, is he?' The humour was getting heavier as Alice played along.

'Must be.' There was a very slight hesitation. 'I got one a couple of weeks ago, as a matter of fact. I must've forgot to mention it. Not that he had anything riveting to say. Must have been the day the post came late.'

'So the secret bit was right, anyway.' Despite the flippancy, the challenge was there in Alice's tone.

'Poor lad's got nobody to write to. No brothers or sisters. Only an old uncle and aunt who he doesn't get on with. And his dad, of course. But he's away at sea all the time.'

'So you're going to be his big sister, are you?'

'Something like that. Sort of doing my bit. You know. They've finished their training, just about. They'll be posted at the end of this month. I'm worried. About Bill, I mean,' she added quickly. 'If he's sent overseas.'

'You want to be careful. I bet this Arty lad doesn't think of you as his sister.'

'So we've *both* got admirers then? You with your Davy . . .'

'Except he knows exactly where he stands with me. I've never tried to string him along. He knows what's what.'

'Does he? *Really*?' Beth was on dangerous ground now, she knew, and it showed in the sudden tension in her voice, the colour that rose to her face. But she couldn't help it. She felt that Al was accusing her of something, throwing up the past at her. 'You think I've been stringing this boy along? Maybe you think I've . . .' let him into my bed, her mind shrieked, like I did with Luke, 'led him on?' she ended. She thought of the kisses, the way he had held her, his body against hers, and how she had let him. 'I've only met him once, for a few days. He was a guest in our home,' she said bitterly.

The shadow of Luke Denby still loomed large between them, though it was almost a year since that traumatic event, and several months since she had even seen him. But it was he, or the memory of him, which played a vital role in the crisis about to descend upon them with such catastrophic force.

CHAPTER NINE

Beth noted the quietness that hung over the clustered groups of pupils as soon as she passed into the impressive entrance hall of Howe Manor. Their voices were hushed, almost whispers, their eyes were big and, in many cases, brimming with tears. Soggy hankies were being clenched or groped for under gymslips, and cold noses sniffled, and not simply because of the bitter February morning. There had been an inch or two of frozen snow on the cobbles, making Beth's journey across the yard to the main building a slow and dangerous one. By the time she had reached the stone steps that led up to the house's front entrance, the stables, with the miniature clock tower that crowned them, were already invisible in the thick white fog. As she came gratefully into the comparative warmth of the hall, the volume of noise increased a little, but it was still muted, the sound of the murmuring made even smaller by the height of the elegant dome above them.

'Oh, miss! It's so awful, isn't it?' Sheila Pincheon was a twelve-year-old, who was in Beth's English class and also in her house. She was a plump girl, who should have been wearing her glasses. Her eyes were slitted, puffed and sore looking, the black lashes spiky with her tears, which glistened on her red cheeks. 'We're all so sorry!' She seemed oblivious to Beth's blank stare of incomprehension.

Beth's heart gave a little flutter of alarm. The girl's sorrowful look was mixed with compassion. Something wrong at home in Margrove? With Bill? But the whole school wouldn't know about it before *she* did? And the whole school wouldn't be devastated by it.

Before she could ask what was wrong, Miss Bell, the headmistress, appeared, standing on the fourth step of the grand staircase, a convenient elevated position for addressing the assembled troops, and, indeed, all the pupils seemed to be concentrated in the hall. Her authoritative voice rose piercingly and stilled the murmurs. 'I think by now you've all heard the sad news concerning Flying Officer Denby.'

Beth gave a small cry. Several heads nearby turned in her direction. She felt a terrible constriction in her chest and throat, the heat sweeping through her. There were some sibilant noises of sympathy around her. Someone reached out from behind, touched her arm. A hand brushed hers, rubbed against it, was withdrawn. For an instant, she was frightened she might swoon. She was giddy, disorientated. Like a True Romance heroine, she thought hysterically, or a Regency maiden. Cut her stays! She had an insane urge to giggle.

Dinger Bell's crisp voice came into focus again. 'Mr and Mrs Denby were of course informed in London. We don't know when they'll be returning, but I should imagine it will be in the next day or two. We must show them all the sympathy and courtesy expected of us. First and foremost, we must respect and not intrude upon their grief. He was a brave young man, like so many others who are serving our cause, and the best thing we can do . . .' her voice rose again, with that imperious note of command, and seemed to pierce Beth's brain, 'is to honour their sacrifice by carrying on, playing our part. Senior Assembly as usual at nine o'clock. Please go to your classrooms, quietly.'

Beth was responsible for one of the most junior forms. She felt pinned under the combined stares as she went through the rituals of the class business.

'Are you all right, miss?'

'Yes, yes! Please! Just be – don't talk. Be quiet. If you wouldn't mind.' Perhaps the rare nature of this murmured plea, so different from the incisive declarations of accustomed authority, shocked them into acquiescence. Certainly, it was far more effective than Beth's normal, increasingly shrill insistences on obedience. They sat in silence, apart from the continual sniffs, and she sat facing them, head down, all of them glad when the hand bell clanged outside to indicate the move to first lesson.

It was an interminable forty-five minutes before Beth could escape to the room on the ground floor, part of the former servants' communal quarters, off the long corridor which led to the kitchen and laundry rooms, which now served as St Anne's staff room. She found Molly Richards there, drawing on a cigarette, in an atmosphere already hazed blue with tobacco smoke. 'What happened?' Beth asked, no longer disguising her dismay. 'I didn't know. I was a bit late. I hadn't heard till the Head spoke in the hall.'

'Oh, you poor kid! You and he – didn't you have a thing with him, back in the summer? My God! You look awful. What a shock! Here. Have a ciggy. Do you the world of good.'

Beth shook her head. *A thing*! The absurd phrase rang round in her head. She felt that threat of hysteria again. Images flashed of his fierce kisses, of his hold on her, the terrifying thrust of his body on hers.

The PE mistress was continuing. 'The news came through the office. First thing. The Denbys must have got in touch with Patrick Barr. They heard yesterday. His plane was shot down some time on Monday night. A raid over France. They mentioned a place – Poissy, I think they said. Apparently he was posted missing. Still is, officially. But then, when all the planes were back – the survivors – they have some sort of briefing. Find out what they can about casualties and so on. The bomber – it was seen in flames, going down. Then it crashed.' She shook her head. 'Definitely no survivors. Nobody parachuted out. And the whole thing . . .' She raised her hands, the right one still holding the cigarette, fingers stiffly extended. The smoke spiralled in a thin trail about her. She gave a great shrug. 'No chance! They confirmed it. What rotten luck, eh?'

Beth nodded. All at once, she felt her legs going and sank on to the nearest chair. She burst into anguished tears.

With a moan of compassion, Polly crouched beside the huddled, sobbing figure, and encircled her with her arms, hugging her tightly. 'There there, baby! I had no idea that you were still keen on him like that.' Her strong hands cradled the blonde head, fingers clamped, pressing it to her almost flat bosom.

The strong smell of nicotine smoke almost made Beth sick. She had to force herself not to struggle wildly to escape. The smothering grip of the would-be comforter was a symbol of the near panic enclosing Beth's mind. *Mea culpa.* The old sacerdotal acknowledgement of sin, so foreign to her background, seemed so much more appropriate than the bleated guilty plea, 'It's all my fault!' She didn't try to reason, or to offer any defence against her self-condemnation. Deeply and primitively, she knew that it was so.

Her misery was a kind of insulation. Normally, she would have been flayed with shame at her behaviour, her abysmal failure to maintain the stiff upper lip, to 'carry on' in the spirit that made Britain great, of drawing such attention to herself. But she clutched her grief like a blanket around her, sat in the chair, huddled forward, her nose red, eyes streaming, moaning softly, hugging her knees, while others hastily solved the problem of covering the lessons she was missing. Some time later, Miss Bell appeared in front of her. Beth stared at the dark, thick stockings, the solid, lace-up shoes, the tweed skirt with its faint horizontal creases in the thick material. 'Go back to your flat. Get yourself a cup of strong tea. An extra spoon of sugar if you've got any left. Here are two Aspro. Take them. Hop into bed. Keep warm. If you're feeling better, come back after lunch. If not, leave it till tomorrow. I'm sorry we can't spare anyone to look after you. You'll be all right, won't you?'

It sounded more like a statement or an instruction, the question tag clearly redundant. Beth nodded. Dinger Bell's crisp speech was delivered in her usual impassive manner, but Beth detected, or fancied, the underlying disapproval of her weakness. Still she couldn't stop the tears from rolling down her cheeks, the sobs that made her incapable of any answer but that dumb nod. She stood, took the proffered tablets, moved out, walking slowly, hunched still, as though she were somehow physically impaired.

When she had left the room, the headmistress turned to Polly Richards. 'P'raps you'd better send one of the fifth form to look for that gardener girl Hobbs lodges with. Tell her what's happened with Hobbs. She can see to her. They seem as thick as thieves, those two.'

Alice had not heard any of the morning's news. She was working out at the edge of the furthest and newest patch of land converted for vegetables, and the figure of the fifth-form girl, wrapped in scarf and woollen pixie hood and top coat, her thin, black stockinged legs protruding from well-muddied wellingtons, loomed out of the mist, her panting breath swirling in billows of white. 'Thank goodness! You're Miss Hobbs's roommate, yes? I've been looking all over for you!' Quickly, she delivered her message.

'Bloody hell! Whoops! Pardon my French, luv!' The fifth-former flashed her a quick grin and disappeared once more. Alice lumbered back towards the greenhouses and the potting sheds, one end of which served as the head gardener's office. Not unexpectedly, Dick Pearson was snugly inside, in a pungent fog of his own creating, from his glowing pipe. Alice stood no nonsense, remembering the petty tyranny of Little Hitler – Mr Johns, the manager of the co-op in Margrove, under whom she had suffered for three long years. 'I've got to go! Elsbeth's been taken bad. I'll be back over later.'

He gaped at her, the hot bowl held in his left hand. 'When?' he grunted, prepared to do battle, but she was already turning, heading back out to the cold.

'When I've seen to her!' she snapped, and was gone.

Rumbling, he got up and banged the door closed again, fastening the sneck. 'Lasses!' He shook his head and settled down with his *Daily Mirror* again, sternly refusing to leap forward to survey the antics of Jane until he had scanned all the articles ahead of the cartoon strip. How many clothes would she have shed today? Steady the Buffs! he admonished himself. Save the best till last. That had always been his motto and he wasn't going to start altering his ways now. Not for some flibbertigibbet of a lass, that's for sure! But he began to scan just a little quicker and to anticipate the delights that waited just a few pages away.

*

Beth was a humped shape under the blankets, blonde hair flowing over the pillow. 'Oh, my love!' Alice had pulled off her boots before mounting the stairs, and she scattered her mittens, hat, scarf and coat across the floor as she raced through to the bedroom. She sat heavily on the side of the bed, put her hands on the covered shoulders. 'Don't upset yourself, sweetheart!' She was startled at the force with which Beth swung round, flung off her grip as she struggled to sit up, to face her.

'He's dead, for God's sake! What do you want? You want me to cheer? Shout hip-hip-hooray?' Her face looked swollen and shiny, red down one side. The yellow hair was lank, strands darkened by sweat were plastered to her brow. Her eyes were bruised, puffed with weeping. The whites showed prominently, giving her a wild look, like a frightened animal, reinforced by the way her lips were pulled back, showing her teeth, that funny little crooked one at the front that protruded slightly. Alice suddenly remembered how, at ten or eleven, Beth's front teeth had projected a little, remembered calling her 'buckteeth' in cruel taunts. Now she almost looked as though she were snarling at her as she glared.

'Don't be daft!' Alice said automatically, staring back in helpless dismay. 'It's terrible, I know. I just don't want you to make yourself bad, love.' She reached out, touched her arm gingerly. Beth was wearing her thick flannelette nightgown with the long sleeves. Alice could feel its warmth, the stale heat rising from the bedclothes. She was totally unprepared for the violence with which Beth shook off her tentative hold, the wild fury that came off her like heat.

'Don't touch me! Leave me alone! I don't want – what are you doing back here? How did you know?'

'Someone from the school told me. Said you were here. I thought . . .' She stood. Her voice tailed away. She felt choked with emotion, racked with pain at Beth's rejection of her. Her arms hung at her side, she felt incapable of speech or movement.

Beth turned her back on her, lay down again, but with her upper body clear of the bedclothes. 'It's my fault,' she said tonelessly. 'My fault that he's dead.'

'Eh?' Alice gaped at her. Speech flowed back. 'How d'you make that out?'

'It's a punishment. For me. Because of – because of what we've done.'

'You what?' Alice's brain was spinning. Her poor darling had somehow flipped. But why? Why should she be sent crazy over Luke Denby's death? It wasn't as though . . . she had said so often how much she hated what he had done to her. And none of that had been her fault. Alice was sorry he was dead, but the lad had been a right bastard. Beth had absolutely nothing to feel guilty about.

In great contrast to her agonized outburst when Alice had laid hands on her, Beth's tone now was flat, almost devoid of emotion, and sounded all the more frighteningly bleak because of it. She lay back on the pillow, still turned away from Alice, one thin hand resting palm uppermost, fingers slightly bent, beside the blonde hair. 'Because of what you and me have done. This is how I'm punished. I'm responsible for Luke's death.'

Alice felt as though she might well be slipping past reason herself. 'How? Who the hell's punishing you?'

'God.'

'Eh?' Alice's shock was genuine, and a long second passed. Inside, she was torn between a wild desire to scream with laughter and to release a flood of tears. 'That's just—'

'Oh! I know, don't talk daft, that's what you'll say, but really it's not daft. It's the truth, and you know it as well as I do, except you'd never admit it. What we do – what we've done. It's against . . . it's wrong! I've always known it. A sin. No good trying to deny it any more. This is God's punishment. I sinned with Luke.' She turned, another sudden movement, and sat up, her arms stretched out behind her, supporting her. Her expression was still wild, despite the quietness of her voice, her eyes fixed on the standing figure. 'But what you and I have done – that's an even bigger sin. This is God's way of punishing us. Me,' she amended.

Alice felt that exclusion more than any other hurt. Her incredulity at Beth's words began to give way to a growing anger. 'Oh aye? You think God's bothered about punishing *you*, with all that's going on in the world now? So he knocks down poor Luke Denby, just to get at you? Or mebbes that's why he started the war in the first place, eh? All so he could wipe out Luke Denby to get back at you! Jesus! And I thought *I* was the one who thought the sun shone out of your arse! By heck, lass, you've got a big opinion of yourself, haven't you?'

Beth kicked her feet free of the blankets, swung them round to place them on the cold floor. She was on the opposite side of the bed to Alice now, presenting her back to her. 'I don't expect you to understand. You've always been proud to boast that you're a heathen. I don't have any excuses. And God has time for everything – and everyone. For individual sins, *and* the sins of the world. He's omnipotent.'

'Your posh fancy words again! You're full of them!' The accusation popped out and for one painful second Alice hoped Beth would laugh, felt the need for her to hear that sound. Nothing came. Instead, her own throat ached, she tried to choke back her grief. 'Still doesn't stop you talking nonsense, does it?'

'You can get back to work. I'm all right. I'd rather be alone, if you don't mind.'

The helplessness welled up within Alice, and a great desperation. 'You bloody stupid little bitch! You want to face up to the truth? Well here it is! You hated him, you hated what he did to you, you told me, you sobbed your guts out while I held you. If God's out there dishing out punishment for sins, then that's why he got Luke Denby, for what he did to you – and a few more like you, make no mistake!'

Beth turned, her eyes wide, her mouth gaping open. At any other time, Al might have laughed, talked about staring fish.

'Aye! You don't want to hear it, mebbes, but that's the real truth, and you've got to face up to it. You and me . . .' She suddenly knelt on the bed, caught hold of Beth's arms and hauled her down to her. They fell together, Alice clinging to her, pinning the twisting figure down, thrusting her face into Beth's damp neck. She felt Beth go limp, all struggle cease.

'Is this what you want?' Beth whispered. 'I didn't fight against Luke, either. I couldn't. Didn't want to, till it was too late. Go ahead.' The trapped eyes looked into Alice's. They stared at each other, their faces inches away. 'The difference was, *he* was a boy. What happened, what we did, was natural.' She lifted her breast, but not in resistance, letting her body touch Alice's through the thickness of their clothing. 'Whatever we do or say, nothing can make it right. It's against nature.' Her voice sank to the softest of whispers. 'We're wrong, Al. Nothing can change that.'

She lay perfectly still, her face smeared with her tears, her lips parted, soft. Alice felt the thin wrists under her hold, their delicate structure, the slim body and limbs outlined under the nightgown, and she ached with tender love and a pounding need. With a harsh cry, part rage and part torment, she levered herself off the supine figure, and turned, scooping up the articles of her discarded clothing as she went. Her eyes were blind with tears as she stumbled down the staircase and fumbled her feet into the cold wellingtons. By the time she got back out into the cold deadness of the fog, the tears were streaming stinging down her cheeks.

CHAPTER TEN

Alice was so deeply hurt by Beth's denial of their love that she compounded their separation by her own withdrawal, and at the very time when that love was needed most, to help both of them through what was the greatest crisis of their young lives. It was worse because Al knew how much Beth was suffering. But still she felt incapable of doing anything to ease that grief, immobilized by that bitter sense of her own injury, even though the sight of Beth's pale, crumpled figure tore at her. She wanted to go to her, to grab her, hold her, shake her out of that crazy assumption of guilt for Luke's death. Smack some sense into the silly bitch! But she couldn't. She cursed the dead young pilot, too, and so felt herself some of the sense of sin which was weighing Beth down. It was all so daft, Alice thought wearily, yet she couldn't drive out the knowledge of Beth's own weary accusation. 'It's wrong, and you know it as well as I do.' I don't believe in you, God! Alice cried inside her head, and hopelessly acknowledged her own madness in her protesting prayer.

That night, Alice sat up, built up the dying fire when Beth went through to the bedroom. They had scarcely exchanged a word, or even a look, since Al's return from work. The cooked 'high tea' had been prepared by Beth. They picked at the meal in a screaming silence, then Beth left to carry out her evening duty of supervising prep. She was away until lights-out at nine. Alice had put the hot water bottle in the bed. She had washed and changed into her pair of man's pyjamas. The cocoa was ready, but of course their routine was shattered. 'I'll take mine to bed,' Beth said, and disappeared. Huh! It speaks! Alice took some comfort from the banality of the childish riposte, even though it was undelivered.

She sat on in front of the banked fire, until, despite her sorrow, her head nodded on her chest. She stirred uncomfortably, but did not get up from her chair. She endured it now, like some squire keeping his last night vigil, felt the cold nipping at the backs of her ankles, while the heat pressed against the front of her legs. She imagined her lover's timid, husky voice, soft with love and repentance. 'Aren't you coming to bed, Al?' But it remained inside her head, a fantasy, and when, after a deeper spell of sleep, she stood, stiffly, the fire was low again, it was after midnight, and Beth was a dark, humped shape on her side of the bed, sniffling genteelly in her own slumber.

'We can't go on like this,' Alice declared the next evening, close to tears and explosion.

'Like what?' Beth muttered, so like a sulky child that Alice would have chuckled, but for a murderous anger that tensed her muscles and made her fingers curl.

'Don't be so bloody daft! You sound like our Doreen!'

Beth looked suitably chastened, and also a little alarmed at Alice's violence. 'I'm sorry. I can't help it. The way I feel.' There was a lengthy pause. 'Listen. I'll see about moving over into the Big House. They might be able to find a room for me again,' she said doubtfully.

The sirens wailed in Alice's mind. 'No, no!' she answered hastily. 'I'll try not to . . . surely we can still put up with each other?' she pleaded.

Beth smiled and nodded. Her telltale gaze flickered away from Alice. 'We can still be chums, can't we? We don't have to fall out.'

And this time the rage and hopelessness was so thick and stifling within Alice's breast that she could only nod in return, and utter a strangulated grunt that was meant to indicate agreement.

Alice commandeered an old single mattress, more like a thin palliasse, whose striped ticking bore some dubious stains, from a storeroom in one of the outbuildings. 'It's Beth's carryings-on in her sleep! She's getting terrible. Tosses and turns, and talks away to herself. Driving me barmy!'

'Ooh! A lovers' tiff, eh?' Evelyn sniggered, but neither of the Land Girls said very much. The news of how badly Elsbeth had been affected by Luke's death had spread through all levels of the inhabitants of Howe Manor, and had stirred memories of a relationship itself long deceased, and resurrected some painful, unfounded rumours.

'She was really in love with him,' Sheila Pincheon, eyes large behind her spectacles, informed her fellow second-formers. 'She didn't want to give him up. Why do you think she took the job here after those evacuees went back home? It was the squire and his wife who split them up. They didn't think she was good enough for him. She's not very well off, you know. Her father's some sort of shopkeeper. And that girl she shares a room with! Have you heard her talk?' There were a few assenting sniggers before Sheila went on quickly, 'Not that I believe in all that rot. I think it's so sad. She's absolutely heartbroken!'

She sighed and the giggles changed to the supportive respirations of tender, blighted romance.

Grimly, Alice staggered up the stairs, fighting her burden before her. With conspicuously new dedication, Beth was finding more and more reasons to be detained over at the school in the evenings. The mattress was already made up, sheet and blankets folded and tucked under its edges, when Beth put in her late appearance.

'I'll pull it round in front of the fire when I'm ready for bed. I'll be snug enough.'

Beth blushed. 'You don't have to.' She cleared her throat. 'The bed's big enough for both of us. There's no need—'

'Yes, there is! It's better to be separate. For *me*, at any rate. Can't you see? Haven't you any idea how I feel, lying there, terrified I might even *touch* you?' Alice's voice was raw with passion.

'I can't help it, the way I feel. You think I don't care? About . . .'

She didn't say any more. She didn't have to. Same old problem, Alice thought sadly. No words for it. No words for any of the agony they were both enduring.

Mr and Mrs Denby returned to Howe Manor. They were seen only as distantly glimpsed figures, kept to the apartments they had selected for their private accommodation, and stayed well clear of the school's areas. Beth wrote out a sympathy card, very brief and formal, and left it with the mail in the estate's office. She could not summon up the courage to call on them, comforting herself with the thought that she was only saving them from mutual embarrassment by not doing so. A memorial service was held in the village church of St John's. The school attended, thus ensuring the fifteenth century building was packed to capacity. 'Are you going?' Beth asked Alice, who shook her head and managed to modify her reply.

'You know me, kidder. Not my cup of tea, all that.' I've got nowt to beat myself with! she thought savagely, and silently.

The mattress had been put aside, propped against a wall of the bedroom. After a few nights, Beth had insisted that she should swap places with Al. 'It's not fair. If you insist on sleeping apart, it's only right we should take turns. You take the bed tonight.'

Alice was woken in the early hours by a shivering, whimpering, icy-footed figure climbing in beside her, and clinging to steal her warmth. 'Oh God, Al! I'm frozen! And my hip's killing me. It's like sleeping on the pavement. How can you stand it? Please don't kick me out, please! Just let me snuggle.'

Alice moved to accommodate her and hugged warmth back into her. She smiled tenderly, but then she lay in the darkness with that beloved head nestled against hers, the wisps of fine hair tickling her face, down which the tears trickled silently. They were together once more but, for Alice at least, still torturously far apart.

Alice had seen at least two more letters arrive for Beth from the soldier friend she had met at Christmas. With difficulty she refrained from any comment. When a third came at the end of February it was Beth who volunteered information, and from her expression Alice could see that she did not consider its news good. 'It's from Arty,' she said needlessly. 'Bill's friend.'

'And yours now!' Alice chipped in, smiling to disguise her true feeling. But Beth was too preoccupied to pick up on it.

'They've been posted. They were hoping they'd both get the same place. They were counting on it. But Bill's going out east. India. Arty's staying in England. Going on some other course. He can't say what it is. Near London, somewhere.'

'You sound as though you're disappointed. You wanted them both to be sent overseas?'

Now Beth recognized the note of reprimand. 'No! I mean – it's just a shame they couldn't have stuck together. You know. Arty sounds quite cut up.' Her tone was defensive. 'He'd rather be going abroad, too. They're good chums.'

Like you and me? Alice managed to stifle the bitter retort. 'Never mind. You might get the chance to meet up with this Arty feller again. He must get leave. What about your brother? Will you get a chance to see him before he goes?'

Beth nodded. 'They get some sort of leave. Embarkation, it's called. Not long. Three days, I think. It's next week.'

'That's quick.'

'I know. I'll have to get home. In any case, I've got to sign on for registration. My birthday's on 7 March.'

'You'll have caught up with me then, you poor ould biddy!'

'I know! Twenty! I can hardly believe it. I hope they'll accept what I'm doing.'

'Listen! If *I* got away with it, you'll have no bother. Teacher! And you've been doing it for eighteen months now. And they know you're a right old brain box, with all them exams you've passed! You'll sail through! St Anne's would fall apart without Miss Hobbs. I can just see you in another twenty years in your twin set and brogues. You'll end up like old Lavvy yet!'

The blue eyes gazed back at Alice, with that vulnerable self-doubt that made her feel all the pangs of love for her again. As though catching something of Alice's mood, the uncertain little smile faded and was replaced by a solemn earnestness. The colour rose pinkly in the lovely features. 'I hope you're right. It's been – we've been happy here. I wouldn't want to leave.'

The smile had gone, but Alice was sensitive to the uncertainty, which was still there in full. Did she really mean that? And for herself, Alice wondered just how long she could bear this situation; this strange limbo, where loving, their true loving, could no longer be expressed, in the way her body and soul cried out for. Could physical separation really be any more painful than this? Her heart insisted that it could, refused to countenance the very notion of living apart, but her treacherous head wondered if she truly knew the answer. If it was down to praying to this God she didn't believe in, she could only hope that, given time, Beth would realize how impossible it was for them to be together and yet stay apart like this. Wasn't there a song about true lovers and friends? As far as Alice was concerned those two things were like the north and south poles and she could never think otherwise.

Beth was a little nervous when she asked to see Miss Bell, though she anticipated no real difficulty. There was a roaring gale blowing. Slates were peeling off the stable roofs, flying about and shattering into pieces on the cobbles of the yard. Black branches whipped through the air which shrieked through the tossing trees. It was a wild confirmation of the old adage of March lions. The wind buffeted, plucked at your clothes, your hair, snatched your breath and sent you scurrying for cover. But there was flashing sunlight and pale blue above the racing white of the clouds, and there was a wild, mad vitality about the day that somehow lifted spirits, in spite of its violence.

It could still be heard battering at the solid old house as Beth entered the small, crowded capsule of order and authority that was the headmistress's office. 'Sit down, Miss Hobbs. I'm glad we've got this opportunity for a chat. I was intending to organize it, but you've beaten me to it. How are you feeling these days? Got over your fit of depression?'

Helplessly, Beth felt the colour rising, felt the heat of its glow, her inadequacy to counter it. 'Yes, thank you, Head. I wanted – I think you know. I have to register. My hometown's Margrove, so I should do it there, I suppose. That's where the papers were sent. I need to go home, just for a night or so. And my brother – he's in the army. He's being sent to India. He'll be home on embarkation leave. It'll be the last chance . . .' Her voice faded. She was gabbling again. Her toes curled in her shoes, and she experienced that familiar surge of anger against herself. Just calm down, she urged herself. 'I'd only be gone two days. Three at the most.'

'Yes. I dare say we'll manage. We've got our end of term to think about. Less than two weeks now.' Beth forced herself to sit still, not to fidget in the hard chair. 'What do you want to do? I'm talking about your registration, of course. What kind of work would you be interested in doing?'

Beth stared at her blankly, unsure whether she had heard right. 'Er . . . why, teaching. Surely that's . . . I mean, it would be accepted . . . as war work. What I'm doing here.'

'First of all, let me make it clear we've been very grateful for what you've done for us, Elsbeth. You don't mind if I call you that? When your Miss Laverton approached me last year, I was only too pleased to take you on board. But I'm afraid as an unqualified assistant, it was always going to be a temporary arrangement. I don't think my board – the governors – would accept any other appointment. In fact, if I might suggest, you could try for a place at college. Get that qualification. I'm sure the authorities would look kindly on your application to complete your studies.'

It still had not properly sunk in that the headmistress was telling her that she was in fact, or would be shortly, out of a job. She blinked, and sat helplessly, her heart racing, and struggled to get her whirling thoughts together. 'You mean I can't stay on here? That I'm finished?'

'Please don't upset yourself, my dear. I'll have the letter ready. You'll be given the requisite month's notice required for an unqualified post. Your salary will be paid until the beginning of next term. And I'll certainly give you a reference to help you to continue your education. I understood that that was your plan, anyway, before you took up the post with the Margrove school? You look rather shocked. I'm sure you've no need to worry. Whatever happens, you'll find something suitable. Chin up!'

Elsbeth found herself outside the office. She was too dazed for tears, she was mentally reeling, while around her the bustle of the school went on unheeding. Somehow she succeeded in getting through the rest of the day. She avoided the staff room, unable to bear the idea of having to announce her dismissal, or, worse, seeing the looks and hearing the false sympathy from those who probably already knew of it.

Her distress would have been all the more acute if she had heard the conversation which took place later between Miss Bell and her deputy, in the same spot where Beth had received the bombshell. 'Not the right background,' the head observed dispassionately. 'It was evident all along. She never carried any real authority, even with the juniors. And she had no chance with the fourth and fifth. They made mincemeat of her! They can tell, you know. Little provincial girl. She might have been all right with those wee ones from her own town, those grubby little evacuees. Though I doubt it, somehow. She's never really fitted in, though, has she? Not with our crew. Rather let herself down over that business with poor Denby. She's far more at home with that funny little Land Army girl she's chums with. Still! We'd better give her some sort of recommendation to take with her. Do her a note, would you, Dee? Usual gubbins, nothing out of the ordinary. I'll put my scrawl on it and send her on her way. *Sic transit ingloria*, eh?'

Beth's face looked drained of colour, except for the dark, bruise-like smudges under her eyes. Even her lips looked pale and dry. Her voice was low and husky, as if she had a bad cold. 'They told me I needn't come back after Friday. They don't even want me till the end of term.'

'They can't just sack you like that!' Alice saw Beth flinch at the harsh word, and cursed herself for her indiscretion. You and your big gob, Glass! But that's what they had done. Alice felt something like a shiver pass through her, as she realized how suspiciously close she was coming to accepting Beth's interpretation of divine retribution for all these things that were happening to them. It all seemed too neatly falling into place, the events stacking up against them. God, you vindictive old sod! Haven't you got enough to do sorting out this war, without picking on us? She was getting as bad as Beth now, accepting him as a reality, shaping our ends, pulling all the strings. If she were telling the truth, she had always believed in his existence, with that mixture of dread and fearful defiance, like a sneaky, sullen child, resentful of his always being there, always knowing what she was up to. 'God be in my head'. That was the prayer they had been taught to sing in Lister Road. It had always scared her.

She had a sick certainty that Beth was feeling exactly the same. Yet again, Alice suffered from a great urge to grab hold of her lovely girl, shake her out of this trance of defeat, this abject, beaten acceptance of the sentence being passed upon them. And it struck her, with the full force of desolation, that this was the end for them.

'Listen,' she said, panic-stricken. 'I can still talk to Mr Barr. Mebbe he can help. Find something. He took *me* on, didn't he? And what the hell do I know about working on the land? I'll go and see him today.' Beth simply looked at her with that drained face and shook her head. Alice saw the ridiculousness of the image of Beth, in overalls and boots, hacking away at the hedging, clearing ditches, muck spreading, hauling at the stinking bins of pig swill. 'You can stay on here, though, can't you? It's nowt to do with the school, is this place. We can't just give up, let them break us up like this!'

But when she gazed into those washed-out blue eyes, she saw only acceptance of the disaster, with no will to resist, and she knew that it was already over, that they had lost the beautiful and precious thing for which there were no words.

PART II

BOMBS FELL ON EBORACUM

CHAPTER ELEVEN

Davy was nearing the end of the late shift, from 2-10 p.m. It was a blustery night, with scudding clouds, through which the moon peeped fitfully. He was glad that it was a quiet weekday night, and also, in the unlikely event of any trouble from the pubs turning out in fifteen minutes or so, he would be safely in the station and making his report before heading home. It would be up to the night-shift lads to deal with any rowdies. On my bike, head down and back to Reeny's cup of tea and a late snack, before a hot water bottled bed and a lie-in in the morning, he thought. He was only a few hundred yards from the station now, as he covered the line of the old city walls along the curve of Paragon Street. He'd had company for a large part of the evening, for he had shared the beat with PC Collins, one of the regulars; a decent enough bloke, who didn't come the old soldier, as too many of his colleagues did with the specials. They had parted at Walmgate Bar, and Collins had very generously opted to carry on up Walmgate towards the River Foss. Walmgate had always had a bit of a reputation: rough houses, both in the accommodation sense and in the fracas that could break out in the pubs and spill out onto the pavements before or after closing time.

'You sure?' Davy had offered, and Collins had sent him cheerily on his way.

'Aye, lad. Be quiet as the grave tonight. Beer the' get nowadays is watered down that much nobody 'cept a bairn could get fighting drunk on it. Get yourself back to the station and away to your bed.'

'Thanks, Ron. You're a scholar and a gentleman!' Ron Collins was right enough. Things were quiet, and no mistake. Too quiet, sometimes, Davy thought. A cuppa in the wardens' hut in Lawrence Street had been the highlight of the shift, and a free half quickly supped in the passageway of the Spotted Cow, after a friendly warning about their less than efficient blackout. People were starting to get careless; it had been so long since they'd heard the siren, though the ARP lads were still active. Truth to tell, life was becoming boring for Davy. He had it too easy. He even got home regularly, almost every other week. His parents lived at Helmsthorpe, ten miles to the east of York, not far from the road to Hull. There was a branch line ran out in that direction, with a station at Fangfoss, less than two miles from his village. In the good weather, if he was feeling energetic enough, he'd be able to cycle out there. And it was beginning to look as though winter, personified in a wickedly bitter, snow laden February, was at last moving aside. These March winds brought blustering rain in, but at least they didn't cut through the thickest clothing with that arctic bite any more.

Life could be a little more exciting, though, he was forced to admit. He wondered how soon it might be before he dared approach Inspector Holden, with a view to the possibility of his move to the plainclothes branch. His three-month probationary period had ended in February. He guessed that it might appear somewhat indecently hasty to contact DI Holden only a matter of three or four weeks later. No, he'd better give it a month or two. Who knows? The suggestion might come from Holden himself, and that would be even better.

The emergence of a pale moon showed the grassy embankment on his right, crowned by the paler stonework of the walls' ramparts. He stepped out a little. He was approaching the looping Foss and the start of Tower Street. One thing was sure, however bored he might be, he didn't want any excitement to intervene right now, between the prospects of a warm fire, hot tea, and bonny Reeny Lumley. And right on cue, from the shadows of a clump of low brushwood at the foot of the walls, he heard a long, shrill wailing, a wavering cry, not particularly loud, more plaintive than a call for help. His first thought was a cat, or some other animal in distress. Then his senses were alerted as he identified it as a child crying.

He moved quickly, dragging out his torch and beaming it at the dark, leafless tangle of the bushes and clumped grass. There it was, a bundled shape, dark clothing, stretched out, no more than a few feet from the narrow pavement. The beam of his torch identified a flash of paleness, and he saw limbs, muddied white ankle socks, black shoes. The girl's face turned up to him, white, but thickly smeared with what transpired to be blood and tears and mud. 'Don't hurt me – please!' she croaked, keeping her voice hushed.

'It's all right, miss. Don't worry. I'm a policeman. What's happened?' Another road casualty, knocked down in the blackout. Hit pretty heavily, he surmised, for no car had passed him for some time. It must have struck her hard enough to fling her from the roadside on to the verge. Surely any driver hitting something with that force would know about it and stop to investigate? 'Was it a car? Where are you hurt? Let's have a look.'

To his surprise, and dismay, the volume of her crying suddenly increased. From that subdued, plaintive moaning, she turned to an anguished sobbing. She squirmed about on the muddy ground, and Davy began to wish fervently that Collins had not left him alone, or that some passer-by would appear to help him. 'Come on, miss. Everything's fine now. Calm down and let's see what's wrong, eh?' He saw her pale legs, bared to the thigh, saw how stained with mud, or something else, they were. As she turned, he noted that her winter coat was open, and that underneath it, her clothes were badly torn. Her dress hung open to the waist, and the whiteness of an undergarment hung down, exposing a breast. Clumsily, he put his arms around her shoulders, attempted to lift her, and she screamed. 'I'm not going to hurt you!' His voice was raised, he spoke sharply, in admonition, and it seemed to do the trick. The weeping intensified, but she moved, awkwardly under his direction, and he helped her to stand. She hung on him now, almost collapsed against him, and he drew the coat about her, to cover the ripped clothing beneath.

'He attacked me!' Davy saw that she had been beaten about the face. Her nose was bloodied, the dark stain spread down over her chin, down her front, and there was a swelling around her right cheek bone. He could feel her trembling violently against him. 'That Sandshoe Charlie feller! He bloody well attacked me.' She leant into him again, her head down. She had no hat on, her dark hair a wild mess. 'He took me bag.'

Davy flashed his torch around them. A headscarf lay in the grass and he picked it up. There was no sign of a handbag. She was a young girl, perhaps in her mid or late teens, he guessed. He slipped his arm firmly round her waist. 'The police station's just along here. Tower Street. We're practically there. Can you walk? Come on. I'll help you. What's your name?'

'Sandra. Sandra Robinson. He – he tried . . .'

'Yes, all right, Sandra. Let's get you to the station. We'll sort everything out there. Come on, I've got you. There's a good girl.'

The station was busy, with the changeover of shifts, and he felt the girl shrink against him as soon as they passed through the small barricade of sandbags, and climbed the stone steps to the heavily screened door at the top. The initial cries of amusement swiftly died. In the light, Davy was fully aware of how bedraggled the girl appeared, and how serious the attack had been. Her coat was filthy and her ripped clothing copiously stained with the profuse bleeding from her nose.

'What on earth's happened to you, luv?' Len Potts was an elderly sergeant brought back from retirement, and was in charge of the front desk. Sandra Robinson calmed down a little and responded to his friendly concern, and his homely, avuncular frame. 'Eh up, Davy, lad. Where'd you find her? Get her through back and sat down. Come on, lass. We'll soon have you right. Look like you could do with a nice cuppa tea, eh?'

She was crying again, but quietly now, with relief rather than fear. She clung to Davy, still, and he kept his arm around her as he steered her through to the corridor and the bare interview room. The lower half of the walls were white tiled, the upper half green paint. It looked bleak under the harsh overhead light, and the much scarred wooden table and battered chairs did little to deflect the harshness, but the weeping figure looked as if she was unconscious of its unattractiveness. She moved slowly and stiffly, groaned as she lowered herself, in obvious pain, on to a wooden chair.

'You stay with me,' Len Potts ordered Davy, and turned back to the doorway. 'Cup of tea here. Quick! And put some sugar in it!' he called, and closed the door. 'Right? Tell me what you know,' he said to Davy. 'We'll get you sorted soon, pet.'

Davy quickly supplied the few details he knew, and Potts began to question the girl. His voice was measured and kind, and she responded to his tone, making a brave effort to suppress her weeping. 'It was that feller,' she repeated strongly. 'The one that's been robbing women. That Sandshoe Charlie bloke. Just like it said in the *Evening Press*. Old macintosh. Black balaclava thing. He pulled it up, off his mouth, while he . . . he started slobbering over me. Trying to kiss me – and . . .' She stopped, stared down at her grubby, folded hands on the table, and the tears took over once more. She shivered more violently. 'The filthy . . .'

'Right, Sandra. This is difficult, I know. Young lass like you, having to tell us all about it. But we have to know, luv. We have to catch the blighter, don't we? What exactly did he do to you? Don't be ashamed. You've done nothing wrong. Just tell us what happened. All of it. We *do* need to know, for when we catch him and put him away. Come on.'

There was a knock at the door before it opened and someone brought in the mug of tea. Davy was feeling a deep embarrassment on the girl's behalf. Why on earth didn't they have a female on hand in the station? Or one that could be made readily available at short notice? They would probably have to summon a doctor to examine Sandra. Why not get some competent woman at the same time? He watched her dirty fingers closing around the mug. The nails were short, the hands roughened by manual work, he guessed. She cupped both hands round the mug, held it close to her chest, as though cradling its warmth to her, holding her battered face to the rising steam. It seemed to calm and comfort her. Her strong local accent, as well as the cheap quality of the clothes she was wearing, were indicative of a humble background, which was confirmed by the address she gave as her home, in one of the many Victorian back-to-backs off Lawrence Street, scarcely more than half a mile from where she had been assaulted.

She made a brave effort to follow Len Potts's direction. 'He tried – you know – but he didn't do it. I was kicking and scratching at him, and shouting for help. But then he started really punching. He hit me in the face, his fists, knocked me flat. He tore me dress, and me vest . .' She put her hand over her bosom, where her coat was closed over the torn garments, 'and he put his hand up, ripped me . . . me drawers . . .' She faltered, drew in a hissing breath, and sniffed, forced herself to continue, while Davy suffered for her and felt he should interrupt, ask Len Potts to leave it, until they could fetch a WPC, or a nurse. Or at least have another woman present, even someone from her own family, perhaps. 'And he was on top of me. He was kicking me – me legs, with his boots. And he was trying . . . his coat was open, he was pushing himself against me . . .'

'Did he rape you, love?' Potts asked, with kind firmness. 'We have to know. Did he actually have intercourse?'

Davy felt helplessly outraged for her, he could feel the heat in his face. Would she even know what Len Potts meant? he thought, then condemned himself for his foolishness. This was not a child. A fifteen-year-old girl, from a background like hers, was wise enough in the ways of the wicked world to know what intercourse meant.

'No! No! He didn't!' She was agitated again now. She stared wildly at them, and she began to cry, speaking against the flood of renewed tears. 'He didn't! He tried – he had his hand on me, down there. He touched me. But he didn't do me.' She cried these last words out harshly, they rang shockingly in the bleak room, and she collapsed in despairing sobs, folding her head on her arms on the table, and Davy reached out, then withdrew his hand quickly. Len was not so hesitant. He stood and put both hands on the heaving shoulders, gripped her tightly.

'There, love. Don't cry. You've been a brave lass. You did very well, you can be very proud of yourself. Now – we're going to have to get the doctor in to have a look at you. Just examine you. We need to have a record of your injuries. And we'll get someone to write out a statement for you, for you to sign. It'll help us catch this feller, Sandra. We'll have him, I promise you. And we need to catch him quick, before he does it to some other poor soul. All right? We'll send word to your folks. Someone can come, your mam, eh? Be with you. I'll see if we can get a car to go round for them. We'll get you sorted. Why don't you come through to the office? You don't want to be sat here on your own, do you? And Constable Brown here can make a start on the statement.' Davy nodded, already resigned to a much longer shift than he had anticipated only a short while ago.

Although he was still on the 2-10 p.m. shift, Davy went back to the station about 9.30 the next morning, in order to complete the paperwork on the Sandra Robinson assault, and to find out what progress if any had been made. What he found made him even more convinced that the present system for dealing with sexual crimes was far from satisfactory – at least at Tower Street, and probably, he surmised, in the majority of stations throughout the county, if not the country. The newly developed prints were still pinned to the notice board in the general office, over the long counter, which ran almost the length of one wall. This was a kind of communal desk, on which three Imperial typewriters stood, and under which several wooden chairs were scattered. It was where the junior ranks dealt with all the lists, reports, and any other written correspondence required. There was a little cluster of bodies round the enlarged photographs, which had clearly just appeared, and been put there to dry.

'Come on, for God's sake!' Davy exploded, and the group had the grace to look suitably chastened. There was a portrait of Sandra Robinson, wrapped in a towel. It covered only her torso, and she was holding it to expose her legs to the tops of her thighs. Her shoulders, arms and legs were covered in dark bruises and weals. There was a back view, where even her skinny buttocks were exposed. They too were well marked. Then there was a close-up of her arms, and another of her legs, and finally, of her swollen, battered face. There was a medical report listing in detail the extent of her wounds. Her nose had not been broken, but she had suffered a suspected fracture of her right cheekbone.

Davy was not surprised to discover that the police photographer was male, as was the doctor. 'Not best pleased to be called out at eleven at night!' the day sergeant on the desk chuckled. Davy thought of that poor kid, beaten, terrified, then having to endure the embarrassment of stripping naked and going through the ordeal of examination, and those photographs.

'Couldn't we have someone – a woman – who can be called to deal with cases like this?'

The sergeant stared at him. 'What? Here? This isn't HQ, mate! Anyway, we're police, aren't we? Got to deal with all sorts we have. That's our job!'

Our job is to catch the criminals, not take pictures of what they've done, or write up reports. The cellar below his feet was full of files, piles of them, stacked high, going back to the beginning of the century.

As if he could read Davy's mind, the sergeant went on, 'And if you'd got round your beat just a bit sooner, my lad, you'd have caught old Charlie on the job! And I hope you wouldn't have been too shocked at seeing them at it to have collared him while his pants were round his knees! Saved us a lot of grief all round, I reckon!'

CHAPTER TWELVE

Sandra Robinson's handbag was handed in to the police later that morning. It had been found just two hundred yards from the spot where the assault had taken place, very near Walmgate Bar, on the grassy bank beneath the walls. There had been no real attempt to hide it. A child out with her mother had spotted it, and the honest citizen had brought it at once to Tower Street. It had been opened – or perhaps had burst open. It could well be that 'Charlie' had flung it violently away as he ran. Sandra's few possessions were there. The woman had gathered up the cigarettes and matches, the cheap compact, even the key to Sandra's locker at work – she worked in the canteen at Rowntree's. The only item missing was the small black purse, containing almost a pound: a ten-bob note, two half-crowns, and some smaller silver and copper coins. 'I didn't see no purse!' the woman insisted, colouring up and beginning to bristle a little. 'I picked up all the stuff that had fallen out. As God's my witness—'

'It's all right, love,' Jim Bloomfield, the sergeant who had earlier been somewhat unappreciative of Davy's part in the proceedings, reassured her. 'No one's suggesting otherwise.' He smiled. 'Be a bit hard to believe you'd have the brass neck to bring the bag in if you'd pinched the purse, eh? 'Specially as there'll be no reward offered, most likely!'

Sergeant Bloomfield seemed to have a gift for 'putting people's backs up', in the local parlance. The conscientious woman, only slightly mollified by his former remarks, now drew herself up with offended dignity. 'That's not the reason I brought it in,' she sniffed. She glanced pointedly at the wall clock and her shuffling daughter. 'And if that's all I'll be on my way, thank you very much!' It had occupied at least half an hour of her valuable time. She'd be way back in the queue at Jackson's now. Any 'extras' at the butcher's would be long gone. She had to wait another fifteen minutes before the report of her action had been written up, with a note of the bag and its contents, and the good citizen's name and address recorded. She inscribed her signature with due solemnity, the pink tip of her tongue peeping forth from the right corner of her mouth, by which time she was feeling less noble at her own actions, and the keen curiosity of her little daughter. 'Next time mind your own business, shite hawk eyes!' she told the aggrieved child.

Foolishly, Davy had lingered a few minutes after he had completed his own paperwork, taking time to chat with the lads who were on their break, and Sgt. Bloomfield was quick to collar him as he was leaving. 'Here! This is all your fault. You're the one who brought her in. Go round to that lass Robinson's place. Tell her her bag's been found. Tell her to come in and verify it's hers. And the contents.'

'I'm back on at two, Sarge! Can't somebody else do it?'

'Hey! There's a war on, tha knows! How many bobbies do you think we've got on our books? It's not far.' He grinned. 'Anyway, you're the big hero, from what I hear. She was hanging all over you when you brought her in.'

'She was terrified out of her wits!' As he recalled the trembling, bedraggled figure, he felt a resurgence of compassion. 'Listen. Can I take her stuff round there? Save her having to come in again.' He thought about what had happened to her here through the long night. She would almost certainly regard the police station very much as part of her prolonged ordeal. 'She's probably feeling very shaky, still.'

The sergeant snorted derisively. 'Take it back to her? You should know better than that, lad! Serious crime is this. Our Charlie's stepped way up the ladder. Not just snatching handbags now. Sex assault, attempted rape, robbery with violence. CID's on it now. It's evidence, is this lot. We'll have the collar and tie lot in on it now. Might be a few double shifts for you flatfoots an' all. He's after more than handbags now. We've got to catch him quick!'

Hudson Terrace was a street of cramped 'two-up-and-two-downs', where you stepped from the street into a tiny vestibule, no more than three feet by two, before you were at the bottom of a narrow staircase and into the main living room, with a large black-leaded range occupying most of one wall. The fire, boiler, oven and hobs were all part of the solid cast iron appliance. A fire glowed now in the high grate, and a huge, chipped brown kettle sputtered in front of it. Davy stood on the doorstep and introduced himself to the tall woman of impressive build and unkempt appearance who filled the doorway. 'Now what?' she glowered at him, and he was relieved to hear Sandra's voice come swiftly from behind the bulk.

'It's all right, Mam. This is the copper – the constable – who took me into the station. The one that found me.'

Davy was shocked anew at the swollen, battered face, bruised spectacularly about the eyes, so that she would have looked like some heavily mascara-ed screen goddess were it not that her youthful features were pitifully distorted by her beating.

'Didn't recognize you without your uniform.' She was wearing an old, thick-knitted woollen cardigan of dark brown. The voluminous way it hung upon her, down almost to her knees, and the thick rolls of turned up material at her wrists, indicated that it had been designed for a much larger frame, and, from the side on which the buttons were fixed, it was clear that that frame had been masculine. Beneath it was a pale, thick shift or nightdress reaching to her ankles; they, too, were covered by men's clothing – a pair of thick grey socks.

Sandra had enough feminine pride to show deep embarrassment, both at her garb and her appearance. 'I'm sorry, er . . . I didn't go in to work. I'll have to get a sick note. I've been in bed.'

'Poor lass is badly!' Mrs Robinson stated, with an emphasis that seemed to suggest that Davy was part of the circumstances causing her daughter's illness. 'And no wonder! She's lucky to be alive, poor thing! Have you got him yet?' she asked fiercely.

'Not yet, Mrs Robinson, but we're doing our best, I can assure you. The detective branch is dealing with it now. I came to tell you . . .' he glanced over the looming shoulder to Sandra's swollen face, 'your handbag has been handed in at the station. It was found near Walmgate Bar.'

'I thought that's what this bugger was after, handbags?' Mrs Robinson queried, still with that aggressive manner. 'Where is it then?' She glanced pointedly at his empty hands.

'I'm afraid we have to hang on to it for a while. The purse was missing, by the way.'

'Oh! So he *is* still at it then, is he? Still robbing, the dirty little bugger!' She mellowed enough to invite Davy to sit at the table and have a cup of tea. She and Sandra were the only visible occupants of the house. The room seemed full enough with only the three of them in it. He wanted to get on home to Dubry Street, for he would scarcely have time to eat and get into uniform to be back for the afternoon shift. But he felt sorry for the young girl, who was so clearly torn between her dismay at being caught in such an unflattering condition and her desire for him to stay. He took his place on the hard wooden chair, and accepted the cup of strong tea from the pot on the lower hob. The liquid looked black and tasted well stewed, and he wondered if it had stood brewing all day. By evening tide it would probably melt the metal spoons. The colour was transformed to an interesting mahogany shade by a trickle of milk from the wide-topped bottle, then fortified with a spoonful of dried milk powder, which floated in little islets, dispersed by a vigorous stirring.

'Sugar?' Mrs Robinson asked, a hand on the old flowered caddy that served as container.

'No thanks, Mrs Robinson,' Davy returned gallantly. 'I've got used to it without,' he lied, and earned at last a genuine smile.

He was somewhat amused, but mostly touched, at Sandra's attitude. Sgt. Bloomfield's mocking gibe about his being a 'hero' came back to him. It soon became apparent that the youngster did indeed regard him in something of that light. She behaved with a mixture of embarrassment and innocent flirtation. Her hands kept moving to her untidy, dark hair, and her unprepossessing clothing, and then to her swollen features. She kept one hand to her face when she spoke, her words coming through her spread fingers. It reminded him of a parody of those powdered coquettes and their fluttering fans, in an eighteenth century court.

He was ashamed of the little fillip it gave to his masculine ego to have this adolescent behaving thus towards him. He was fully aware of how ridiculous it was to allow his male vanity to be flattered by something so pathetic. For some reason Alice Glass popped into his mind. He recalled her youthful wisdom at the ways of the world, learnt no doubt in circumstances not much different from this kid's environment. The wisdom of the 'school of hard knocks'. He remembered the rough directness of Sandra's speech as she had described the attack, and its embarrassing details. At fifteen she was already out of school and into the adult world and all that it entailed. Youthful she might be, but her innocence was doubtless already qualified.

As if to support his private speculation, she suddenly gave a dramatic little squeak, put her hand on his arm, then withdrew it to her bruised face again. Her sudden wide-eyed discomfiture had more than a trace of artifice in it. 'Eh! You haven't seen them pictures they took of me, have you? Oh my God! Me showing practically all I've got! I didn't know where to put meself!'

He felt he was the one who was blushing as he recalled that clustered group around the prints, and the salacious comments. 'Oh, that's all in the confidential file,' he answered her swiftly and falsely. 'For evidence, if necessary. Nobody sees those.'

'Thank God for that!' She rolled her eyes expressively and sighed with relief. A little too theatrically? Davy wondered, and was saddened by his cynicism. Yet even her display of coquettishness had a trace of artlessness about it still, he extenuated. She still retained enough of the child in the budding woman to cause him to be a little charmed.

Mrs Robinson evidently found nothing to be too upset about in this exchange. 'She'll have to see how she feels,' she said, bringing the conversation back to the point of his visit. 'I might have a walk down with her this afternoon, if she's up to it.'

'Will *you* be there?' Sandra asked, her bruised eyes fixed on him, with the hint of a plea in her tone.

'I'm on from two today. In fact, I'll have to get a move on. I've got to get back to my digs and eat. Get changed.'

'Oh, you're not from round here then? I didn't think you were, like. You talk far too posh. I thought you were from down south somewhere.'

Sandra gazed at him with that look again. Artlessness or artifice? He explained about his parents living in Helmsthorpe. She looked blankly at him, as though she had never heard of it. Ten miles, he guessed, was far distant in her narrow life. He felt himself moved with sympathy for her once more. She *was* just a kid after all, and it was a terrible thing to have happened to her. 'I'll probably be on the beat by 2.15, but I'll keep an eye out. It won't take you long, though. All you have to do is check the bag and its contents. Sign a paper to say they're yours. They might even take your fingerprints,' he added, as though he were offering a child a treat.

'Here! I'm not the one who's a bad 'un, am I?'

He laughed, shook his head. 'No, but they'll want to know which prints are yours. If they check for prints. If there's any that aren't, well that could be our man's. The so-and-so who attacked you. You said he had like fingerless glove things on, didn't you? Finger prints could help to prove he did it.'

Sandra nodded, impressed, but her mother gave a worldly-wise sniff. 'Aye. But you've got to catch the bugger first, haven't you?'

There was another attack, only five nights later. This time it took place near one of the city's other ancient gateways, or bars, as they were called: Micklegate Bar. The victim was a married woman in her thirties: a cashier from the Northern cinema, making her way after the evening show to the nearby Windmill pub, where she normally joined her railwayman husband and his mates for a late drink before they escorted her homeward. She had almost reached her destination, and was waiting to cross the road to the dark shape of the pub, when she was grabbed from behind, an arm circling her throat and pulling her head back, the other hand smothering her cry of alarm. She was pulled back into the shadows, to the muddy foot of the wall only a few yards from the projecting bar. Badly frightened, she had made no further attempt to scream – 'He said he'd kill me if I made a noise' – and she had lain whimpering and begging him not to hurt her, handing over the purse from her coat pocket. But once again it was clear that robbery was not his sole purpose. Leaving her in her opened winter coat, he had ripped apart the cardigan and blouse, baring her breasts, clawing at her flesh, then hauling up her skirt, continuing his assault. She lay, 'expecting the worst', as she told the police afterwards. 'I was just terrified he'd kill me, like he said. But then he just suddenly rolled off me. Got up and ran, without a word.' Some men passing by, on their own way to the pub, heard her crying, found her lying in the little, muddy patch, half naked.

It led to Davy's meeting Detective Inspector Norman Holden again, for he visited the station to help coordinate efforts to catch the attacker. There was a detective sergeant in charge of the case at Tower Street, but Inspector Holden was the overall senior officer. 'Mrs Wright wasn't beaten like your girl Miss Robinson,' Holden told the assembled crew, who were crammed into the general office. 'Because she didn't put up a fight like the Robinson girl did. Same bloke, though, undoubtedly. Old mac, balaclava, fingerless mittens. And he got a lot more of what he was after, this time – and I don't mean the money,' he added significantly. There was a burst of deep laughter, which faded uncertainly as the inspector's face remained impassively serious. 'In fact, it's a bit of a mystery why he didn't get everything he wanted. Mrs Wright reckons it was quite a while – a good few minutes, maybe five – before the folks who found her came along. Our Charlie was on top of her, having a good grope, if you'll pardon the expression, then he just suddenly ups and offs, like a bat out of hell. Maybe he heard something, somebody coming along. Nobody we can trace, though. He just takes off, down towards the sheds and the station yard, Mrs Wright thinks, but she's not too sure. Makes sense though. Quieter down there at that time of night. If he'd turned back up to Blossom Street or Micklegate he'd have likely run into someone. Anyway, that's a line I want you to pursue. You lads,' he grinned at the uniformed figures, 'chance for you to make a name for yourselves, get a bit of overtime in. I want you up there asking questions. See if you can track down his movements, ask around. We've got to get this pervert, and quick. He's tried twice and not hit the jackpot. He's not going to stop. And some poor lass, or somebody's wife, or, worse still, some poor kid, isn't going to be as lucky as these two.' He pointed to the names on the blackboard.

When the meeting had ended, he called Davy over to where he stood chatting with the detective sergeant. 'You know Special Constable Brown?' Detective Sergeant Baxter nodded. 'This lad's already had a bit of plain clothes experience,' Holden smiled. 'He helped to nab that mob over in the Dales last year. The ones that led us up to Teesside.' Again Baxter nodded, waiting. 'Use him on Sandshoe Charlie, Tommy. He'll be coming over to the branch soon. Give him a bit of real experience, eh? Give him a taste for it, I reckon.'

Tommy Baxter's fleshy face broke into a sudden grin. 'Aye, happen. Or put him off for life!'

CHAPTER THIRTEEN

Alice felt the heaviness of spirits weigh upon her as she unlocked the door of the flat, like the chill she knew would be waiting for her inside. She pictured the sooty detritus of last night's fire, which would be waiting in the grate, and which she would have to deal with before she could light another. The trouble was, it was still too chilly to do without one, unless she stayed muffled up to the eyeballs, grabbed a quick bite and jumped straight into bed. And that was something she shied away from, too. She kept out of bed as long as she could these days. It was lonelier than anywhere else in the flat.

She saw the envelope lying on the doormat, recognized the writing as Davy's. A pang of guilt swept over her. She had written a short note around the time that Beth had left, and had not answered the two letters she had received from him since. This would be the third. She stooped and picked it up, shook her cold feet out of the rubber boots, and left them leaning drunkenly against the damp wall as she climbed the stairs. The silence wrapped itself around her like the damp chill.

You'd think she'd be used to it by now. It was three weeks since Beth had departed, a lifetime, practically, but still she hated this moment, entering the tomblike hush, the deadness of the empty rooms. Davy's letter would have been lying on the table, beside her place set for the meal; the fire would have been glowing red, or pale flames licking round a fresh log, Beth's voice teasing as she announced the arrival of the missive from Davy. But that was in another lifetime, twenty-one long days ago.

She pulled off the woollen hat, shrugged off the heavy coat and the dirty mittens. Through in the tiny scullery she put the kettle on, rinsed out the mug she had used early that morning, dumped a single spoonful of tea from the shrinking pile into the teapot. It was amazing how much less than half a single ration book provided compared with two. And she didn't have Beth's pretty smile and gentrified voice to wheedle those 'little extras' out of Mrs Floyd at the village shop.

Really, she must think about doing something with her life. The self-contempt surged again at that tightness in her chest, the sting of unshed tears behind her eyes. Beth was gone. She'd lost her, and she must stop being this inert lump of misery, and *do* something. This place, its dead emptiness, was stifling her. She had already vowed she wouldn't just stay on here, pining for her lost love. And it was lost, no doubt about it. Beth was not going to come waltzing back through that door; the days of twinkling fire and waiting cuppa were gone, and she should be, too, instead of sitting here on her backside like one o'clock half struck!

The cruel little madam hadn't even written to her, not a line, in the eternity of the days that had passed. And Alice had forced herself not to write, either. Well, not strictly true. She *had* written, several letters, with heartbroken, lovelorn pleas, splashed with tears, and then furious vituperation at Beth's cruelty – but none of them had been sent. They all finished up crumpled and consumed in the lonely flames. She knew that Beth was hurting, too. She could see all too clearly still that stricken, chalk-white face, the blue eyes lost in the watery sadness that engulfed them. They had clung, speechless, both shaking, torn with their grief, and Al had fled, and not from selfish motives either, so that she would not be around when Mr Hobbs came to collect his daughter for the last time. It had taken real nerve for Alice to come back that first evening to the empty flat. And it still tore at her each time she had to do so. She had vowed she would move. The Forces, a factory – anything. What did it matter? Yet still she hadn't summoned up enough will to do something about it. She was just hanging about here like some forlorn ghost haunting an empty house.

She forced herself to clear out the grate and lay a new fire, with paper, sticks and coal, and at least sweep the dusty hearth. She held a newspaper over the opening until the new flames were roaring and the paper showed signs of scorching, then carried the big pan of hot water through from the stove to the enamel bowl on the towel spread on the rug. She stripped, knelt, and stood, as she comprehensively washed herself, and tried not to recollect how much more pleasurable such ablutions used to be when shared with her partner. In her pyjamas, and with the dressing gown (another gift of Beth's) wrapped around her, she ate the meal of reheated minced meat, fortified with the remains of a tin of *Woppa* peas, and, finally, with resurrected guilt, settled down in front of the fire with Davy's letter.

My Dear Alice,
Remember me? I'm beginning to wonder if you do, it's been so long since I heard from you. I guessed you would be feeling a bit low after your friend Elsbeth left, but would

it make you feel any worse if you wrote to me once in a while? You could get things off your chest that way. You said we were 'mates' and that's what mates are for, to tell our troubles to. I always did, didn't I? And I'm not going to stop now, so here goes.

Remember I told you about that young girl, Sandra Robinson, getting attacked and having her handbag taken, and getting quite badly beaten up in the process? Well, things have got a lot worse. This Sandshoe Charlie (that's what we call him) has been pinching bags for quite a while – a few months now – always after dark. He started before Christmas. Obviously the blackout suits him. And not just him! Burglaries shot up last year, when the sirens were going practically every night and people were out in the shelters. The numbers have dropped a lot since the nightly air raid warnings have stopped. But now this Charlie character has turned really nasty. Before, he always used to just leap on women, grab their purse or bag and tear off again. Bad enough, I know. He made one poor old lady really ill, gave her some sort of heart attack. But with Sandra it was different. He took her bag – we found it later, with her purse missing – but that wasn't all. He attacked her, really badly, punched her and kicked her, then tore her clothes. I don't need to tell you what he was trying to do. There've been two more attacks like that on women out alone, both sex assaults. The last one was another young girl, another of the Rowntree's girls, where Sandra Robinson works. She was on her way home from working a late shift and he dragged her down on to the towpath by the river – half throttled her, pulled her off one of the bridges, down some steps to the bank. She was absolutely terrified, poor kid. Didn't put up much of a struggle but he still battered her about the face and body. Knocked out a tooth and split her lip. Ripped off most of her clothes.

Some animal, eh? Don't know why I'm telling you about this stuff, except that it's been on my mind a lot, as I'm quite involved in it now. We've had to do extra shifts, and we've had to patrol round the factory when the girls finish their late shift and watch the main routes home. Inspector Holden has got me attached to the team – I've even been out in plain clothes. I would be chuffed, if it wasn't for the fact that these are such awful crimes. I don't feel good about getting a chance to do detective work through something like this.

I didn't really mean to unburden myself so much, but, as I said, we're chums – I hope! Now then, the real point of writing. I've got some leave over Easter. A whole week! I'm sure you must get some time off, so I thought it would be a great chance for us to get together again. I don't suppose I could persuade you to come through to York, so I thought I'd come to Howbeck. I could do with breathing some of that wonderful air again. A good day's hike on the Tops would do me the world of good. And I could look up some old chums – like Vera Rhodes!!! I'm sure they'd all be delighted to see me in the bar of the Oddfellows!

What sayest thou? Make it a yes, please! Seriously, I do very much want to see you. I promise to behave myself and not start any spoony nonsense again. I give you my word on that. You're still a very dear friend to me, though – best I've got, so don't turn me down. Write quick – just scribble a note saying how much you're looking forward to it. I can get away on the Thursday, and we could spend Good Friday and Easter Saturday together. I could even travel to Margrove with you if you've arranged to go home. I could even meet you there, so we could spend at least a few hours together. I'm counting on you to make a lonely bobby happy!

Love,

Davy xxx (matey kisses only)

He could still make her smile, in spite of herself. And he did a pretty good job of rekindling the fires of guilt, too. She ought to have written to him, she knew. But she'd been feeling so low. Low? Come off it, Al! Rock bottom and then down a bit, you mean, lass! In fact there was no bottom – it had fallen out of her world with Beth's departure, and she didn't care how melodramatic that sounded, because it was all too true. Maybe it would be good to see him again, though. Of course, she couldn't 'unburden' herself, even to him. For a few seconds, she found herself, nevertheless, exploring the shocking thought of doing just that. But no. Not even Davy would be able to take it. The girls had found it hard to talk about, even between themselves, even when the whole rapturous, dizzy glory of it was bursting all over them. Her beloved Beth practically writhed in torment whenever Al stumblingly tried to do so. *Wrong. Unnatural.* The old words came tolling up in her mind, with all the old, measured monotony of the funeral bell.

But it *would* be good to see him again. She had practically buried herself for the past three weeks. Nobody had got more than a few begrudging words from her, until Evelyn and Beryl had virtually given up on her, and even grumpy old Dick Pearson was wary of challenging her. 'Bear with a sore head!' he chided, mildly for him, and left it at that. Perhaps seeing Davy would snap her out of this lethargy, make her take stock and actually do something about lifting herself out of her torpor.

Quickly she reached for pencil and paper and wrote her compliance with his plans. She could, in fact, have had the Easter weekend free, to go home to Margrove, but the idea of being so near to Beth had made her sick with need for her, and she had volunteered to stay and help out with the few necessary chores, thus allowing both the Land Girls to take leave instead. It would make up to some extent for her general grumpiness.

Next day, after she had posted the letter to Davy, she asked Evelyn if she would 'do something' with her hair for her, for the following week, and both the girls stared at her in some surprise. 'Thought you were staying here over Easter?' Their look conveyed their anxiety.

'I am. It's just . . .' To her surprise, she felt herself reddening a little. 'Davy Brown's coming through to stay for a couple of days, next Thursday.'

Both girls stared in amazement. 'My God! You crafty little bitch!'

Beryl's eyes widened. 'Ooh, do you think he'll be all right? I mean at the Oddfellows. With Vera. She won't turn him away, will she? She'll give him a room?'

'She won't get the chance to say no!' Alice answered. 'He'll stay here, of course. In the flat. With me.'

'Ooh! But you've only the one room! The one bed!'

And for an instant, the old, wicked Al appeared, in her sparkle-eyed vivacity. 'I know. I hope to God he doesn't snore, eh?'

Alice was touched by the way his eyes lit up, that dark, serious look of his transformed by the radiant smile as he stepped from the train and saw her standing by the way out. He still thinks a lot of me! She was shamed by the way the thought stirred her vanity for an instant, but then dismissed the accompanying sense of disloyalty she felt at it. Who else was there to care about her these days? Several passengers from the Middlesborough train had alighted at Howbeck, all of them locals, all of them recognizing the figure of Alice, and several of them the young man in civilian clothing who eagerly embraced her. She accepted his kiss on her lips, hugged him in return. 'That'll set a few tongues gossiping!' She smiled, aware of turning heads and prolonged stares.

'Good! Take their minds off the war, eh? My God, Alice! You look good, you really do. A sight for sore eyes, you are!'

She blushed visibly. Again she felt a flash of discomfiture at the pleasure she took from his words, and his look. She had made the effort, a considerable one, to smarten herself up. Hair done, make-up on, best clothes, practically all provided by Beth, who had refurbished Al's wardrobe with her 'cast-offs', many of which Alice had suspected were new rather than good as: the fawn twin set under the red winter coat, the heather-check skirt and the precious rayon stockings; even the petticoat. An extra smile tugged at the corners of her mouth. Not what was under that, though. She was wearing the silk underwear that the Big Swede, alias Gus Rielke, had presented to her last year in the bar of the Oddfellows. It made her want to giggle at the knowledge that Davy had already seen the article, having been there with her when the gift was given. She was glad now she *had* made the effort, she thought defiantly. And to hell with Beth, the chief benefactress of the feast. And feasting Davy was, his eyes were still all over her, and he was hanging on to her arm as though he feared she might run off, as they left the station and picked their way down the rough lane to the road, in the afternoon sunshine.

'I'd nowt better to do,' she told him, in response to his expressed surprise and pleasure to find her waiting on the platform. 'I guessed you'd be on this one or the next. The 4.45.'

He was heartened to see her looking so well, and with so much of her old animation. He had not expected it. She grinned and her nose wrinkled endearingly, when he nodded at the pub as they passed it, just after they crossed the humped stone bridge over the Howe. 'You reckon Vera would have turned me away? I doubt it. She always had her head screwed on as far as brass was concerned.'

She squeezed his arm. 'Aye, but God knows what she'd have popped in your beer or your Victory Pie! Anyways, we'll give 'em summat much better to talk about, lad, you staying at the flat. One bedroom – one bed! Evelyn and Beryl's eyes nearly fell out when I told them!'

'I must admit, it made *my* poor old heart flutter. You're absolutely sure it'll be all right?'

'Of course! And who cares what their mucky minds make of it? And before you get all hot under that clean collar of yours, I can tell you I'll be very snug and cosy on a shake-me-down in front of the fire.'

She thought of the old, striped mattress still propped against the wall of the bedroom. As he began a gallant protest about his occupying the spot in front of the fire and not dreaming of putting her out of her own bed, she said brightly, 'Don't fret yourself! I've done it before, loads of times!'

And for the first time, the perceptive Davy saw just the flicker of a shadow in those grey eyes, and saw it flit across the determined brightness of the smile she offered him.

CHAPTER FOURTEEN

Alice spread her oilskin cape with its wet side down on their favourite flat surface of the rocky outcrop. They had been caught by a short, heavy shower on their climb on to the moor, but the steady wind had quickly dried them again, and the rocks on which they now rested. They had been up here several times when Davy was working at Howe Manor. From this high point you could see right across to the coast and the grey sea, if the weather was clear enough. It was today, now that the shower had passed, and Davy lay back, breathing deeply, enjoying the ride of the white clouds over the vast expanse. Behind them, just over the curve of the heather-covered slope, lay High Top farm, where the cache of stolen goods had been found, which Rielke and the tenant farmer, Bob Symmonds, guarded and distributed as part of a well-organized criminal network. Alice had brought Davy here on one of their first excursions with the ulterior motive of getting him to help explore the outbuildings where, among other things, a store of illegal petrol lay hidden.

Davy's mind was clearly dwelling on their past adventure, too. 'Do you ever see Mrs Symmonds?' he asked. 'How is she managing with that brood of hers?' He still felt somewhat guilty at the way Bob Symmonds had borne the brunt of the punishment, both legal and illegal, that was meted out those months ago. It had been an extremely unequal relationship between the Norwegian and the hill farmer. Rielke was very much the senior partner, who made all the decisions. He it was who, through greed, had taken the risk of stealing sheep from their neighbours, and, typically, he it was who had escaped the police trap, disappearing from the area for good. Bob Symmonds was not so lucky. It was the sheep stealing which had, reluctantly in many cases, swung the majority of village opinion in favour of Davy's pivotal action in the police operation. In fact, the farming community had not waited for the due process of the law to take its course. For two days, it appeared that Symmonds had, like Rielke, eluded the authorities, but then he was discovered, trussed up and naked on the roadside at the approach to Howbeck, so badly beaten that he spent several weeks in hospital. He was still serving a long term in gaol.

'She's doing better than when her hubby was running things,' Alice told Davy, in answer to his query. 'The two oldest lads are running the place and making a better go of it than their dad ever did. Mind you, he had his mind on other things! And his missus – well, she was hardly ever seen in the village anyway. But I reckon she must have had the good sense to hang on to a fair bit of the black market money Bob was making. Somebody was saying she's spruced up a bit, her and the bairns. Baby's doing fine, an' all. I reckon we did her a favour getting shot of her old man for her.' She grinned over at him and pulled a comic face. 'Mind you, I wouldn't go out of me way to run into her. She'd probably give me a right good hiding!'

She dug into the rucksack and took out the wrapped sandwiches and the thermos. 'Clever things, eh?' She held up the metal flask. 'I still don't understand how they work, though. Beth left it with me.' Again, Davy saw that flash of hesitation, and pain, before she ploughed on. 'She gave me all sorts. Half the clothes on me back came from her. More than half, if I'm being honest.'

'She was a good mate,' Davy said quietly. Now it was he who paused, before he added, 'You miss her very much, don't you?'

Alice ducked her head down. She felt a kind of panic as her throat closed, and her eyes filled with tears. It washed right over her, caught her helpless in its power, like the tide of colour flooding up into her face. She swallowed, her head down, nodded. A sob caught in her throat and as she tried to choke it back, she made a curious hiccupping sound, like fizzy pop getting up her nose. Oh God! It must be something to do with coming up here again, bringing it all back to her.

Suddenly he was up, kneeling, taking hold of her, his arms tight about her, cradling her into him. The bastard! It was all his fault! If it hadn't been for that warm kindness in his voice, the compassion in it. She began to sob, the great welling of grief erupting from her, shaking her whole frame. She gave way, let it carry her, folded into his embrace, her head on his chest as he nursed her like an infant and the tears streamed down her face, a massive release of anguish and sorrow.

He rocked her slowly, holding her against him, his mouth in the burnished, wind blown curls, and murmured as though soothing a child, 'There there, my love.'

It was a considerable while before she quietened. Part of her was almost reluctant to resume control, for it had been a great release and relief to let the true extent of her desolation and loss show at last. And she was very glad that he was there. She needed his care, and his understanding. How complete that was, she remained unsure. And embarrassment came as she finally recovered from her emotional outburst, but still she was glad of his presence, and of his sheltering arms, in which she rested far longer than she felt she had a right to.

She took his handkerchief, wiped her wet face, sniffed and blew her nose vigorously, the sobs toned down to gusty sighs. Calm was restored but she couldn't bring herself to look at him. 'Don't look at me!' she croaked, still busy with her red face, and was angry with herself for her girly soppiness. 'Sorry about that!' Time of the month, she almost added, to excuse her lapse, but held the lie back. She'd embarrassed the poor lad enough. 'Oh God! We haven't even had our bait, have we? Come on, tuck in. Pour the tea, there's a good lad.'

She made a valiant effort to act as though her weeping fit had never happened, asking him about his work in York and the Sandshoe Charlie case he was part of. He went along with it, talking easily about his life in the police force, and the city, and she gave him her full, even eager, attention. But those washed out grey eyes did not hold his for long, darted away again, and his heart went out to her as he chatted, and made her smile, then laugh, until he was sure she had fully recovered.

He made certain the conversation remained on safe ground, describing his work mates and their foibles, the funny things that had happened to him since he had begun his new career. All the while, he was trying in his mind to comprehend the nature of her outburst, the reason for the very real grief she had displayed. He felt more than a little out of his depth. Girls were more intense, their emotions more volatile, closer to the surface. He understood that much, though his experience was, he was the first to admit, somewhat limited. An only child, he had had no close relationships with the opposite sex, except for his passionate but unfulfilled feeling for Lou, the French girl; and, before that, the girl in Spain during the war, his comrade-in-arms, literally, for a while. But Meleta had been far from typical of her sex. For all the physical loving they had shared, emotionally she had been as dispassionate as any barrack room neighbour, so matter-of-fact about their sexual activity that privately he had swiftly become disenchanted, and considered her something of an aberration. Alice's grief at the loss of her friend confused him. One thing he was sure of, though, it was genuine, and therefore it hurt him to see her hurting so much. He was determined to take away that pain if he could.

Good Friday had always had that austere Sunday feeling about it, that he remembered from childhood, though, during their long day's ramble across the moor towards the east, and then the long loop back towards Howedale, they passed a surprising number of hikers. There were even one or two private motor cars parked off the narrow road cutting across to the coast, with families picnicking on the turf, cloths spread out and children playing and running over the dark, springy tussocks of the young heather. Davy remarked on the sight, as they passed one such scene, the children's screeches seeming small against the great open space. 'The war's changing so many things. We were never allowed out, except to the Meeting. Maybe a walk but we wouldn't dare make a row or race around like that lot.' He nodded back to the now distant group. 'Best Sunday suits, ties. I hated it. Bottle green, my suit was, scratched like hell. The short pants used to chafe my legs!'

Alice smiled, but his words served to remind her of the sorrow, like a solid lump, forced back down to the middle of her chest now, but still there, in the centre of her, immutable as always. Church, Sunday best, parents laying down the law. That was just how Beth must have gone on when she was a kid! And Alice saw vividly the picture of that golden haired child – pretty dress, shiny shoes, spotless white socks. How could she ever have expected to share a world like that? Davy, canny lad that he was, was from that world too – a world, of cleanliness and comfort, smart clothes, Sunday school and church, caring parents. They were two of a kind, Beth and Davy. And here she was, piggy-in-the-middle. What right had she to be mixing with the likes of them, to be trying to break into their privileged world? Once more, she felt that encroaching despond, like a blurring of vision at the edges of her sight, and she trudged on, savouring the weariness of her legs, hearing his well modulated tones, the 'posh, fancy voice' he shared with her Beth, letting it drift over her as she clung to his clammy hand and strode forward.

It was nearing dark when they got back to the flat. 'Pity the pub's shut!' He grinned. 'But I'm determined we'll go for a drink tomorrow, right? I want to see Ma Rhodes's face when we walk in!'

'Listen, don't you kid yourself, she knows already. I bet there's not many that don't know you're here by now.'

'You're probably right. I bet her face will still be a picture, though. Now, let's put a match to the fire, get the place cosy again.'

The night before, he had won the battle over who should sleep on the thin mattress, and she had woken this morning to the sound of the grate being cleared. He was kneeling, with his braces over his singlet, hands blackened as he finished laying the new fire. The mattress had been put aside, by the dresser, the sheets and blankets folded neatly on top. 'You're thin as a lat!' she had observed, studying his pale bare arms and lean body. She pulled the brown checked dressing gown tighter around her. 'Wash your hands and get your shirt on before you freeze to death. Are you sure that landlady of yours is feeding you properly?'

'Mrs L treats us like kings! It's a real home from home,' he said warmly. 'You must come and meet her. She's really great.'

She had made no answer, aware of the more serious intent behind his casual invitation. Now, twelve hours later, as they sat either side of the new blaze and stretched their stockinged feet towards it with a luxurious sense of ease, which their aching muscles seemed only to enhance, he renewed his exhortation with more determined purpose. 'Listen. Why don't you come through to York one weekend? I'll be able to get time off. Swap my shift with somebody. I can find you somewhere to stay near my digs. It'll be my treat. My turn, anyway, after you having me here.' He sensed the demurral in her movement, and hastened on. 'It's a great place, you know. Loads to see. The Minster, the walls. The river. You've never been, have you?'

'No. But I'm not one for gadding about much. This is the furthest I've ever been from Margrove. I'm not one of your travelling types.'

'The change would do you good.' He hesitated, and all at once the embarrassment of her outpouring up on the high moor lay between them once more, in all its starkness. 'Do *me* good, anyway.' He leant forward, put his hand with gentle diffidence on her trousered knee and withdrew it again. 'I still feel – you're still my best mate. You know that, don't you?'

There was that choking lump again, lodged in her throat, and the stinging behind her eyes. Why did that rich, gentle voice of his affect her like this? For a second she felt a blaze of real anger, a wish that she could be alone again, in the cold mausoleum of her grief, but then she was ashamed of her thought. She cleared her throat, tried to make her tone gruff and casual. 'By heck! You must be hard up for friends then!' She sipped at her cooling mug of tea, bent and placed it on the floor beside the scuffed wooden fender. 'You never know. I might take you up on it one of these days.' She paused. 'I'm thinking of doing a bit more travelling, any road. Mebbes a lot more. I'm thinking of packing in this job. Bit of a dead hole is Howbeck these days. I might find summat else. Factory work. Mebbe the ATS. Imagine me in uniform, eh? I bet I'd look a right clip, wouldn't I?'

He stifled his shock. 'You'll never get me to agree with you there.' A sudden idea and hope flickered in his brain. 'But, listen, if you're serious let me see what I can do. I could find out – maybe you could get a job in one of the York factories. I know quite a few people who work at Rowntree's—'

'What? Making cocoa and chocolate? That's not essential war work, surely?'

'They do all kinds of things nowadays. There's other places. There's a place out near the racecourse. They make all sorts of service equipment. Tents and things. I'm sure you'd find something. Will you let me try? Ask around?' Once again, he sensed her lack of enthusiasm. 'At least we could see each other.' He strove, not altogether successfully, to curb his own almost desperate eagerness. His voice lowered to a hesitant softness. 'If you wanted to, that is. I didn't mean . . . I'm not trying . . . I wouldn't pester you if you didn't want, you know, to be bothered. But now and then . . . it would be smashing . . . for me!'

There was a long instant of silence before she answered. And this time it was she who reached out, rested her hand on his knee, left it there, until he covered it with his own. 'Don't be daft. Of course I'd want to see you. We'll always be pals, won't we? Who else could I blub me heart out to?'

It was the first time she had referred to what had happened up on the moors, and with instinctive understanding of what it cost her, Davy made no reference to it. She jumped up, leant over him from behind his chair and kissed the top of his tousled dark head. 'Now you go over and get your bath. And take the torch with you. You might think you know your way around this place, but you'd be amazed how many bruised shins and bumps on the head I've given meself coming back in the dark.'

Again he refused to yield to her pleas that she should be allowed to sleep on the mattress in the living room. 'I'm not that stupid! You think I'm going to give up this beautiful warm hearth for an ice-cold bed?'

'There's a hot water bottle in there!' she urged, in vain. She had changed into her night things and he went into the bedroom to follow suit. He came out shivering exaggeratedly.

'No wonder you're trying to get me to swap with you! It's freezing in there!' He thought she was about to make up his temporary bed for him, as she went to the pile of bedclothes against the wall, but she seized the two pillows and disappeared into her bedroom. 'Oh no! You're not going to pinch my bedclothes as well, are you?'

'Just hang on a minute!' she called back through the closed door. He sat on, bare feet stretched to the embers, curling his toes in luxury at the feeling of tired contentment. God! I love you, Alice Glass, he thought, and wished that she could feel the same way about him, but even his sadness that it was not so seemed gently familiar and bearable tonight. He could only bless his good fortune at being allowed back into her life, if only for a brief interlude. He tried to damp down the spark of excitement at the thought of their earlier talk, to steer his mind away from the hope that shimmered, of her moving to York, and the possibility of seeing much more of her.

'Right-oh! Come here, you!'

The voice came through to him. All at once his whole body was alert, his nerves taut. He stood, went through into the bedroom, full of shadows, lit only by the dim lamp beside the bed. She was sitting up, in the striped pyjama jacket that hung on her. She was in bed, and he saw the humped shapes of pillows at her side, running down the length of the bed, hidden under the blankets. Her eyes looked huge, her face solemn. Her voice was husky with embarrassment. 'It's daft you sleeping on the floor when there's this bed in here. There's loads of room.' She patted the empty space on the other side of the barrier of pillows. 'Why don't you get in? I don't know what you'll think of me. But I don't mean . . . I'm not after . . . you know. I've never slept with a feller in me life, apart from our little Algy, and he'll be seven next birthday. But I know I can trust you. It's up to you.'

His heart was thumping, his body trembling. He struggled valiantly for lightness. He pretended to stroke his chin. 'Well . . . it's probably the best offer I'm going to get tonight, so all right. I'll risk it!'

Quickly, he shed his dressing-gown and slid carefully beneath the covers. The hot water bottle was there, on his side.

'Don't say I'm not good to you,' she said, trying to match his lightness. Her voice was a little breathless.

When the lamp was out, he felt her hand groping, touching his arm. 'Thanks for today,' she whispered. 'You really are my best mate. Hold my hand, will you, just for a bit?'

He reached for her and found her. They held hands over the yielding hump of the pillow. 'Goodnight. God bless,' she said, and he answered with the same formula.

He lay clasping her in the darkness, deeply moved with her sweetness, and her innocent trust, and deeply shamed at the quivering desire spreading throughout his frame, and the hard, clean ache of his need for her.

CHAPTER FIFTEEN

Davy spent most of Saturday with Alice. He caught the 5.30 p.m. train into Whitby. It was the latest time he could leave and still make a connection to Scarborough and thence to York. 'I promised my folks I'd meet them on Sunday. They're coming into York for the Meeting, then I'll go home with them and spend a few days at Helmsthorpe. Back to work on Wednesday.'

It had all been very strange. Alice was amazed at how quickly she had drifted off to sleep on Friday night, still clutching his hand, despite the fact that it was the first time she had slept with a grown man. How could she have done that, invited him into her bed so brazenly? What on earth must he have thought of her? And worse still, what must he have expected of her? She remembered the sweet agony of those last nights with Beth, when she had lain there ill with longing at her side. How could Davy possibly believe that Alice's motives were innocent, begging him to hold her hand? She was just incredibly lucky that he was such a thoroughly decent boy, and behaved like the gentleman, the gentle man, she had always thought him.

She had woken in the pre-dawn blackness, all at once, completely alert and very much aware of who it was lying a couple of feet from her, of what she had done, and not done. She turned her head, slowly, and could see the indistinct shape of his upper body, his arms out above the eiderdown, his dark head on the pillow, turned away from her, as though anxious to avoid making contact. She lay absolutely motionless, staring up into the darkness, scarcely breathing, listening to the sound of his deep breaths.

So he didn't snore, after all! But she did not smile at the memory of her bold words to Beryl. She could feel the stickiness of perspiration on her body. It seemed at one with the deep sense of mortification she was suffering. And suddenly another even more disturbing thought crept into her mind: that she should atone for her wicked, wayward selfishness by allowing him to possess her body. For surely it was a greater sin not to let him do so, having brought him to lie by her side like this? Maybe that was how it was meant to be; that she should put an end to this unnatural love she had been carrying around inside her for so long. Do what God intended, be the woman that God had made her.

Davy was a good man, she knew that. She also knew he felt something for her, something deep. Go on, she admonished herself. *Love.* He had said it to her, written it to her, and however much she argued with herself against it, she believed it to be true. Maybe not as he had felt it for that French lass he had told her of. But it was strong enough, and true enough, for him to stick by her, and always do right by her. He would never let her down. They could even be happy together. Except. . . .

There were those tolling words again, clanging round inside her brain. *Unnatural. Wrong.* Damn you, Beth Hobbs! Poisoning what had been so beautiful and good and true – for both of us, not just for me.

And Alice thought of having sex with Davy, felt her whole body, even her inner muscles, clench with tension, but desire wasn't there – only fear, and even revulsion. How could she do that to Davy, whom she did love, but not in that way? Which was the greater lie, the bigger sin? All at once she moved, slid her body carefully out of her side of the bed, eased away from her sleeping companion, and padded barefoot, with accustomed skill as she had done so many times when she didn't want to awaken Beth, out of the darkened room.

It was daylight when he emerged from the bedroom. She was dressed and preparing their breakfast. His hair was sticking up all over the place, and his face looked creased and tired still. She guessed he had not slept very well either, cursed herself for her well meaning, impulsive foolishness in asking him into her bed. So many wrongs done with so many good intentions. Speech was a minefield.

'Sleep all right? I didn't snore, did I? Beth used to talk to herself . . .' Bang! she thought, writhing inwardly with shame.

But, typically, he dealt with it, smoothly, easily, with that smile of his. 'If you did, I didn't hear a thing. My goodness! Something smells good. I think I must have died and gone to heaven. Sleeping with a beautiful girl and waking up to find her cooking breakfast for me!'

And she responded in kind. 'Nay, lad! You must have been dreaming all right! Now you wake up to me and the smell of burnt porridge, eh? What a come down!'

The rest of the morning passed quickly and pleasantly, with Alice firmly shutting her mind to the strange night and her wayward behaviour. There would be plenty of time to torment herself over it in retrospection when he had left her. True to his promise, he insisted on going to the Oddfellows and, in spite of her misgiving, she accompanied him. The holiday Saturday ensured that it was quite crowded. Perhaps people felt an extra need for some cheer with the disappointments of the war news, though the continuing successes of the Japanese in the Pacific and in Burma, and even General Rommel's impressive sweep eastward against the Eighth Army in the desert in the shuttle-cock of campaigns, were all too far away to merit more than a passing mention, and not even that for many of the inhabitants of Howbeck. Davy had forgotten how insular these dales folk could be. Even events in Whitby, a half-hour train ride away, could seem distant. He recalled a knowing shake of the head, and the dismissive remark of a villager in the bar at the mention of some occurrence in the nearby port. 'Aye, well, that's Whitby folk for yer. Funny lot down there!'

Alice was surprised at the reception they got when they entered the bar. There were several calls of welcome, many gracious nods of recognition, and though the steel glittered in the heavily made-up eyes of the landlady, Vera Rhodes managed a grimace that might well have passed muster as a smile. Even Derek Aygarth, Big Malcolm's nephew, who had made a nuisance of himself on New Year's Eve, until Alice had taken firm hold of him in a very private place and reduced him to kneeling, whimpering impotence, waved and grinned and offered to buy both of them a drink.

'How's crime in the city of York then, constable?' Vera asked challengingly. 'Making sure those city tykes are sticking to the letter of the law, are you?'

'Doing my best, Mrs Rhodes,' Davy answered easily. 'You're looking well, as ever.' He beamed at her and moved away from the counter with their drinks. His head bent close to Alice's, he murmured, 'So, who's the latest candidate to fill the Big Swede's boots then?'

She giggled, waited until they were well away from the busy bar before she replied. 'I haven't been in here for ages. We used to pop in now and then with Beryl and Evelyn when we were going to the Saturday hop. I wouldn't be any more welcome than you. Still, she didn't order us out, did she? We should be thankful for small mercies. Drink up. We're not staying for another!'

'I should have asked her if she'd heard from Gus lately. But I suppose that would have been a bit below the belt.'

They didn't linger, and after the Oddfellows, they made their way round to Northend Cottage to collect Doreen, who was spending part of the afternoon with Alice and her visitor. Alice had already explained the position in her earlier letters, and she was ready to unburden her worries about her younger sister. 'She hasn't even gone back to Margrove over Easter. In fact she hasn't been back home since the beginning of January – and that was only for the night. Truth is,' Alice continued bitterly, 'she thinks *this* is her home now. It is an' all, I guess. Miss Ramsay – *Aunt* Elizabeth! – has taken mam and dad's place. Those papers they signed – she's our Doreen's legal guardian or summat.'

'They could contest it, I'm sure. She's only – how old?'

'Twelve coming up. Her birthday is next week. She won't even be home for that. Some sort of do here, apparently. Miss Ramsay's taking her and some of her posh mates from school to tea in Whitby.' She sighed and shook her head. 'Trouble is, it's what she wants.' She waved a hand at the tranquil scene around them. 'All this. The grammar school. That's why they did it, mam and dad. It's her big chance. They couldn't ever give her anything like this. She's a bright kid. *Too* bright, mebbes. But she's dead set on making the most of herself. You can't blame her for that, can you?'

Her voice sounded so wrought with uncertainty and regret that Davy reached out, flung his arm over her shoulders in a comradely gesture, pulled her in close as they walked. 'No, of course not. But she shouldn't forget where she came from. Her own roots. She's got nothing to be ashamed of there. After all, look what they've produced. She'll be lucky if she turns out to be half the girl her big sister is!' He aimed a clumsy, swift kiss at the side of her curly brow. He saw her gaze up at him, her eyes crinkling and suspiciously bright with tears. Her voice had that rusty quality that signified the heightened emotion once more.

'You *are* daft sometimes, Davy Brown! But it's been nice having you around. I really have missed you, you know.'

Doreen was waiting by the gate of Northend and walked sedately to meet them. She was smartly turned out, in tam and new coat, with nipped in waist and short, flaring skirts. She opened it to show off the new jumper and skirt, and bright red woollen stockings beneath. 'Look! My new Easter outfit! Do you like it? Hello, Mr Brown. It's so nice to see you again. How are you?'

'Hey! We're old mates, remember? The name's Davy. And you look fantastic! And so grown up! A real lady!'

'Don't tell her that! She's bigheaded enough as it is! Thinks she's God's gift, don't you, kidder?'

There was a lot of talk and playful teasing between Davy and Doreen, while Alice kept largely silent. When she did speak, her accent seemed almost deliberately coarsened, as though to challenge the youngster's more modified and softened cadences. Davy became more and more aware and uncomfortable at Alice's withdrawal. He was relieved when, after eating heartily of the scones and cakes her sister provided, Doreen took her leave. 'You'll be coming through again soon to see us, won't you?' she said pleadingly. 'It's been great fun, Alice! Make him promise to come again? You must!'

She spun around towards her sister, making the skirt twirl out from the red stockinged legs, with her hands clasped under her chin, elbows flying. You little bloody Shirley Temple! Alice thought, almost admiringly, despite her irritation.

'Remember last Easter?' Doreen burbled on, turning her attention back to an amused Davy. 'When we had that day out in Whitby? In Luke Denby's car . . .' Her voice faltered just for a second, then picked up once more. 'Maybe we could arrange something like that again? A picnic.'

The shadow of the name had fallen on the two adults, and when Doreen had taken her leave, Davy felt its chill, and was seized by a kind of desperation. 'I'd better get myself sorted. Can you be bothered to walk me to the station?'

'Of course. So, what do you think of her? Coming on a treat, eh?'

'She's still just a kiddie, Alice. It's all a bit much for her now. When she's older . . .'

'Oh, aye.' Alice's tone was full of cynicism, and Davy was sad to hear it. 'Mebbes it's all for the best. There'll be nowt like this for her back in Margrove.'

He could feel the tension between them as they headed back through the village and up the slope towards the railway station. 'Look,' she said abruptly, withdrawing her arm, which had been linked in his, and halting for a second to gaze bravely up at him. 'I'm sorry about last night. It was a rotten thing for me to do to you. A bloody stupid thing. Asking you to my bed like that. I'm ashamed. I don't know what you thought of me. But I didn't mean . . . I didn't want what . . . girls usually want, doing something like that. But I know how unfair it was. How you must have felt.'

The lips quivered a little and the grey eyes filled, and suddenly his feelings were too intense to continue gazing at her. He clasped her hand tightly, using his arm to hold it against him, and turned, began walking again, a slow stroll through the cloudy afternoon. 'I felt honoured. And very glad just to be with you. Near you. I know you're feeling very blue just now, and I wish there was some way I could make you happy. That's all I want, Al.'

The diminutive of her name smote her, like a sharp little needle. She swallowed hard, the scene in front of her dissolving in the shimmer of the tears she fought to hold back.

'I'm ready to be whatever you want me to be,' he was continuing. 'I just don't want to be cut out of your life. I do love you. I know you don't like me saying it, and I really try hard not to, but just this once I need to remind you of it. But all I'm asking is to be part of your life – as a friend, or whatever. That's it.'

'You bugger!' Her head was down, she was sniffling now. They had reached the small cobbled forecourt, and the open gate, badly in need of a coat of paint, that led on to the deserted platform. 'I never have a hankie with me when I need it.' He dug one from his pocket, and she dabbed and blew noisily. 'I'll keep it and wash it. I'll return it.'

'In person would be nice.'

They were on the platform when Mr Lonsdale the porter appeared from the ticket office. 'On time.' He glanced at Davy's ticket, grinned at him. 'Enjoy your stay?' Then he saw Alice's tear stained face and moved hastily away, trying to look officious.

'Please, Al! I meant what I said. Do think about moving to York. And let me know. I can find out what's going on. Ask around. Us coppers know everything.' He managed to smile and tapped the side of his nose with a finger. But he felt close to tears himself, and swallowed hard. He didn't want to leave her – ever, 'Please! Promise me you will think about it. I'm not expecting . . . anything out of it for myself. Except for just being able to see you now and then. To look after you, when you need it.'

'Oh God! I've done nowt but bubble, have I? Thanks for coming, Davy love! And yes, I will think about it, I do promise. I'll write in a day or two. You really are my best mate. My real friend, and I do love you!' She held up her face, pressed her mouth against his, felt the sharpness of their teeth pressing through the softness of lips, the wet warmth of tongues as her mouth opened, their faces crushed together. She stared up at him when they broke the kiss, both gasping for breath, and she could feel her heart thumping in her breast, his chest against hers. 'Take care. I'll see you again – soon.'

He released her and her gaze left his, she blushed, her head down, until they heard the warning blast of the whistle, and both looked to where the puffs of black smoke forewarned of the approaching train.

She stood, waving vigorously, his handkerchief fluttering like a favour in her hand, and he hung from the open window, defying the LNER's written warning against such dangerous conduct until she faded from his sight.

CHAPTER SIXTEEN

It was after 11 p.m. when Davy let himself in to 25 Dubry Street, and he was surprised to find Reeny Lumley and her husband, Dick, sitting in front of the kitchen range, at the end of the long passageway from the front entrance. Her dark honey hair was attractively waved, and she was wearing a pretty floral dress, with diamante earrings, and a matching necklace glinting at her throat. Dick was in a pair of good flannels, with dark, narrow braces over a clean white shirt. The stiff collar and tie he had only recently discarded hung over the back of his chair and a pair of highly polished 'best' shoes stood beside him. Reeny was wearing make-up, her lips glossed, and her face looked animated, a blush that did not entirely owe its existence to rouge highlighting her cheeks. Davy wanted to tell her how good she looked, but at the affable greeting from her husband, he exercised circumspection, and settled for, 'You two look very smart. Been out wining and dining?'

'No. We had the Morrises round, and one of Dick's inspectors from the works. A game of cards, and a bit of a laugh. There's still some fresh tea in the pot. Or something stronger, if you fancy a nightcap. You can have a drop of Dick's whisky. Can't he?' She turned to her husband, her laugh girlish, and Davy saw how buoyant she was. 'Or there's a bottle of pale ale in the pantry, isn't there, Dick? Come on, pull a chair up, get yourself warm. How did you go on? Did you have a nice time with your young lady?'

Her husband chuckled. 'You'd better sit yourself down, lass, afore you fall down. She can't take her drink nowadays.' He grinned at Davy. 'I hope it won't put you off, seeing your landlady drunk like this.'

'How dare you!' She drew herself up in a parody of righteous outrage. 'A couple of port and lemons, that's all I've had. Drunk indeed!' She swigged down the remains in the glass she took from the table. 'I'm behaving like a perfect lady, aren't I, Davy?' She dropped a little curtsey and gave a genteel little stagger. Davy wondered if it was entirely deliberate.

He settled for the tea. He was suddenly aware how glad he was that he had found the Lumleys still up, and he basked in the easy domesticity of their company. It had been a long and chilly journey, changing trains, waiting in the evening cold, first at Whitby, then at Scarborough. It had taken six hours to cover a modest distance. An express from York to London could do the trip to the capital in far less time. In theory, anyway. Wartime travel was a prolonged and painful business. No wonder they had coined the slogan, *Is your journey really necessary?*

At least it had given him plenty of time to ruminate on the events of the past forty-eight hours. Too much time, perhaps, to brood on the strange moods that affected Alice these days. At first, he had been very pleasantly surprised, finding her far less depressed than he had anticipated. He had felt it was touch and go whether she consented to his visit or no, so he was even more relieved when, finding her waiting eagerly on the platform to meet him, she appeared to be pretty much her own lively, lovable self.

But it had turned out to be something of a façade, a brave show for his benefit. Up on the Tops, back at one of their favourite spots, he had seen that façade crumble, and the abandon of her grief had touched his heart – and made him feel fairly useless, too, despite her reassurance later of the comfort he provided for her. Apart from suffering on her behalf, he was disturbed by the depth of the loss she felt at Elsbeth Hobbs's departure. He had always been intrigued by the closeness of their attachment to each another. On the surface they were very much chalk and cheese. Elsbeth so delicate, refined, with that lower middle-class background; Alice so much the down-to-earth product of her working-class roots. That rough diamond, take-me-as-I-am-or-be-damned attitude he had so much admired, and come to love her for. Of the two girls, he had always thought Alice the far more striking in every way. Well, he had to concede that Elsbeth did have that chocolate box, conventional beauty that men were attracted to. But, underneath that soft, flowing yellow hair and the pretty face was a rather vapid, tame personality, compared with the wonderful vigour of Alice's indomitable character. In fact, it was small wonder that the Hobbs girl should have found herself so influenced by Alice's magnetism. And yet she had moved on, was getting on with her life, without any qualms, while, in her wake, Alice seemed lost and utterly desolate at losing her.

It was strange. And, more than that, oddly disturbing to him. It was as though a certain element in Alice's natural development had been missing, or was arrested. All right, it was hurtful for him to have to admit that she had not found him attractive, in a physical sense, had not felt the sexual as well as spiritual pull that was necessary for two people to come together. But, as far as he could tell, and he believed Alice had been honest with him, it was not simply he as an individual to whom she failed to respond in that way. She had never felt that kind of attraction, for any male. 'I can't be doing with all that,' she had told him quite straightforwardly. Sad as the thought made him, he had hoped that she would one day find that special someone with whom she could settle down, mate with for life. Discovering now just how deep her friendship with Elsbeth went, how much it meant to her, he felt dismayed and anxious for her. And more than ever determined if he could to bring her to the awareness of that aspect of love that somehow lay completely dormant within her. He would do all that he could to awaken it within her.

The thought of the night spent lying beside her haunted him again; the tormenting hunger for her that racked his body; the terrible suspicion of doubt gnawing at him that he could have brought about the transformation he sought, in one decisive move, if he had not lacked the courage to act, to move, to claim her body instead of that proffered hand. Was she, in fact, asking him to make that move, begging for him to awaken her to sex?

All these speculations had rolled around throughout the lengthy journey back to York, and he was greatly relieved to find the Lumleys awake, and so ready to welcome him to their warm fireside – and the easy, steady warmth of their relationship: the blessed normality of their domestic scene, the solid strength of the family home they had created between them.

'Well, we'd best get off to bed, eh, lass?' Dick stood and stretched, giving a theatrical yawn, his arms way above his head. Something behind the casual words, a look, a quiver of instinctive communication, passed between them, or so Davy fancied, his own senses alert to it, so that he throbbed with envy and with affection towards them.

'Aye, go on, love. I'll be up in a minute. I'll just set the table for Bob's breakfast. He's on early shift. I hope I don't sleep in for him. And you be quiet when you go up, mind,' she warned Davy. 'Get undressed in the bathroom. You can have a good lie-in in the morning, lucky lad!'

Dick Lumley said his goodnight to Davy and left the kitchen. 'He's a lucky man!' The words escaped, and Davy was a little startled himself at his remark, for usually he was far from forward in offering such comments. Its untypical flavour made her pause for just an instant as she was reaching for the things on the table, and slighty deepened the colour in her cheeks.

'Try telling *him* that!' She laughed, easing the instant of tension, and then, intuitively aware of his mood, she said, 'Everything all right with your trip? With . . . Alice, is it?'

He was greatly tempted to try to explain. But not now, at this late hour, and, in any case, he was far from sure that he *could* explain it, even to himself. 'Yes, it was lovely to see her again. We had a really nice time, thanks.' He hesitated, then went on, 'I'm hoping I can persuade her to move to York. To find work here. She's a bit fed up with Howbeck just now. I might have to look for a job for her.'

'She must be mad, giving up all that lovely countryside for this place! But then, maybe it's not the place that's the attraction, eh?' She gave a gurgling laugh.

'Oh, I don't know about that, Mrs L.'

Something of the wistfulness of his tone got through to her. He was startled when she turned towards him, and very gently raised her right hand, let her cool fingers brush very lightly and quickly across his cheek. 'Don't worry, Davy. She'll come to her senses soon. She's a bright girl, you said. She'd be daft not to.'

The quiet interlude spent at his parents' home in Helmsthorpe gave Davy plenty of time for further reflection on Alice's present situation, and his feelings for her. And hers for him. Could he still justify clinging to the hope that he might one day mean much more than a good friend? The whole complexity of their relationship seemed to be encapsulated in that strange night they had spent, sharing her bed in celibate intimacy. He was strongly tempted to refer to it in a letter. It would be easier to discuss his feelings, and his restraint, by written word, free of her presence. But he knew she could be startlingly thin skinned for such a robust character. Besides, she had promised that she would think about moving to York. It was essential he did nothing to jeopardize the chance to have her close to him, to share at least a part of her life again. He decided it would be better to wait a while, before bringing up the intricacies of their night together.

He built up his hopes that there would be a letter waiting for him at his lodgings when he returned to the city on the Wednesday morning. Alice was typically impulsive – she would not sit for days on end before she made up her mind, one way or the other. He could only hope and pray she would make the decision he wanted so much for her to make.

It was there, waiting for him, lying on his neatly made-up bed, with some other correspondence he cast aside. He felt the unsteadiness of his hands as he tore open the envelope, fumbled out the two folded sheets from the writing pad. He scanned hastily the opening lines, expressing her pleasure at seeing him again, apologizing for not being able to offer him an exciting time, for her mood, and her outburst on the moor:

You were so good to me, putting up with my weeping and wailing and soaking your shirtfront! But you've always been good to me and don't think I don't appreciate it. I may not show it but I do. There's no one else I would have wanted around to see me like that.

The long and short of all this is to tell you I'd like you to see if there's anything going work-wise in York or round about, as you said you would. I've told Mr Barr I'll be leaving and I can go at the end of next week, that'll be Friday, April 10. There! Burnt my boats now, haven't I? I hope you're pleased and not thinking, oh God! What have I done to deserve this? I just want to thank you for being so good to me, and for helping to make me get off my behind and do something. I'll have to let the National Registry lot know, so if you can find something that will be taken as war work I'll be ever so grateful. But don't worry if not. Main thing I've been and gone and done it at last! Thanks to you, my very best mate. I wouldn't be that bothered if they sent me to the ATS or WAAFs, but it would be nice if I could get something that meant we'd be near enough to see something of each other now and then. Anything would do me – scrubbing and cleaning, cooking – I'm a dab hand at anything like that, anything that doesn't involve brains, eh? So don't go trying to put my name down for jobs where you need certificates and things – remember how thick I am. They never let me take exams at school.

He smiled at her cheerful admission, yet felt that tug at his heart, his pain at the blasé front she put up, and the injustices of a social system that wrote off people like Alice, whose native intelligence he would match against most of her contemporaries. Like the decorative Miss Hobbs, the erstwhile boon companion, who had taken off so blithely, who had failed to contact her former soulmate in a month or more, and for whom tough little nut Alice Glass had sobbed heartbrokenly on his breast.

Never mind. She was coming! Coming to York, to be near him – at least if he had anything to do with it, and he would do his damnedest! He'd begin this very day, when he got into work for his two-till-ten. He hoped Len Potts would be in charge of the desk. Davy got on well with him, and he had spent years on the force, knew just about everything there was to know about the city. He would be a good source for beginning the search for employment for Alice.

He was feeling buoyed up when he entered the kitchen again. Mrs L had gone out to the shops with Micky, and Bob Noone was the sole occupant, sitting with his feet up on the brass rim of the fireguard, and leafing through the *Daily Mirror*. 'Same shift as you, old son,' he said in answer to Davy's query. 'So! How's the blue-eyed boy after his little holiday then? When they gonna give you your sergeant's stripes, eh? Hope you won't forget your old mates when you're up there with the big boys!'

Davy stared in surprise and hurt at his roommate's obvious tone of sarcasm. 'What the hell are you going on about?'

'Come off it! Don't play the innocent with me! They don't call you Brown for nothing, eh? DI Holden's little golden boy, mate!' When Davy, his face red, continued to protest that his innocence in this case was completely genuine, Bob Noone explained. 'You've been taken off the roster, as from today. Seconded over to CID. Working with Tommy Baxter on Sandshoe Charlie, till further notice. All right for some! We're short enough of bobbies as it is. But still, that won't bother you, will it, sunshine?'

'I didn't ask for this!' Davy protested. 'You can ask Tommy Baxter himself if you don't believe me!'

'Baxter just takes his bloody orders like any of us, doesn't he? Like I said, this has come down from Holden and his crew. And you've been his bright-eyed boy since you came here, and don't make out otherwise! You've gone on often enough how you want to get over into Plain Clothes!'

Davy was dismayed by the vehemence of Bob's attack, and completely floored by it. He had had no inkling of any resentment at the station, or of the fact that he had been marked down as a favourite of DI Holden. He found himself almost resenting the inspector's patronage, which, he had to acknowledge, had been instrumental in securing him his present position as Special Constable in York. But then he was ashamed of his own ingratitude. He thought of his life over the past two years: his time in prison, and the demoralized state in which he had emerged from the experience. He had been utterly beaten, ready to crawl away and hide somewhere, anywhere. He reminded himself how lucky he had been that Howbeck had been his bolthole, and that he had met Alice there, who had been so instrumental in his revival. She had reawakened him as a caring person, made him look around, participate in life again instead of shrinking away, dying inside. And DI Holden had been part of that renaissance as well. He should only remain indebted to him, not ungrateful or resentful.

'Yes, it's what I want,' he said quietly. 'I'm glad I've got this chance to work with CID. I'm not going to turn it down. I'm sorry you feel I've been picked because of some unfair favours from DI Holden, or anybody else. I don't want to fall out with you, or anyone else at the station because of this. But it's not promotion, is it? I'm still an SC. It won't get me permanently out of uniform.' Suddenly he gave a grin, inviting Bob to help dissipate the tension which had flared between them. 'In fact, I'm not sure if this whole thing isn't just a big bloody send-up on your part, you devious blighter. How do I know you're not just pulling my leg about the whole thing? You know what day it is?' He nodded towards the flip-up calendar on the narrow mantelshelf, behind the hanging clothes rack. The bold figure 1 stood out. '1 April. And it isn't even twelve o' clock yet.'

CHAPTER SEVENTEEN

It was strange for Alice, being back in Margrove, and 19 Maudsley Street, the house she had spent all of her remembered life in, except for the last eventful year and a half. In those eighteen months she had spent very little time at home. Now, she was reminded painfully of just how much she had grown away from her former life, and the communal existence she had grown up in, with its almost total lack of privacy. True, the little terraced house was not as crowded as it had been then. George, her brother, had celebrated his eighteenth birthday in February, and two weeks later was called on to report at the huge training camp at Catterick, conscripted into the army. His mother still harboured bitter feelings of betrayal towards her husband, for Fred Glass had confidently reassured her many a time that George, having been taken on as a labourer at the steelworks where his father worked, would be protected from call-up by a classification of Reserved Occupation. However, George himself did not appear to regard his summons as the disaster his mother considered it, and went off cheerfully enough, to 'do his bit'.

And of course Doreen was yet another absentee, perhaps even more permanently. She had been even more eager to flee the familial hearth for the glittering opportunity provided her by her benefactress, Miss Ramsay. After only a few days back home herself, Alice grudgingly had to recognize the fortune that had fallen Doreen's way, and to accept that maybe her parents had not acted solely from mercenary callousness in surrendering up their ten-year-old child so readily. Though, to be honest, she was far less inclined to give her father the benefit of the doubt. Her mother, she knew, had put a brave face on it when Doreen had been handed into Miss Ramsay's care, and Alice was prepared to acknowledge the wrench it must have cost her mam to sign those guardianship papers. But Maggie had, as always, gone along with her husband's wishes, even though she had doubtless shed more than a few tears over it since. Not that she would ever admit it outright, even to Alice. But as for Fred – his sanctimonious bleating about 'doing the best for the lass' made Alice's hackles rise. If only they hadn't taken the considerable – and never divulged – financial inducement Miss Ramsay offered, Alice might have been more inclined to allow him a modicum of paternal magnanimity. But inside, she could never get rid of the idea that for him Miss Ramsay's intervention had been a double stroke of luck: an offloading of responsibility and a generous payment for it.

With two fewer bodies about the place, the house was less crowded. But as far as fourteen-year-old Ethel was concerned, Alice's return to the fold meant a re-addition to the household which she clearly resented. 'I'm not sharing with *her* again!' Ethel said, the ferocious scowl transforming her delicate features to a look of narrow meanness. 'I've just got used to being on me own!'

Maggie, whose greatest wish was that she could have all her offspring back under her roof, was furious with her. 'You'll do as you're told, my lady! Getting far too big for your boots, you are! You haven't even left school yet, so watch your mouth, you hear?' Ethel would be leaving Lister Road in the summer, and 'couldn't wait' for the happy day when she would be seeking work. When George had left for the army in February, six-year-old Algy had been moved into the small room his older brother had vacated, leaving Ethel to recline in solitary luxury in the big old bed which in former times all three sisters had shared, with Algy in an ancient cot at its foot.

'Welcome home!' Alice grunted sardonically. 'You can go in our George's room if you're so bothered, and Algy can come in with me.'

'You can't swing a cat in the little bedroom! All me things are in the back.'

'I'll skelp your bloody backside for you if you don't shut up!' Maggie exploded. 'And don't think you're too big, neither! You should be glad our Alice is back home, you selfish little bugger!'

But, sad though it was to admit it, Alice herself was far from happy to be back in Maudsley Street. It pained her to face up to the fact that she could hardly wait herself to be free again. She had written to tell Davy to contact her at her home address. She had parted quite amicably from Mr Barr, who had given her a good reference. She had felt sad when she closed the door on the stables flat for the last time, but only for the precious memories it held of the happiest time of her young life, which had been spent there. But that happiness had gone with Beth's departure. Since then, the flat had been a place of loneliness all the more painful because of what had gone before.

Now she tried to be patient as she hoped that Davy would be in touch soon. Not as cocky as you thought you were, are you, madam? she taunted herself. And it was true, she would be happy if Davy could find her something in York.

She valued him dearly as her friend, so much so that her conscience pricked her when she thought of how much closer he would have liked them to be, how much more than friendship he wished for from her. But it would be good to keep him as her friend, to have him near. She'd had enough of loneliness these past weeks.

Such speculation led her to the painful feelings that were never far from her mind. Her beloved Beth had changed her life for ever. Alice had known so little about herself. She had been awakened by Beth in so many ways. It was their love which made Alice realize now the difference within her which made it so difficult to fit back into the existence of Maudsley Street and its narrow environs. She had to get away. She couldn't wait too long for Davy to find her something. In any case, the Registration Board wouldn't wait too long, either. They might give her a month's leeway, but no more.

And that led her back, of course, to Beth. It was well over a month since they had separated. What was she doing now? And, more important, why hadn't she been in touch? It was difficult to accept that she was probably no further than two miles away, up by the park. That knowledge added tenfold to the pain she was already carrying, had endured for all these weeks. She vowed that she would simply walk the long mile up to the park, to Elton Grove and knock on the front door. One of the first questions she had asked Ethel had been to ascertain whether Elsbeth had taken up a teaching post again in the Infants' Department of the school. She was unsure whether she felt disappointed or relieved when Ethel confirmed that she had not. If the answer had been yes, Alice knew she would have had a great struggle against her own temptation to contact the headmistress, or Miss Laverton, to see if there was any menial work they could offer. It would mean having to stay at home; but it would also mean that she could at least be in Beth's proximity, see her again, have the chance to talk to her.

She felt her stomach dissolve in quavers of sick excitement at the image of Beth coming in person to the door in answer to her knock. Pictured the look on that endearing face, the way they would simply gaze at each other in silence, before . . . what? Falling in blessed, penitent tears in each other's arms? Or would she see that look, of shame, of pain, in the blue eyes? Alice despised herself for the untypical fear that made her hesitate, equivocate with herself as she sat at home for the first days, and avoid even walking up Park Road in case she might encounter Beth and face that rejection once more.

It was, perhaps, symbolic of the star-crossed fate of their relationship that Beth's first letter in the long weeks of their separation should have arrived at Howe Manor for Alice on Saturday, 11 April, the day after Alice's departure.

Someone in the Estate Office had found it on the Monday, and had re-addressed it to Maudsley Street. It went out with the outgoing mail on Tuesday.

When it was delivered on a dull Wednesday morning, Alice recognized the neat hand that had written, *Miss A. Glass*, and the crossed out address beneath, and her fingers shook, and her heart hammered. Glancing fearfully at the post-mark, she felt her heart leap again, with a tremendous surge of joy as she saw the Margrove GPO frank. Thank God! She spun away, called out to her mam that she would be down in a minute and raced up the stairs, away from the morning hullabaloo in the kitchen, and sprawled across the unmade double bed. At last! Beth had written. And she was still here, in Margrove! She would see her again. She was filled with resolve. Even if it was just to talk, to meet up for a chat. She tore open the envelope, dragged out the single sheet of classy notepaper, smelt its restrained fragrance. She smiled, through the film of tears in her eyes. It was typical of her dear Beth. Her eyes swept over the lines of the familiar handwriting.

When Elsbeth came back from Howbeck, her parents were swiftly aware that things were not right with their normally pliable daughter. In fact, Cedric Hobbs was aware of it before she arrived, for he it was who came to collect her on the wet last day of February, hurrying across the slippery cobbles of the stable yard to pile her abundant luggage into the car. 'Alice not around?' he asked. 'You've said your goodbyes?' He had thought nothing of the hurried way she had answered.

'She has to work on a Saturday. I saw her when she went off to work.'

He attributed her quietness during the journey home to natural sadness at leaving the place and the work where she had found so much pleasure. Although she had sounded philosophical enough when she telephoned to tell them that her post at St Anne's was being terminated – 'I didn't think for one minute there was much chance of them keeping me on once I had to register. I *am* unqualified, after all' – Mr Hobbs guessed she must feel regret at leaving, especially as she had got on so well with the Glass girl. He'd been proud of her, the way she'd mucked in so well. He'd been more than a bit worried, from the moment when she'd gone off with the Lister Road contingent a couple of years ago. Such a rough lot.

Uncomfortably, he remembered how as a kiddie she had had some bother during the brief time she had spent there as a pupil, before she had won a scholarship and moved on to the girls' grammar. He had always felt bad about having to let Elsbeth go to Lister Road, especially with William being away at boarding school. But the business hadn't been doing at all well, back in 1930.

Things in the north-east hadn't even begun to pick up. Little Robert had arrived by then. It had taken Cedric all his time to pay the modest fees for Rosebank, the little private kindergarten up on the Dalby road she had gone to when she was five. Things had got worse. When she was eight, he couldn't afford to keep her there any longer – it was touch and go whether he would be able to keep William at his prep school – and Lister Road was the only school in their area with a place in Standard III. At the time he had countered his wife's worries with a robust, 'It'll do her good, Mildred. Teach her to stand up for herself.' But he had never ceased to feel guilty about it.

But maybe it had paid dividends, after all. She'd never looked back after getting that scholarship, and had done very well for herself. If she was a bit quiet today, it was only natural. She'd made a right go of it at Howbeck, and settled in extremely well. Mildred had had a few anxieties about her sharing with Alice Glass. Maudsley Street was not the most salubrious of neighbourhoods and certainly not one from which they would have expected her daughter to choose her friends. But the girls had got on so well together. He had been quite impressed with Alice, when he had given her a lift home once. And as for her younger sister, Doreen. Well, her manner had been excellent, and even from the way she spoke it was clear that the removal to Howbeck had done naught but good for the child. The lady she'd been billeted with, Miss Ramsay, was top drawer. At least the war had done some good as far as the Glass family were concerned.

So, Elsbeth's preoccupation during the drive home did not cause him too much anxiety. Apart from feeling a bit down at leaving, the foul weather had given her a cold. She spent most of the journey sniffling into her handkerchief, and her poor nose was distinctly pink. But her mood of brooding withdrawal persisted, until they could not help but be concerned. It wasn't as though they didn't have enough on their plate as it was. William came home for his brief embarkation leave, before he set off by troopship to India – and then, probably, Burma, where the Japanese were forging ahead. Cedric himself was almost swamped by work. The business now was booming, but he had to be there practically day and night, what with staff shortages, worry over materials and urgent government deadlines.

When he got home, worn out and longing only for a few hours peace and quiet, and sleep, he had Mildred, her voice low and urgent, haranguing him on the pillow: 'I don't know what's wrong with her. I've never known her like this. You don't think it's some boy, do you? Someone back in Howbeck? Or maybe that poor Luke Denby? I thought there was nothing in it, after that time she brought him here. She soon gave up seeing him. She seemed to have got over him easily enough. But I think it knocked her for six, him getting killed. She must have thought an awful lot more of him than we realized. You know, it could have been *him* that broke off with *her*. You hear so many tales these days – especially with those RAF boys! We've got to talk to her. Once Bill's gone . . .' Her voice wavered and he reached compassionately to hold her. 'On Friday. Try and make some time for her. So we can both be there.'

Coming as it did, when all three were tense after saying farewell to son and brother, the talk did not go well. In fact, Elsbeth, white faced, and soon pink-eyed, looked as if she might flee the room at any second. Every suggestion was met with abrupt dissent: return to her studies, another teaching post at Lister Road, her father's approach to the growing number of influential acquaintances to find her some suitable office post – all were summarily rejected.

'I've managed on my own for the past eighteen months. I'll just see what they offer when I sign up.'

'You might be sent away! I mean far away. In the forces! You just don't know – some of the girls they get – where they come from . . .'

Her face flushed, she looked at them strangely, her eyes glinting. 'Like Alice Glass, you mean? I can look after myself! I've been doing it quite a while now.'

They were startled to be informed, when she came home after the medical examination and interview: 'I've put my name down for the Wrens. They'll let me know soon. I was told I'd stand a good chance with my School Cert and Higher.'

'She could do worse, love,' Cedric tried to console his wife, who looked far from convinced. The tears trickled readily from her puffed up eyes.

'We'll have nobody at home now. Only Rob for the holidays. And he's war mad. Can't wait to join up. And you away all day and half the night. How's it all going to end, Ced?'

A good question, he thought, as he took her trim frame into his pyjama-ed embrace.

Events seemed to progress with indecent haste. Elsbeth was accepted for service in the WRNS, which involved more interviews and a comprehensive medical, in Newcastle. She was one of a long line of young ladies waiting to be seen. On entering the harassed doctor's presence, he glanced up from form filling, snapped, 'Clothes off. On the chair,' and hurried out with a fistful of documents. When he re-entered the room, he stared, wide-eyed and open mouthed, at the fetching spectacle of a blushing Elsbeth, clad only in her panties, perched on the wooden chair like a marble nymph on her plinth. 'Good God!' He roared with laughter. 'I meant *clothes* on the chair. Come down before you get us both arrested!'

She was too embarrassed to tell a soul of her gaffe, but reflected with some pain how Alice would have howled with laughter at the tale. And as the cogs of officialdom ground with surprising speed until the eve of her departure came, she at last yielded to the dictates of her troubled conscience, and wrote a brief, stiff note to her dearest friend and former lover, to let her know of the dramatic change in her circumstances.

Dear Alice,
This is just to let you know that I've finally got my call-up, to the Wrens. I have to report down in London on Monday, (the 13th – I hope that's not an omen), but then I think I'll be posted to Portsmouth for basic training. About twelve weeks, I think, but there may be more training after that, depending what branch they put me in. I'm looking forward to it really, but a few butterflies in the tummy as well! Still, it's got to be done and I'll feel I'm doing my bit, just as you are, working on the land. I will write later and give you my more permanent address in Portsmouth, or Pompey, as the sailors call it. Give my regards to Beryl and Evelyn, and anyone else who remembers me. Take care,

Love,
Elsbeth x

The names hurt Alice as much as anything. No more Al and Beth. After all the days of silence, this was cruel, and Alice wept. But the most cruel thing of all was that, until two days ago, Beth had been there, less than two miles away from her, and Alice had failed to find the courage to seek her out – and now she was far away, out of reach, and out of her life for good.

CHAPTER EIGHTEEN

It was not after all Sergeant Len Potts who proved to be the key to finding employment for Alice, but the amiable Dick Lumley, train driver husband of Davy's landlady. True, he required a gentle nudge, and then a more vigorous push, from Reeny, but his status on the footplate and his seventeen year, boy and man service with the company had earned him respect. The inspector who had been one of the card players at Dubry Street the night Davy had returned from Howbeck had even greater influence, and was a personal friend of Dick's. The upshot of these connections meant that, two weeks after receiving Alice's letter on April Fool's Day, he was able to write to her at her Margrove home to inform her that if she could present herself in York for an interview at 9 a.m. on Wednesday, 22 April, at the Depot Offices behind the railway station, she had every likelihood of being offered employment as a domestic assistant for LNER's Railways Canteen Services:

'Your vast experience of cooking for Lister Road School's evacuees in Howbeck, plus your more recent experience of growing the d. . .d stuff at Howe Manor, should ensure it's a foregone conclusion that they'll offer you the job. Apart from the fact that Mr Mears, the inspector who's fixed it up, already guarantees it. There's nowt like a bit of nepotism and intrigue when you want something done!'

And what the hell's them when they're at home? Alice wondered, as she read these lines.

It's best if you can travel down next Tuesday – you'll have to change at Darlington or Middlesborough, and try to arrive in the afternoon if you can, preferably after two. I'll meet you at the station. Don't be mad – I've enclosed this for the fare. Don't worry, just a loan, you can pay me back out of your wages. You can stay at our place, Tuesday night – Mrs L's. You'll like her, she's really nice – I think I've told you that before. Just one thing, though, I don't know if she'd be all that keen on our sleeping together, so you'll have to manage on your own!

Cheeky bugger! She felt her face grow hot, and her heart quicken with agitation at the memory of that strange night. It was difficult to clarify just how she *did* feel at its recall. But then she could identify clearly enough the beat of excitement that stirred her at the prospect of an early escape from her present gloom.

It was only two days since she had received that note from Beth, which had driven her out to walk the streets for hours, in spite of the cold April showers. She just could not stand the claustrophobic little house, or having to face her family. She didn't want to talk to anyone, and, in spite of her best efforts, she could not dispel the fit of despair, which brought tears to add to the clinging wetness on her cheeks. She even trailed the length of Park Road, then through the drab neatness of the park itself, with little sign of spring yet, its sombreness thoroughly in keeping with her mood. She was brave enough to continue now, past the pond and through the gate on the far side, to the neat houses, each nestled in the seclusion of its garden, among which was 'Holmlea'. No need to fear running into Beth now. She was already far away, much further than York, away in distant London, or maybe even further than that, on the south coast.

Now, she almost felt guilty at the lift of spirits this news from Davy gave her, and, yet again, she felt her heart warm towards him for his loving care. Even sending her money for her ticket! That was so typical of him. She could manage the fare on her own, of course – but it would make considerable inroads to her modest savings. She was a little nervous at the thought of the interview, but what the heck! They wouldn't expect a brain box for a job in a canteen. Cleaning, cooking, serving meals. She'd done plenty of that, and a railway works canteen wasn't exactly the Grand Hotel! She'd be all right. In fact, she'd be fine, with Davy to smooth things for her, finding her lodgings and being there for her to talk to whenever they could get together.

Her thoughts returned to her beloved Beth. And not with bitterness this time, but with a churning anxiety and concern for her. She's no rough diamond, not like me. How would she get on, going off all by herself, with no one to look out for her? Flung in with a barrack room full of strangers. She'd been shy enough with Alice at first, until . . . She tried not to let her mind dwell on the intimate happiness they had shared. But her heart was full, and the tears were back again, to blur the image of the neat house, behind its hedges and low wall, whose gate she had never opened, and never would.

Her mother was tearfully upset when Alice announced her intention to try for the job in York. 'There's plenty of places round here where you could find summat,' Maggie remonstrated. 'They've even started taking on lasses at Gray's now.'

'You'd like to see me working in the shipyard, would you, mam? Catching red-hot rivets, coming home black as the ace of spades! You might as well ask me dad to fix me with a job at the works, while you're on!'

But then Maggie's thoughts were less painfully diverted. 'Here! This lad – that copper, Davy What's-his-name. You're not sweet on him, are you?' A knowing smile formed instead of the ready tears. 'He's a bit keen, isn't he? Our Doreen hinted as much last time we saw her.'

'Don't be daft, mam!' Alice hoped her dismissal of the notion was convincing.

'He's going to a lot of trouble, though, isn't he? He sounds like a nice lad.' Then the clouds were back in her face again. 'He was a conchie though, wasn't he?' Thoughts of her son's recent departure for Catterick Camp stirred her resentment. 'Be a fine how d'you do if everyone felt like that. Where'd we be with Hitler then, eh?'

'I told you,' Alice answered wearily. 'He did more than his share of fighting in Spain, against that Franco feller. Anyway, he's medically unfit for the army now. They wouldn't have him, even if he wanted to go.'

'Lucky him!' Her mother's tone was bitterly sarcastic.

'He's still doing his bit. It's dangerous enough being a bobby. He's out all weathers, and in air raids and all that. They have to stop out on the streets. And there's all kinds of bad 'uns out in the blackout. Thieves – and worse. They've got this Sandshoe Charlie – remember the feller we had round here, grabbing handbags? Well this one's far worse. He attacks women.' She gave a meaningful look. 'You know what I mean. He's after them, for . . . you know.' Another significant nod. 'He beats them up, badly. Davy's been put on plain clothes – detective work, to help catch him.'

'That's what I mean! What do you want to be going off to a big place like that for, where you're not safe going out of your door? Daft, I call it.'

Her father, too, was not happy about her leaving home again so soon, but for a rather different reason. 'You've only just come home. And your mam could do with you chipping in with a bit. We've lost our George's wage, you know. We haven't had a penny from him since he joined up, and when they get his allotment sorted it won't be much. They hardly pay them 'owt in the army.'

'I'll bet! Nowt like what you lot at the steelworks make, eh? With all that overtime!'

'You cheeky monkey! It's not easy keeping a family – there's our Algy, and Ethel. It's hard.'

'Good job you got shot of Doreen then, eh? One less to worry about. And don't worry. As you're having such a struggle, I'll try to keep on sending summat out of me wages – the way I always have! Though it's not much, I know. Not as much as you hand over the bar in the Black Oss every week!'

'You insolent young bugger! You always did have too much mouth on you.'

As she had so often, Maggie Glass stepped in with accustomed skill like a referee to separate the squaring up opponents. There was almost an element of nostalgia as she did so, but there was resignation, too, as she reflected that maybe it was just as well that her eldest child was not going to remain in the family home. Things were no easier between Alice and Fred now that his daughter was grown up. Maggie hoped this chance of a new job would work out for her, and she was confident the lass would continue to send what she could to ease the burdens of her mam's housekeeping.

And as for this business of this Davy chap, he sounded keen enough, to Maggie's mind, fixing things up the way he had. Even sorting out lodgings – not that she'd got the job yet, though Maggie wouldn't mind betting it was in the bag, reading between the lines. There were plenty of folk speaking out for her, by the sound of it, including this railway feller where Davy Brown was lodging. They were putting up Alice there on Tuesday night, before she had her interview on Wednesday morning. Maggie wasn't sure if that was the right way to be going about it, staying under the same roof as a young chap who had his eye on her. Goodness knows what might go on. And for all her brass neck, Alice had never had much to do with lads and courting and all that malarkey. She always gave the impression she could hold her own anywhere, but with lads she'd never been one for sparking and messing about. Maggie wondered just how much she *did* know. Maybe she should have a talk. But the lass might take things the wrong way and fly off the handle with her – she'd always been a bit funny about things like that. She thought of her own ignorant, eager youth. Nobody had ever talked about such things with her. There was only that fearsome THOU SHALT NOT emblazoned in her mind, and for all the fears it hadn't stopped her. And for all his faults, numerous as they were, Fred had done the decent thing, and stood by her after getting her into trouble. At least this Davy sounded a decent sort. From a good background, maybe even gentry. She could only hope he'd do the decent thing and all, if things got that far.

The thought kept occurring to Alice that everything was going far too smoothly, slipping into place far too easily. She got on well with the Lumleys, or, rather, Reeny Lumley. Her husband, Dick, one of Alice's chief benefactors, was away when she first stayed at Dubry Street, and wasn't expected home for two days. 'They're all over the place these days,' Reeny explained. 'Goods and stuff. Troops and munitions trains – I don't like to think of what he's carrying half the time! But you'll meet him soon enough. He's looking forward to it. We've heard so much about you from Davy.'

Alice was sleeping in the little front bedroom where Micky normally slept. His cot stood dismantled against the wall, to make room for the iron single bed, which had been set up for Alice. Reeny had interrupted Davy before he could complete his sentence, when he referred to the cost of his friend's stay, before her arrival: 'For goodness' sake! She's your friend! It's only for a few nights. It's no bother, so just be quiet. Now then. There's some digs in Cook Street. With a Mrs Douglas. Her husband's away in the army. She's got a couple of kids, one at infant school, the other's a few months younger than Micky. But that won't bother your lass, will it? She's used to kids, working at that school. And there's youngsters in her own family, you said? I'll take you round and you can take a look before she gets here. See what you reckon.'

That was one of the things that made Alice just a little uneasy: the extent to which Davy had paved and smoothed her way. He was instrumental in finding her this opportunity; he had found a place for her to stay, hardly more than two minutes away. The interview, about which she was far more nervous than she showed – she slept very little in the comfortable but strange bed – was so relaxed and went so smoothly that it seemed little more than a friendly, welcoming chat, as though the whole thing had been decided before they'd met her, so that she was far less surprised than she would normally have been when the friendly man who'd led the interview said as he steered her out of the door on to the cobbled yard of the station annexe, 'Well, I hope you'll be happy here, Alice. I'm sure you'll fit in very well.' He grinned at her. 'We'll just pop over to the clerical office and get things signed up.'

'I've got the job then? I thought I might have to wait – to hear, like.'

'Nay! If George Mears thinks you'll do, that's good enough for us. And I'm sure you *will* do. Very nicely!'

'They think I'm your girlfriend!' she said to the grinning Davy, when she finally emerged to find him waiting for her. He had rearranged shifts so that he could be off on the Wednesday morning.

'Is that so terrible?' His tone was light, but then he caught her serious look. 'No, Alice! Really. I've told Mrs L often enough, don't worry. But we *are* friends, eh? Good friends. She knows I think a lot about you. But I've made it clear that we are just friends. That there's nothing – else between us.'

His expression of embarrassment, and of regret, stirred her feelings of guilt. 'All right then.' She grabbed his arm, linked hers in it and smiled at him. 'I've a feeling she'd be a bit of a matchmaker if she had the chance!'

'Well, let's face it. I need all the help I can get!' She stopped in her stride and turned to him, and he grinned again, with humorous ruefulness. 'Come on! Only joking! Anyway, you know how I feel – all right! I'm not going to start again. But I can't help being glad I'm going to be seeing a lot more of you. And I promise I won't make a nuisance of myself. It'll be good, you'll see.'

Yes, it would, she thought penitently, and she *was* grateful to him for making all this possible. He was special to her, no doubt of it. And she strove, bravely, to push the thoughts of her secret sorrow away from the forefront of her mind. Davy had persuaded her to stay in York on the Wednesday night, too. He had swapped a shift, so that he did not have to report for duty until 10 p.m. The interview and the brief bureaucracy involved in being signed up for employment were all done before noon. 'You wouldn't think there was a war on, would you?' Davy grinned. 'Now I can show you some of the sights.'

They headed to the centre, and he led her through the narrow medieval street of the Shambles, and on into College Street, towards the dark twin towers of the Minster, showing above the jutting, steep rooftops. 'It's like something out of an old history book!' Alice marvelled, as they passed the College of St William, and the timbered Treasurer's House, though the sandbags piled at the entrance were an ugly reminder of present grim times. Beyond that was a handsome, much newer building, whose stone and brickwork had yet to show the layers of city soot and grime.

'The new deanery,' Davy told her. 'And it is. Brand new. Just built. The old one was knocked down a couple of years ago. Just before the war.'

As they came round the south side, they saw the long queue of people waiting to file into the Minster, and Davy hurried forward to join them. He felt her slight resistance, her arm linked in his. She glanced up at the massive structure, its soaring stone projections, the fierce, monstrous carvings grinning and snarling over their heads. 'You must see inside. It's magnificent. Just a quick look. We'll come out again if you don't like it.'

It was dim inside, a murky twilight filtering through the high windows, the dust floating visibly in the falling rays, like searchlight beams, she thought. Much of the great stained glass had been removed, the boarded up gaps shocking and ugly. But the nave was almost full. They stood to one side at the back, and Alice stared in awestruck wonder at the vast height, dwarfed by its size. Her mind reeled at the way such lofty, solid dimensions could at the same time suggest a delicacy and lightness.

A sidesman whispered that the service was a celebration of the appointment of their archbishop, William Temple, to the See of Canterbury, which had been announced only a few days ago. They did not join the seated congregation, but stayed where they were, listening to the organ filling the great cavern of stone with its sound, and then the singing during the processional, and the opening hymn, 'Now thank we all our God'. 'A German hymn,' Davy said, glancing at her with a wry smile.

She gave a little shiver. 'Let's get out of here.' She glanced back at the cathedral with some relief when they were out in the bright morning once more, and heading for Stonegate. 'I don't really belong back there,' she added feelingly.

'You belong anywhere today. You look wonderful!'

'Now don't start being daft. I've warned you about that!' She was irritated by the instinctive feeling of pleasure and vanity his words had sparked. To be honest, though, she did think herself that she looked pretty good, with her (Beth's) best red coat over her costume and the smart little beret pulled at an angle across her carefully tweaked curls. She had wondered privately as she made herself ready earlier that morning, whether she was going just a wee bit overboard for an interview for a job serving in a railway canteen. But what the heck! She had got the job, hadn't she? Even if it had been virtually decided before they ever clapped eyes on her! There was nothing wrong with looking her best, was there?

'And now we've done the Minster, I'm taking you to another famous place in town. Betty's Bar. Also known as the Dive, because of all the notorious types who frequent it. A lot of the Brylcreem Boys get in there – the bomber lads from the aerodromes round about – and the young ladies who keep them company! So stay close to me. They'll be round you like flies round a honey pot.'

'Don't you worry, kidder!' There was an edge beneath her flippant reply. 'I've dealt with types like them before.'

There were similarly dashing types, handsome fly-boys in smart uniforms, proud, shy, some convinced they were indestructible, others who struggled hard always to stop their fear from showing or from overwhelming them, who would soon be studying the mapped layout of the ancient city with avid interest, but with a far more sinister purpose than the sightseers who had gazed at the old Baedeker travel guides from which the information had been gleaned.

CHAPTER NINETEEN

Mary Douglas was a garrulous little woman, just a year younger than Reeny Lumley, though from her stature and appearance she might well be mistaken for a schoolgirl. No more than five feet in height, and almost painfully thin – ‘a spelk of a body’ as Reeny had accurately described her – she had an amazingly deep, throaty voice, and a laugh which tended to slide into a wheezing gargle of a cough which made the hearer feel the urge to clear the throat in sympathy. The Wild Woodbine cigarettes, which quivered on her lips the vast majority of the time, no doubt contributed to the asthmatic nature of her habitual jollity. They also added to the sharp, foxy look of her pointed features, which were generally screwed up against the spidery trail of acrid smoke that hung about her turbaned head.

‘Doctor’s orders,’ she cackled, on first meeting Alice and Davy. ‘Good for me nerves, he reckons, me tabs. It’s just since me hubby, Terry, went away. It’s hard being on me own, with the bairns.’ Gerald was six, attending the neighbouring school, and Tony was a grubby three-year-old, who spent most of his time bumping about from one sharp article of furniture to another. As the weather became more clement, he was often to be found tethered to a vertical drainpipe in the back yard, by means of a long rope, the other end of which was fastened to the leather harness buckled about his shoulders and chest, adorned with rusty tinkling little bells. The rope was long enough to allow him the freedom of most of the long, narrow yard. The end of his tether took him, frustratingly, to a few feet from the entrance to the Anderson shelter, fixed into the corner of the wall dividing the yard from the neighbouring property, and the higher brick wall leading, via a wooden door, into the tiled back lane.

Alice noted the involuntary and swiftly disguised glance of dismay that crossed Davy’s face at first sight of the crowded, untidy kitchen, where every surface seemed to be covered with a miscellany of objects, while two lines of garments hung like a complicated naval flag signal over their heads. He said nothing while Alice declared it would suit her 'down to the ground'. He insisted on carrying her single suitcase up the narrow stairs to her little room at the front of the terraced house, directly over the small vestibule. There was just enough space for the iron bed to fit behind the door. Its foot rail rested against the opposite wall, in which was situated the narrow window, with its criss-crossed strips of anti-blast tape behind the white net curtains, and the inevitable blackout drape. Against the wall that ran parallel to the bed stood a solid cupboard, with two shelves above it, which left a gap of slightly less than two feet between it and the bed, the only free floor space, covered by a threadbare blue rug.

Alice was well aware of what was passing through Davy's mind after they left the terraced house on the Sunday afternoon. 'I'll unpack me stuff later,' Alice had told her new landlady. 'I'll not be late.'

'Oh, you don't need worry, luv. I sit up half the night anyway, usually. I still haven't got used to sleeping on me own, even though our Terry's been gone since last year. That's why I'm glad to have Geraldo back in with me – even though he does kick me black and blue. That's our Terry's nickname for him. Geraldo – after the band leader.' This was followed by the usual wheezing, spluttery chuckle.

'Are you absolutely sure it's all right for you?' Davy asked dubiously, as they made their way through the identical streets back towards his own digs.

Alice was amused, and also a little saddened, by his obvious unease. It reminded her all too vividly of Beth. She would probably have seen the same ill-disguised look of dismay on Beth's features at sight of Mary Douglas's cluttered little abode. It brought home once more to Alice the similarity between Davy's and Beth's more privileged backgrounds and her own rough-and-ready origins. 'Hey, it'll be just fine. Honest. It'll be like home from home. She seems a canny little soul.' She laughed. 'And I don't think I'll have much time to feel lonely, do you? She looks like she could talk the hind legs off a donkey.' She saw just the flash of another expression pass over his face, as though she had said something hurtful, and yet again was reminded powerfully of Beth. These bloody thin-skinned, sensitive types! she thought, with a mixture of whimsical humour and regret. She knew it was her reference to feeling lonely that had caused that fleeting look. He wanted so much to be the one who would make her loneliness go away. Maybe her time with Beth had made her more perceptive to these things. Maybe she was getting more like them after all, she reflected wryly.

For all her brave face, she was undeniably nervous when she reported for her first day of duty the following morning, at 7.30. The staff canteen was a large one, situated behind the station, near the marshalling yards, with their lines of clanking, shunting wagons day and night, and the big carriage works, which had its own separate canteen and employed its own army of workers. 'You might have to spell out over there sometimes,' her immediate supervisor told her, a grim faced, solid figure of a woman, called Ethel Bloom. 'And you'll have to do some shift work when you've got used to being here. Late shift about every three weeks or so. Two till ten. No nights, though. Be all right, won't it?' Despite her forbidding appearance, Ethel Bloom proved to be a fair and even quite pleasant character, as long as you pulled your weight and weren't 'lippy'. Alice acknowledged that the colloquial term might well have applied to herself two or three years back. She thought of the clashes she'd had with Mr Johns, Little Hitler, and some of the more senior staff back at the co-op. Those days were long gone, though. She'd learnt a lot since then, about others, and about herself. And inevitably such thoughts led very quickly to Elsbeth Hobbs, and brought that closing lump to her throat, which had to be swiftly swallowed, and pushed back, down to her chest. To her heart.

Davy was still working with the plain clothes squad, under the immediate direction of Sgt Baxter, and he contrived to be waiting outside the entrance to the works canteen, when Alice emerged, red faced, the bronze curls at her brow damp and limp, from her first shift at 5 p.m. Hastily, she snatched the ugly green mob cap from her head and thrust her fingers through her tangled curls. The hem of the green overall hung below the belted winter coat. She wasn't wearing stockings, and the old, scuffed, solid lace-up black shoes with their low heels made her pale ankles look ugly. But who the hell cares? she chided herself, with a touch of irritation. The involuntary, tender look on Davy's face as he greeted her added to it, and she smothered her annoyance guiltily.

'How did it go?'

'Fine! That's more like it, eh?' She held up her reddened hands, and grinned at him. 'Me feet are killing me and me back's aching, but that's just cos I've been taking it easy for a couple of weeks. Soon get back into the swing of things. Peeling spuds, hands in greasy water washing mucky pots! Just up my street!' She cut him off quickly as she saw the beginnings of that rueful, apologetic expression. 'Really. It couldn't be better. Indoors all day, all the grub I can eat, and no more old misery guts, Dick Pearson, griping on at me. Heaven!'

'You want to soak in a nice hot bath this evening,' he advised her, and made her smile again. He hadn't even noticed; it hadn't even occurred to him. Cook Street might be only a few minutes away from his own digs, but it was a very different, humbler proposition than Dubry Street. The 'bathroom' was either out in the chilly 'back kitchen', beside the bricked-in copper beneath which a fire had to be lit, or in front of the luxurious warmth of the kitchen range, with sheets or towels draped over a wooden clothes-horse for modesty. But why disabuse the poor boy?

'Aye. Good idea. And if you don't mind, I think I'll have an early night. Get settled in, like.' She pulled a grinning, mock-rueful face. 'Little Mary's expecting a bit of a heart-to-heart, I think. Getting to know one another, she calls it. And I've got a bit of sorting out to do. How about tomorrow? Will I see you after work?'

Once more, he thought he had successfully concealed his disappointment. 'Yes, sure. I can be there to meet you, if you like.' He glanced at her, added hastily, 'Or leave it till later, if you like. After you've had your di— tea.'

'No. As long as you don't mind seeing me in all me muck and glory, like this. They'll all think I'm going steady, you waiting outside every night.' Clumsy! She admonished herself at seeing the touch of heightened colour in his face. Foot in mouth again!

Davy knew several of the railway police, and on Wednesday he met one in the station concourse. There was over an hour to go before Alice would finish her shift, and Davy had intended to fill in time in the restaurant for travellers, but the fellow policeman invited him to a cuppa in the small office at one end of the high vaulted station, over the footbridge from the main forecourt.

'Here! You lot haven't heard any buzz about something special going on?' his colleague asked. Davy's mystified look was answer enough. 'It's just . . . there's a whisper going on that there might be summat up. Some sort of enemy action coming soon.'

'What? You mean an air raid? There hasn't been any of that for ages, has there?'

'No. But . . . there was a warning last night. Three or four bombers, that's all. Over the Esk valley. Following the railway line, they reckon. Thought they were going for Whitby. But they vanished. Might have got lost. No bombs dropped anywhere, as far as we know.' He sipped at his mug of tea and grimaced. 'God! Sorry, this brew's been on a while, eh? And then they've started up down south, haven't they? That raid on Exeter a week ago.' He leant closer, lowered his voice, as though he were about to impart some high level, top security information. 'We heard they might be starting up reprisals. For that RAF raid last month. On that Jerry place. What was it?'

'Lubeck,' Davy supplied. As a secret it was not a well-kept one that the RAF had set the ancient city ablaze and destroyed practically the whole of its medieval wooden buildings.

'Bombers' moon tonight, an' all. At the full. Let's hope we get a few clouds, eh?' He laughed, and by the time Davy met Alice coming from work, he had all but forgotten the gloomy warnings. There were always such predictions flying from tongue to tongue, especially since so many people insisted on tuning in to listen to 'Lord Haw-Haw' and his 'Germany calling' propaganda. They were as ready to believe his broadcasts as they were the news from the BBC.

Alice had quickly got over any embarrassment at his seeing her in her unbecoming working attire, after giving herself a sound mental ticking-off for displaying such vanity. What do you want? Want him to go on fancying you, do you, even when you know there's no hope for him? So now she cheerfully linked her arm through his and matched his stride as they climbed up the hill from the station, towards Micklegate Bar, following the line of the medieval city walls, and continuing along Nunnery Lane towards Clementhorpe, where they lived. 'How are you getting on with your case?' she asked. 'Have you caught him yet?'

He grinned. 'Give us a chance. They've only had me on the case less than a month! He's been quiet for a while. He must have heard about them putting me on the team. There's been nothing since that attack I told you about, on that Rowntree girl. And the light nights have helped. We'll still get the blighter, though. He deserves to be locked up for what he put those three women through.'

'Mebbes he's been scared off all together?'

Davy shook his head. 'I don't know. Those last three attacks. They weren't just robberies. I mean – he really attacked them. It's sort of . . . well, it's more to do with something wrong in him. I don't know if he *can* stop.'

'You'd better hurry up and get him then, hadn't you? Before he has another go at some other poor lass.'

He had no idea how soon her words were to return so painfully to his mind.

They went to the Northern Picture House for the evening show. The cinema was packed as usual, and they waited patiently in the long queue. 'Listen, I want to pay my way!' Alice tried to insist, and they had quite a fierce little argument, conducted in hissed whispers.

The tips of Davy's ears were burning red. 'For goodness' sake! What do you take me for? I don't ask a girl out to the pictures and then expect her to pay for herself! What sort of bloke do you think I am?'

'It's not like we're – courting or anything.' Even as she said it, she knew how it would hurt him, but she was feeling quite upset herself at being put on the defensive. She hated this idea of the conventional boy-girl business. She hated the way the usherette guided them towards the back rows, which seemed to be automatically reserved for 'canoodling'. She gave in with as much good grace as she could muster, and was grateful when he did not attempt to slip his arm around her shoulder or to hold her hand – by the sound of the heavy breathing, there was plenty of that, and worse, going on in their vicinity.

When they came out, the night was dark after the smoky, flickering half-light inside, but as their eyes became accustomed to the change they saw that in fact there was a bright full moon, and all at once Davy remembered the words of the railway policeman in the station earlier that day. He decided it was not worth repeating to Alice, and they headed up the steep Micklegate Hill towards the Bar. He wondered if it was worth calling in at the Windmill to see if they could get a quick drink before closing time, which was imminent. He decided against it. He would much rather spend the remainder of the evening enjoying Alice's exclusive company. He had been very much aware of her sweet, close proximity to him in the cinema, and how frustrating it had been not to touch her, not even to talk to her while the frothy nonsense of Hollywood babbled on the screen. Determinedly, he pushed away the increased sense of dismay at how far short of his hopes this relationship fell. You were the one who was so keen to get her here, he reprimanded himself. So you've got her! For better, for worse. And this is better, you reckoned, than not seeing her at all. So shut up and be thankful!

At that second he was diverted from his inner debate by a startlingly sudden deep roar, a thunder of engines deafening them out of nowhere, so that they, and the other pedestrians on the dark street, cowered, thinking a plane was about to crash right on top of them. There seemed to be a heat in the roar, and the crescendo died, just as suddenly, and Davy, glancing up, saw the dark, indistinct shapes frighteningly low in the sky, sweeping over them. Still it didn't occur to him that these were not friendly aircraft. They were gone, but before the engine sound had faded quite away, there were two loud, heavy detonations, over the rooftops to their right, and the reverberations made the pavement beneath them tremble. The echoing bang which followed an instant later seemed even louder, and was accompanied by a hideous noise of shattering glass, which seemed to be taking place all round them.

Davy dragged Alice bodily down, one hand dug into her head, displacing the woollen beret, dragging it down over her neck. He buried her face into his chest, flung his body over hers, covering her and hugging her down onto the hard ground, shielding her as comprehensively as he could. Then the whole world erupted in a continued burst of noise, and his reeling senses acknowledged they were caught in the middle of a sustained bombing raid right on the centre of the city.

CHAPTER TWENTY

'Get off the street, quick!'

'Where was the warning? There was no bloody siren!'

Around them, people picked themselves up from the ground and began to run. 'There's a shelter at the end of Priory Street!' Davy called, assuming the now familiar mantle of authority, though several people glanced at him askance. Just then there was another burst of detonations, fearful in volume, from down towards the river. There was a series of almost simultaneous flashes, which lit up the sky and the buildings all around them, and they cowered once more.

'They're after the Minster! By God, they've hit it.'

A flurry of Bonfire Night sparks erupted, immediately followed by tongues of flame, making the high black rooftops of the buildings across the road stand out against the lurid glow. 'No! They've missed. That's not the Minster. It's right by the river. Coney Street, I reckon.'

'Let's get you to the shelter.'

Alice felt the pressure of his hand in the small of her back, urging her forward. His other arm was still wrapped protectively across her shoulders. Something in his tone prompted her to ask, 'Why? What you gonna do? I can help and all.'

As he opened his mouth to remonstrate, there came the terrifying sound of roaring, straining aircraft engines again, and more explosions ahead of them. They dropped on the ground once more, against the wall of Holy Trinity church. Many of those caught on the street had scrambled through the gateway to take shelter among the tombstones, while others made for the porch of the soot-encrusted building itself. As a counter point to the explosive crumps of the bombs, they heard a rapid hammering. Davy recognized immediately its repetitive drilling as machine gun fire. 'Stay down! Stay where you are!' he yelled urgently, and again covered Alice's body as well as he could, pressing her against the foot of the wall. She turned with a little whimper in towards him, burying her face under his chin and flinging an arm around his neck, squeezing him convulsively. The mad stuttering of gunfire ended, and the roar of engines faded.

They stood. Now the sky behind them and ahead to their right was lit by flames, and thick, rearing clouds of smoke could be seen, dark against the fires and the moonlight. There was a fierce, acrid stench of burning. Then came the tardy wail of the sirens, and a waggish voice called out, 'Better late than never, eh?'

'They've hit the station by the look of it.'

Alice firmly refused to seek the dubious safety of the communal shelter, and clung tightly to Davy's hand as they made their way up the remainder of the hill to the Bar and the turreted walls. The white helmets of the ARP wardens began to appear, yelling at people to get off the streets, and adding the whirr of their rattles to the general chaos and the crump of the still falling bombs. Several people ignored them, their curiosity and desire for excitement stronger than their fear, and climbed the steps up to the ramparts of the wall to the right of the Bar. Alice and Davy joined them.

'Look! They got the station all right!' The impressive block of the offices were apparently untouched, but they could see a shattered section of the station roof, behind which the area of the railway stables was well ablaze. The towers of the Minster stood out, lit by flames which seemed perilously close, but the cathedral appeared unscathed.

'Bugger me!' a cloth-capped figure declared feelingly beside them. He apologized when he noticed Alice, and pointed his arm to a distant building whose roof was engulfed with fire. 'They've only gone and bombed the Guildhall! We've just spent nigh on three years redoing the whole place. Riddled with death watch, it was.'

'Never mind, mate! Looks like you've got another three years' work waiting for you tomorrow.'

A little further down from the Guildhall, which stood at the top of Coney Street, the church of St Martin's was another prominent casualty, and just across the river from them, the great Rowntree's warehouse was already well ablaze.

'They're after the station all right! Leeman Road's copped a packet, see?' Fires were burning from the closely packed houses near the railway lines. 'I bet there's a few poor souls caught in that lot.'

Just then above the general clamour they heard the sound of aircraft again, this time a deep, steadier throb that indicated they were flying at a greater height than the earlier attacks. 'Don't need to come down so low. They've already got the fires to guide them!' Discretion overcame valour or inquisitiveness and the walls rapidly emptied, as the spectators stumbled down the narrow steps and fled.

'Look! I'm getting you home – to *my* place!' Davy declared almost desperately, pulling at Alice's hand. 'I'll have to report to the station. Tower Street,' he added in explanation. 'I'll have to get into uniform and sign in. They'll need all the help they can get. Poor Mrs L will be going frantic. She's on her own with the kiddies. Dick's away, of course.' He hoped this argument would help to persuade Alice to agree.

'Little Mary'll be terrified and all. I ought to make sure she's all right. I hope they're in the shelter.'

'Right! Come on.' As they ran down the length of Nunnery Lane, the old city walls on their left, fire engines and ambulances began to hurtle past them, bells clanging, heading in the direction they had come from. The thuds of further detonations came, thankfully, from behind them, and as they raced across Bishopthorpe Road and into the narrow streets of Clementhorpe they noted with relief that there was no sign of bomb damage. 'Are you sure you won't come to our place?' Davy asked again, but Alice tugged against his tight hold.

'No. I'd best go to Mary's. She'll be petrified. You get on. I'm all right from here.'

'Don't be daft! I'll see you home. After all, I asked you out.' He grinned tightly, and they jogged the final yards to Cook Street.

'Mary's left the back door open.' Alice led him into the cobbled lane to the rear, and they slipped into the walled-in yard. At once there came a rusty cry from within the humped shape of the Anderson shelter just inside the rear door. Mary Douglas's sharp little, turbaned head appeared in the dimness of the low entrance to the shelter, the red tip of her Woodbine bobbing furiously. She was so overwhelmed she actually withdrew it from her lips.

'Oh God, my God!' she sobbed, reaching out frantically for Alice's embrace. 'This is it, me luv! Our time's up, I reckon. Oh God! Am I glad to see you, pet!'

Alice's arms enfolded her. 'You're all right, Mary. Don't upset yourself, come on now.'

Behind them the dark, cramped interior of the tunnel-like shelter billowed with blue smoke, and both youngsters coughed heartily. 'You get on.' Alice threw a worried, bravely comic look over the diminutive clinging figure of her landlady, and Davy stood awkwardly on the threshold.

'If you're sure. I'll come round as soon as I can in the morning. Stay inside here, whatever happens.'

As though only just aware of his presence, Mary gave a fresh wail and flung away the stub of her cigarette in her agitation. 'You're never going out again in this? For God's sake be careful, man! You've got to come back to this lass, you know.' Suddenly she swivelled and threw an arm round the startled Davy's neck, the other clamped about Alice's, and sandwiched herself between them, her pointed, pallid face gazing up from their intimately close chest level, hanging like a drunken midget between them. 'Give her a proper kiss, damn it!' Mary croaked, pulling their heads together, and their lips met clumsily over her brow.

'Be careful!' Alice called, as he turned away.

'He thinks the world of you, that lad!' Mary said, with conviction, as he left the yard.

Alice could still feel the raw stab of his lips against hers. She opened her mouth in automatic denial, but then stayed silent. At least the force of her landlady's terror had been diverted somewhat by the romantic interlude. And besides, Alice had the sweet but sad feeling that she had spoken nothing but the truth.

Although it was not quite dawn, the sky was rosy with the burning fires, even though the all-clear had sounded a while ago. First estimates calculated the raid had been a heavy one, with more than fifty bombers involved. There was still an argument raging as to its main purpose. Some were already insisting that the prime target had been the Minster, and were already talking of a 'miraculous escape' on a par with that of St Paul's during the blitz of '40. Others stated that the aim had been to disable the railway, in which case the enemy could claim at least partial success. The signal box at the southern edge of the station approach had been put out of action, the large stables had been destroyed, and the station itself damaged. Trains into York had been delayed further up the line, both north and south, and nothing was leaving the station. The nearby residential area of Leeman Road had been hit, and this was where many of the casualties had occurred. Again, rough estimates at this stage put the fatality figures at 'more than fifty'. A conservative estimate, Davy thought privately, when he was directed to the area to assist the rescue services and the fire crews.

The machine-gun firing he had heard had taken place near the same area. The Cooperative Wholesale Society's large central store had had all its windows smashed, and goods were scattered over the roadway, in among the countless shards of glass. One of Davy's tasks, along with his colleagues, was to ensure there was no looting, but though there had been some rumours of a few youths making off with some tins, when the police arrived on the scene they found some people gingerly picking the items from the broken glass and placing them back in the window spaces.

When the grey light of Thursday morning broke, most of the fires were under control. Davy helped in a careful search of the blackened ruins of the terraced houses for any more survivors or bodies, and was on hand to assist in the removal of three corpses, badly mutilated by fire and by bomb blast, from the smouldering heap of bricks and blackened timbers that was the remains of a dry-cleaner's shop. The three dead, a grandmother, her daughter and the daughter's child, a girl of eleven, were from the flat above the shop. The rescue workers discovered the names of the victims by questioning the neighbours who had managed to make the dash to the nearby concrete shelter. The grisly remains, which had to be gathered into sacks, gave little clue. Worst of all for Davy was the sickeningly sweet smell of burnt flesh, which, no matter how many times he hawked and spat, and blew his nose, or how many mugs of scalding tea he drank, he seemed unable to get rid of. He thought there was nothing left of the dreadful night which could shock him, but he was proved wrong.

He was on his own this time. As the morning light grew stronger, and the new working day began, he was ordered by his sergeant to take over a beat which covered the area around the destroyed and still smouldering stable yards, adjacent to the station itself. 'Transport police are strapped just now. They've got the goods yard, and there's trains still stuck outside town. Some passengers have been walking in down the lines, from miles out. Make sure everything's all right around the stables, and up Station Road. Call in from railway offices if you find 'owt. I'll try and get a relief for you for dinner time.'

He took the chance to call at the staff canteen, where, to his great relief, he found Alice already at work in the busy kitchen, clad in her green cap and overall, swilling out the tiled floor around the vast metal sinks. In spite of her tired look, and shadowed eyes, she gave him her cockiest grin and gave a mock salute with her heavy broom. 'Caught me in all me glory! How are you doing? You look as though you could do with a good wash and brush up.' She flourished the broom at him. 'Can I do yer now, sir?' Her imitation of Itma's Mrs Mop was a fair one.

'Glad you're safe and sound.' He blushed, remembering their snatched kiss.

'Aye. They should put our wee Mary in the forces. Send her over to Germany. She'd talk 'em all to death! I'm right glad to see you're all right an' all, kidder.'

They stared at each other, wordlessly, for a second. 'Right. I'd better get on then. I'm on duty till lunchtime at least. Look, I'll try to be here for when you finish work.'

'Nay, don't be daft. I'll pop round after tea to see you. Don't worry if you're busy.' She pulled a face. 'Unless they come back again tonight. You never know what the heck's gonna happen, eh?'

He realized how much better he felt, despite his aching weariness, for seeing her. Once again, he fell to wishing he could find the secret to winning her, to rouse in her the same feeling she had awakened in him. More and more he was being forced to acknowledge his love for her. A rough diamond. Those were her own words to describe herself. And she was right. Diamond was the word that mattered most to him, for she was just that, precious to him. Rough? It disturbed him to acknowledge that, too. Undoubtedly, in some ways people would agree with her assessment. Her background was humble, no way could he argue against that. When he had first discovered how attracted to her he was, he had dwelt upon how awkward things might be, for both their families. His parents would welcome her, at first for his sake, but he was convinced they would soon come to recognize her true worth. All the differences of background were superficial: education, the way they spoke, the refinements of privilege and upbringing. None of that really mattered. She could learn – it made him guilty and ashamed even to think of it – but it was true. There was nothing wrong with polishing some of those rough edges off. She would still be the same, lovable Alice. She would never lose that fierce, independent spirit of hers, that tomboyish wholeheartedness, which was one of the qualities he loved most in her. She would never be 'girlish', in that sense that so many females traded on – that 'goo-goo eyed' helplessness designed to ensnare their man, and pander to that outdated caveman egoism. 'Me Tarzan you Jane'. A bit like that fluttering little, pretty butterfly, her one time closest buddy, Elsbeth Hobbs.

He felt his own hesitance in pursuing that area again; a no-go area, as far as Alice was concerned, for she had scarcely referred to her – in fact never, of her own volition. And she had very swiftly choked off any queries on his part, refusing to entertain any talk of her friend, making it a taboo subject. What on earth could have happened between them? What sort of falling out could have caused such a complete separation, mental as well as physical? His thoughts kept returning to that day up on the High Tops, and Alice's atypical breakdown, betraying a genuine grief, which had alarmed him, and still made him uneasy to explore the reasons for it. It was so intense – like the bitter tears for a lost love. He could identify with it so vividly. It was the way he had felt when Lou had so gently rejected his love.

He was so distracted by his musing that he was almost surprised to find himself circling the charred remains and broken roofless walls, the blackened, skeletal timbers, of the stable yard. The smell of burning was still very strong, but not unpleasant, except by association with what had caused it. The smell in fact stirred memories of bonfires, of autumn, and woodland walks. At the furthest end from the wide entrance on to the road was a long, brick shed, which looked as if it had taken a direct hit. Part of its outer walls were standing, jagged as broken teeth, the long, narrow windows were glassless, with traces of their blackened wooden frames. The rubble of bricks, along with the charred roof beams, had collapsed in heaps, and he picked his way around them, about to turn back towards the distant entrance, which would lead round the side of the railway tracks and through the little tunnel back to Station Road. He had picked his way past the piled rubble into the wide doorway, now gaping emptily, of the shed, or store, when he saw something – a long, pale object, projecting from the collapsed bricks inside the building. It was almost hidden in the dimness, but it didn't seem to fit with the tumbled ruins on which it nestled. He turned back, moved further in, glancing up at the morning sky through the missing roof, making sure there were no further dangers of collapsing walls. He eased off his cap, wiped his sweating forehead. It was odd being back in uniform again. The high, buttoned collar, the roughness of the serge, chafed at his neck. He moved closer, peering, then stopped in disbelief. He could see a pair of long, pale legs, and haunches, jutting from the bricks. He ran forward, saw that the upper half of the body was partially hidden under a loose pile of rubble. He moved the bricks covering it. He saw black hair, curled, stiff with blood, a purple blouse, or the remains of a dress, covering the shoulders and the upper back. It was a young woman, and she was dead. There was no doubt of that when he finally, with difficulty, turned her over, and recoiled with a gasp of shock and revulsion. The eyes stared wildly, were bugged, almost as though they would protrude from the contorted features. The face was a deep red purple, and the tongue lolled sickeningly, obscenely projecting from the gaping mouth. The head had been battered. The front of the skull had a deep concave depression, and the dark hair and one side of the terrible face was caked with dried blood. She was naked except for the blouse or dress, which gaped at the front, exposing her breasts and the pitiful flapping remnant of some undergarment. The dark bush of her pubis stood out against the paleness of her thin frame. There were marks on the inside of her thighs, which were parted, but not gaping. There were marks on her buttocks and her legs, but definitely not consistent with having been caught up in the terrible destruction of the raid. Could it have been blast which had killed her, stripped her of her clothing? He had heard of casualties being found naked, with no marks on their bodies. But then there was that hideous disfigurement of her face. He forced himself to bend close, to touch her. Her flesh was cold and hard as marble. Only those features stared at him, in that rictus, that gargoyle of final agony. That one blow that had crushed in the skull. One unlucky blow? Then he saw the neck, and either side the deep, black bruised, symmetrical indentations, and he knew that the life had been murderously throttled out of her.

PART III

YOUR EYES WILL TELL ME

CHAPTER TWENTY-ONE

'Hey! Hobbsy-Nobbsy! I dunno why you hide yourself away under that towel, mate! You ain't got nothing different to us common lot, you know!'

The speaker was Pat Eaves, a petite platinum blonde with facial features of arresting beauty but whose full-bosomed figure was almost too much for her height of five foot four. It was a figure she proudly if not carelessly displayed as she entered the steamy, wet tiled communal bathroom of Drake Accommodation Block, HMS *Victory*, the naval shore establishment in Portsmouth. Her towel was slung over her right shoulder and she carried her service issue toilet bag in her right hand.

'Take no notice, Elsbeth!' Norma Richardson advised coolly. As always, the willowy Norma managed to look poised and perfectly at ease even though she herself was nude. She wrapped her own towel around herself and tucked it into her breast. 'Some of us just don't feel the need to flaunt what we've got in front of all and sundry, Eaves.'

Even after almost three months of living day and night with each other, the girls of Class DIIIC still tended to use surnames only, except where real bonds of friendship had been forged. It still jarred on Elsbeth's ear. It sounded so harsh, so unfeminine. Thank goodness she had quickly found a rapport with Norma Richardson, otherwise the long weeks of basic training in Portsmouth barracks might have been a lot harder to endure. On the whole, it had not been too bad. Certainly not as difficult as she had anticipated, once she became inured to the communal nature of practically every aspect of her life, from washing and bathing, and even going to the toilet, to sleeping in company with thirty-five others, in creaking, double-tiered bunks in the vast bareness of a dormitory which had to be referred to as a 'mess', with its great black stove at one end, which could not be lit now, because, as far as the Royal Navy was concerned, summer began on 1 May and ended on 30 September.

To be fair, not all the girls were as common – the adjective made Elsbeth blush inwardly but, truth to tell, it was the only fitting word to describe Pat Eaves – as the platinum blonde. There were even two who, like Norma, had been to private boarding schools, and another couple like herself who had attended grammar schools, which meant that half of Class DIIIC were from similar (or better) backgrounds than her own. It was painfully disturbing to her to reflect that the year she had spent living in such close partnership with Alice had also contributed considerably towards making her less unworldly and naïve. Nevertheless, barrack room life had been enough of a shock to make her glad of Norma's presence, and her cavalier, protective personality.

They had hit it off from that first rather frightening day, during the train ride from the capital to Portsmouth Harbour station and the ride in the back of a naval truck to the intimidating RN barracks, with its stern rows of Victorian accommodation blocks, and the vast open plain of the parade ground, which they were to get to know far too well as they wheeled and stamped and marched all over its bleak surface in the weeks that followed. A little judicious wangling, and Norma managed to install herself in the upper berth a few squeaking feet above Elsbeth, who took comfort from the sagging springs overhead, which were the last thing she saw before weariness eased her into sleep each night.

They were, of course, soon on first name terms, though Elsbeth had a moment of intense discomfort when Norma said, 'Elsbeth! That sounds a bit formal. Can we shorten it a bit? How about Beth? That's a really pretty name. It suits you to a T.'

'Oh, I've always been Elsbeth,' she lied, reddening slightly. 'I couldn't ever get used to anything else.' Even her prudery gave her conscience some intense moments of angst as she reviewed the many, many moments of abandon she had so willingly surrendered to under the encouragement and guidance of Alice. But most of the time she was able to shut such painful memories out of her mind and convince herself that the shyness and reserve displayed by Wren Hobbs E., Service No. PM9118, in the company of her fellow trainees was the real her.

She was prepared to make an exception, up to a point, with Norma Richardson. She needed a bosom pal, an 'oppo', in the naval parlance they were all so desperately trying to acquire and to use as naturally as possible. Even so, she was sometimes seriously disquieted at the warmth of friendship she experienced and the attraction she felt for her lively chum, and would pull herself up short, to curb her enthusiasm and affection. 'You're a moody little mare sometimes, aren't you?' Norma would remark at such times, prompting Elsbeth to feel even guiltier.

But it was true what Arty Clark had written:

'It's probably as well not to get too friendly – I mean real chums, you know – with your mates in the services. You've got to remember, especially in the early stages when you're still doing your training, that you'll most likely all be split up and scattered to the four corners of the globe – not that you're likely to find many corners on a globe!'

She was sure that he was thinking of her brother, Bill. They had been close, and she knew Arty really missed him, as well as feeling bad about his own appointment to the War Office in London, while Bill had been posted to the Far East. She corresponded regularly with Arty now. People like Eaves teased her almost every time they saw the envelope laid out on the mess table with all the others. 'Another little pash piece from your pongo, Hobbsy! You can see the scorch marks on the paper! Letting the side down you are, going out with a brown job. No sense of shame!'

She let them think what they liked. She was more than pleased that they should assume that he was her 'boyfriend', with all that it signified. Somehow, the subterfuge was an aid towards her aim of achieving the 'normality' she desperately sought after. And anyway, she really *did* like Arty. He was the kind of young man she would have an affinity with: shy, rather reserved, with a touch of diffidence. They were all traits she recognized in herself. Which was why the passionate, unholy attachment that had flared up between her and Alice Glass had been so shocking.

It was Arty who had come up with the idea which had helped her to decide on the next step in her military career. He was already involved himself in the complex and secretive branch of ciphering and deciphering signals, and had written enthusiastically of how, if she applied at the end of her basic training, she might even find herself posted to the Admiralty in London: 'Or there's a place near Reading, in the country. Very hush-hush. But not bad for getting up to London when you're free.'

She caught something of his enthusiasm. She was well aware that his motivation in encouraging her to apply for the Signals Branch was the hope that they might thus be closer, within easy reach to see each other. She didn't mind at all. In fact she was keen for that reason, too, she told herself. And firmly pushed away the idea that she was running away from rather than towards something. So she applied to join the communications branch as soon as they were allowed to state a preference, and was encouraged by the jovial remarks of her divisional officer. 'So! Fancy getting yourself a nice little billet up in the Smoke, eh? Join the other glamour pusses in the typing pool in the Admiralty?

Angels dining at the Ritz and nightingales singing in Berkeley Square!' Reality would, at first, be a hard slog of almost another twelve weeks at a place not far from Pompey, at HMS *Mercury*, but it would, she hoped, lead to far better things.

After four weeks of their basic training, they were given a forty-eight hour leave, and she smothered her feelings of guilt at deciding not to go home by telling herself that it was too great a distance to travel, especially given the exigencies of wartime train timetables. Going 'up the line' to London was a much less fraught trip, of less than two hours. And besides, having been given plenty of warning, 2nd Lt. Arty Clark was able to make himself available to squire her for the weekend.

One of the most powerful bonds uniting them was their concern for Elsbeth's brother, Bill. The Japanese had captured Mandalay on May Day, three weeks ago. Bill's unit was stationed in the Chin Hills, on the Indian border, though he could not inform them of his precise whereabouts because of security. In any case, they had not received news of him since before the fall of Mandalay, so he could well have moved, either towards the encroaching front or further west. 'I don't think he'd be involved in the ground fighting. I mean right in the thick, front line stuff, so to speak,' Arty told her. She hoped he was not merely trying to comfort her – or himself. 'I mean he's attached to a command HQ. They don't normally get mixed up in the rough stuff.' But the surrender of Singapore three months previously, and Hong Kong on Christmas Day before that, and the stories that had filtered back from those disasters, were disturbing enough. Not only front-line troops were involved, but staff officers, auxiliaries, even civilians – women and children – had been taken prisoner, were being held in camps.

But their worry over Bill, great as it was, did not overshadow their brief interlude. It strengthened greatly the closeness of their friendship, which had been established by their regular correspondence. Arty was waiting, as promised, at the barrier at Waterloo. Both blushed at the good-natured cheers from the milling throng of fellow servicemen as the couple self-consciously hugged and pecked at awkward cheeks in greeting. 'I'm sorry. I look a bit of a mess in uniform. I don't think I exactly look the martial type.' Privately, she thought rather differently, and hoped that he did, too. She wished she could have had the advantage of wearing the individually tailored and finer material of the officers' rig, with their smart hats instead of the round, stiff little pillbox of the ratings' cap, with its black ribbon and the little gold lettering, WRNS, like a brand across her brow. However, like Norma, and many of the other girls, she had paid to have what alterations she could, and was permitted, to make the skirt hang more flatteringly and her jacket fit more snugly. From Arty's expression, she decided it had been well worth it, as had the extortionate price she had paid one of her 'shipmates' for some precious items of make-up, from a source which was described vaguely, with a knowing wink, as 'a good mate'. The girl was making a small fortune, and what else from her source 'the mind boggled', as Norma said. Elsbeth was reminded of her adventures in Howbeck, and Alice's determined pursuit of Gus Rielke and his nefarious dealings. She was, she supposed, no better than those villagers who had been only too willing to take advantage of the Big Swede's black marketeering. But then, she reflected soberly, she had learnt a lot of things about life, and not least about herself, in the quiet dales village.

Such thoughts helped to accelerate the pace at which her relationship developed with the quiet, fair haired young man who spent every minute he could at her side during their two days together. He had booked her into the Ladies' Army and Navy Club in St James's Square and himself into the British Empire Club in the neighbouring square. She protested, blushing charmingly, when he assured her he had already settled the bill for her stay. 'Look. It's the least I can do after the splendid hospitality you and your family showed me at Christmas. Taking me in like that – a perfect stranger. I'll never forget it.'

'Well, you're not a stranger now, are you?' Elsbeth said, in a tone and with a look that, for her, was distinctly coquettish.

'I hope not,' he answered, equally meaningfully, and equally unsteadily. They were both remembering the sudden flare of passion that had caught them by surprise in the Hobbs's kitchen the last night of his brief stay. He was recalling with beating hope the eagerness with which she had returned his kiss, despite her protest. She was recalling that moment, too, with some embarrassment, but also with a sense of something she shied away from exploring too closely, but which came near to atone for that secret, perverse lapse of character and conduct over the past year that weighed so heavily on her.

So, in the dark, smoky comfort of the West End cinema, while Tara blazed in glorious Technicolor on the big screen and her eyes filled with tears, she was glad of the distraction of his hand searching out hers, and then the hesitant but brave snaking of his right arm across her shoulder and the discreet tilt and touch of their heads. It was true. Tomorrow *was* another day, and she would spend almost all of it in his company. Before then, in a dark doorway, while the slit-lamped traffic crawled past them, desperation conquered diffidence, and he gripped her tightly enough to make breathing difficult for both of them, and she could feel his quivering passion through the layers of their uniforms and other, invisible items, and his leg thrust hard against hers, rucking her skirt.

She twisted a little in his embrace, felt the pop of a suspender almost at the instant she felt his hand on her left buttock, encountering the thick serge skirt and the unyielding rigidity of the girdle beneath it. Armoured plating! Would it prove impenetrable? She blushed at her own indecorous mental wanderings as she dragged her scraped lips away from their contact with his, not through protest but for a need for air, which was suddenly in frightfully short supply.

'I'm sorry, Elsbeth!' he was babbling almost, in her ear. 'I can't help – you're such a wonderful girl! I've never – I mean I've never, you know, had a proper girlfriend before. Never . . . this damned war!' he swore, with dire unoriginality, but with the most sincere feeling.

Poor boy! She felt him relaxing his crushing hold on her, preparing to release her. 'Neither have I!' she panted, and as she said it she realized the lewd, music hall comic impropriety of her words. The name ALICE blazed as high as the doomed township on the screen epic they had just witnessed, and she almost cried aloud in shame and despair. Instead, she reached for him, searched for his mouth and clamped hers fiercely against it once more, and thrust her body blatantly against his until she felt sealed to it. She felt the delicate parting of another suspender clip. To hell with it! Let her stockings slip down to her ankles, and, to borrow his mild oath, be damned!

On the Sunday, he took her on a guided tour of much of the war torn capital, and she stared in awe at the great gaps where the rubble of bombed buildings had been cleared away, and at roofless, glassless shells of other ruins that bore testament to the assaults from the air. 'It's a while since we've had any heavy raids here. But I saw there was one up in your part of the world a few weeks ago. On York. Seems like Jerry's been going for our old, historic towns. Bath, York, Exeter. What on earth can be the military purpose behind that, eh?'

She stopped herself from commenting unpatriotically on their own efforts, and rumours of bigger and bigger bomber strengths being assembled for raids on Germany and its occupied territories. The allies, the Yanks, were very much in evidence nowadays, especially in the capital, where they wandered like uniformed tourists, with cameras at the ready despite official restrictions.

'Let's walk up the Mall to the palace,' Arty suggested, holding her arm in his as though he expected her to flee any second. And she had no intention of doing that.

'Oh, yes, that'll be great! Maybe we'll catch sight of the king and queen.' They didn't, but afterwards they rested in St James's Park, which was so full of people strolling they failed to find a bench to themselves.

'Grass is a bit damp for sitting,' he said apologetically, as though it was somehow his fault, and she smiled fondly.

'How about a café? I could do with a sit down somewhere.'

Again he started to apologize, and tenderly she stopped him in mid-stream. 'Look! I'm having the most marvellous time. It's been absolutely wonderful.' Her voice dropped a little, and she felt the colour on her cheeks. 'It's been so nice seeing you again. I wish . . . I didn't have to go back tonight. You've made . . . you've given me such a good time.' She smiled fondly at the way he glanced round before he hurriedly and clumsily kissed her quickly on the mouth.

At Waterloo, he eyed the surging masses of uniformed figures dubiously. 'Why don't you let me get you a first-class seat?'

'Don't be daft. I've got my Forces Special. Can't waste it. Anyway, I'd only get funny looks from your fellow officers! They think first-class is only for them. Not for lowly matelots like me!'

'You're neither of those things!'

She blushed and allowed him to manoeuvre her against an ugly, white-tiled wall out of the path of the streaming horde. He leant in close, and she put her arms up around his neck, felt their knees bump, his body press intimately against hers as their mouths met and stayed together as long as possible. 'I've had to wear garters,' she panted daringly. 'I don't think my suspenders will stand up to the strain.'

'You *do* know how I feel about you?' he implored, his fair skin pink with embarrassment and desperate need. 'I think you're the most marvellous girl I've ever known.'

'Oh yes? And just how long is the list?' she teased. She felt heady at the novelty of feeling in control, and excited by it. She pushed away the intrusive spectral thought of Luke Denby.

'Can I – I mean, is there any hope for me? That you could feel something?'

'I do. I like you very much,' she offered, and was confused by her own sudden uncertainty. 'Don't let's rush things.'

'We have to!'

The raw feeling in his voice shocked her. She knew he was referring to the terrible insecurity of the times they were living through. But she had a vivid sense of how his words applied very personally to her own life and the direction or misdirection she had taken. She stared at him, her eyes intent on his delicate features. She nodded. 'You're a very sweet boy. I'm very fond of you.'

They kissed once more, in their exclusive, private huddle, as the war and the world swept by them. 'I'm in love with you, Elsbeth.'

His words repeated in her head as he steered her through the barrier to the platform, and the packed train. She didn't bother looking for a seat, but stood, jostled in the corridor, gazing at him, putting a hand to her mouth and blowing him a last kiss as the train began to puff noisily out of the station. *In love?* Why hadn't he said, I love you, Elsbeth? Yet she took strange comfort from his clichéd phrase. Only one person in her brief adult span had told her she loved her, and it hurt too much to think about that.

CHAPTER TWENTY-TWO

It took them a long time to identify the body Davy had found in the smouldering ruins of the Baedeker raid. Not unnaturally, his immediate thought had been that this was another victim of Sandshoe Charlie. He was certain of one thing. No bomb had yet been invented which could strangle people to death, and those terribly distorted, discoloured features, as well as those deep, indented bruises at the front of her neck, indicated that strangulation had caused her death – or at least contributed significantly to it, along with that terrible blow to her skull. There was no doubt in his mind, or in those of the medical experts who examined her later, that she had been slain by deliberate and individual intent.

Davy had made a quick examination of the vicinity of the body as best he could with the aid of his torch to find any further clues relating to the corpse or the incident, but found nothing. No handbag, no clothing, no obvious signs of struggle, though given the environment in which she had been found – a building demolished by an air raid – the chances of discovering such clues were negligible. This done, he had then searched frantically for help, which he found in the form of a couple of ARP wardens nearer to the station where the main area of damage had been caused, and swiftly apprised them of the few facts, stressing that they should not allow anyone near the shed, while he hurried through to the railway police office to call his station and to set the official wheels in motion. It took a further hour before DI Holden and Sgt Baxter arrived on the scene.

'Good lad,' Holden told him, when he described briefly what he had done. 'You found nothing at all? You touched her?'

Davy explained that he had turned her over, to ascertain that she was indeed dead. 'There were a few bricks piled on top of her shoulders and back, as though someone had made some attempt to hide her. But then the body practically from the waist down was fully exposed. That's how I saw it – her –

I saw something pale in the darkness.'

'You sure she hadn't just been caught by a bomb? Was inside here when it hit?'

Davy was startled at the question, which seemed to him quite superfluous. Only later did he reflect that it was Holden's testing of his ability and observation that had prompted it. 'No, sir. There were just a few loose bricks dumped over her. You can see – there's far more rubble under her than there was on top. If she'd been here when this lot went up she'd be in a hell of a worse state than this.' He blushed, realizing how silly that sounded, and added feebly, 'Than the body is, I mean.'

Sgt Baxter was already chuckling. 'Aye, lad. I don't really think she could be much worse off, eh?'

'No, sergeant.'

'All right, Tommy. Get a couple of the lads in. Let's have a thorough scour of the place. I know it's in a mess, and I'm sure Brown here has not missed anything obvious. Start close in. Looks like a blouse or what's left of it she's wearing. And a vest. Her clothing might be around somewhere.' He nodded at the tumbled masonry and jagged, windowless walls around them.

'You think it's Charlie, sir?' Davy asked.

'Mustn't jump to conclusions, son.' He nodded down at the lifeless form. 'Some mad bugger, that's for sure. And he was after more than her purse. That bash on her head. That would be enough to do her in, judging by the amount of blood, without him throttling her. And see the marks on her legs, and on her behind? Some pretty rough stuff went on, and nothing to do with the raid, I'd say. We'll know more when the doc's had a proper look at her. Meanwhile, we've got to find out who the poor soul is. Everything's chaotic after the raid still. Be a while probably before we can check missing persons. You can start by contacting the AFS and ARP lot. See who was first on the scene last night. There's always a chance someone might have noticed something. A woman hanging about. Or a couple. Get started, Brown. Wilson, you go with him. Ask anyone else who was about – station staff, the transport boys.'

But all enquiries revealed nothing which could help them with identifying the body. Even when the casualty lists from the raid had been drawn up there were no people of either sex unaccounted for, and no reports of a missing female.

By the time Davy got back to his digs on Thursday afternoon, he was almost out on his feet, but he appreciated the fuss made by Reeny Lumley. Quickly she prepared a meal for him, and roused him from his seat in front of the range to eat it. While he did so she ran a hot bath for him. 'Don't lock the door, mind! I'll not have you drowning on me. Keep singing so's I'll know you're awake. I'd hate to have to come in and rescue you!'

'Promises, promises, Mrs L.'

'Watch it, my lad! You're getting as gobby as that roommate of yours. Go on, up you get, then get yourself into bed, before you fall down.'

'How about you? I'm sorry, I never even asked. How did you manage?'

'Well, we got a bit of a fright when the bombs started. No warning or anything. But we were straight into the shelter, as you know. And your pal came soon after you. You know how he goes on! I tell you, I began to wish a bomb would land, just to shut him up! But we were back in bed again not so long after midnight. And slept in this morning. Trust our Dick to be away for it all. George Mears got a message through to him, to let him know we're all all right. He'll be home late tonight. Unless the beggars come back again. Fingers crossed, eh? Now get up them stairs and get some rest!'

The pathologist's report confirmed the obvious conclusion that their unidentified victim had been murdered. The blow to the head, severe and disabling as it was, had not caused death. She had been killed by manual strangulation. There were no signs of any blast damage, or any other injuries resulting from the air raid.

'It's quite clear that she was not present in the shed when it was hit during the attack.' DI Holden announced to his squad. 'The contusions and scratches on the body were the result of an assault by someone, most likely part of a sexual assault. There was no indication that coitus occurred recently. By that we mean during the assault or during the hours prior to it. But there were signs – traces of semen around the pubis, the nature of the marks on the inner upper thighs, to indicate an attempt was made at sexual penetration.'

There was a kind of collective response, a sighing of breath, exchanged looks and nodding of heads. 'It's our boy again!' someone said firmly.

DI Holden waited patiently until the reaction had died down. 'Time of death estimated at just before or maybe even during the raid, but certainly before midnight. She'd been dead at least ten hours when PC Brown found her, at 8.25 a.m. Chances are the murder took place somewhere nearby, but not in the shed itself. The murderer could have lugged the body in there, but not from far away. Even in an air raid you wouldn't rate the chances of hauling a body undetected through the streets. There's plenty of places around the stables there where the attack could have taken place. Maybe he panicked when the raid started, dragged the body in the shed and legged it. He didn't have time to make a proper job of hiding her, but at least it gave him plenty of time – at least eight hours – to get away.'

'What would a woman be doing wandering about round there at night? Up to no good, I'd say.'

'Have we tried the local pros? One of them would know her, surely, if she was doing a turn?'

Tommy Baxter answered the speaker. 'We've made a few discreet enquiries so far. None of the regulars reported anyone missing.'

Holden took charge again. 'It's tricky, with all the confusion the raid's caused. Casualty lists are complete now. No females reported as missing. As for our Madam X, she's no virgin, but no traces of sexual disease, nothing to suggest she was on the game. She was in her early thirties, borne at least one child. Nothing to indicate she put up much of a fight, no blood or skin under her fingernails and so on, but we can't be sure. Mind you, once he'd bashed her head in – a stone or more likely a brick is the doc's favourite guess – she wouldn't be capable of doing anything. Even if he hadn't throttled her, she might well have died anyway. She was losing a lot of blood. Especially as he hid the body away where no one would find her for hours.'

'Good old Bulldog Brown!' someone called raucously. 'Sniff out a naked dolly anywhere – even if she *is* a stiff!' The burst of laughter was stifled by Holden's curt reprimand.

'Let's have some respect, eh? Read the report.' He flourished his copy. 'Discolouration and signs of indentation on the third finger, left hand. Suggests a ring was forcibly removed. Wedding? Engagement?' There was a further shuffling of feet, and suitably chastened looks. 'Brown and Bloomfield. Next step, you check on trains leaving York after 8 p.m. Wednesday. Destinations. We'll have to start checking, see if there's any female missing persons in any of them. Or anybody trying to offload a ring or other jewellery. Get round the jewellers, the usual fences.'

'What about the press, sir?'

'I've had a word with the locals. They've had enough on their hands with the raid. But they won't keep quiet much longer. And once the nationals get wind of it they'll be down on us like a ton of bricks. I'm thinking we might need the publicity, anyway, to track down the victim. *And* to put the fear of God into the womenfolk again. They've all but forgotten our Sandshoe Charlie. And now what we were afraid of has happened. At least the news might keep them from going out alone at night.'

It was a sentiment wholeheartedly supported by both Reeny Lumley and Alice's diminutive landlady. 'I daren't put me nose out the door after teatime!' Mary Douglas confessed readily. 'Eeh, I'm glad I've got your bonny lass with me, I can tell you!' she told Davy, who smiled propitiously across at Alice, lest the 'your lass' might disturb her. She went on yet again in fulsome praise of Alice's reassuring presence during the air raid. 'I don't know what me and the bairns would have done without her, bless her!'

It was Saturday evening, and Davy had just accompanied Alice home from work. Both Alice and Mary were avid for more news about the murder case, which had just been blazoned forth in lurid headlines in the *Evening Press* and in several national dailies. 'Why don't you show a picture of her? Someone might recognize her?' Mary asked.

Davy repressed a shudder as the all too vivid picture of her head came into his mind. 'We don't have one. Except for . . . well, the body. We couldn't show that.'

'Oh aye, of course not!' Mary declared, not understanding his real meaning. 'Wouldn't be right, would it?'

Unobtrusively, Alice went upstairs to change from her work clothes, and to take the opportunity to gather up towel and wash things. Dick Lumley had a rare weekend free, and Alice and Davy were babysitting for the Lumleys while they enjoyed a night out at the Engineers' Club, with some of their friends. 'Give you a chance to do a bit of courting, eh?' Reeny had grinned. 'Tell Alice she can have a bath if she wants.'

Alice had jumped at the chance, but she didn't want Mary to feel slighted. It wasn't as though Alice was embarrassed at the sociability of bathing chez Douglas. In fact, she quite enjoyed sitting, knees drawn up in the small zinc bathtub in front of the fire, while Mary companionably scrubbed her back for her, nor did she mind the long, cosy, intimate chats, while her toes wrinkled and the water cooled and Mary perched on the low stool and talked incessantly. She *was* slightly less at ease when the cosy circle of two was increased by the arrival of the six-year-old George and his three-year-old brother, their bright eyes curious and piercingly direct. The luxury of stretching out in a proper bathtub, in glorious solitude, was a chance not to be missed.

'We'll not be back before ten.' Reeny grinned and winked at Davy. 'Don't forget what I told the bairns. Be good!'

'As if I'd ever be anything else!' Davy quipped, but when the Lumleys had departed, there was an awkward moment as they gazed at each other, until Bob Noone came singing down the stairs, hair slicked and smart suited for his own evening's diversion.

'I'll hang on if you want me to scrub your back for you.' He, too, grinned at Alice, but in a different way from Mrs L. 'I know Davy's too much of a gent to offer, but I don't mind. I know what little girls are made of. And big 'uns, and all!' The grin was now a leer.

'You look very nice, Bob,' she countered. 'All dolled up. You look the business. You remind me of a film star.'

'Oh aye?' He waited, still smiling cockily, but warily.

'Aye. George Formby. Turned out nice again!'

'Needs a firm hand, does this lass of yours, Davy! Put a bit of colour in her cheeks, I would!'

'That right?' she called to his retreating back. 'You and whose army?'

There was another awkward pause as the front door closed, and they were alone, except for the two infants up in their beds. 'Everyone seems to have got it into their heads I'm your lass.'

'Do you mind?'

'Not if you don't, kidder. Come and light that geyser thing for me. I don't want to blow us all to kingdom come!'

'You can use my room, if you like,' he said, when the hot water was running, and over the hearty roar of the geyser. 'To change, or whatever.'

'Don't build your hopes up, sunshine! I've only brought my siren suit. Not exactly glamorous, I'm afraid.'

He strove to keep his tone light. 'Do you need any assistance, madam? How about Bob's suggestion?'

He saw her grey eyes turned directly on him. He felt himself reddening. 'Sorry. That was *infra dig*.'

'Was it?' Her eyes were still holding him. He recognized their hardening, defiant expression.

'A cheap shot. I'm sorry, Alice.' He blushed some more. 'Just turn that knob to stop the water. Shout if you need anything.'

She moved quickly, and very lightly put her left hand on his shoulder and quickly withdrew it. 'It's all right, mate. You go and put the kettle on. I won't be long. You'll be surprised how clean I scrub up.'

When she came down again, he was sitting at the kitchen table, the tea made, the pot cosied, the cups ready. She was towelling her curls, which were still darkened by the dampness. 'By! That was good.' She was barefoot, her face pink. She looked very young in the baggy suit.

'You look great. Shall I be mum?' He started to pour.

She took her place near him, picked at the loose sleeve of the top. 'I've had this ages. It's the one Beth . . . gave me.'

He noticed the pause, sensed the reluctance to pronounce the name. He was aware she had not meant to say it. In an effort not to make it significant, he said casually, 'Have you heard from her yet?'

'No. Not a word. Nothing since that note, nearly a month ago now. She'll be well into her training. Wherever she is.'

'Why not drop a line to her home address? They'll forward it to her.'

'Oh, I'm not much of a hand with a pen, as you well know. Not like you – and her. She's probably forgotten all about me by now.'

'I doubt that very much. She was very fond of you. You were very close, weren't you?'

She gave a short, hard laugh. 'Not any more!'

He could see the forced effort she made to be dismissive, and wisely decided not to probe any further.

'We haven't missed Vera Lynn's show, have we? Look at us, sat round the fire, me with my hair drying, dressed like this. You in your shirtsleeves. Cups of tea, listening to the wireless. We're like an old married couple.'

'Tell me when it's time for bed!' The words came out involuntarily, and the smile which followed was painful.

She looked at him, and her eyes this time were large and full of sadness. 'Don't, Davy!' she whispered huskily, her voice pleading, and he apologized once more.

CHAPTER TWENTY-THREE

Bob Noone was drafted in as part of the team putting in some overtime by sifting through the ruin of the stable store, piece by piece and brick by brick, searching for any clue which might lessen the mystery of the crime. It paid off, after three dusty, grumbling days of searching on hands and knees, when they found a half brick near the top of the heap of rubble in a corner of the building's shell. It was heavily crusted with dark, dried blood, and a forensic expert quickly confirmed that he believed it to be the makeshift weapon which had inflicted the blow to the victim's skull.

'So, she was alive when she was brought into the shed, and that was most likely after it had been damaged by the bomb. There's a crater only a few yards from the building, and the explosion blew off the roof, and a good section of two of the upper walls, most of which collapsed inwards. If our couple had been in there when it happened, there's very little chance either of them would have escaped, or come out unscathed.' Holden looked round at his select audience. 'But there's not a trace of anything else to help us. Not a stitch of clothing, not even a fag end. So what *do* we know?

'More about the perpetrator than the victim, I'd say. I'll stake my pension on it being the same bloke who attacked the three others – Sandra Robinson, Anne Wright, and Margaret Collier. From the descriptions all three gave, the clothes et cetera, the old mac, the balaclava, the mittens, it was our Charlie all right who had a go at them. Except that up to just after Christmas, all he was after was handbags. Poor old Mrs Lewis, the OAP, took a nasty fall, and it set her heart condition off. But it was only because she wouldn't let him have her bag. She held on to it, and he gave her a mighty shove. But he didn't hang about, he took off as fast as he could. And after that there was a bit of a pause. I must admit I thought our Charlie was suffering from a dose of bad conscience, and not before time. After all, Mrs Lewis got quite a lot of attention in the Press.

'Then in March we get our last three. And the prime motive in each case is sexual. All three victims young – the oldest 33. All right, he robbed them as well – old habits die hard, eh? But he wasn't only after money. And what's the one other thing the attacks all have in common?' He looked around, waiting for an answer.

When no one else volunteered, Davy cleared his throat and spoke out, despite his feeling that he was stating the obvious. 'They all failed. I mean, he didn't get what he wanted, sir.'

'You might well be right, lad. If you go back over those three cases, the interviews with all three victims, you find none of them was raped. And yet in all three cases he could have done. He had time and opportunity to do it. Brown here found Sandra Robinson a good ten to fifteen minutes after the assault, with Charlie well out of the way. No one else had heard a thing. The Robinson girl described how she struggled with him, how he interfered with her, how he knocked her about and kicked her. Then he just took off. Ran for it.

'Mrs Wright, the woman attacked up by Micklegate Bar, just across from the Windmill, where she was going to meet her husband – she reckoned it was five minutes or more after Charlie had run off before anyone found her. And by her own admission she didn't put up much of a fight. "I was too frightened", she said.

'And Margaret Collier, the other Rowntree's lass. She was petrified, hardly struggled when he pulled her off Lendal and down to the riverside. Stripped her and tried to have intercourse with her. She was weeping and begging him not to hurt her, but she didn't put up a fight. He was on top of her, then suddenly he started cursing and punching at her before he ran off down the towpath. From the description she gave of the assault, it's fairly clear that Charlie is impotent. To put it crudely, he can't get it up.' He stared round at them, challenging them to snigger or make some uncouth comment. Though several pairs of eyes avoided contact with his, everyone kept silence.

'I think he tried again with our murder victim, and this time his rage got the better of him. He lost his rag completely. Instead of beating her up, he smashed her head in and throttled her. He likes hurting and terrifying women, does our Charlie. But he can't get what he really wants, and that's to have sex with them.'

There was another long, shuffling, coughing silence, before Tommy Baxter took up the theme. 'Interesting point. We thought he might be targeting Rowntree's lasses, but I think it's just a case of there's a lot of them about.' His comment eased the tension, and there were a few grateful laughs.

'One thing worth noting. Margaret Wright was attacked by Micklegate Bar. Top of Station Road. Not so far from the station and the yards, the stables. We want all the beat bobbies keeping their eyes peeled. Our Charlie's crossed the line now. He's mebbe got his biggest thrill. Taken someone's life. We've got to stop him before he decides he wants to do it again.'

Dave Wilson, the detective constable Davy had been working with, said, 'We've no evidence as yet, sir, that Charlie is our man.'

'Except for the fact that our corpse was definitely roughed up and her killer tried to have his wicked way with her, and failed. Just as Charlie's done three times already!' Sgt Baxter ended scathingly.

'You're right, son,' Holden answered reasonably. 'No hard evidence. First and foremost, we still need to find out who Madam X is. Seems increasingly unlikely she's local. So, you and Brown get back to your list. Chivvy the coppers at all those stations, get on to them again. See if they've come up with anything that could remotely fit in with our lady. *Somebody* must know her. And she's been missing, what? Five nights, and at least four days now. To work, lads!'

That night a letter arrived at the North Yorkshire Constabulary HQ. Though it was not addressed to any individual, it very swiftly found its way to DI Holden. It was a single sheet of cheap lined paper torn from an exercise book. It read simply: 'Check for Mrs Helena Duckworth, 15A Darwin Grove, Beeston, Leeds.'

A telephone call to Leeds police brought the news that no person of that name had been reported as missing. The inspector politely refused a friendly offer of help. Davy was woken, via an alarmed Reeny, by a bicycle-clipped special constable from Tower Street around seven in the morning, with orders for him to report in as soon as possible. A rather bleary-eyed, hairnetted Mrs L, in dressing gown and slippers, tried to insist she should cook him breakfast.

'No, it's fine, honestly. I'm still half asleep. I'll get something in the canteen when it opens.'

'It'll be this blooming murder, I suppose?'

He nodded. 'I guess so. Something must have come up. Bit of a flap on.'

'I wish we could get a telephone in. It'd be really useful, not just for you and Bob. For Dick as well.' She yawned, her hand delicately covering her mouth. 'Sorry. Don't worry. Time I was up anyway. Got to get our Micky up for school soon. Take care.'

DI Holden was waiting at Tower Street. Dave Wilson arrived a short while after Davy, and they were both called in to the inspector's office. He showed them the note and its envelope. 'Post mark York. Night before last. Could be a complete waste of time, some joker wanting to give us the run around, old score to settle, but you never know. I want you two to check it out. Be as discreet as you can. Find out if this is our Madam X. Be careful. If it is, it's bloody odd that no one's reported her missing. Don't give the game away. See if you can get a look at a photo of this Duckworth woman. Spin a yarn, see how the land lies.' He handed a warrant over to Wilson. 'Here's a chit for travel. I'm afraid we can't spare a car. Train at 8.30. If you run you should just make it. Good luck, lads. We'll keep our fingers crossed. Phone in if there's anything tricky – or if you get a result. I'll be here, or Tommy will be.'

They made the 8.30. Two hours later they had tracked down Darwin Grove in the intersected forest of humble terraced dwellings of Beeston. The A after the 15 owed its existence to the fact that two of the Victorian in-off-the-street houses had been knocked into one, and divided into two flats, an upper and a lower. 15A stood at the terrace end, and its entrance lay up a short flight of iron stairs, with a tiny railinged balcony before its front door. 'You do the talking, mate,' Dave Wilson grinned. 'Good practice for you. Besides, your posh voice'll put the fear of God into them!'

The woman who answered their knock was a short, square, grim-faced individual, with wisps of grey hair showing beneath her headscarf. There was no need for an accent to instil fear. It was already there, stamped into her heavily lined features as soon as she caught sight of the two strangers, intimidatingly dressed in jackets, collars and ties, standing at her doorstep. Davy was startled at the degree of her alarm, and smiled reassuringly. 'Good morning, madam. Could we speak to Mrs Helena Duckworth, please?'

'Who are yer? Wod yer want? She's not here.'

'We're from York Police, madam. It's very important we contact someone who knows Mrs Duckworth. You know her, madam?'

Davy grew even more alarmed at the pallor which spread over the rather florid countenance. She gave a kind of muffled whimper. A work-worn hand rose to her throat. 'Oh God! What's happened? Is she all right? Has she been hurt? I haven't seen her since . . . since last Wednesday. She should've been back by now.'

'Look, can we come in, er. . . ? We might have some bad news. You are?'

'Deighton. Lily Deighton. I'm her mam. For God's sake! I've told her time and time no good would come of it. Oh God!' She began to sniffle, lifting the corner of her grubby, flowered pinny to her nose. 'Come in. You'll have to forgive the mess, like. I wasn't expecting company. Come into the front room.'

The small room had that unused, Sunday air, and smelt of dust and soot. A fire was laid, unlit, in the mall grate. 'Please mister, tell us what's wrong. *Is* it to do with the air raid? Has she been hurt? If that bugger's caused any harm to fall her—'

'Oh aye?' Dave Wilson jumped in with brutal quickness. 'What bugger's that then?'

'I never wanted her – I told her she should put a stop to it. To *him*! I warned her. And now her work's been after her. She's missed that many shifts chasing after him. . .'

'Who?' Dave Wilson demanded aggressively, and Davy shot him a reproachful glance.

'Sit down, Mrs Deighton. We need to explain. First of all, have you a picture of your daughter? A photograph? A fairly recent one?'

Her lips were quivering, the tears spilling from her wrinkled eyes. She glanced round, and Davy saw a framed wedding picture standing on the sideboard. 'May I?' He reached out for it, studied the bride, dressed in traditional white, dark hair showing beneath the white headdress. He tried to superimpose the timidly smiling young woman's face over the hideous features of the corpse he had found. They could be one and the same. He held it towards his partner, who studied it equally carefully, before nodding. 'It's her, I reckon.'

'Tell me what's happened? Is she . . . ?' Mrs Deighton was too afraid to complete her sentence, preferring the unfinished uncertainty.

'Please bear with us,' Davy said, compassionately. 'Any more snaps? Holidays, maybe?'

Frantic now, she opened the sideboard doors beneath the twin drawers, scrabbled, pulled out a small album. 'Here. There's loads in there. Her as a kiddie, then near the back . . . a holiday trip they had, to Scarborough, just before Eddie, her husband, joined up.' She flicked the stiff pages with trembling fingers, found the shots of the grinning, pretty, dark haired girl, in a bathing suit, with an infant struggling to escape from her lap. He studied the lean features, the slightly prominent long nose, envisioned again the twisted mouth, the bugged eyes. Yes. He was almost sure.

At his elbow, Wilson said impatiently, 'It's her, man. Got to be.' He turned to the distressed figure in the pinny and headscarf, and thick stockings and scuffed shoes. 'What was she doing in York, your daughter? Why haven't you reported her missing?'

Mrs Deighton gave a groan and burst into a loud wailing. She sank onto the edge of an old armchair, her gnarled fists clenched on her lap, gently swaying backwards and forwards. 'What's happened to her, for God's sake? Is she hurt bad? I'm her mother, for God's sake!'

Davy crouched beside her, put a hand on her shoulder. He spoke softly, his voice full of compassion. 'Mrs Deighton. We think your daughter Helena might have been a casualty. We found a body, on Thursday morning, after the raid. Not far from the station.'

She gave a loud cry, and stared at him, her eyes pleading, full of tears. 'Oh God! No! Not dead, is she? Please God, no!' She slumped suddenly, her head down, her shoulders heaving as the sobs racked through her. 'I told her! Told her she should put a stop to it. To *him*, the wicked swine. We had a terrible row about it. Before she went off, last . . .' Her voice choked, and the low sobs shook through her again.

Davy stayed kneeling by her, his hand resting still on the heaving shoulder. He wanted to say we're not sure yet. It might not be her. But the more he looked at the smiling figure on the sand at Scarborough the surer he was that it was the woman he had found. 'Look, can I get you something? Maybe a cup . . .'

Dave Wilson was not so patient. 'Who's the feller you're on about? The *wicked swine*? Someone through in York?'

She raised her face, suffused with colour, glistening with tears. 'If she hadn't been carrying on she'd never have been through there. Seeing him. She'd never have been caught in the bombing.'

'She wasn't. Leastways, it wasn't the raid that did for her. She was strangled to death.'

Mrs Deighton stared, open mouthed, her expression one of utter disbelief, and Davy's muscles tensed in disgust with his colleague at his lack of feeling. 'Hold on a minute, Dave,' he said, but Mrs Deighton gave a kind of horrified snort, thrust herself upright, her eyes wild.

'You what? He's killed her? You've got him, have you?'

'Who?' Dave pursued relentlessly, and she screeched her answer back at him.

'*Him*! Her fancy man, the feller she's been carrying on with! Running around with for the past year, nearly! While our poor Eddie's out there in the desert, been away fighting for his country for two year. Leaving me to look after little Malcolm, while she leaves everything, traipsing off with him, staying away night after night. Well, just make sure he swings for it! The rope's too good for his sort!'

The hysterical anger flowed from her, and she collapsed, sank back in the chair, crying noisily, her face buried in the pinafore she held before her. Davy gave another glare at his companion before moving back across the narrow passage to the kitchen, where he filled a kettle, lit the gas ring and searched for tea and pot. He heard Wilson's belated, gruff efforts at sympathy. 'Come on now, luv. Pull yourself together. We need some questions answered, quick like, if you want us to catch him.'

At least his words had the effect of breaking through the wall of her grief. She gaped at him once more. 'You haven't got him? I thought you said—'

'We don't even know who you're on about, missus. So, come on. Start at the beginning and tell us everything.'

It was a considerable time before they had the means to piece her story together, and they had all supped several cups of the weak tea Davy had made before they were done. Eddie Duckworth had been away in the army since 1940, sent to North Africa, then to Greece, Crete, and back to the desert again. They had a son, Malcolm, who was now nearly seven. 'I see far more of him than his mother does,' Mrs Deighton told them. 'She got a job in the aircraft works at Yeadon, more than a year ago. She didn't have to, but she was all for it, and she had muggins here to look after the bairn. Not that I minded. I love him, bless him.' She broke down again at this point. 'I'm all he's got now, God love him! Except his dad, and God knows when he'll get back!' Davy gave his partner a warning look as he saw Wilson's mouth open for another impatient protest, and it closed again, unwillingly.

She resumed her sad tale after a few weeping moments. 'She met this bloke last year. He was through working at the factory, doing something, I don't know. They were installing some machinery. According to our Helena he's some engineer or summat. He started taking her out for drinks. He had digs somewhere over Yeadon way. Then it got nearly every night, then she started stopping out. Supposed to be on night shift herself, some of the time!' She sniffed in eloquent scepticism. 'Turns out of course that the bugger was married himself, with a wife and a kid somewhere near York. I don't know where,' she said. 'I was never that interested. All I wanted was for her to stop seeing him. I don't know his name or nowt about him. But even after he went back to York, they met up. She'd go through to see him, stay over somewhere. I thought that's what had happened this time. That's why I've been waiting. Why I didn't go to t'police or 'owt. I kept thinking she was just stopping through there with him. She's been right daft about him. Got worse the more it's gone on.' Her vehemence ran down, she sagged back in her chair again, then stared up in ruinous puzzlement. 'But if you haven't caught him, if you don't even know his name, how the heck have you got here?'

They told her about the anonymous note. 'Could we have a look through her room, missus? Search around a bit? We might find something, a clue, like.'

They found nothing that would help to trace the unknown adulterer. They left a stricken Lily Deighton to her grief and the grim prospect of her having to make a journey through to York at police expense to make an identification of her daughter. That anonymous note had firmly crushed any hope of the body being anyone other than Helena Duckworth.

When they were on their way back to the railway station, Davy said, 'Surely they could find some other relative to make the identification? Having to see her own daughter like that?' He still could not rid himself of the mental vision of that terrible face.

'Oh, I wouldn't worry, mate,' Wilson said with callous indifference. 'Them co-op undertakers can work wonders. Probably make the lass look like a fillum star when they've finished with her.'

CHAPTER TWENTY-FOUR

The sensation of the German raid on York continued to vie with Helena Duckworth's murder for attention in local minds during the month of May, as the funerals of the eighty victims of the bombing took place, and the 'miracle' of the survival of the Minster was emphasized. The picture of the slim, youthful bride appeared in the local papers, and one or two of the national dailies, along with her name and address, together with an urgent request from the police that a local man who 'may have been in touch with us already' should contact them again to help with their inquiries, and that any information he might be able to supply would be 'dealt with in the strictest confidence'.

Sandshoe Charlie remained their chief suspect, though one or two entertained some speculative doubts. 'Could have been her lover boy,' Dave Wilson offered at the morning briefing the day after Mrs Deighton had made her formal identification. It was rumoured that the husband, Private Eddie Duckworth, was to be brought home on compassionate leave, but thus far there had been no sign of him, and they wanted to get things moving. 'Mebbe she'd took notice of her mam's warnings and told him she was jacking it in. Mebbe he's a crafty sod. Took advantage of the raid and made it look like our Charlie did her in.'

DI Holden was unimpressed. 'Too clever – and too risky. Hide the body or chuck it in the river. Much easier. I still think he's the one who sent us the note. Must have been worried when he didn't hear from her. Then when he read about the murder, it must have clicked straight away.'

'But then why bother to tell us who she was?' Dave Wilson queried in genuine puzzlement. 'I mean he'd just keep quiet, say nowt. It doesn't make sense.'

DI Holden grimaced. 'Well, just maybe, he had a smattering of conscience left. Maybe he really did have some genuine feeling for her. It does happen, Wilson, believe it or not.' His last sentence, heavy with irony, earned a few cheers at Wilson's expense.

Davy was ashamed of the disloyal thought that he should not be discussing the case with Alice. 'Listen, don't say anything about any of this at work – or to Mary Douglas,' he added, and then felt doubly ashamed at her accusing look. 'I haven't told anybody, not even Mrs L. Even Bob doesn't know the ins and outs of it all.'

'P'raps you shouldn't be telling *me* then!' she said challengingly, staring very directly at him. 'If you don't think you can trust me. I can keep secrets if I have to.'

'I know. Sorry, Al.' He moved penitently towards her and caught hold of her hand. She didn't return his grip, just let her hand hang in his.

'Don't call me that!' she said sharply. 'I'm not a lad.'

'I'm well aware of that!' His tone was astringent, too. He released his hold on her, and just for an instant derived a mean satisfaction from seeing the colour mount as she clearly understood his meaning. 'I thought you liked it,' he added, with a touching air of sulkiness.

Her expression remained hard. 'That was a long while back. I've grown up a bit now.'

True, Davy thought, but kept his reflections to himself. He was being unfair. He was doing the very thing he had promised himself he would not do. Alice had been here just over a month now. He had so looked forward to her coming, been delighted at having her so close, so much a part again of his daily living. Scarcely a single day had gone by without his seeing her at some point. They had spent evenings together, weekends when he was free, had explored the old city together, shared the terror of the raid. They had even enjoyed the warm comfort of the Lumleys' firelit kitchen in splendid isolation, child minding while Reeny took the chance to visit her family or to have a night out with friends or, occasionally, with her husband. They had held hands in the smoke filled darkness of the pictures – she had allowed that, if nothing else. He felt his bitterness rise, and the shame again that came with it. What had he told her, and written to her, before she committed herself to the move he so longed for her to make? 'I promise I won't make a nuisance of myself.'

He hadn't. At least he hoped he hadn't. But was she really aware of how difficult it was for him, not to tell her, or show her, how he *really* felt? Why was it she could not respond to those feelings? Their friendship was so strong, so firmly planted after all the time they had known each other at Howbeck. She had shown such kindness to him, been such a stout defender of his right to his pacifist viewpoint. All along he had clung to his hope that one day that friendship would develop, transform into something even tenderer, more binding.

'I can't be doing with all that.' Her phrase had stuck with him, kept recurring every time he thought about the possibility of their love. It had even been part of her attraction for him, that careless disregard of matters sexual and the artifices of femininity that was part of her ingenuous honesty. He had told himself that it had something to do with her background, humble and 'rough and ready', as she was so keen to describe it. He had even hoped, in all humility, that she might come to learn tenderness and sensual love through his example and guidance.

His hopes had soared at her sudden acceptance of his proposal that she should move to York, and her apparent willingness that their lives should be so closely allied once more. But in the weeks which had followed, he had been forced to dwell on some painful inner thoughts. The reason for her abrupt decision to come here had clearly had its roots in the emotional outburst on the High Tops during his visit to Howbeck. They had never discussed it; sensitively attuned to her as he was, he respected her reluctance to do so. It was one of those things he had reassured himself would be resolved later. But it had remained painfully in his mind. The depth of loss she felt at Elsbeth Hobbs's departure had confused him, despite all his attempts to rationalize it. He could not forget how he had held her in his arms, felt her whole body shaking, racked with despairing grief as she lay helpless in his embrace. Now the recall of such passionate grief disturbed him, the notion of such intensity. Why couldn't she feel with that same intensity for him?

May ended on a note of optimism on the warfront, at least for the majority of people at home. The first thousand-bomber raid took place on Cologne, and 'serve 'em jolly well right, too!' was the general righteous reaction. And the British government signed a twenty-year mutual aid agreement with Soviet Russia, who was still putting up a gallant resistance on the eastern front, and whose bluff leader was being transformed rapidly from former demon to jovial 'Uncle Joe'.

On the smaller and more local level, the efforts to solve Helena Duckworth's murder were yielding slow progress. The widower, despite his desert tan and khaki uniform, looked beaten and too bemused to cut a heroic or even angry figure when he appeared at the police HQ in York. He had not even made it home in time for his wife's burial. They actually managed to spare a car to take him back to Beeston – he was staying at his mother-in-law's – and Davy and Wilson accompanied him back there. There was an ulterior motive. Enquiries were laboriously going ahead to investigate the backgrounds of all the migrant and subcontracted workers at the Yeadon aircraft factory, to locate the 'fancy man', so far without success. 'Just a matter of patience,' Holden told his subordinates. 'That's what detective work is all about.'

They had said little of this to Private Duckworth, who had in any case seemed apathetic about the whole business. 'I think *I'd* be a bit more upset if it was *my* missus,' asserted Dave Wilson critically, out of the widower's hearing.

'He's just learnt that she was having an affair, practically since he went overseas. I think that's probably knocked him for six.'

'It's his missus who should have been knocked for six!'

Davy stared at him. Dave's thick skin could still sometimes surprise him. 'I think she was!'

But still Wilson succeeded in startling him when, as they dropped the soldier at the end of Darwin Grove, the detective leant out of the car and bellowed cheerfully, 'Enjoy the rest of your leave, mate! Make the most of it, eh?'

DI Holden had put out several carefully worded appeals in the *Evening Press* for their mystery informant to get in touch with them. He was convinced that it was the adulterer himself, and not someone who simply knew about the affair. 'No reason for them to keep quiet and give nothing else away, if it's not her lover.' He had tried in these subsequent press statements to imply that even the identity of the informant might be kept secret, but still his efforts so far had borne no fruit.

The greatest fear was that Charlie would strike again. 'Like a bloody unexploded bomb!' Tommy Baxter observed.

But then, six weeks to the day since the raid, there *was* progress, and it was spectacular. Davy had just completed the two-minute journey from Cook Street to his own digs. His thoughts as so often nowadays were oppressive and were not concerned with work or with the fate of the late Helena Duckworth. Alice had seemed listless and 'down'. She sprawled before Mary's kitchen range, the fire still burning despite the warmth of the June evening, in order to supply the heat for the oven and the hot water. She had eaten her tea, had not bothered to wash but reclined in slacks and green overall, curls a dark tangle, stockinged feet stretched towards the glow of the coals in the high grate. Mary's wheezing, cackling tones dragged on and on incessantly, except when interrupted by her mewling infant, the younger of the two children, and Alice seemed content just to slump there and listen, throwing in an occasional comment, or to relate some inane event which had taken place at work. Davy felt excluded, and, more hurtfully, felt that Alice didn't care. She would rather sit there and indulge in the trivial chatter with the tiny woman who, quite frankly, was getting on his nerves. Another seriously black mark against Mary was that she had been responsible for Alice's starting smoking, and the two of them filled the kitchen with the pungent swirls of their Woodbines as they talked.

He had remonstrated with Alice in private about the habit, which he deplored. Of course, he realized he was very much in the minority in his objection to cigarettes, and was frequently reminded of how odd he was, especially by his work colleagues. Alice was no less tolerant of his singular behaviour. 'Listen. I used to smoke regular when I was at school, when I was twelve and thirteen. It's good for you, man. Even the doctors'll tell you! Calms the nerves. You should try it.'

'*I* don't need it! I don't need drugs and stimulants to keep *me* going!'

'What you on about? Who's talking about drugs? You'll be signing the pledge next! Here, you're not going back to that Holy Joe religion of yours you told me about?'

The light dismissiveness of her tone added to the hurtfulness of her comment. He had to struggle to keep silent, not to strike back at her. Suddenly he felt the distance between them, and it disturbed him greatly.

Alice's voice cut in on his sombre thoughts now. She yawned, rather theatrically. 'Listen, I think I'll have a wash and get off up to bed. You look as though you could do with an early night and all. You through at Leeds again tomorrow? Don't worry if you're late getting back. I guess I can survive going one whole day without seeing you! Come round Friday, if you're off.'

The diminutive Mary rose, flung her fag end into the fire and moved round behind Alice's chair. She leant over and put her hands on Alice's shoulders, squeezed her gently. There was something possessively intimate about the action. Davy was startled by the strength of his adverse reaction to it, and to the way Alice's left hand moved to close over Mary's thin fingers, in acceptance of it. 'Right! I'll leave you two to it then. Good night.'

He hurried out into the dim remains of the twilight. It wasn't yet nine o'clock. He was aware of the abruptness of his leave taking, and the uncomfortable atmosphere, and was certain Alice would be well aware of it, too. But then, why shouldn't she feel it? His cheeks were hot at the sudden vision of the two of them laughing and sniggering at the way he had marched out. You're like a spoilt kid, Brown! he reprimanded himself, but he couldn't get rid of his sense of injured innocence.

He was soothed by his landlady's warm sympathy, as though she were intuitively conscious of his sober mood but without the selfish curiosity to probe for its reason, and by the time he had sat and drunk yet another cup of tea in her calming presence, he was feeling much better. He was surprised by the sudden clatter of Bob Noone's arrival off duty and his hurried entrance into the kitchen. 'What's up?' He glanced at his watch. 'You're nearly an hour early. Villains all gone on strike, have they?'

'They sent me to tell you!' Bob answered eagerly. 'You're wanted down there, pronto, mate! They've got him. Charlie. He's in the cells at Tower Street right now. Somebody turned him in. It's over. They've got him!'

Davy's immediate impression when he eventually came face to face with Maurice Bramley was that no way could he have committed the murder, or the assaults on the other females. He was five foot five in height and his frame was so thin he looked scarcely more robust than Alice's landlady, Mary Douglas. In addition, his left foot was turned inward slightly, which gave him not a limp but a strange, unevenly loping gait. His face looked almost emaciated, his sallow skin marred by several fierce pimples; his big nose, aggrandized by the pinched face, seemed to be so frequently dew-dropped that it caused him to sniff, loudly and maddeningly, to punctuate every phrase he delivered.

He was just twenty-one. He had failed his medical at call-up, and worked part time as a porter at Bootham Park hospital. His mother was dead, his father had abandoned the family when Maurice was a toddler. Taken into care, he had been brought up in the workhouse, then left from his mid-teens to look after himself, until his sister, Aggie, two years his senior, in service in the city, had been impregnated by a young man named Bert Foulkes, who had fortuitously decided that the prospect of enjoying hectically pleasurable nights in bed with Aggie, free from interruption, was worth the price of matrimony. By the time she was twenty, Aggie was the mother of two, and Bert had decided that a soldier's life, while it might be 'terrible hard', was reasonably well paid, and with war threatening daily, it was, in one sense, a secure enough occupation. Plucked from the water at Dunkirk, Bert had swiftly been posted to North Africa, and Aggie had been glad to offer her brother a roof, humble as it was, covering two rooms, and a scullery, in a street off Bootham. The lavatory in the yard was shared with three other families. Aggie was happy. Maurice brought in a little money, and, more importantly, was able to look after her two youngsters while she went out cleaning and working at the hospital laundry.

She was usually too tired to worry about her brother's strange habit of disappearing for half or sometimes the whole of the blackout night, returning with the dawn, or his weirdly alarming appearance in the trailing ancient mackintosh and the black balaclava, and his fingerless mittens. 'You must give folk a terrible fright sometimes!' she chided affably, having little idea how right she was. Until the tales of 'Sandshoe Charlie' began to spread abroad.

She warned him he should be careful, but sometimes he handed over a sum of money which added considerably to their standard of comfort, and both of them were comfortable with her mild admonitions. Then old Mrs Lewis had her fall and her heart attack, and she warned him seriously to 'pack it in'. He swore to her that he had done so.

In March, when the assaults began, she was truly alarmed. She threatened first to inform the police, then to evict him, but he swore, tearfully in turn, that he was not responsible. The trouble was, he was still often missing half the night, and still thieving, or robbing. His contribution to the household economy was acceptable, though, even more so as Aggie had found herself a romantic attraction and distraction, which made shorter working hours even more desirable. She tried to put her fears out of her mind, telling herself that Maurice might be a thief, but he was not, could not, be an attacker of women.

After the terror of the raid, and then a few days later the even more frightening news of the murder, spread over the *Evening Press*, she tried desperately to cling to her belief in her brother's assurances of his innocence. But, significantly, he had not been with her during the air raid. She'd had to grab her two children and flee with other inhabitants of the street to the communal shelter. Maurice had not shown up until almost midday the following day. He was filthy and even more bedraggled than usual. His old mac was ripped at the sleeve, and there was blood from a long scratch on his left arm, staining the frayed shirt cuff.

He was nearly hysterical. 'It wasn't me! It wasn't me!'

She had striven so hard to believe him. Day on day she lived with it, wrestled with it. Then she read about Helena Duckworth, about her child, the husband home from the desert, the grandmother who insisted on looking after the little boy. The inspector said in the paper how important it was to catch the killer, that he was somebody obviously mentally ill, who had to be locked up, before he struck again.

When Maurice was out at work, she searched through his things, in the untidy corner where he slept on a battered bed-settee. The mac, the woollen balaclava, the mittens, the frayed sandshoes: they had all been bundled up, hidden in the innards of the bed-settee. There was no sign of the shirt, but there were spots of blood on a dirty shoe, and on the torn sleeve of the raincoat. She thought of the picture of the young bride she had stared at in the paper, the little boy, the bewildered soldier husband. She thought of her Bert, at danger like this poor man in the paper, maybe even a comrade of his, in the desert. Bert had done the right thing by her. He still sent her money – not much it was true, but it came, every month. And here she was, betraying him, letting someone have what she had no right to give. She belonged to Bert, just as that poor Duckworth woman had belonged to *her* man. Well, there was one way she could make up for the sin she had committed, and maybe save some other poor soul into the bargain. Weeping silently, she grabbed her coat and pulled it round her, hurrying out before she should change her mind.

CHAPTER TWENTY-FIVE

Even Inspector Holden seemed uncharacteristically inclined to go along with the general air of euphoria that pervaded the department. Davy found himself with a familiar sense of isolation in his deep-felt doubts of Maurice Bramley's guilt. 'God! Davy, lad! It's as plain as the snotty nose on Charlie's face! He's as guilty as sin. His own sister's the one that's shopped him. You're telling me she doesn't know her own brother? What he's been up to? She says he was out all night the night of the raid, that he was wearing his gear and that he had blood on his clothes.' Wilson shook his head in disgust at Davy's intransigence. 'You're just being bloody awkward for awkward's sake. What's wrong with you? A couple more days and we'll have a confession out of him,' he declared confidently. 'He's ready to crack any minute.'

'That's another thing,' Davy argued. 'He's retarded. Not all there. He's scared out of his wits and doesn't know what he's saying half the time.'

'Of course he's scared out of his wits! Because he knows the game's up. Probably putting on that daftie act cos he's trying to avoid the rope! Fat chance!'

DI Holden listened more sympathetically to Davy's reservations, when he had the chance to express them to his superior in private. 'He hasn't got the temperament for that kind of violence, sir. He's hardly got the physique, come to that.'

'You can't judge everything by appearances, Brown,' Holden countered reasonably. 'I've seen some villains who looked as though a breath of wind would blow them over, carve out a regular bloodbath. And what about the sister's statement? The blood on the shirt he got rid of?'

'He could be telling the truth when he said he went out thieving when the bombs started. That place in Ropery Lane. It *had* been broken into. The back door had been forced.'

'Nothing to show he'd cut himself, according to the crime sheet. And you know what these tea leaves are like. He'd probably heard somebody talking. He had nothing to show for his night out, had he? He might even have been there, like he said. Before he ran into Helena Duckworth – or after. He might be a lot brighter than he's making out.'

But another ten minutes of sitting in on one of the brutal interrogations of the snivelling, sniffing suspect ensured that Davy remained entirely unconvinced that Bramley was the murderer. The trouble was, Davy thought sombrely, Wilson was right, damn him. The poor, lost, inadequate soul was so bemused, and so weary, and so afraid of the aggressive captors who bawled and bullied and threatened physical violence that he would soon confess to anything to end the persecution. British justice? Davy wondered bitterly how many dubious confessions were elicited under similar conditions.

Davy renewed his acquaintance with Sandra Robinson, when he was detailed to escort her to a so-called identity parade, which consisted of the hapless Maurice flanked by two smiling members of the force. In spite of their civilian clothing, their confident direct gaze ahead proclaimed loudly that the woebegone figure between them was the felon-in-the-middle. Sandra, a pert young lady now, dressed for the part and her lips reddened with the beet juice which substituted for lipstick, gave every indication that the attack which had taken place four months ago had left no permanent mark on her lively personality, while the slightest hint of a tilt in the alignment of her nose took nothing from her vivacious prettiness. Davy could not help but be lifted by her warmth of greeting, and the appreciation he discerned in her brown eyes.

She peeked through the door of the inspector's room at the trio lined up in the outer office and shook her head doubtfully. 'He looks a bit small,' she offered uncertainly. They made him dress in Sandshoe Charlie's props: the mac and balaclava and mittens, but only succeeded in eliciting a tentative, 'Could be, I suppose,' for which Davy silently blessed her.

But it was the married woman, Anne Wright, the cinema cashier and wife of the railwayman, who finally and firmly quashed any hope of an early conviction. In total contrast to the weeping, terrified figure she had presented on the night of her attack, she insisted on marching boldly close to Bramley in the line-up, thrusting out her proud bosom almost under his damp nose, and declaring roundly, 'Naw! No chance! Not him! Could have been *'im,*' pointing at one of the policemen, 'but definitely not the one in the middle!' She explained more fully when she was back in the inspector's office behind closed doors. 'Too little. That feller couldn't've grabbed me and got on me the way Charlie did.' She stuck her impressive chest out once more. 'That poor thing in there would get lost under this lot!'

The pathologist brought further grief to those who wished to bring a firm charge against Bramley. 'The measurements and size of the neck wounds suggest that it would be difficult for someone with Bramley's hand span to have strangled her.'

'Give us a bit longer, sir! Just a few more goes at him!' Wilson pleaded, and, for a while, Davy was afraid that Inspector Holden was about to cave in to the pressure of Wilson and his ilk. In fact, he allowed the suspect to be held for one more day, during which his interrogators reduced Maurice to incontinent and incoherent sobbing, but not to confessing. Holden ordered his release, much to Wilson's vociferous disgust, though not in his boss's hearing. 'We'll have the snidy little bastard yet!' Wilson fumed. Wisely, Davy kept his relief and his thoughts to himself, but 'beyond reasonable doubt' had acquired a whole new meaning for him.

At the end of June, Class DIIIC came to the end of its twelve weeks of training. Elsbeth learnt that she had been successful in her request for entry into the communications branch and was posted to HMS *Mercury*, but not before a very welcome seven days' leave. She had spent another weekend with Arty Clark up in London, during the remainder of the basic training. She was happy to ascribe to him the semi-official title of 'boyfriend'. She could not help feeling immensely flattered by his declared love for her. His letters were passionate, though never beyond the bounds of decency, while the couple's amorous clinches during their brief meet-up were not really struggles. She was not as afraid as she had feared she would be, when her mind had dwelt on the dark events of that fateful assault on her innocence carried out in that grim little bedroom in Howe Manor. Luke Denby had paid the ultimate price for his conquest. That was how she saw it, in spite of all the logical protests of her brain at believing such nonsense. He had been wrong, done her wrong, though even that had sat uneasily on her conscience. She was the one who had changed her mind, who had finally invited him to come to her room and sat waiting for him like a slut, in that stupid silk underwear he had given her. It was too late when she had realized she did not want to go through with it, was terrified at the nightmare of surrendering her virginity to the young pilot. But she had not prevented him – had not fought against it.

And now Luke was dead. Not only because of that – but because of the far greater sin she had committed with Alice, with her true lover, night after night. Logic was helpless against her deep-seated conviction that her perversion had caused Luke's death, not his taking of her unwilling body.

Arty Clark loved her. He kept insisting it, eloquently on paper, and stammeringly sincerely in her ear. She strove hard to convince herself that she returned his love. She *was* fond of him; he was dearer to her than anyone, except her family. Still she had to keep pushing those intensely sweet, painful memories of Al – Alice! she corrected herself furiously – away from her. They could make her whimper softly to herself, no matter how much she tried to flee them. There was a certain desperation in her turning towards Arty, so that her need became as obsessive as his to put their relationship on an unshakable footing. She agreed to meet up with him at the end of her leave. She would cut short her stay at home, lie to them and return to the capital three days early. She was shaking, literally, as she wrote: 'Is there somewhere where we could be together? I mean, stay together? I want to be yours truly, as the letters say. Please don't be shocked, but I want to belong to you properly, and, as you say, time is precious, we can't waste it.'

Mary Douglas caught sight of herself in the narrow wall mirror of Alice's bedroom, and studied her reflection with new critical awareness, her hands on her prominently jutting hipbones, turning to one side then the other. 'God! I'm a skinny little bitch, aren't I? Not a picking on me! It nearly killed us having the kids! I'm not built for all that. I just hope our Terry doesn't want any more when he comes home.' She turned her gaze to Alice, who was sitting up in the single bed watching her. 'Anyway, I might be past it by then, eh? I'm nearly thirty.'

'You look more like thirteen. Specially like that! Stop flaunting yourself like one of them mucky magazines and get back into bed.' Alice held back the blankets and Mary eased herself into the tiny space and snuggled her naked body into Alice's. The narrowness of the bed necessitated the intimate entanglement of bodies and limbs, but neither objected.

'You're a wicked lass, you are, Alice Glass! And you've made me wicked and all! Eeh! What would that nice lad of yours say if he could see us?' The idea thrilled her and she gave a throaty giggle.

'It's nowt to do with him. Nowt to do with anybody but us.' Alice had spoken more strongly than she had intended. 'He's not saying much to anybody about anything these days,' she went on quietly. 'I think he's a bit upset about them not catching that Charlie feller. Or about them getting the wrong one. Funny business, that. Means the real killer's still around somewhere. Mind, Davy knew all along it wasn't that daft lad they picked up.'

'He's a clever lad, your Davy. A real gentleman and all. Speaks ever so nice. You met his folks yet?'

Alice gave a harsh laugh. 'You're joking, aren't you? They're real toffs. You can imagine what they'd make of me, eh?'

'He's mad about you. You could have him tomorrow – I mean proper like, wedding ring and all that.'

'I've told you umpteen times. It's nothing like that. We're just good mates. From when we were up in the dales.'

'Does he know about this? You know?' Mary's limp hair brushed Alice's shoulder as she ducked, squirmed closer, and her hands moved illustratively over Alice's warm flesh.

Alice gave a snort, caught a thin wrist, held it detainingly. 'Don't be daft! He'd have a fit if he did! Not that he'd ever believe it.'

'It takes *me* all me time!' Mary chuckled. 'You're wicked, you are. Thank God!' She wriggled again and clung like a limpet.

'Well, you're gonna have to do without me for a few nights,' Alice said. 'I'm off home on Friday. I've got a weekend off, and I haven't been home since I came here, nearly three months gone.' She lay back, enjoying the comforting feel of Mary's form wrapped so closely against hers, the warmth of her cheek, the soft whisper of her breath on her right breast. 'Do Davy good to have a break, as well as me. Time he found himself a *real* girlfriend. Know what I mean?' She returned Mary's hug. 'One that can give him what he wants.'

She felt Mary's head lift, her voice croaked in her ear. 'You can be a right hard little bitch at times, can't you?'

Alice sighed. 'I've had to be, Mary. Otherwise you just get kicked hard – where it hurts most.'

Alice was not familiar with the Biblical proverb which declared 'out of the mouths of babes and suckling . . .' but she recognized the innocence with which her little brother Algy, delighted to see her, announced, 'I saw Miss 'Obbs up at school today. She was in one of them lady sailor uniforms. She'd come to see Miss Laverton. She didn't see me, though.'

Alice felt it was not the best news to be greeted with almost as soon as she stepped through the door of 19 Maudsley Street, though she struggled hard to disguise the effect it had on her. The novelty of being back in the familial bosom for the first time in months helped to distract, but the consciousness that Beth was once more close could not be pushed aside, nor the fact that last time it had happened Alice's timidity and failure to act had meant that she had lost the opportunity to see her again. Unsure as she was, and unable to see what good could come of meeting her again, she was determined not to display cowardice a second time, and on Saturday morning, in bright sunshine, she headed off up Park Road, her stomach swirling and her heart pounding almost as loudly as her resolute steps. She fumbled with the latch of the wooden gate and almost ran up the path between the colourful flowerbeds, so that she would not lose her nerve and do what her muscles were urging – turn and flee. She was a little breathless when the door opened, and Mildred Hobbs stared politely, without recognition. 'Yes? Can I help you?'

'Hello. My name's Alice. Alice Glass. I heard Elsbeth's home.'

Elsbeth's father appeared, stepping into the porch and peering over his wife's shoulder. 'Alice? It's good to see you! How are you keeping? Everyone all right? How's that bright sister of yours? Still doing well, is she? Come to see Elsbeth? She's just about up, I think.' He laughed indulgently. 'Having a bit of a lie-in. She just got back a couple of days ago. Just finished her basic training. Come in, I'll give her a shout. I think she's in the bath.'

Mrs Hobbs was far more restrained, but she ushered Alice into a large drawing room, whose bay window looked out onto the front garden. Her husband was already calling upstairs. 'Elsbeth! Someone here to see you, love! You'll never guess!' He came into the room to chat. Alice refused his offer of coffee or tea, which had not come from his wife, who had made an excuse and left. A few endless minutes later, Elsbeth came into the room. She was wearing a pale lilac, quilted dressing gown, and her short yellow hair, crimped in metal curlers, was hidden in a silk, knotted turban. Her clear face was devoid of make-up, and Alice felt her breath caught by that familiar beauty.

A tide of colour swept up the slender neck, engulfed the flawless countenance. The blue eyes, caught in Alice's intense stare, were large with vulnerable helplessness, then they flickered away from contact, fixed somewhere around Alice's shoulder. 'Oh, hullo, Alice. Long time no see, eh?'

She made a jerky move forward, and Alice thought she was coming to embrace her, and her own muscles tightened, her hands half rose to anticipate it, but the slim figure stopped. They faced each other several feet apart. 'I meant to write. They keep us pretty busy. How have you been keeping? Still at the Big House?'

Alice could hardly speak against the clogging restriction of her throat, and her voice came in a husky half-whisper. 'I left not long after you did. I'm in York. Working there.'

'Ah! With Davy Brown?'

Now it was Alice's turn to blush. 'I see quite a lot of him, yes. I live not far from him.'

'I'll leave you two girls to catch up on the news.' Mr Hobbs left them alone.

Alice moved involuntarily, taking a step towards Elsbeth, who stiffened. All at once the atmosphere was stifling. Alice swallowed hard, blinked back the stinging tears. 'I had to see you,' she said helplessly. She glanced around at this strange, luxurious room, as though she were trapped. 'Can we go somewhere? Get out of here? I have to talk to you.'

'I don't want a scene.' Elsbeth's face was white now. She looked frightened. 'I don't know what there is to say.'

'Please! Just half an hour. Surely you can spare me that much time?'

'All right. Just give me five minutes. I'll put some clothes on.'

CHAPTER TWENTY-SIX

'You look different with your hair short. Nice though,' Alice added swiftly. 'Waved like that.' Most of it, except for a curl or two at the brow, was hidden by a soft felt cap, with a large peak.

'It's easier to manage. They don't like long hair in the service.'

It felt strange to Alice not to be linking arms as they walked the short distance to the park and passed though the gateless pillars to the wide stretch of grass, and the paths between the green, mid-summer trees. They headed past the pond, and the long embankment of the air raid shelter, to the rose garden. 'I'm surprised they haven't turned it over to spuds and cabbages!' Alice made a brave attempt at humour, despite the heaviness in her chest. She moved towards an empty bench and sat, Elsbeth following. 'You look different,' Alice repeated quietly. 'More grown up. As lovely as ever, though.'

'Don't.' Beth was staring straight ahead, avoiding looking at her.

Alice watched the colour mounting up the slender neck, the pinkness of the face, and felt the ache of loss and loving so painfully she was afraid the tears might spill over. 'I've missed you so much. You should have written. Let me know where you were. How you were getting on. You don't know what I've been going through, Beth. It was wrong of you to do that to me . . . after everything.'

'No! What's the use? You know how I felt – feel!' She gave a kind of convulsive movement, almost as though she were about to leap up and run. The thin hands waved agitatedly. 'It was no good . . . there was nothing else to do. I've put it behind me.' Her face was paper white, and she was still staring directly ahead. Her eyes, devoid of any make-up, were crinkled, and Alice could see the sparkle of tears on the soft, fair curl of lashes. 'It's the only thing I can do. Please leave me alone, that's all I want.' Now she did turn towards her, and a drop detached itself from the eyelashes, sparkled still on the high cheek. The blue eyes were swimming in tears. They reflected the anguish, and the appeal.

The vision of her face dissolved in the mist of Alice's own grief. 'Damn you, Beth Hobbs! You're the one who can make me really cry.' Beth turned away again. The pale hands were still, curled, rested on her knee, on the patterned flowers of her summer dress. Alice stared at them, and at the pale round of the knee beneath them, and felt a shocking spasm of desire, knife sharp, through the pain of her sorrow. She compressed her lips, sealing in the moan of despair and need inside. 'What we had. What we did. Don't spoil it, Beth. Don't mucky it, turn it into something bad. Because that would be a bloody lie. And you know it!' She reached out, unable to stop herself, caught those cool hands in her own.

Elsbeth did not try to snatch them away, but kept them closed into fists, resting on her lap still. 'Please don't touch me,' she murmured, staring down at Alice's strong, reddened, work toughened hands.

'Touch you? I'd like to bloody *throttle* you!' The shocking words rang out, a violent obscenity against the bright, colourful peacefulness of the day, and against her own intense feeling of love for the figure beside her. Alice had a sudden vision of Davy, that poor strangled corpse he had found. She recalled the feel of his body pressing hers to the ground while the planes roared and guns clattered nearby. She snatched her hands away, but, still helpless against the riptide of her emotion, she reached again, for that beloved face, turning it towards her. 'Look at me! Look at me! Tell me you don't – didn't – love me!'

Their eyes met, for the last time. Alice saw the pleading yet again, the helplessness in those blue orbs, and the fear there also; the fear of what she was denying in that shaking of the head. 'Let me go!'

Alice released her hold. Her arms fell leadenly, as heavy as the despair which struck her. 'Go on!' she whispered. 'Bugger off!'

Elsbeth sprang up, ran off down the path and the few steps which led from the terrace. Back towards the pond, and the far side of the pond, and her comfortable home. Alice watched her through her blurred vision: the slender form, the pale legs under the shortness of the utility hemline, the feet turned out to the side, high. Still runs like a daft lass! She felt the tugging of a tender smile, in spite of her tears.

In her mind, Alice carried on the conversation with the vanished girl. It's yourself you're lying to more than me, Beth. Denying what you are, what you really feel. It's not something that will go away, that you've caught, that you'll get better from.

The trouble was, Alice could understand the pain, even the horror, of being so different. She knew all too well the shock of her own self-discovery. It hadn't struck her in any comprehensible way until the full force of her feeling for Beth had overwhelmed her, and, more importantly, the astounding joy of being able to express that feeling in the physical passion they had shared. She must always be grateful for that; for those wonderful months they'd had together. She couldn't imagine ever losing the strength of that love, or the knowledge and memory of its power over them. Writers wrote about it, crooners sang about it: 'Till the seas run dry'. That's how it was for her.

And the ache she felt now wasn't only for herself. It was for Beth, and the hurt she was doing to herself by trying so hard to deny it. Of course Alice knew why. She wasn't that thick. She knew how shocking it was in the eyes of the world, knew fine well what Beth meant by 'perverted'. She'd been shocked herself at her feeling before they had come together, the glorious urgency which drew them, literally, together.

Alice had tried to talk, to put it into words, but always Beth had stopped her, sometimes with a kiss, it was true, but nevertheless she was the one, the golden girl, who should have been able to express their love, who shied away from such a recognition. And who, now, had, also literally, run away from it. What was so wrong about it, so wicked? They made jokes about men doing it to each other. Fairies, queers, puffs. A string of names. And a law against it, too. Was there a law against women? She only knew the term 'lesbian', and that only because Beth had explained where it came from. They didn't make jokes about them, not like they did about the men. Didn't talk about it. Why not? Because it was even more shocking? Well, no one would ever in a million years convince her that anything that she and Beth had shared had been wrong, or anything other than wonderful. If it was a sin, so be it. She'd go to hell for it and be damned!

She stood up, turned to stride out in the opposite direction, back to the gate that led out onto Park Road, and the long descent back to her own crowded world of narrow streets. For the first time she noticed three scruffy kids, two girls, aged about ten or eleven, and a smaller lad, maybe a couple of years younger. They were staring with avid curiosity. Alice wondered how long they had been observers. 'Didn't no one ever tell you it's rude to stare at people?' she growled, rubbing at her wet cheeks.

'Garn!' they yelled at her retreating back. 'Who'd yer think you are? Bugger off!' flinging her own words after her as she hurried away.

'What's the matter, pet?' Maggie Glass asked her eldest daughter. 'Something's not right, is it, luv? You're not in any bother, are you?'

'What sort of bother? What do you mean, mam? I'm not knocked up, if that's what you're getting at.' It was Sunday night, and Alice was packing her suitcase, ready for a dawn start on the morrow – the milk train to Middlesborough, and then an early morning train to York. She could go straight into work without going back to her digs. She had told them she would be in by mid-morning.

'No need to bite me head off, lass! I didn't mean 'owt like that at all! But you've been as miserable as sin all weekend. And when we haven't seen you for so long . . . it's nowt to do with that lad? Davy?'

Alice shook her head, gave a crooked smile. 'Nay, mam. I don't know why you won't believe us, none of you. There's nothing between him and me. We're just good mates.'

Her mother clicked her tongue impatiently. 'Aye. Well, that's another thing. A lass like you – your age. And a young feller. It's not natural, is it? You can't be mates!' She paused, and Alice fought down the anger she could feel ready to burst out. It's not me mam's fault! she kept reprimanding herself. 'Unless . . . he's not a bit funny, is he? You know – a bit like that? Why hasn't he got a lass of his own? He's not . . .'

'A puff, you mean? I'll have to ask him, mam! Or mebbes it's not him at all. Mebbes it's me who's queer. How about that then?'

'There's no talking to you! Whatever it is, you want to get yourself sorted out, my girl! If it's the job you don't like, pack it in! Get yourself in the forces, like that fancy mate of yours, Elsbeth Hobbs! Then you'd know what hit you!'

Her mother retired in high dudgeon, and Alice found herself sitting weeping yet again, in spite of her fury with her own weakness. But she couldn't escape it. Even her mother had unwittingly brought up the name. And her mother was right. She had indeed to get sorted. She had to face up to life after Elsbeth, and it had taken that short, painful confrontation in the park to drive home once and for all the inescapable fact that it was over. She had to pick up the pieces of her shattered life. Since her lover had left her she had been in limbo. And, sadly, she was forced to admit that the move to York had been part of that. It had not marked the new step she had tried to convince herself it was, but merely a temporary diversion; an escape from the pain Elsbeth's departure had caused. She had used Davy, too, as an escape mechanism. She must have put the poor lad through torture, with all her talk of 'good mates'. Her mother was right. It wasn't natural to expect a lad like Davy, a normal lad, to play such a role – as unnatural as her own inclination, and her heartbreak.

She made tearful peace with her mother before she left the next day. After all, her mother had pointed the way forward for her, albeit entirely unintentionally, when she had burst out with, 'Get yourself in the forces'. Elsbeth had done it, and in spite of all Alice's private worries for her, appeared to be thriving on it. So be it. One of the armed services would have her, she was sure. Probably the ATS. She didn't mind. She sternly pushed aside the temptation to try for the WRNS. Of course, there would be little chance of their paths crossing, even if she did become a Wren, especially as Elsbeth was already going on to do something brainy, to do with radio or something. But no! A clean break it had to be, and if she ever came across Elsbeth Hobbs again, it would only mean pain – for both of them.

There were more than a few painful steps along the way to carrying out her new resolve. Her employers at the railway canteen were disappointed when, at the first opportunity, she sought out her supervisor and declared her intention of leaving. 'I thought you were settled in real well. What's that young man of yours got to say about it? You could end up anywhere, you know, in the forces. You might even get posted overseas.'

Reeny Lumley was upset on her lodger's behalf, and even reproachful. 'He really cares for you, you know,' she chided. 'I thought you two got on so well?' She hesitated. 'It doesn't always have to be violins and all that – swept off your feet from the word go. You need something solid to build on – someone you can rely on. Being together makes you stronger. It's something that grows. If you're with the right feller.'

'That's right, Mrs L., I know that. And I just know – Davy's not the right one for me. He'll find someone. He's a lovely lad.' Reeny's expressive eyes were full of concern and gentle rebuke.

Another casualty of Alice's newfound determination was her own landlady. Mary shed ready tears, and sniffled close for comfort in the private, late night moments together, when the children were asleep. 'Eeh, I'll miss you, pet!' the slight figure sighed, snuggling in the cocooning bed. 'I don't know what I'm gonna do when you've gone. For this,' she added graphically, indicating their entwined bodies. 'You've kept me on the straight and narrer, you have. Kept me faithful to my Terry.'

Alice was too diverted to be offended by Mary's odd notions of sexual morality. She took comfort from the fact that it would be her landlady's narrow loins rather than heart that would miss her attentions. But this odd and unlooked for alliance with the older woman had created some further uncomfortable heart and soul searching for Alice during its brief history. First, it had brought home very strongly the disturbing fact of the sexual nature of her orientation. It was an urge that, certainly post-Beth, could not be denied. Deep and abiding as her love for Beth was, sensuality was also a powerful element in the relationship and her memory of it. Her heart might ache for her lost lover, but so did her body, almost as unbearably. She was ashamed at the notion that it was this urge that had driven her to take solace with Mary Douglas, but she had to acknowledge it as the truth. And who was to say it might not happen again, wherever she found herself? And it would not mean that her love for her dear Beth would be any the less because of it. And that left only Davy.

He had been of course the first she told, the very day she returned from her weekend in Margrove and handed in her notice at the works canteen. She grew increasingly angry with herself as the hours ticked by towards the end of her shift at her mounting nervousness and reluctance to face him with her news. She was relieved when there was no sign of him waiting in the sunshine when she emerged from the canteen into the busy cobbled forecourt. But it only meant an extension of her discomfort. At Cook Street, she picked at her tea, then washed hurriedly out in the back, hardly able to concentrate enough on Mary's incessant chatter to punctuate it with appropriate monosyllabic replies.

She had to sit and endure a further interlude of polite conversation with Reeny Lumley before at last she and Davy were alone, except for the busy city's life flowing unseeing around them in the pleasant summer evening. They threaded their way through the maze of neighbouring streets that made up South Bank, heading towards the open country around the Knavesmire and the Race Course. Unobtrusively she had slipped her hand from the crook of his arm as they walked.

'What's wrong?' he asked, after they had been moving for several minutes and he had found himself stepping out briskly in order to keep up with her. 'What's happened? Something at home?'

She detected that concern, and the warmth of care in his voice, that made her sigh at the difficulty of the task that lay ahead. 'I saw Beth – Elsbeth – on Saturday. She was home, on leave.' For an instant she wondered why she had told him that first, instead of just blurting out her announcement that she was leaving work – and him. But it was all one, really; all deeply connected.

'Oh yes?' He had picked up on something in the way she had offered this information, as she had guessed he would. 'How is she? Is she enjoying the Wrens?'

'Oh aye! Looked a treat. Not that I saw her in her uniform, mind. She's thriving on it, I'd say.'

'That's good. I'm glad. I must say it was quite a surprise, her joining up. It's not the sort of life I'd imagine she'd take to.'

'Oh, don't worry. She's a bit tougher than she looks, is our Beth.'

The bitterness of her tone alerted him. 'Well, I'm glad, for her sake. You had a good heart-to-heart, did you? Did you manage to get her address out of her this time?'

She ignored his question. 'Set me off thinking, though. About my own plans. What to do about meself.'

He felt suddenly that he had stumbled into a verbal minefield once more. 'What? You're not going after her, are you? Don't tell me *you're* running off to sea as well!' His pathetic attempt at jocularity failed miserably. She didn't even notice it.

'Oh no! It wouldn't do me any good, going after her. Not that I could, anyways. But joining up on me own, aye. The ATS, mebbe. They'd take us, I reckon.'

He was so dismayed by her disclosure that he failed to register the strangeness of her statement about going after Elsbeth. 'Why? What's set you off on this tack? We've only – you've only been here a couple of months. Is it the job? There must be other work you could find . . .'

'The job's fine, as far as jobs go. But I don't feel like I'm getting anywhere. You know, With my life. What I'm doing here.'

'Listen, Alice! I thought this was what you wanted. Making a fresh start, getting away from Howbeck. I've kept quiet. Haven't bothered you with . . . any of that personal stuff, how I feel about you.' He felt a little lost, and very confused, as though danger was suddenly looming all around him. He strove hard to stem the rising sense of desperation. 'I've got to speak out – and please listen. Just hear me out, for the sake of our friendship. Please?'

She kept her troubled gaze down towards her feet, and kept silent, allowing him to recapture her hand, to link it with his again. 'Nothing's changed about the way I feel about you. It never will. I know you say you don't love me – not the way I'm talking about, and I've accepted that. But Alice, I *do* care about you – love you – enough to know that I want to spend my life with you, be together with you, always. I'd look after you, provide for you. We get on well together, don't we? That would be enough for me. And maybe one day you'd feel different, something deeper. Alice, I want to give you a home – a family—'

'No!' Her cry was piercing. It shocked him. She had halted, and snatched her hand from his hold. He saw her face, stamped with raw emotion, the glitter of her eyes. 'I *can't* – couldn't ever – do any of that. Couldn't love you, not that way!' She saw the stricken look, and stretched out her hands, touched his arms as though she would shake him. 'It's not just you! Don't you see? It's any lad. I don't want – I can't – love any lad like that. Can you not tell?'

She turned those tearful, pleading eyes away from him, and her hands dropped to her side. Her voice sank to a croaky murmur. 'It's Beth. She's the only one I want, have ever wanted, and I've lost her.'

CHAPTER TWENTY-SEVEN

Shocked was an inadequate word to describe Davy's reaction to Alice's bald declaration of her homosexuality. Stunned would be nearer the mark. He found he could not gather his scattered wits sufficiently to put forward any persuasive counter-argument, or even to dredge up any anodyne remarks to proffer into the gaping social crater of a wound her announcement had caused. He groped and flustered along the stricken way until Alice rapidly put an end to the awful hiatus by breaking away from him. 'I'd better go. I'll see you tomorrow, after work. I'll come round after tea. If you want. I'm sorry. I should've told you.'

He didn't object when she turned away and hurried from him. He even continued walking slowly in the direction they had been heading, while the shadows lengthened and the lowering sun continued to shine on a tranquil evening that seemed to have forgotten there was a war on.

He was glad of the distraction work offered the next day, when he got orders to report to HQ. DI Holden arrived soon afterwards. Helena Duckworth's lover, her 'fancy man', the adulterer, had turned up, volunteered himself at the station after all this time they had spent searching for him. 'He heard about us going through records over at Yeadon. Probably thought he'd better come forward before we got on to him. You can sit in with me, son. Good experience for you.'

Geoffrey Skinner was tall, dark *and* handsome, in a fleshy, matinee idol kind of way, Davy conceded when he sat at his chief's side opposite the badly frightened individual. Holden was right. It was clear that Skinner had belatedly offered himself only when it became apparent that there was every chance the police would track him down through their own enquiries. 'I've been away, down in Derby. I'm away a lot. I'm a hydraulic engineer. We do a lot of work at the aircraft and armaments factories, all over the place. I'd have been in touch sooner if I'd realized . . .'

'Realized what, Mr Skinner? That we were nearly on to you? Why has it taken you so long?'

The strong features under the brilliantined, sleekly swept back hair, coloured deeply. 'Like I said, I'm away a lot.'

'It's a while since you sent us that little note, giving us Mrs Duckworth's name and address. Why didn't you come in then? Or send us *your* name?'

'It's difficult.' The brown eyes flicked around, as though he were afraid others might be listening, or his words were somehow being recorded. 'I'm married. I didn't want . . . my wife . . . I've got two kids, a boy and a girl. Please! They don't have to know?'

Holden pursed his lips, shook his head doubtfully. 'It's aroused a lot of interest, as you must know. The press are very keen, they're on to everything.'

'Look! I've come forward now, haven't I? All right, I'm sorry. I should have been in touch earlier—'

'About two months earlier, I'd say!'

'But I'm here now, aren't I?' His voice rose unpleasantly, his desperation naked now. 'I'll help in any way I can. I want to catch this bastard as much as anyone! I'll tell you anything. Whatever I can.'

'Just the one thing, really, Mr Skinner. Did you kill Helena Duckworth?' The sudden transformation, from gentle dispassion to the fierce bark of interrogator in the question made Davy's muscles clench involuntarily. Geoffrey Skinner's face twisted in a mask of disbelieving horror. His eyes bulged.

'Good God! You can't think – I've come here in all good faith, prepared to do what I can to help. I loved – I was very fond of her!'

'Prepared to say so in the witness box, are you? We may need you to corroborate a few things when we catch our man. Assuming you're telling the truth, of course, and you didn't do it, as you claim.'

Skinner's face turned a sickly grey, and his gaze was full of horror. 'Please, inspector. I swear to God! I had nothing – I was with Helena that night. We'd spent all day together. I left her by Micklegate Bar. Outside the Windmill. She was just off to catch her train back to Leeds. I had to get back out to Heslington. We live in the village. I should've stayed with her, seen her on to the train. But I never thought . . .' He shook his head. 'We'd only just said cheerio when the raid started. All at once, all hell was breaking loose. I wanted to go down to the station. But they wouldn't let us through. Made us get off the road. It took me half the night to get home.'

He sighed, sat back. Davy noted how he kept twitching, his big hands clasping and unclasping on the stained wooden surface of the table, thick fingers interlaced. Well groomed, the nails impeccably clean; not the sort of hands he would have imagined to be an engineer's. But big, certainly. Strong. Capable of squeezing the life out of Helena's long neck.

'What made you send us the note? What made you think it might be her?'

'We had an arrangement. She used to write. I had a place I could pick up her notes, letters. And a phone number at work. We had a sort of code. She always rang after we'd had a meet-up. If she couldn't get me she'd leave a message. Just to let me know things were all right. When she didn't write, or telephone . . . I just had a feeling. I'd been worried sick.'

'Not enough to get in touch with us since, though, eh? Nine weeks, isn't it?'

His shoulders dipped, he shuffled his feet under the table. 'Well, once you knew who it was . . . I mean there was nothing much I could tell you. Nothing of any use. We said cheerio, and she went off down Station Road. I didn't see anything, anyone suspicious. You know what it's like in the blackout. I just wish to God I'd gone with her. Stayed with her.'

'We'll need a written statement of the last time you met Mrs Duckworth, including the hours prior to your leaving her. And we'll need to be in touch. Let us know if you have to leave the area again in the near future. I'd hate to have to come looking for you, knocking on your door, eh?' The frightened eyes told all too well how the DI's shot had found its mark.

After they left Skinner with Sgt Baxter to make his statement, Davy asked, 'You're not going to go along with him, are you, sir? I mean, keep it from his wife?'

Holden gazed at him thoughtfully. 'Dunno. Probably turn out to be pretty difficult to keep her from finding out, eventually. We'll need him to establish the time when he left Helena Duckworth, when she set off down Station Road. If we ever catch the blighter who did it,' he ended, even more thoughtfully.

'You accept it wasn't him then?'

'Do you?'

Davy, taken aback by his superior's return question, nodded a little reluctantly. 'I think so. He might be a devious, lying swine, but I don't think he's our murderer.'

'Ah! The black and white focus of youth!' Holden sighed with mock nostalgia. 'I refer to your remarks about his infidelity, of course. Give you another ten to fifteen years, and a wife and kids round your neck, and see if you're as quick to condemn.' Davy stifled his reply, as it was clear DI Holden did not expect one. 'You're right about his not being our man – unless he's a very clever cove indeed! My money's still on our Charlie. Not poor Bramley – I mean our Charlie Mark Two. I've already checked, by the way. Mr Skinner's got a cast iron alibi for two of the other assaults. Your little Sandra and Mrs

Wright. He was over in Sheffield, and actually working at those times. And I'm still betting their attacker and our strangler are one and the same.'

After the briefing in the CID office, which followed the interview, Dave Wilson said to Davy, 'What's up? You look like you lost a tanner and found a farthing. That lass of yours playing up, is she?'

'For God's sake! I've told you hundreds of times! She's not my lass! She never was.'

'Hey! Keep your hair on, mate! A bit bloody touchy, aren't you? Maybe that's what's wrong with you, eh? You fancy her but she doesn't fancy you! That's it, isn't it? I'm right, aren't I? Well, it's no good running after her, like a dog with its dick hanging out. The more keen you are, the more she'll give you the run around. You want to take it easy. Make out like you're not bothered. Leave her alone for a while. She'll soon come running after you. You take my word for it. Get yourself down the Palace Sat'd'y night. Have a few jars. Plenty of totty down there. Queuing up for it at the last waltz – and I don't mean dancing!'

He had to get out quickly, otherwise he would smash his fist into that grinning red visage. He could feel his nails digging into his palms, his muscles trembling with the effort not to erupt into violence.

'Oy! Where you off to?' Wilson's aggrieved cry faded as Davy made his escape, out through the enfilade of sandbags into the busy morning traffic along Tower Street. He dodged across the road through the vehicles to Clifford's Tower and the castle green behind it. He was supposed to be working this morning, with Wilson and another constable on bicycle thefts. There had been a spate of them from Rowntree's, and they were supposed to be going round the other big employers, like the carriage works and railway sheds, and the sugar factory, to check on and warn about bicycle thieves. 'Life goes on, in spite of our murderer,' Holden had said philosophically. 'And let's hope the summer light nights have given us a bit of a reprieve. We're cutting down on the Duckworth case, till Sgt Baxter and I can come up with some fresh leads. Let's hope it's before the nights start drawing in.'

Davy's pace eased as his temper cooled. Perhaps this was a further test, pairing him off with Wilson. Maybe Holden knew just how obnoxious Wilson could be sometimes. If so, Davy was failing that test at the moment. But really, his partner could be insufferable, as he was this morning, for instance.

But was that really true? Honesty forced Davy to examine his conscience. He'd had an almost sleepless night, and then woken around dawn from a dream, part graphically sexual, part nightmare, in which he had been lying beside the churchyard wall with Alice, his body thrust intimately against hers, not through the layers of their clothing, but warm, yielding flesh on flesh. Then the bombs had started bursting, flashing and thundering all about them, in a swirl of acrid smoke and fierce flame. He had reached out for Alice, to hold her close, his hands closing about her shoulders, her neck, and suddenly, rearing up against him, was her transformed face, bulging, purple, those terrible staring, sightless eyes, the dark, lolling tongue of the corpse he had discovered. He had jerked to consciousness, damp with sweat and shaking with terror, even as his body was still roused and hard.

She had stood his world on end. He felt completely lost, bewildered. At first, he even tried to convince himself that she had lied, had deliberately thought of the most shocking thing to confront him with, in order to ensure he would give up all hope and thought of a loving relationship with her. But of course he could not deceive himself. That was not Alice's way. If he knew anything about her, it was her essential honesty, her truth. She would never make up a lie as profane as that. And it was that knowledge that filled him with the greatest despair of all.

Desperately he sought for explanation, and extenuation. He focused on Elsbeth Hobbs, her delicate looks, the peaches and cream skin, the wide, ingenuous, blue-eyed stare, the rose lips, so often slightly parted with that little girl, naïve expression. As though she was somehow so wonderingly innocent of the ways of the world. And all the time living that lie, corrupting the loving, straightforward Alice, the protecting and trusting Alice, who was so admiring of her friend's beauty, her unworldliness.

But once more he was too honest himself to hold on to his wishful thinking. He knew that the young teacher had had some sort of affair with poor Luke Denby. How far it had gone he was never sure; he only knew how fiercely protective of her Alice had been. Nor could he forget how happy she had been living with her 'Beth' in that little flat over the stables – *we should be able to stay here as long as the war lasts*, she had written to him. *I do hope so, as I'm so happy with the way things are here*. She had added kindly, *except for missing you, of course,* and had even put an x after it, but he had known even then it was just for his benefit, not hers.

She had always maintained, from their first acquaintance, that she could never be doing 'with all that boy and girl stuff'. He had put it down to her robust, tomboy nature – it was one of the things that had so attracted him to her in the first place. She had only to learn what a true, loving relationship could mean. Now, he saw things so differently. *He* was the innocent, the naïve one all along. She was not some unschooled schoolgirl. She was a young woman of twenty, well able to take care of herself. All at once, he felt as though he had never known her, and with it came a deep sense of betrayal. Worst of all, it was not something he could ever accept. Forgive, yes, but only with her agreed acknowledgement that it was wrong, a grievous sin.

He had rebelled himself, quite spectacularly, against what he saw as the narrowness of the strict religion he had been brought up in. God knew, he would never be one to take the moral high ground, to preach against the wrongs of others. He could hardly cast the last stone, never mind the first. But now he saw his own youthful attempts at debauchery, the drinking and the lechery, as a pitiful rebellion against what he knew in his heart was a code which was necessary to a better way of life. There was no way forward for them, for her, without acknowledging the fact of her perversity, and striving in every way possible to resist it.

The first meeting after her disclosure was fraught with danger and with pain. 'You're still speaking to us then?' Alice said, when she found him waiting outside the canteen. 'I wasn't sure if you would be.' She was stating the truth.

By tacit consent, they made their way through the disordered remnants of the stable yards, passing very close by the ruin of the shed where Davy had found Helena Duckworth's body, and through the narrow lane that led uphill, to emerge near the rear of the Odeon picture house, and on to Blossom Street. They strolled seemingly aimlessly along the wide thoroughfare that led out towards the racecourse, both aware that they needed both the time and the privacy the open air afforded them to deal with their crisis. If anything Davy was the more reluctant to begin.

'I've not told another soul,' Alice said. 'But I don't want to lie to you, of all people. You matter too much to me. And I'm sick of lying to you – or of not telling the truth.' He understood the difference and nodded his acquiescence. When he continued to keep silence, she ploughed on with unsteady determination. 'I know you're shocked.' She gave a grunt of harsh laughter. 'I was shocked meself when it all started. But then I realized that's how I am. With Beth it started ages ago, when we first met up again, back in Margrove. I never thought 'owt could happen, you know. But then last year, after the kids went back home, and Beth and me were on our own, when we moved in up at t'Big 'Ouse, it all just happened. Like a miracle. It was marvellous. I couldn't believe . . . we could both feel like that.'

The word miracle had jarred him. 'But it couldn't go on. You couldn't go on living like that.' His voice was gentle, still full of tender concern for her. 'That's why Elsbeth . . . she realizes . . .'

'She blames us for Luke Denby's death!' she burst out angrily. 'That's all it is. She thinks somehow God punished her for his death, because she once slept with him – I mean he had his mucky way with her! And she hated it – and him! I told her. If God was after anybody it was for what Luke did to her!' The passion suddenly died from her voice and she sounded tired with defeat. 'She's got it into her head that it's wrong for us to love each another. You know what I mean. To be lovers.'

'She's right, Alice.' His voice was quiet, too, but there was the passion of conviction in his tone. 'You've got to accept that. You must see . . .'

'What? That this old God of yours is right? How do you know, any of you, what it's like? What we had?'

'There are people who can help you. I don't mean priests. There are doctors. We all have urges. Sex can be wonderful. But we're not animals. I want you, Alice. Want to make love to you, *with* you. But I know I can't have you. Can't force myself on you, if you don't want me.' He nodded vaguely back the way they had come. 'Like that poor woman back there, brutally attacked.'

'I love her!' The cry was torn from her, and the pain in her voice was evident. It shocked Davy all over again. 'I didn't force her to do anything. Any of it. It was love. Everything we did. And she loved me, I know it. I'm not clever, not like she is, or you are. But I still know what's right. And what we had was right, for her and for me. It's not some disease that's got to be cured!' He began to protest, but she swept on, over his effort to interrupt her. '*She's* the one who's wrong, and she'll find that out, no matter what she thinks!'

CHAPTER TWENTY-EIGHT

The first class compartment at York, where Elsbeth changed trains for the long last lap of her journey to London, was almost full, but there was a corner seat free on the corridor side, next to the sliding door. There were three uniformed officers already seated on the banquette, one an RAF man, the other two army. She was pleased at her recently acquired knowledge of ranks, which allowed her to recognize that the airman was a flight lieutenant, and the 'brown jobs' a captain and a major. The other occupants, a matronly lady over by the far window, and two men in dark sober suits and trilbies, crackled their newspapers, and one of them shot her a quick, hard glance which made her blush self-consciously as it occurred to her they might well be wondering what a girl of such lowly military status was doing travelling first class. Then the blush deepened as she wondered in turn what the protocol was for acknowledging officer rank in such circumstances. But already the flight lieutenant, who would be her immediate neighbour, had sprung up and democratically reached for her service case and swung it up to the luggage rack.

'Allow me, miss. Welcome aboard!' He grinned. 'All we need now is a marine and we've got the full set!'

She smiled with due gratitude, while there was a faint, neutral stir of sound from the others, and a further fluttering of papers. She eased herself into her seat, slipped off her cap and crossed her legs. Still self-conscious, she tugged at the hem of her skirt, which had ridden up with her movement to expose the round of her raised knee in its dark rayon covering. She acknowledged the ambivalence of her action and her embarrassment, given the fact that she had paid quite handsomely, along with many others of her contemporaries at *Victory*, to have the garment's length shortened from its original dimensions.

'Back to duty?' the flight lieutenant asked with another flashing smile. Clearly, he considered himself a 'ladies' man', but then, who didn't these days, particularly among the Brylcreem Boys? The two more senior warriors simultaneously cleared their throats in what was meant to indicate their disapproval, then went back to discussing, with even clearer dismay, the appointment of this new Yankee general with the German sounding name as C-in-C, Europe, slightly more *sotto voce*, of course, being aware of their responsibilities and the adage about 'careless talk'.

'My name's Peter Buck, by the way. How do you do?' The airman held out his hand, his grin ever widening, and Elsbeth proffered her cool, limp fingers for a quick grip.

'Pleased to meet you. I'm Elsbeth Hobbs.' She answered his question with some reluctance, and, to her chagrin, with persistently pink features at her dishonesty. 'Yes, that's right. I've just been at home for leave.'

She half turned from him and rummaged busily in her shoulder bag, taking out the paperback novel she had brought for the journey. *Death and Mary Dazill* was one of the latest detective novels by Mary Fitt, another mystery centring on Superintendent Mallet, and his assistant, Dr Fitzbrown. She was in danger of becoming addicted to crime fiction, particularly Mary Fitt's works involving these two police heroes. Though she opened it with a great show of eagerness, it was merely part of her continued deception to prevent the flight lieutenant from persisting in his efforts to strike up a conversation – 'coming on', as Norma Richardson would have said. Thankfully, he took the hint.

She hoped he wouldn't decide to make one last try when the train arrived at King's Cross. It was a pity that Arty wasn't able to meet her. If she could fling herself enthusiastically into the waiting arms of her fiancé, it should get the message across fairly explicitly that she was not available. She was a little ashamed of her readiness to elevate Arty to that position, when nothing had been formally arranged or declared. But then they were as good as engaged, even though no announcement had been made to anyone and despite her ringless finger.

However, that was about to change. She felt another clenching discomfort of her tummy as she thought of what the evening, and the night, would bring. Where would they spend the night together? He had said there were places – there would be no problem about finding a room to share, where identity would not be a difficulty, where the landlady or landlord would not worry about proof that she was 'Mrs Clark'. *I'm longing for the day when it will be true*, Arty had written. And she believed him. She wanted it, too. So why then did she feel the need to convince herself that it was true for her? It would be, it *will* be, after tonight! she urged herself, and that hollow churning came again, so uncomfortably that she squirmed, and moved, recrossed her legs, and felt the smooth silk, the damp warmth beneath the hot serge.

She thought of that hidden silk and lace, so delicately far from the ugly plainness of the service issue. Her mind locked vividly onto the recall of the scene in the little room in Howe Manor, the sickness of waiting for Luke Denby's furtive tap, and the horror of what had followed. No, no! It would *not* be like that, not this time, not with Arty. He loved her, deeply – as she did him. But once again she felt that need to reiterate that final part of the avowal, and to agonize over the uncertainty it caused her.

'What's wrong? Can't get into it?'

She jumped at the voice in her ear. The book's black cover lay on her lap, held by the tightly clenched fist resting on it. She had been staring sightlessly out into the corridor, and the countryside steaming past the long window on its further side. 'Er, no.' She stood abruptly and dropped the novel on the cushioned space. 'Excuse me. I must – won't be a minute.' She turned, scrabbled clumsily, and he was up, brushing against her swivelling hip as she dragged at the awkward door. She stumbled out, feeling the tears perilously close and wanting to scream at her foolishness, her total, fumbling inadequacy, wishing she were anywhere except here, on this train, beet red and hopeless. She fled, lurching down the corridor, squeezing past several figures standing leaning against the outer windows, or even squatting on their luggage, mostly kitbags. They were fugitives from the overcrowded third-class carriages. The guard should have cleared them, but often they didn't bother, unless their number became too large. Thankfully the lavatory was free, though she was painfully conscious of the smiling stares of two soldiers sprawled nearby. In third class, the toilets were usually occupied the whole time, not only for the purpose for which they were intended, but as another space in which to travel.

Safely behind the bolted door of the little compartment, she stared miserably at herself in the mirror over the washbasin. She leant forward wearily, until her hatless gold head brushed against its reflection, and waited, struggling to prevent the tears from falling, and from the welling tide of near panic waiting to engulf her; all those 'what-ifs'.

What if having sex with Arty *was* after all as terrible as it had been with Luke? What if she couldn't stand the thought of repeating it, the way she had felt after Luke had done it to her? What if Arty knew, when they did it, that she was not a virgin? Should she pretend? How could she? What must she do?

What if she told him the truth, about Luke, about . . . about Al?

She lifted her head, stared again at herself, saw with surprise that the tears were falling, her make-up streaking, ugly, about her eyes. What if she simply ran away, failed to show up at the Corner House where she was meant to wait for Arty to come for her?

It was a long time before she re-emerged, freshly groomed and fragrant, make-up restored, and made her way back, past the staring eyes along the swaying corridor to her compartment. Poised, recovered, cool. No more schoolgirl blushes. But one look from the airman's amused and penetrating eyes and she failed, sat humiliatingly enduring the come-on for practically the whole of the long remainder of the journey to their destination.

The boarding house was quite respectable, a mid-terrace Victorian house, the furniture basic, solidly old-fashioned, the bed linen clean. The room was on the third floor, nicely tucked away at the end of a landing, up three narrowly carpeted stairs, and not far from the bathroom. Arty had already popped the question, in Lyon's Corner House, and produced a ring, with a simple cluster of three small diamonds. 'My mother's,' Arty told her, a little huskily, for which she loved him. 'My dad gave it to me some time ago. For . . . you know, the right time. And this is it. You *will* marry me, won't you, Elsbeth?' She had nodded, and they had held hands among the teacups, jugs and teapot, and the sad little efforts that were known as cakes. He slipped the ring on her finger, while the trio were playing over the voices and chinking crockery a selection from 'The Student Prince'. It all felt a little distant from her; calm and ordinary, despite the uniforms they wore and the similar garb all around them, and the make-do cakes. They had talked and talked, still filling in details of their previous lives and plans for their rosy, unspecified future. It still somehow didn't seem real to her.

Then it had become real, frighteningly so, as she nervously stripped to her underwear across the wide bed from him, and sat on the curving wicker-backed chair to unclip her stockings and slip them off, while he sat on the far edge of the bed and removed his shoes and collar and tie, and slid the khaki canvas braces from his shoulders. She kept her girdle on, pulled on her dressing gown and grabbed towel and wash bag. 'I won't be long.'

He was in pyjamas and dressing gown when she returned, and left to take his turn in the bathroom. She had plenty of time to complete her undressing and slip the short silk nightdress over her head and be sitting up in bed awaiting him. When he came back, he eased himself carefully in beside her, taking care not to displace the covers at her side. There was a long, long moment of silence, as they sat, motionless and untouching. Her hair was a yellow-gold, soft cap about the edges of her solemn, tense face, fine filaments of gold standing out against the lamplight.

'I love you,' he murmured hoarsely, gazing at her sadly with brown eyes that were luminous with tears. 'I'm so scared. I don't know anything about all this, and I so want it to be right.' He took her hand, didn't look away from her, and she moved, placed it over her left breast, the soft swell of it under the smooth pale blue silk.

'It will be.' She moved over to him, felt her legs touch his, let their bodies slowly make contact as she held out her arms and they lay together, facing each other, gently joined from head to toe as they kissed.

It *was* all right. It was gentle, and timeless. They lay, just kissing and tasting each other, and whispering, lips moving against lips, and she guided his hands over her body, until she was shivering and wanting him. Even the ignorance, the lack of skill and clumsiness became part of the pattern of the night, and part of the love that wrapped them both together. Some time, she didn't know how long into the night it was, their flesh really did join, he was in her, not for long, and not with that wild, plunging rut she remembered so fearfully from Luke Denby.

He wept, lying on her, and she felt his tears against her cheek, and on her damp breast, and the wetness at their loins, and all at once she felt a great surge of relief and happiness – and love. And some time, later still, again she didn't know when, she took his hand in the dark and put it to her, and felt the slow rise of her desire and its enflaming to urgency and final satisfaction, and she cried, too, and he held her on *his* breast and felt *her* tears.

In the morning, when Arty woke, the daylight was flooding in through the white net and the diagonal crosses of the anti-blast tape over the small, sooty squares of the window. Elsbeth was sitting with her legs drawn up under her, on the wicker-backed chair, which she had moved nearer to the window, letting the early sun fall on her naked body. He came to join her, unclothed, too, and knelt before her, and she turned to face him, unfolding her legs and stretching them out to the floor, either side of him. He bent his head, which she stroked as he softly kissed the tops of her thighs until she was shivering with her need to be loved. They moved back to the bed, but did not get under the covers but spread themselves on top. She groaned as his mouth and hands made their gentle exploration of her proffered flesh and her head swam with visions and memories of Alice at the sweet, slow remorselessness of her hunger and the climax of its satiation.

They were the last ones into breakfast in the narrow basement dining room, and at the end of the meal Elsbeth found herself momentarily alone with the landlady, a small Welsh woman, with a sharp face and masses of black hair. 'It's all right, love,' she said matter-of-factly. 'You don't have to kid on you're married, you and your boyfriend.' She nodded at the ring, which Elsbeth had turned so that the diamonds were hidden. 'You'd hardly be married being in the forces, would you?' Though they were wearing civilian clothes now, they had arrived the evening before in uniform. 'Doesn't bother me, my love,' the woman continued, ignoring Elsbeth's discomfort. 'Your young man's a gent, and I can see you're no trollop. I keep a respectable house here. Not like some not so far away that I could mention! Good luck to you, the pair of you. I hope you do get to tie the knot one of these days, when this blasted war's over.'

By the end of their brief time together, Elsbeth felt committed, and certain that she wanted to be Mrs Clark. She was convinced that she could make him happy, and, in turn, she would feel cherished and safe. It disturbed her that the ghost of the love she had known with Alice Glass was not laid to rest; that their forbidden passion was powerfully resurrected in a way by many aspects of Arty's reverential handling of her. But there was a profound relief, too, that she could find such release and return his love in a manner so evidently satisfying to him.

By the autumn of 1942, Elsbeth had completed her training at HMS *Mercury* and achieved her cherished ambition of a posting to the Admiralty. It meant that she and Arty could be together much of the time, and he managed to rent a room in Bermondsey, almost within sight of Tower Bridge, over the jagged gaps and level waste spaces of property destroyed by the blitz of two years previously. It was small and shabby, but it was a cheap haven, and they spent many idyllic nights there.

'We ought to do something. Take precautions,' Arty said, with customary diffidence, which secretly pleased her. He could blush as readily as she, and she loved his gentle bashfulness, which felt so familiar to her.

'We do,' she said mischievously. 'We hardly see each other more than four nights a week at the most.' She even went along to a Marie Stopes' clinic, bold as brass, and lied blatantly. 'My husband's come home from overseas. But we don't want to start a family. Not in the present circumstances.' She received advice, and leaflets, sheaths, and a cream to go with a rubber device to fit inside herself, to seal off the neck of the womb during intercourse. She tried it once, with difficulty and discomfort during a long solitary session in the dingy communal bathroom of their lodging. It made her sore and rendered her incapable of feeling anything except her painful awareness of its invisible presence during their lovemaking, and she swiftly let it remain invisible instead inside her wash bag, and lied once or twice to an artless Arty. He was as unenthusiastic, and ashamed, of his lack of manipulative prowess with a condom, and so they went back to a blissful reliance on the fate that proves so often unreliable to lovers.

Their 'luck' held until late November, when, as Benghazi fell at last to the Allied forces, Elsbeth knew she had fallen, too, to a more personal invasion. Yet again, her relief was greater than her fear, though her knees trembled and she wept at the scourging verbal assault delivered by her superior officers, before they bitterly acknowledged a fait very much *accompli* and gave her a medical discharge from the Wrens, though the 'dishonour' was kept as private as possible.

A wedding was swiftly arranged. The engagement had been official since the summer, and the Hobbs were perfectly willing to accept Arty into the family, though his assumption of the title of son-in-law came rather suddenly and more precipitately than they had anticipated. As usual Captain Clark was absent from the ceremony, though he sent his blessing and a very practical gift of a considerable sum of money. 'I hope I'll get to meet him before we have a host of grandchildren to introduce him to,' Elsbeth joked.

The date was fixed for 18 December, a Friday. 'A Christmas wedding! How romantic!' friends and relations enthused, and accepted its relative suddenness. 'Well, these days, you know. You never know what's going to happen.' If Elsbeth's mother guessed at the reason for haste – and Elsbeth was inclined to think she had – she never gave voice to her speculation. 'You're looking very well, Elsbeth. Positively blooming.'

And she did for some time. She even stayed in the Bermondsey bed-sit through a wet, chilly winter. In spite of a persistent sniffly cold and some attacks of nausea, it was in many ways a continuation and extension of the idyll. Because of his married status, Arty received permission to billet with his wife when duties permitted. Elsbeth spent long mornings in bed after he had departed in the winter dark. She wore a flannel nightie and dressing gown and a pair of Arty's thick army socks. She roused herself to tidy the room and prepare the evening meal, after which it was time for bed again, snuggling and listening to the wireless. With the electric fire on, and engendered mutual warmth, there was no need to wrap up, and Elsbeth's body blossomed and bloomed in the rosy glow. Arty's lovemaking was selfless and rapturously slow and gentle, and she responded to it with a fervour and abandon which reduced her to tears of dazed gratitude and wonder. In the languorous afterglow of these tender intimacies, she would caress her rounded belly and swear that she had never been happier. At times she could almost believe it.

CHAPTER TWENTY-NINE

'Mail up, corp! Bumper bundle for you, by the looks of it. You want them now or shall I put them in the hut?'

'No, I'll take them, thanks. I'll nip off to the NAAFI and have a skive. What's the point of having stripes up if there's no perks to go with them?'

'Fair enough.' The duty 'postie' handed Alice three of the Forces' blue envelopes and moved on across the dusty compound. Alice squinted at the names and addresses of the senders written on the back of each one. Doreen: the script was neat and flowing; *Northend Cottage, Howbeck, N. Yorks*. Already mature, confident, in keeping with her new life and home. Well, hardly new any more. Doreen had been with Miss Ramsay almost three years now, and at thirteen was still living up to her promise, and making the most of the opportunity she had been granted. However stuck up the well-off spinster might be, she had certainly taken Doreen to her heart, even if she *had* paid handsomely for the right to do so. No doubt Doreen would end with her usual fib – *Aunt Elizabeth sends her love*. Fat chance! No love to spare for any of the Glasses, apart from her protégée and adoptive daughter. Fair enough.

Doreen had written to her eldest sister at least three times in the six and a half months Alice had been out here, and not only through a sense of duty reinforced by her guardian's encouragement. At least Alice hoped not. Her letters were lively and well written. The cocky little madam could always make her smile, and often laugh out loud at her witty resumés of school and dales' life, as well as news about the family. Alice was glad to read it, for her mam had written only twice herself: short, laboured notes, which had no doubt taken her long enough to compose, but saying very little in their stilted phrases: *I hope this find you well, we are all well as can be expected, George your brother* – as though Alice might have forgotten who he was! – *is well, still down south but may be posted abroad any day. Ethel still working at The Groves skivvying but can't wait to get into war work.*

Take care, all our love, Mam. There was no *and Dad* before the x's. It didn't upset Alice. He had never told her he loved her, not that she could remember. Which was, again, fair enough, for she couldn't remember ever saying it to him.

The second letter was from Davy, her most regular and faithful correspondent. She had not expected that he would be, given the circumstances in which she had left York, and him, a year ago. She had shaken him; shocked him rigid, to be honest, as she was well aware. There were times during that final week, while she was working out her notice at the canteen, when she cried to herself in the dark, her grief only temporarily assuaged by the eager diversions afforded by Mary's hot, scrawny little frame.

He had never known how close she came to his way of thinking in those solitary times. If only she could be different – *normal.* And then she would grow angry all over again at her own intransigence. I'm *me*! she chided herself bitterly. Why should I want to be different? And when the tears came again, they were softer this time, tears of sadness for the splendour of the love lost, and for her golden girl.

He had seen her onto the train for Margrove, though there was little either of them had left to say. He knew it was useless to try to make her change her mind, if that was the right phrase for the very essence of what she really was. He had the goodness not to try, though she could guess how much he was hurting. She was hurting, too, knowing how sincere he was when he told her he loved her. The tears were there in his eyes as he stood looking up at her from the platform and she leant out towards him. And she couldn't keep hers from falling, even though she dashed them fiercely away with the back of her hand, and smiled through them. The words she had spoken only a week or so ago to Beth – among their last words – came powerfully back to her. 'You're the only one who can really make me cry!' Not true, not true! she admitted, and longed for the train to pull out. 'Come on then! Give us a kiss!' she cried as at last the guard shouted and doors slammed and whistle shrieked. 'I still want you for my mate. Will you write to me?' Their faces brushed together, swiftly, inadequately, lips made fleeting contact. He nodded, unable to answer in words, and she watched him diminish, dissolve through the shimmering haze, and fade out of sight.

The script on the third envelope stood out, round and still ingenuous, and had the most powerful effect of all in the North African sun as Alice recognized Beth's handwriting. She felt the tightness of her chest, the hollowing in her stomach. Her instant desire and need to tear open the envelope made her fingers tingle, then was replaced immediately by a kind of dread, an unwillingness to learn what Beth had to tell her.

The only other letter she had received from Beth had been waiting for her when the troopship had docked in Alexandria, the day before Christmas Eve. Its content, devoured in the topsy-turvy swirl of the new, utterly alien and chaotic world of Egypt fiercely assaulting them with its heat, sights, sounds, and smells waiting for them down the gangway, seemed as incomprehensible as her surroundings.

> *Sorry I haven't written sooner. I didn't know whether you'd want to hear from me to be honest, but then I just felt I had to let you know what has happened, and what is happening. I got engaged to Arty Clark just a few days after I saw you. We stayed together in London. I got posted up here to the Admiralty after I finished my communications course in September, so we've been seeing a lot more of each other. I'm going to have his baby! I haven't told a single soul, except for Arty, of course. We're getting married, quickly – on 18 December – please be happy for me and say prayers for us on the day. I'm truly happy, Al, and wish that you could be, for both of us – or all three of us, I should say! It would mean so much to me. I'm sorry for any hurt I caused you, you will always be special to me.*

18 December. Almost a week before Alice had got the letter, which had been forwarded from the depot at Nottingham. Married in white? Alice had wondered, ashamed of her cynicism, and her empty-gutted desolation, yet helpless against it. She had replied as soon as she could find the time, the second day after their landing, which was Christmas Day itself. She was tipsy on fizzy foreign beer, and on some strong red wine they said came from Syria. Perhaps that was why she couldn't say any of the things she felt. Or perhaps it was just because there had never been words to express them. Beth had said there was no need for words. Maybe she was right. Certainly Alice had never found them. Or maybe they were both just too scared to utter or hear them. And it didn't matter now, anyway. It was far too late. So she had written a short, stilted acknowledgement and *best wishes to both of you*. She had heard nothing since, for six months.

The address on the letter in her hand now was Beth's home. *Mrs A. Clark, 'Holmlea', Elton Grove, Margrove, Co. Durham.* She must have had the baby by now. Suddenly Alice felt afraid, and found herself praying, her insides twisted with anxiety. Oh God! Let everything be all right. Please! Don't take it out on her, please, God! The fight between her dread and the need to know her darling was safe was instantly resolved, and she tore clumsily at the flap of the envelope, dragged out the thin sheets. The top one was dated, 25 June.

I thought you would want to know that we have a lovely daughter. Our little girl was born two days ago (23) and is well and beautiful. 5lb. 12oz., so small but perfect. I'm fine, too, but exhausted, and very sore, so this won't be a long letter. I wanted you to know, though. Arty couldn't be here of course, but he will arrive tomorrow (Saturday) and I can't wait for him to see her. He's overjoyed, as am I. I hope you get this news quickly. Arty says that mail is going out to North Africa by air these days. Isn't it strange? I thought I would be the one going off to exotic places, and here I am back in my old bedroom and you're out there in the desert!

Take care of yourself, won't you? Maybe you'll be home soon, now that we're doing so well out there and Tunisia has been won. I'm very proud of you. Please write soon,

All my love,
Elsbeth x

PS. We'd already decided if it was a girl she'd be called Elaine Ruth.

Alice wiped at her sunburnt cheeks and blinked rapidly. She squinted up into the blinding, fierce glare of brassy sky. Thank you, Lord. Little Elaine Ruth would be two weeks old now. I might even go to church parade on Sunday instead of skiving off, she half promised. She felt odd, not quite sure how. A bit light headed, and queasy in the gut. Sympathy pains for poor old Beth! And she tried not to let her mind dwell on the thought of Beth's lovely slim form distorted by pregnancy, or the bloody unspeakable details of the birth. But then she pictured the tiny baby, suckling at Beth's breast, and a differently strange feeling possessed her, a tender longing to be near, to share. She drifted away from the fierce beating heat, the damp cling of sweat and parching dust, and dreamt of the three of them, she and Beth and the baby, snug in the flat over the stables at t'Big 'Ouse. Beth propped up in the big old bed, feeding the infant, Al lying loving and protective beside them. A family . . .

She couldn't face the canteen. There was always someone to chat, to distract. She was assailed by a rare longing to escape, to be out of all this, the camp she had known as home for the last six months and more. She made her way to the long wooden accommodation huts by the perimeter fence. Their hut would most likely be empty at this time of the morning, but even if it weren't, she had her own partitioned little caboose at one end, the luxury of a semblance of privacy, as the NCO of the hut.

The rows of beds, facing each other across the wide central aisle, were indeed unoccupied. The place was airless, the heat enveloping as the interior of an oven, and Alice felt a nostalgia for the bell tents they had slept in when they had first arrived last Christmas, with the eight beds radiating like spokes from the central pole, and the flapping of the turned-back canvas sheets, even the streaming water which had sometimes flowed through them, soaking camp beds and all their belongings when the Nile delta rains had struck.

She went through to her little cabin at the end of the low building, left the thin door wide open and peeled off the khaki slacks and short sleeved shirt, kicked off the heavy boots. She sprawled on her creaking bed, dressed only in the singlet and panties, also khaki, and her socks. The underwear was summer issue, lightweight cotton, but there were darkened stains between her shoulders and her breasts. She could feel the perspiration drying on her now that she had removed her outer clothing. She lay back, the letters scattered across her midriff, and stared at the thin iron bars overhead and the high ridge of the roof.

'Stop feeling sorry for yourself, Glass!' she whispered aloud, and felt the tears rising again, that ache which could catch her unawares when her thoughts turned like this to Beth. 'Go away!' she added, even more softly and wriggled up on her elbow and took up Davy's envelope with sudden determination.

Davy had felt wretched when Alice had left York and, what was worse, guilty, for he accepted that somehow he had let her down. He should have been able to help her, convince her of the error of her inclination, or aberration, or . . . sickness. He hardly knew what to call it. But whatever it was, he should not have run away from it; should not have let it render him useless and incapable of any action against it. The trouble was, he had been stunned into a paralysing helplessness, a fatal weakness, which had made him unable to put up any kind of fight. So he had watched her go, the girl he had asked to marry him, and he had let her go without even putting up a fight.

In the first weeks after her departure, his paralysis of will had continued, and with it came an uncharacteristic self-pity. He relied on, and took advantage of, his landlady's obvious, deep sympathy. Whenever the opportunity occurred, he would sit up late with her, sitting before the glowing range in the kitchen, sharing a late-night pot of tea, or mugs of cocoa, and relishing the soothing balm of her gentle concern. There were times when he had the grace to feel ashamed at his weakness, and his exploitation of Mrs L's compassion. A level of innocent intimacy developed between them until he realized that he was in some ways transferring his tender feelings for his lost love over to her. Except that Alice had never been his 'love', except in his own heart and mind. Surely he was not now replacing her with Reeny Lumley? Of course not! She would be horrified if she ever had an inkling of his deviant ponderings. A happily married wife and mother. But he was not strong enough to resist the vicarious pleasure her compassionate warmth gave him, and the innocent examples of her concern in the light touch of her hand on his shoulder, the regard of her dark eyes so full of solicitude.

He was relieved when, after a lengthy period, Alice's first letter arrived. *Private A. Glass, Service No. A5196M, Auxiliary Territorial Service.* She had done it! Why should he be so surprised? She could do anything she set her heart on, that girl! She was doing some basic training in West Yorkshire, and would then go on to do a driver/mechanic's course. So now she was part of it; part of the whole great fighting machine which had enveloped the whole nation – including women. The press were trumpeting the fact that three-quarters of the womenfolk, married and unmarried, were engaged in some kind of war work.

For a moment, Alice's letter opened the secret wound of his own history of non-involvement, and the subsequent horrors of his punishment for it. How tarnished were his principles now? He wondered if there was anything rock solid left in him to believe in? Pacifism? The faith he had been brought up in, and its moral tenets? There were even elements of sexual lust – stronger than he would care to admit – in his feeling for Reeny Lumley. As for Alice's deviation . . . his automatic reaction of repugnance, his righteous outrage, had swiftly withered during her absence. Terrible things were being done in the world right now, some of them in the name of 'justice'. God on our side. Who knew what truth was any more? Maybe feeling love for someone of one's own sex, however sordid it might seem in bodily terms, might not be the abomination we held it to be. He smiled at the whimsical aptness of the term 'glass house', which came into his mind. The house of Private Alice Glass was solid enough in its certainty. That night he sat on after Mrs L had retired and wrote the first of many long letters to his 'mate', to let her know that he was still humbly happy to be awarded that title.

CHAPTER THIRTY

In November 1942, the now unfamiliar sound of York Minster's bells was heard, not as a warning of enemy invasion, but in celebration of a victory and a turning point at the Battle of El Alamein. There was victory of another more local and personal kind, and recognizable 'justice', too, in the capture of Helena Duckworth's killer, who had eluded the police for seven months.

He had lain dormant all that time, as far as the police knew. When he struck, he was no longer wearing his Sandshoe Charlie guise. In October, with the return of the dark nights, just as DI Holden had feared, there was a serious attack on a young woman, not long after dark. It took place hardly more than a hundred yards from where the first assault had occurred on Sandra Robinson. The victim, 21-year-old Brenda Harrison, who worked as a sales girl in an ironmonger's on Foss Islands Road, had been for drinks with some colleagues, and stayed later than she intended. She lived with her parents in Cardigan Street, off Wellington Street, no more than two stones' throws away from Sandra Robinson's home. She was a plump, plain and jolly lass, single but courting an RAF lad, an aircraftsman stationed down in Lincolnshire.

She had just crossed the now quiet junction in front of Walmgate Bar, and had reached the outer boundary of the cattle market pens on her left when the attacker loomed out of the darkness and pounced on her before she saw him, and dragged her off her feet, a filthy, evil smelling hand clamped over her mouth. He wore coarse woollen gloves, but his thick fingers were bare, and brutal as they dug into her jaw, and smotheringly crushed her nose.

He pulled her down and hauled her under the metal bar of the cattle pen, on to the straw scattered sandy stones, swept after the day's business but smelling strongly of dung and urine still. 'Keep still or I'll kill you. I've got a knife.'

She whimpered and pleaded with him not to hurt her, then she discovered that there was no sign of the knife he had threatened her with. Both his hands were busy, turning her on her back, clawing open her coat and tearing at her cardigan and the blouse beneath it, dragging her skirt up around her hips before ripping at the difficult tangle of her underclothing. At first she was too shocked and terrified to do anything more than whimper, but then her terror was not strong enough to overcome her natural outrage and revulsion, and she began to writhe and kick against his pinning weight, arching her back to permit the piercing screams to emerge. The world exploded in pain as his fist crashed into the side of her face, while his other hand dug into her hair. Her scalp lifted agonizingly as he tugged, bending her head back to expose her bare throat. No! She wouldn't let him have her, and she fought against the throbbing pain and the taste of her blood to get her hands up, fingers hooked, her nails digging into those great, brutal hands which were striking and now scrabbling frantically to lock around her neck, to squeeze the life from her. She managed to keep her head wildly threshing from side to side on the damp ground, her limbs kicking under him, her fingers digging, raking, so that the pressure eased a fraction, then one hand moved from her throat, to clamp round her face. But not before she had released another frantic yell.

It was still early enough in the evening to be fatal to his design. The night watchman for the cattle mart had not even begun to settle himself in his home-made kiosk for the night, and, to Brenda Harrison's great good fortune, one of the bored air raid wardens from the nearby Lawrence Street post had stopped to chat to him. Their slit torches bobbing in the darkness, they ran through the network of cattle pens, calling out as loudly and courageously as they could manage, in the direction of Paragon Street and the shocking screams they had heard.

And now Brenda, aware of his sudden uplifting thrust away from her, dimly acknowledged that rescue was at hand, and made a last brave, determined effort to detain him, and earned the most serious physical injury of all as she reached up to hold on to his clothed figure. The brutal fist smashed into her once more, splitting her cheek and slamming her head back down on the hard earth, and his boot thudded into her. The two men were within yards, close enough to get a glimpse of his dark shape as he broke free and ran off.

DI Holden steadfastly insisted on maximum publicity for the attack against the initial ire of his superiors. 'Makes us look damned inefficient!' his superintendent remonstrated, passing on the ticking-off he had received from the assistant chief constable. 'Stirs up the whole business of this Sandshoe Charlie thing. Reminds everyone that we've still got an unsolved murder on our hands from months back. Gets everybody panicking all over again!'

'That's what I want, sir,' Holden maintained stubbornly. 'I want everyone so het up they'll shop their own fathers, brothers, or boyfriends if they've the least suspicion of anything fishy. I want to give them every detail about this assault we can. When, where, what he did and tried to do to her. How she fought, how she might have marked him. It's the only way we're going to get him, sir, believe me. I don't care if the whole town's baying for our blood as long as they give him up to us!'

Unpalatable as his view was, it proved to be correct. A load of information came in: from irate, voluble women, from husky anonymous telephone calls and unsigned notes. They sifted through it all, working round the clock, wearing themselves out, for they knew they would not have much time. And soon it led to a one room lodging in one of the old tenements close to Walmgate Bar itself, and to Arthur Conlon, a reclusive loner, from Middlesborough originally, where he had failed to comply with the National Registration Act and whose identity card falsely declared him to be medically unfit for service in the armed forces.

His room was a fetid bolthole, full of lewd pictures from magazines, with articles of female clothing and a scrapbook of newspaper cut outs of everything written about the Sandshoe Charlie assaults in the city. The scratches on those big, raw hands, and the bruised knuckles, made the other evidence peripheral. For a day or so, he struggled and bellowed like the cornered animal he was, in futile denial, but under the harsh, continual interrogations conducted by CID, led by Holden and Tommy Baxter, and by others like Dave Wilson during the long night, which were even more brutal, he was ground down to sobbing confession to Helena Duckworth's murder, and the other four assaults.

'She laughed at me.' His big red face, smeared with tears and mucus, gazed up at them in hopeless pleading, as he spoke, not of his latest victim, but of the long unsolved murder. 'She was half pissed, and she laughed at me, even when I slapped her and had her down on the ground, over in the stables yard. All hell was breaking loose, the bombs started going off, and she was laughing, saying wicked, filthy things about me. Filthy things.'

He gave a shrill yelp as Wilson leant over him and seized him by the back of his hair, slammed his face down on the table, so that vivid red blood was added to the snot and the tears. 'What? Like you couldn't get it up, you sick pervert? Eh?' He smacked the lifted face hard and grunted with satisfaction. 'The sooner they string you up the better!'

Davy shared in the general rejoicing and the euphoria of relief, but by the time he wrote about it to Alice, he'd had time for some uneasy and uncertain reflection: '*The chances are he'll get the death sentence when his trial comes up in the new year, but I wonder if that's the solution, having seen him at close quarters and how sad and twisted his life has been.*' All at once it struck him with distressing force that to some a shocking parallel might be drawn between this frighteningly debased murderer and the girl to whom Davy was writing and whom he loved. How hopelessly wrong he had been to classify her love for Elsbeth Hobbs as perverse. He remembered DI Holden's wry observation on Davy's judgmental comment about Geoffrey Skinner, the dead woman's lover: his narrow, conventional viewpoint, the rigidity of black and white, of right and wrong.

He was doubly shamed that he, of all people, who had stood against the storm of patriotism that had mobilized almost the entire world into two opposed camps, should have so readily been duped into such unbending judgement of Alice, an error equally as grave as 'my country right or wrong'.

Seven months later, in the baking heat of the camp at Burg el Arab, Alice lay back on her bed, with the pages of Davy's latest letter scattered beside her. Her eyes were moist again, and she was moved with tenderness. This must be the day for having heartstrings tugged! Even Doreen's news had raised smiles of warm affection at the memories of the village where she had lived so happily and been a part of the close knit, enduring community. And now the steadfastness of Davy's love for her warmed her heart. He had remained her stalwart comrade, her 'best mate', in spite of all she had done, and not done, for him. She should never have confessed to him about Beth, knowing the way he felt about her, the hopeless hopes he had cherished. If only they could forget about all this bed and sex and babies business, she would love to live with him, somewhere out in the country, miles from anywhere; kindred spirits, good mates. Dream on! She thought suddenly of that strange night in the flat, when they had shared the bed, and she had woken, and seen his face in the dim light, on the pillow where Beth's head used to rest. She felt a deep sadness for him, and regret. Could she have made things different, would it have been so bad, terrible for her, if she had simply turned and opened her arms, her body, to him? But that would not have been honest, would not have been *her* that she was offering. And how did Beth feel now; Mrs A. Clark, mother of Baby Elaine Ruth?

At least between Alice and Davy there was real honesty now. She had been down in the dumps quite a few times, despite the novelties of her new surroundings, the excitement of the hard work involved in helping to keep the supply lines flowing for the troops advancing to the west. She had told him about Beth; about the marriage, her pregnancy, her own sense of loss. She hadn't kept much back, just let it all pour out onto the flimsy sheets of paper. And good old faithful Davy had not after all let her down.

She searched again in this latest missive for the lines that had touched her most.

> *You said not long ago that you felt very much like 'a broken glass' these days. Doesn't sound like you at all! I'll tell you what came to my mind. Remember the yard at the end of Dubry Street, next to the garages? The one with the high wall? I passed it on the way back from work this afternoon. Remember the top of the wall, what they've got to keep kids and thieves out? Those little jagged pieces of broken glass, all colours, bits of old bottles I guess, all set in cement? Tough and indomitable ('you and your posh fancy words,' I can just hear you saying!). That's you, my little soldier girl!*

Right you are! With energy recharged, she pushed herself up off the squeaking bed and pulled on her shirt and trousers once more, slid her feet into the scuffed and oil-stained boots. A few minutes later, she saw a similar pair, gaping unlaced, on the ends of a thin pair of very brown bare legs projecting from underneath a one-ton truck, a battered veteran in the pale shades of desert camouflage. There was a shrill cry, followed by a squeaky, heartfelt litany of curses. 'Oh, you effin', bastard shitty bugger of a bastard!'

Alice bent, caught hold of the skinny ankles where they emerged from the boots, and hauled vigorously. The thin figure lying on the sheet of canvas slid easily on the cement floor and popped into view. 'I hope you're not talking to me, Private Manning.'

'Whoops! Sorry, corp! It's the blankety sump! I can't shift the nut.' The speaker was a short, thin girl, clad in a pair of baggy shorts which had ridden way up her slender thighs, and a khaki shirt, whose short sleeves were rolled nearly to the shoulders. The arms, legs, and every other visible area of skin was of a deep brown, and glistened with sweat and with great smears of oil, which extended to her brief articles of clothing. The khaki handkerchief she had knotted about her head was already tumbling free, to expose hair of a lustrous blackness, cut short about the neck and ears. Together with her slight figure, any femininity disguised by the stained clothes, it gave her the appearance of an adolescent boy. The teeth against the dark tan showed a brilliant white as she grinned up at Alice, who reached down, a hand extended. When the prone figure took it she hauled her easily to her feet.

Lynne Manning shook and dusted herself down, and used the discarded kerchief to wipe her sweaty brow and face. Her real name was Evelyn, but she preferred Lynne, which was the name everyone knew her as. 'I used to know an Evelyn,' Alice had confided once, remembering the attractive Land Girl, in Howbeck. 'She wasn't a bit like you, though. For a start, she wasn't a midget. She was tall, and beautiful.'

Alice always thought of her as the 'young-un', though Manning was only a couple of years younger than she was. She was treated as a youngster by most of the girls in Alice's section, a kind of mascot, and she played up to the role. 'Kid' was the term most people applied when addressing her. She was warned countless times of the danger of exposing her skin to the fierce sun, but she wore shorts whenever she could, and spent hours at the recreation beach lying out in her swimming costume. She had quickly taken to wearing a long white *thobe*, the gown favoured by the Egyptian men, and with her dark complexion and short, brilliant black hair, looked remarkably like an Arab youth. 'You could be mistaken for Ahmed!' Alice had joked, referring to the mess boy who tidied the hut and the area around it, and made tea and ran errands for them. 'What do you wear under that thing?' And with a quick, mischievous glance around to make sure no one was watching, Lynne hoisted up the gown above her narrow hips and swiftly let it fall again. 'You little hussy!' Alice breathed appreciatively.

'Out of the way, kid! Let's have a look.' Alice lay on the strip of canvas and manoeuvred herself under the jacked up vehicle. A few grunting, sweating minutes later, she re-emerged triumphantly, a long streak of oil down the side of her face. 'There you go!'

'Ooh, bless you, corp! I could kiss you!'

'Careful, kid. I might take you up on that!' Alice saw something in the dark, dancing eyes, and felt her pulse rate quicken.

'Any time, corp!' The brown gaze held her, the dazzling white teeth parted. There was an electric contact in the air between them. The slim, dirty hand reached across, touched Alice's bare arm. 'You're so strong!' Lynne Manning murmured, her voice seductive, her eyes dancing mischievously.

'That's me. Indomitable, I am!' She winked at the girl. 'Knock off now. Go and get cleaned up. I might buy you a beer at the canteen later on. If you're a good girl!'

'I could be – for you, corp.'

Alice stood and watched the thin figure as she walked away.